UNCLE GRANDPA
AND THE TIME CASSEROLE

CREATED BY
PETER BROWNGARDT

ROSS RICHIE CEO & Founder
MATT GAGNON Editor-In-Chief
FILIP SABLIK President of Publishing & Marketing
STEPHEN CHRISTY President of Development
LANCE KREITER VP of Licensing & Merchandising
PHIL BARBARO VP of Finance
BRYCE CARLSON Managing Editor
MEL CAYLO Marketing Manager
SCOTT NEWMAN Production Design Manager
IRENE BRADISH Operations Manager
CHRISTINE DINH Brand Communications Manager
SIERRA HAHN Senior Editor
DAFNA PLEBAN Editor
SHANNON WATTERS Editor
ERIC HARBURN Editor
WHITNEY LEOPARD Associate Editor
JASMINE AMIRI Associate Editor
CHRIS ROSA Associate Editor
ALEX GALER Assistant Editor
CAMERON CHITTOCK Assistant Editor
MARY GUMPORT Assistant Editor
MATTHEW LEVINE Assistant Editor
KELSEY DIETERICH Production Designer
JILLIAN CRAB Production Designer
MICHELLE ANKLEY Production Design Assistant
GRACE PARK Production Design Assistant
AARON FERRARA Operations Coordinator
ELIZABETH LOUGHRIDGE Accounting Coordinator
JOSÉ MEZA Sales Assistant
JAMES ARRIOLA Mailroom Assistant
HOLLY AITCHISON Operations Assistant
STEPHANIE HOCUTT Marketing Assistant
SAM KUSEK Direct Market Representative

UNCLE GRANDPA AND THE TIME CASSEROLE, March 2016.
Published by KaBOOM!, a division of Boom Entertainment,
Inc. UNCLE GRANDPA, CARTOON NETWORK, the logos, and
all related characters and elements are trademarks of Cartoon
Network. (S16) All rights reserved. KaBOOM!™ and the
KaBOOM! logo are trademarks of Boom Entertainment, Inc.,
registered in various countries and categories. All characters,
events, and institutions depicted herein are fictional. Any
similarity between any of the names, characters, persons,
events, and/or institutions in this publication to actual names,
characters, and persons, whether living or dead, events, and/
or institutions is unintended and purely coincidental. KaBOOM!
does not read or accept unsolicited submissions of ideas, stories,
or artwork.

For information regarding the CPSIA on this printed material,
call: (203) 595-3636 and provide reference #RICH – 665289.
A catalog record of this book is available from OCLC and from the
KaBOOM! website, www.kaboom.com, on the Librarians Page.

BOOM! Studios, 5670 Wilshire Boulevard, Suite 450, Los
Angeles, CA 90036-5679. Printed in USA. First Printing.

ISBN: 978-1-60886-791-2, eISBN: 978-1-61398-462-8

UNCLE GRANDPA

AND THE TIME CASSEROLE
CREATED BY PETER BROWNGARDT

Story by
PETER BROWNGARDT
& KELSY ABBOTT

Written by
PRANAS T. NAUJOKAITIS

PRESENT DAY
Art by **PHILIP MURPHY**
with colors by **CASSIE KELLY**
& MADDI GONZALEZ

MOON CITY
Art by **ALEXIS ZIRITT**
with colors by
KATHARINE EFIRD

THE '90S
Art by **DAVID DEGRAND**

ANCIENT ROME
Art by **CHRISTINE LARSEN**
with colors by
KATHARINE EFIRD

ANCIENT EGYPT
Art by **GEORGE MAGER**

5TH CENTURY ENGLAND
Art by **MATTHEW SMIGIEL**

CAVEMAN TIMES
Art by **PRANAS T. NAUJOKAITIS**
with colors by
WYETH YATES

Letters by
TAYLOR ESPOSITO

Cover by
PETER BROWNGARDT

Designer
KELSEY DIETERICH

Assistant Editor
ALEX GALER

Editor
SHANNON WATTERS

With Special Thanks to Marisa Marionakis, Rick Blanco, Curtis Lelash,
Conrad Montgomery, Meghan Bradley, Rossitza Lazarova and the wonderful
folks at Cartoon Network.

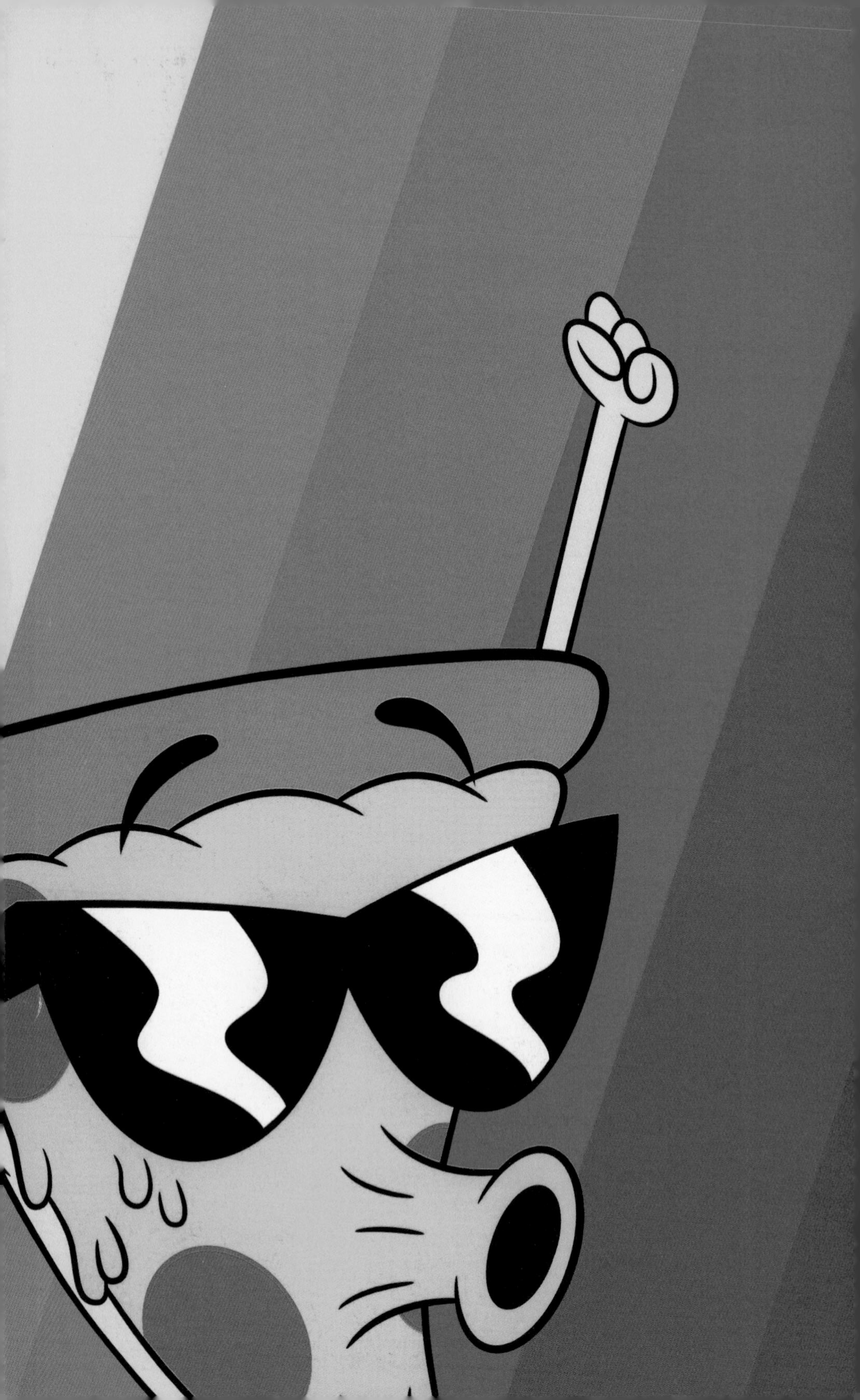

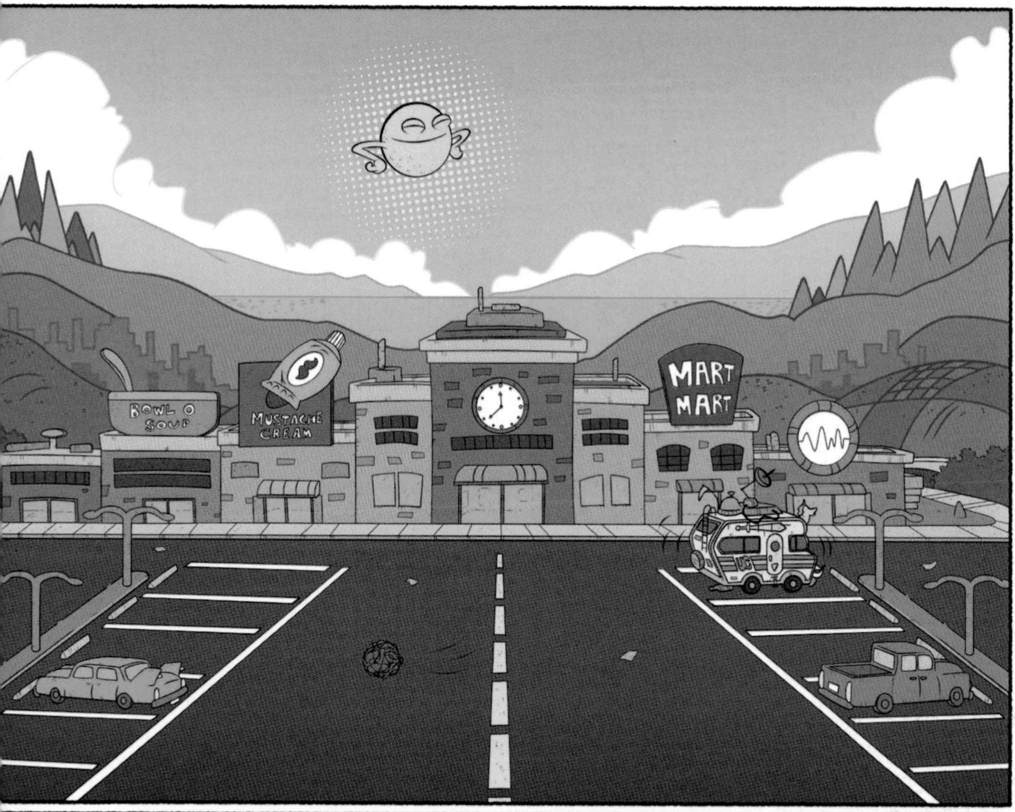
BOWL O SOUP
MUSTACHE CREAM
MART MART

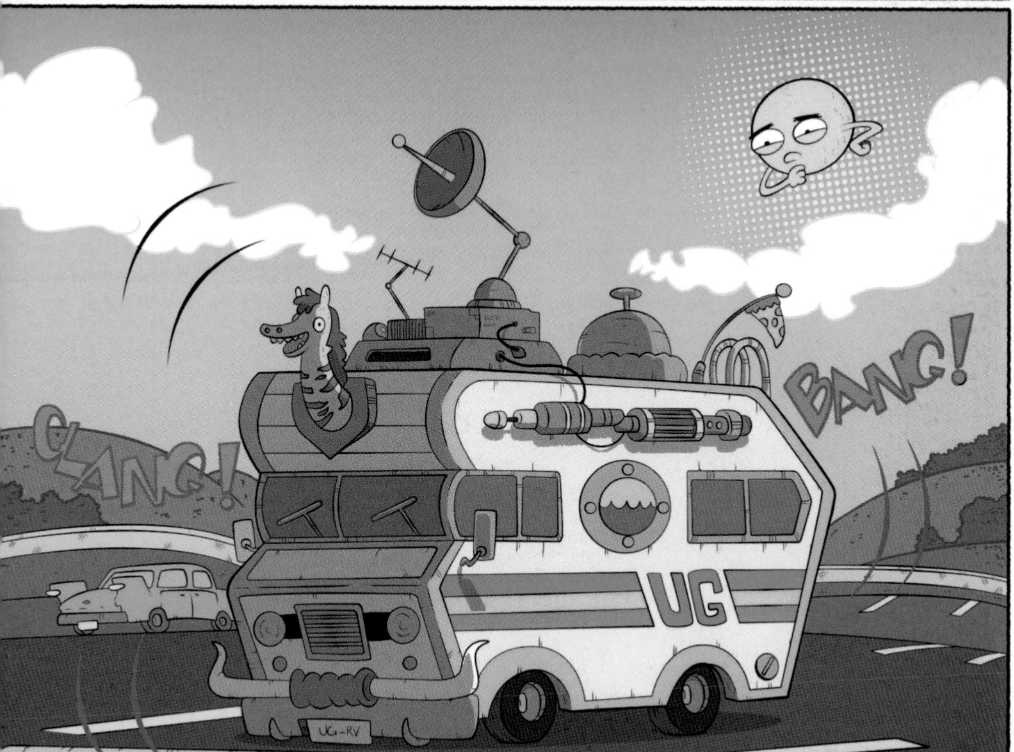
CLANG!
BANG!
UG
UG-RV

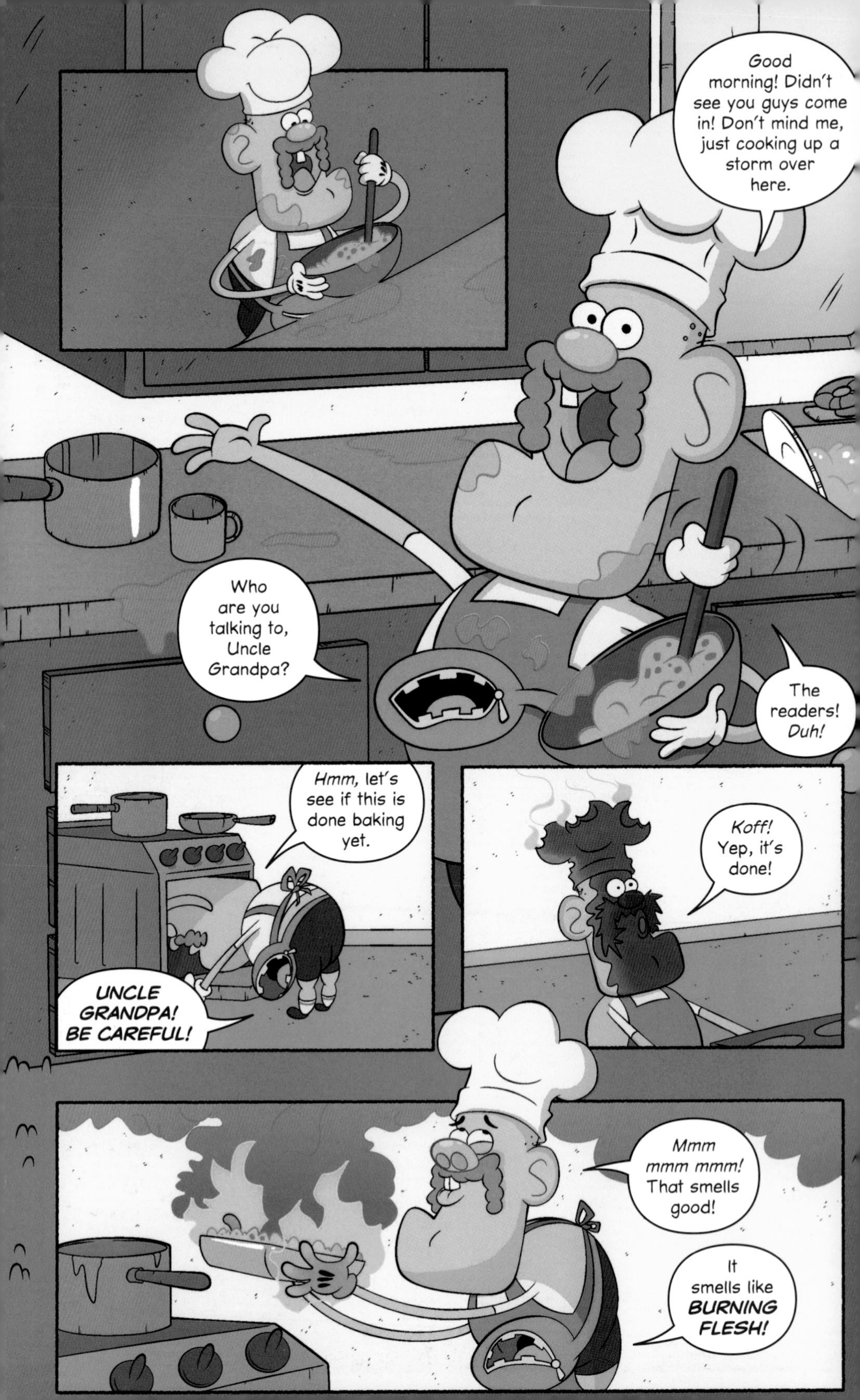
Good morning! Didn't see you guys come in! Don't mind me, just cooking up a storm over here.
Who are you talking to, Uncle Grandpa?
The readers! *Duh!*
Hmm, let's see if this is done baking yet.
UNCLE GRANDPA! BE CAREFUL!
Koff! Yep, it's done!
Mmm mmm mmm! That smells good!
It smells like **BURNING FLESH!**

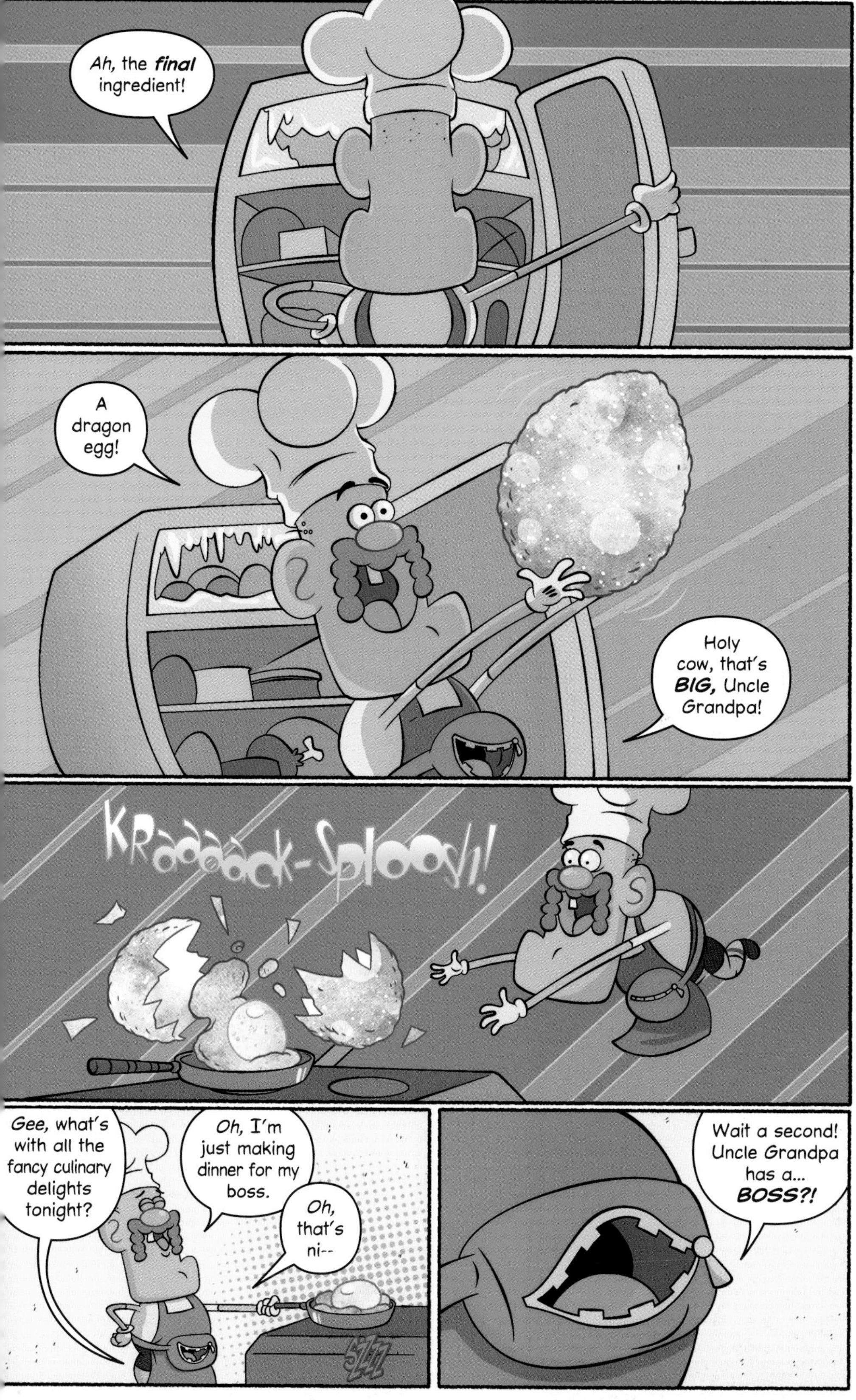

Ah, the final ingredient!
A dragon egg!
Holy cow, that's BIG, Uncle Grandpa!
KRaaaack-Sploosh!
Gee, what's with all the fancy culinary delights tonight?
Oh, I'm just making dinner for my boss.
Oh, that's ni--
SIZZ
Wait a second! Uncle Grandpa has a... BOSS?!

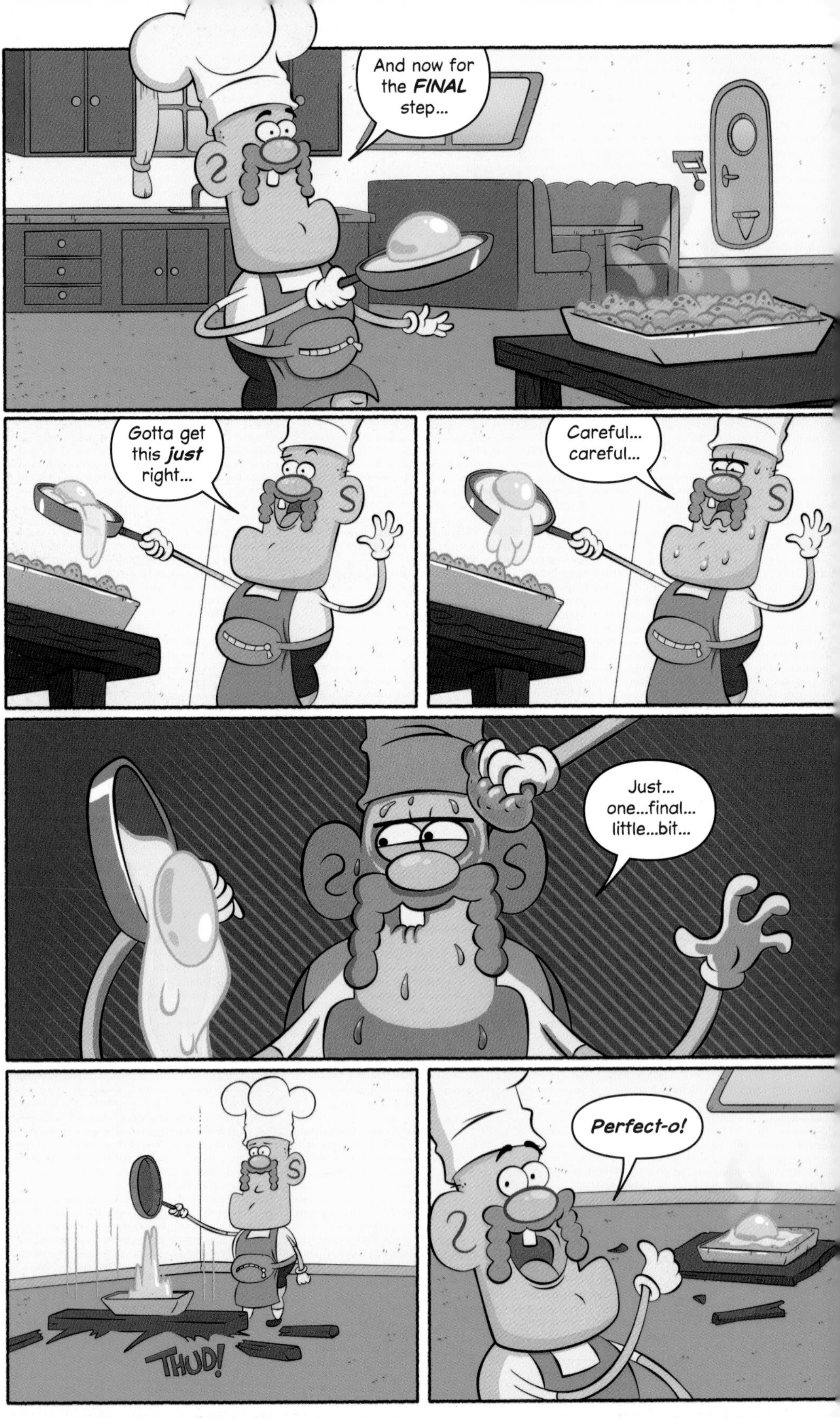
And now for the ***FINAL*** step...
Gotta get this ***just*** right...
Careful... careful...
Just... one...final... little...bit...
THUD!
Perfect-o!

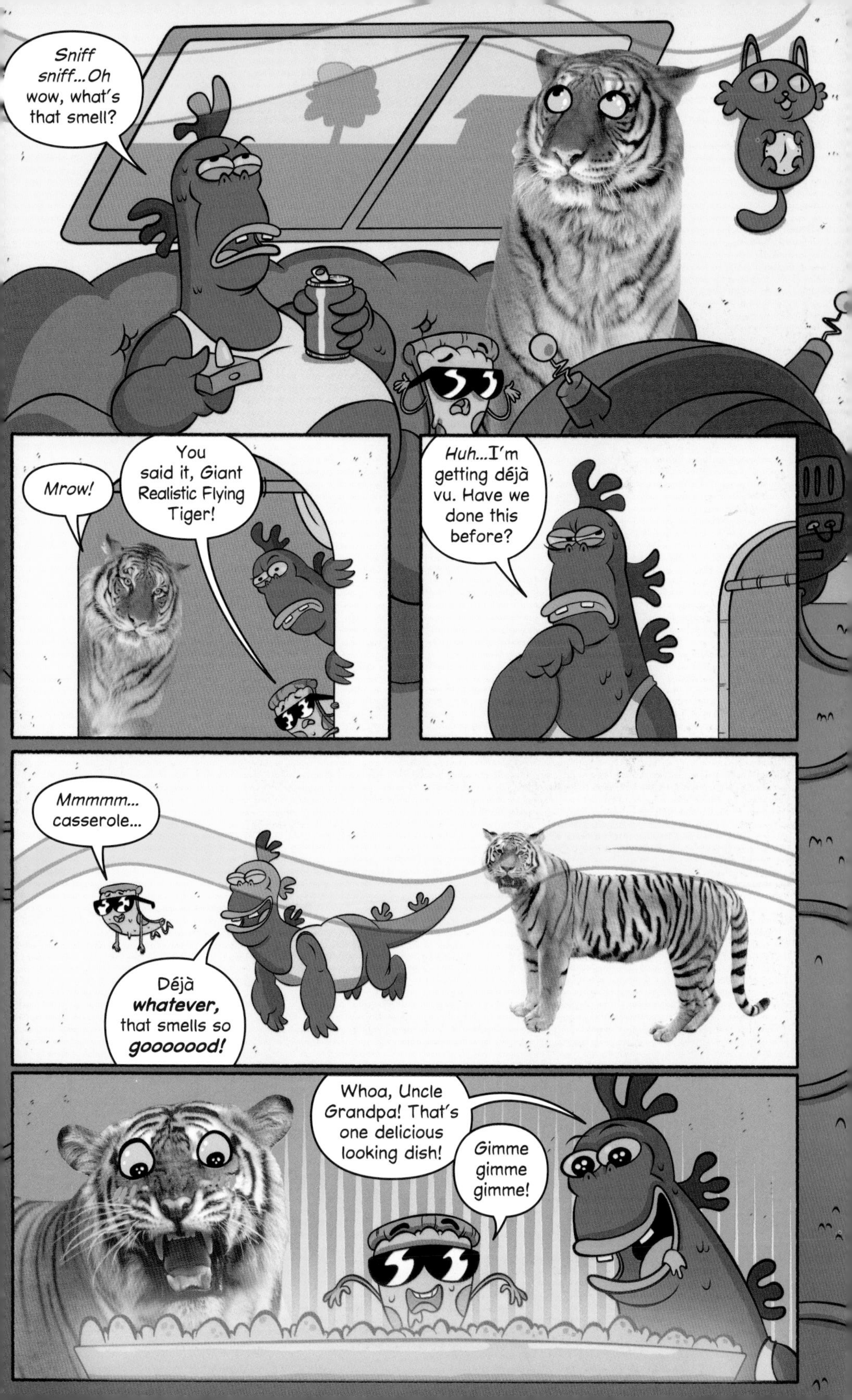
Sniff sniff...Oh wow, what's that smell?
Mrow!
You said it, Giant Realistic Flying Tiger!
Huh...I'm getting déjà vu. Have we done this before?
Mmmmm... casserole...
Déjà **whatever,** that smells so ***goooooood!***
Whoa, Uncle Grandpa! That's one delicious looking dish!
Gimme gimme gimme!

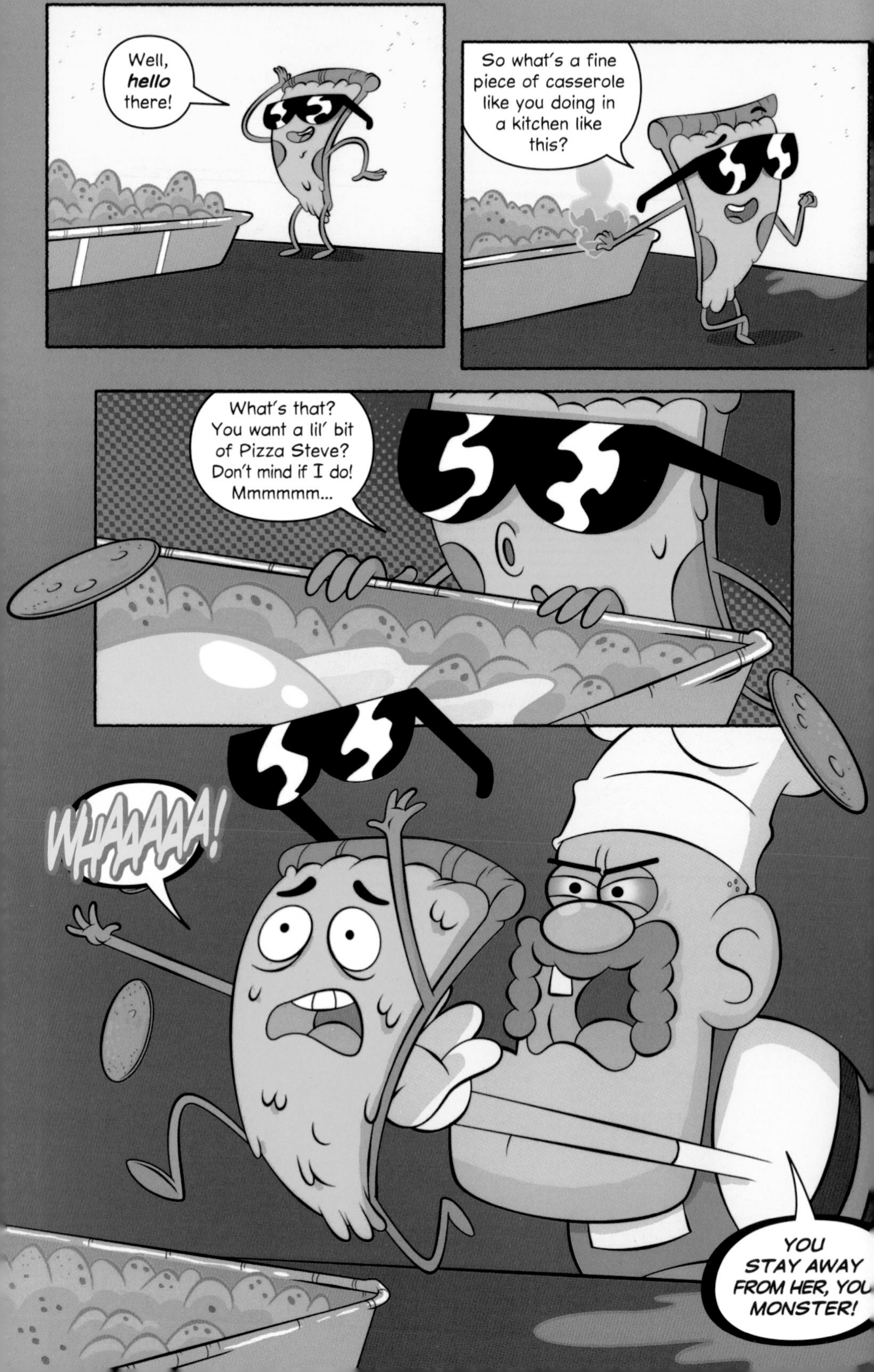
Well, *hello* there!
So what's a fine piece of casserole like you doing in a kitchen like this?
What's that? You want a lil' bit of Pizza Steve? Don't mind if I do! Mmmmmm...
WHAAAAA!
YOU STAY AWAY FROM HER, YOU MONSTER!

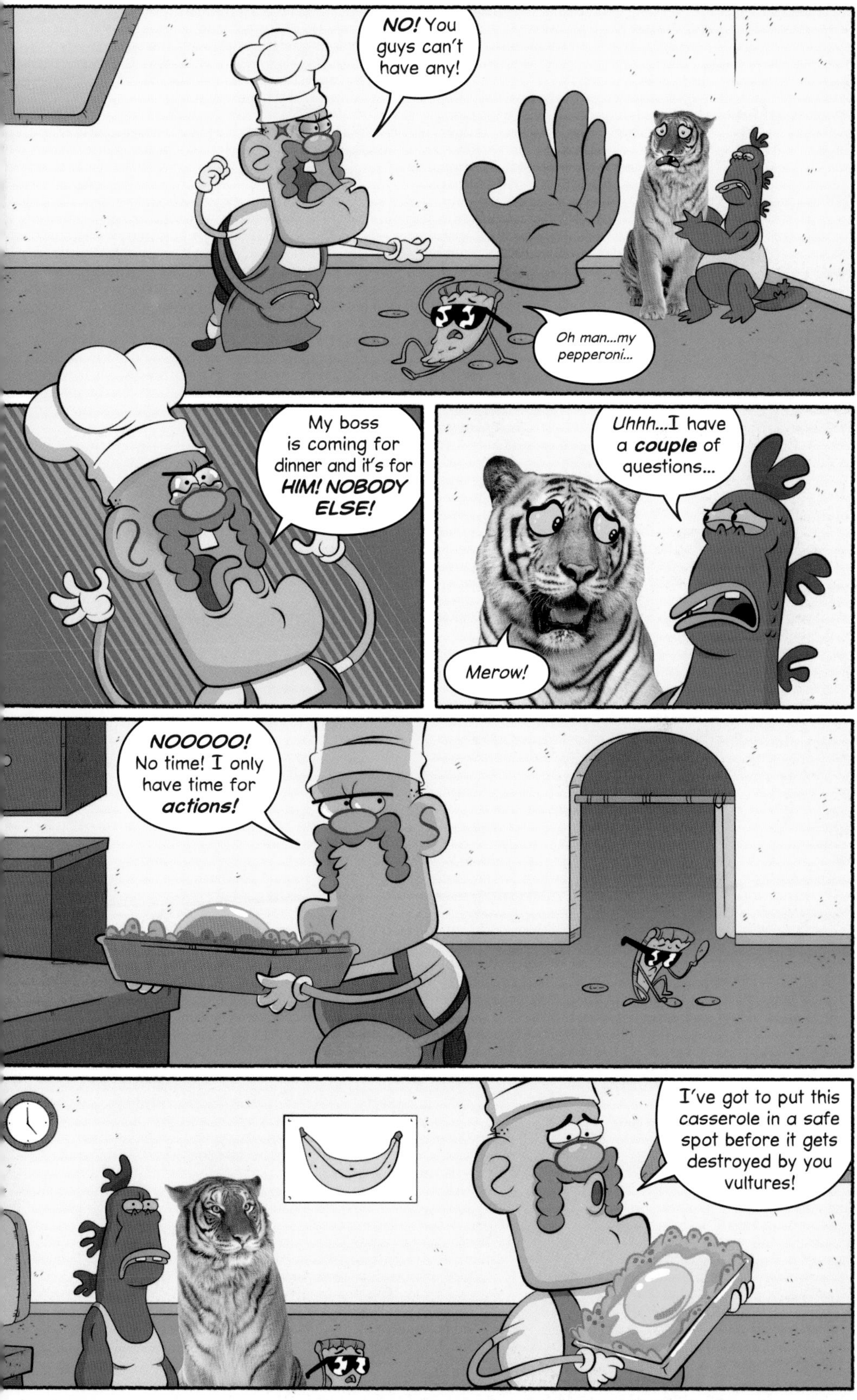
NO! You guys can't have any!
Oh man...my pepperoni...
My boss is coming for dinner and it's for HIM! NOBODY ELSE!
Uhhh...I have a couple of questions...
Merow!
NOOOOO! No time! I only have time for actions!
I've got to put this casserole in a safe spot before it gets destroyed by you vultures!

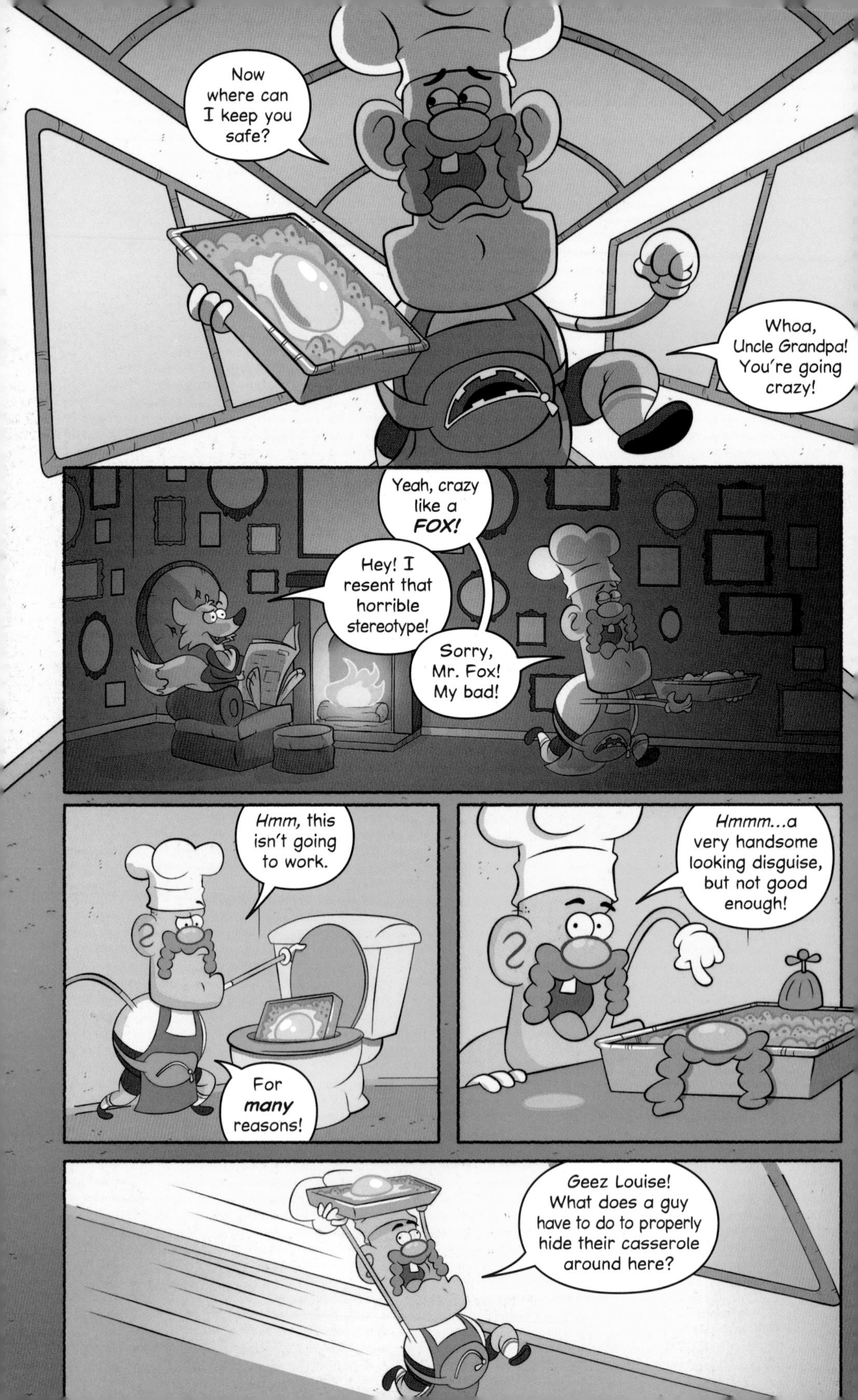
Now where can I keep you safe?
Whoa, Uncle Grandpa! You're going crazy!
Yeah, crazy like a *FOX!*
Hey! I resent that horrible stereotype!
Sorry, Mr. Fox! My bad!
Hmm, this isn't going to work.
For *many* reasons!
*Hmmm...*a very handsome looking disguise, but not good enough!
Geez Louise! What does a guy have to do to properly hide their casserole around here?

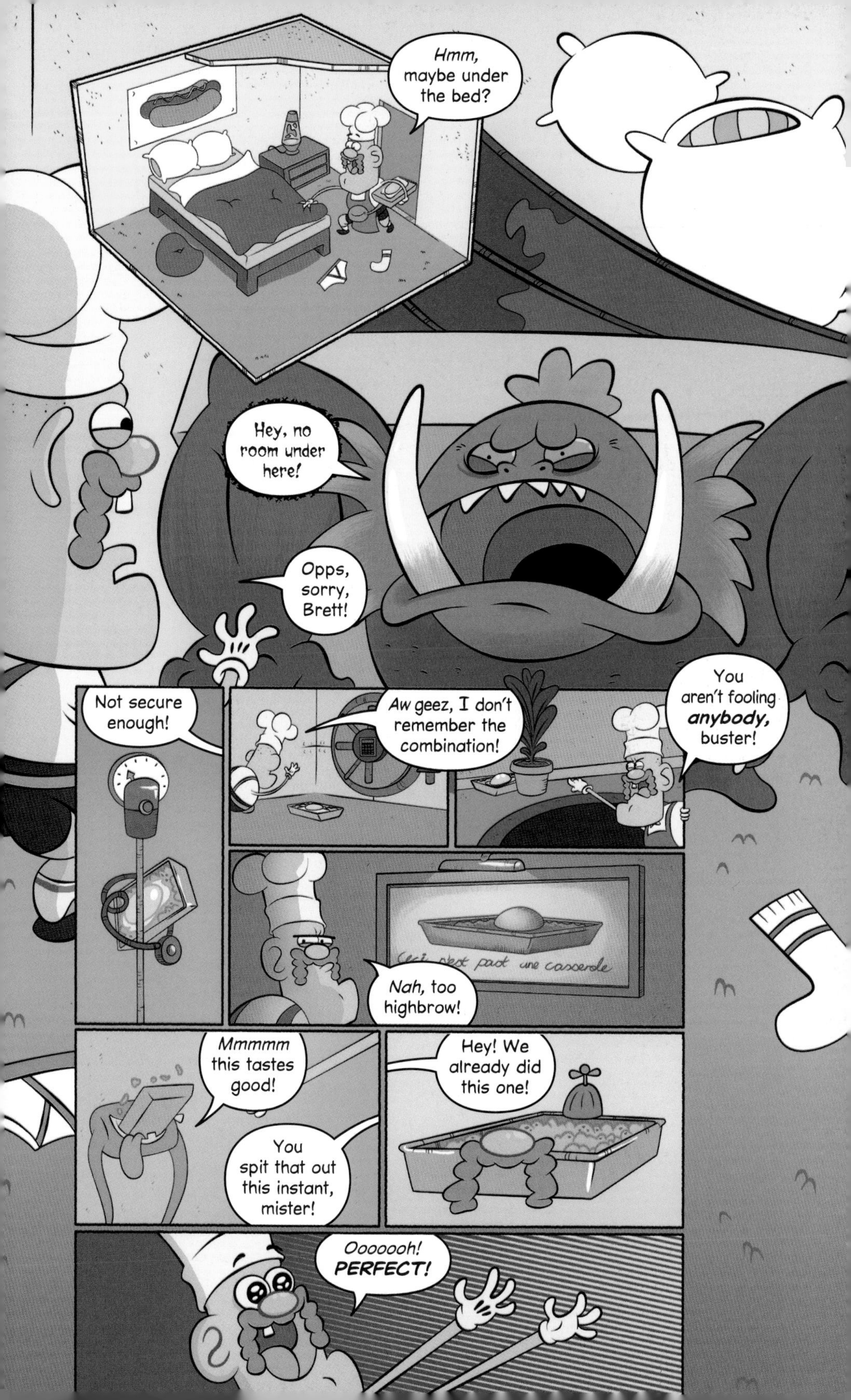

Hmm, maybe under the bed?
Hey, no room under here!
Opps, sorry, Brett!
Not secure enough!
Aw geez, I don't remember the combination!
You aren't fooling **anybody,** buster!
pas une casserole
Nah, too highbrow!
Mmmmm this tastes good!
You spit that out this instant, mister!
Hey! We already did this one!
Ooooooh! **PERFECT!**

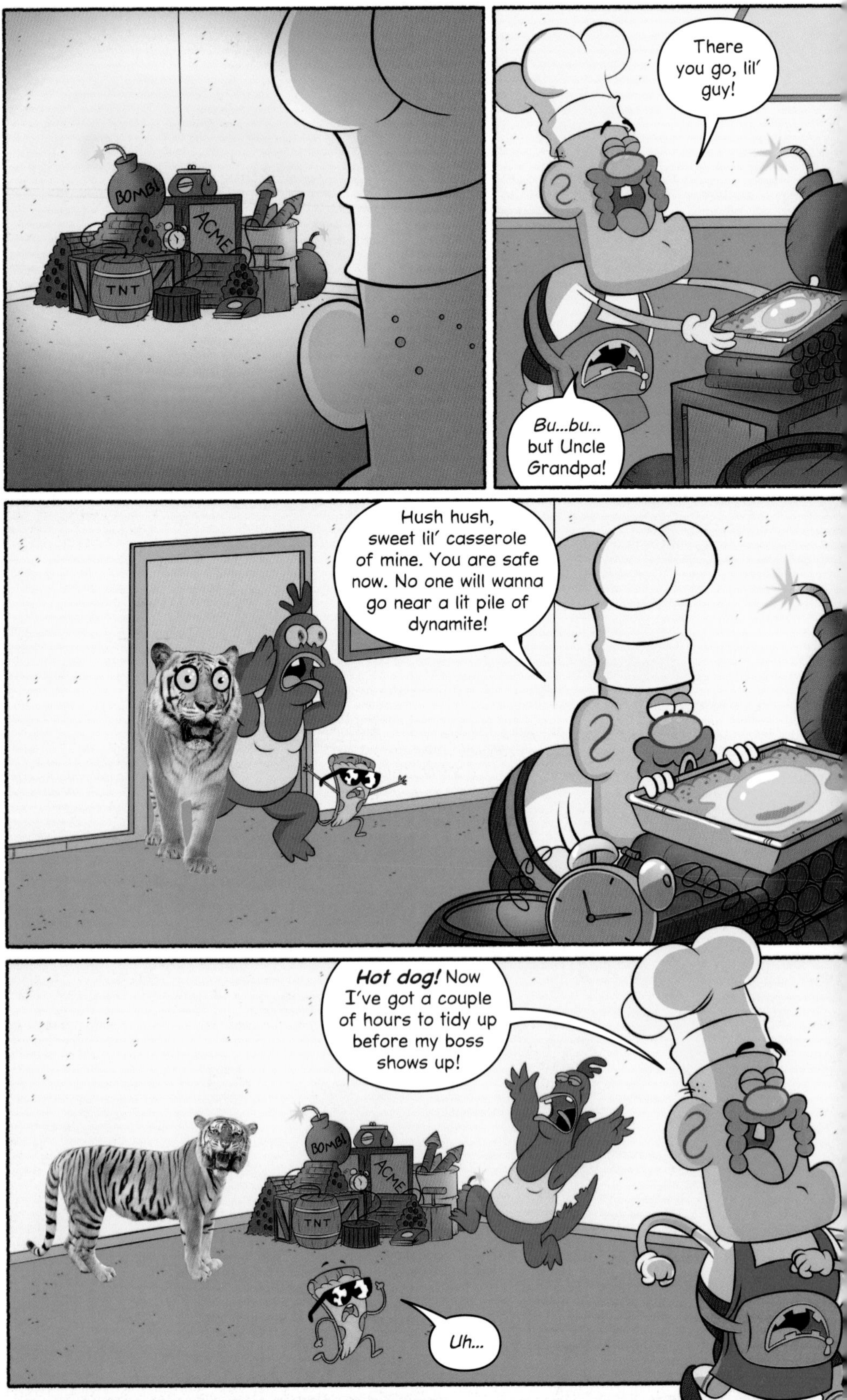
BOMB!
ACME
TNT
There you go, lil' guy!
Bu...bu... but Uncle Grandpa!
Hush hush, sweet lil' casserole of mine. You are safe now. No one will wanna go near a lit pile of dynamite!
Hot dog! Now I've got a couple of hours to tidy up before my boss shows up!
BOMB!
ACME
TNT
Uh...

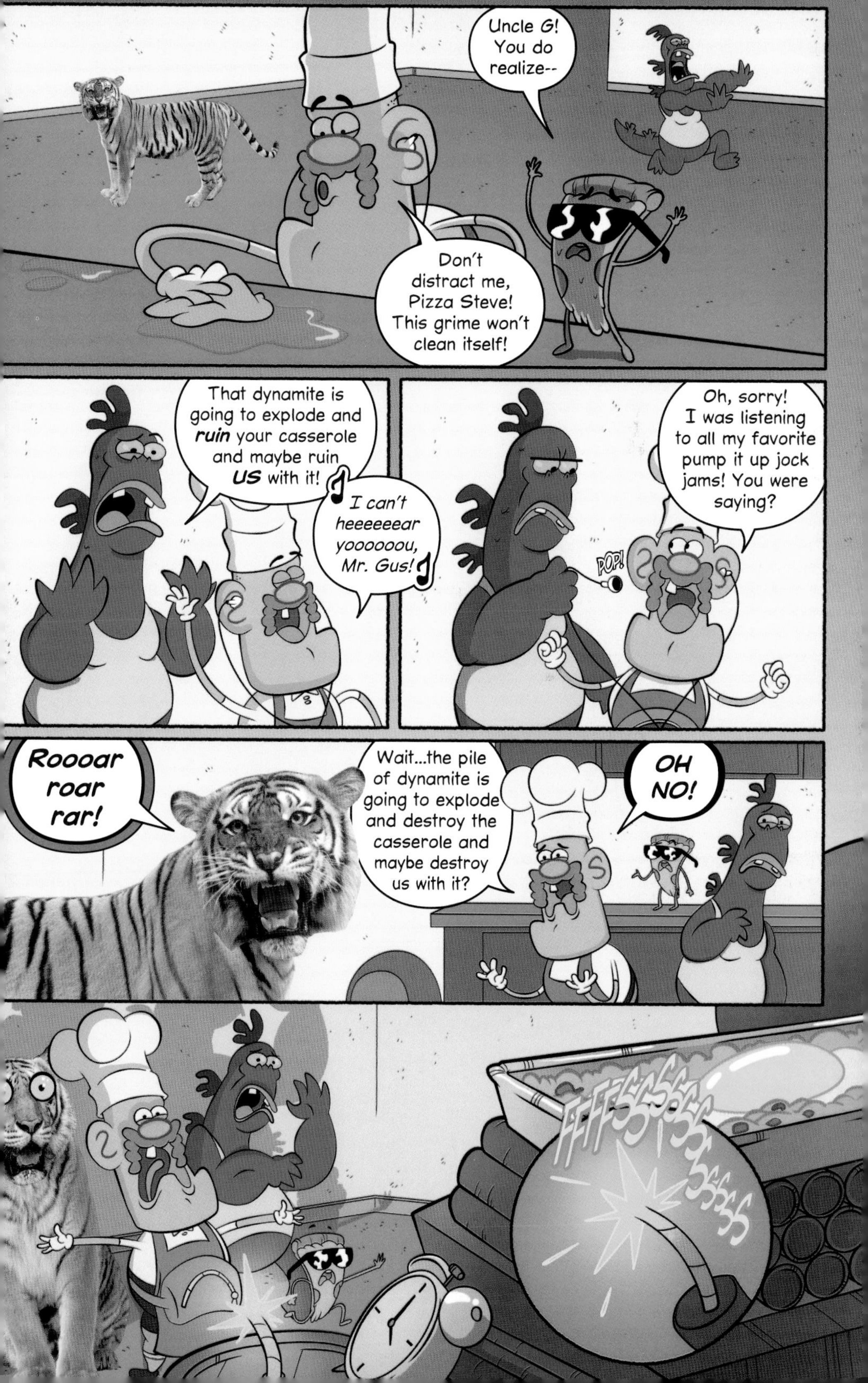

Uncle G! You do realize--
Don't distract me, Pizza Steve! This grime won't clean itself!
That dynamite is going to explode and ruin your casserole and maybe ruin US with it!
I can't heeeeeear yoooooou, Mr. Gus!
POP!
Oh, sorry! I was listening to all my favorite pump it up jock jams! You were saying?
Roooar roar rar!
Wait...the pile of dynamite is going to explode and destroy the casserole and maybe destroy us with it?
OH NO!
FFFFSSSSSSSSSSSS

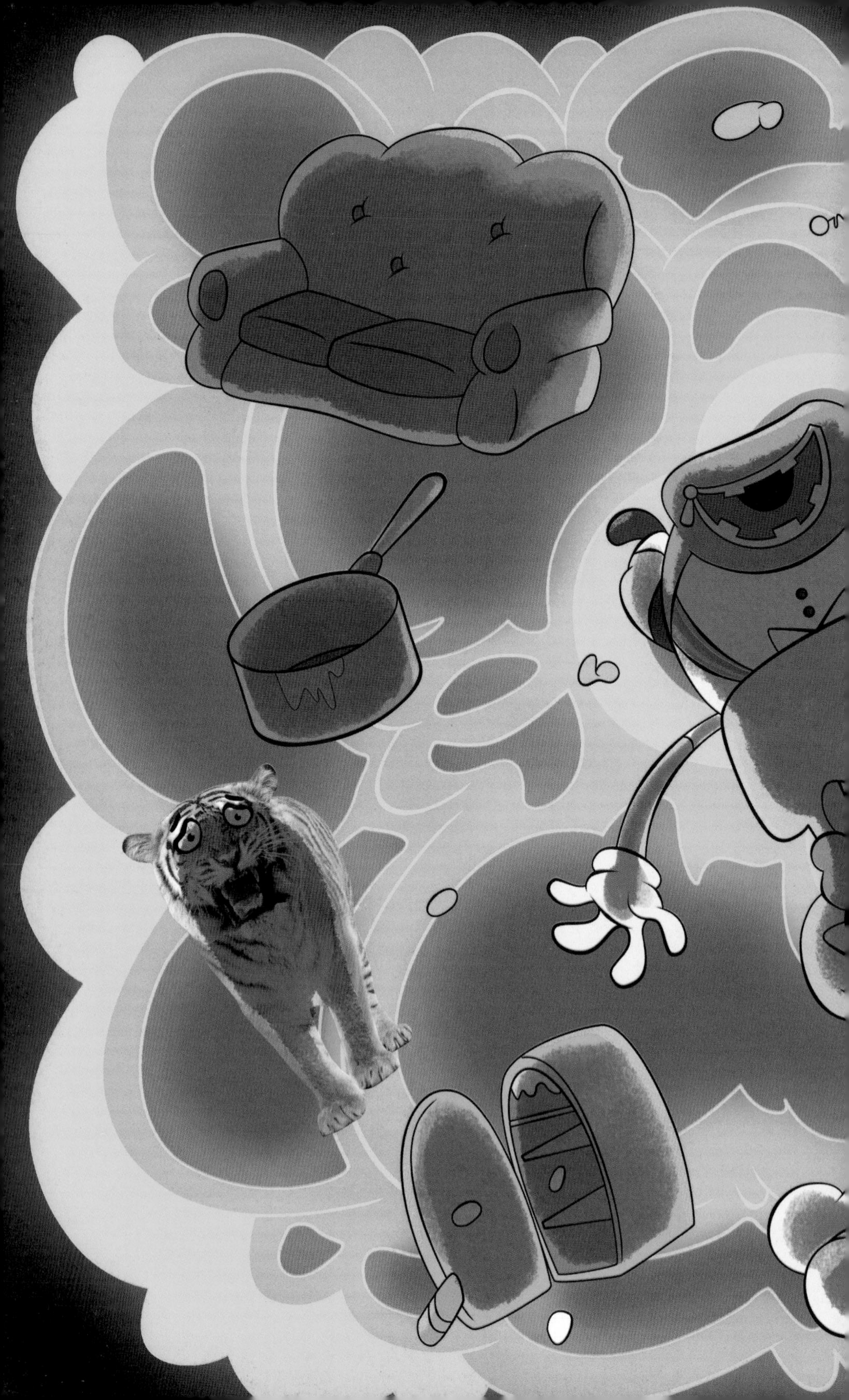

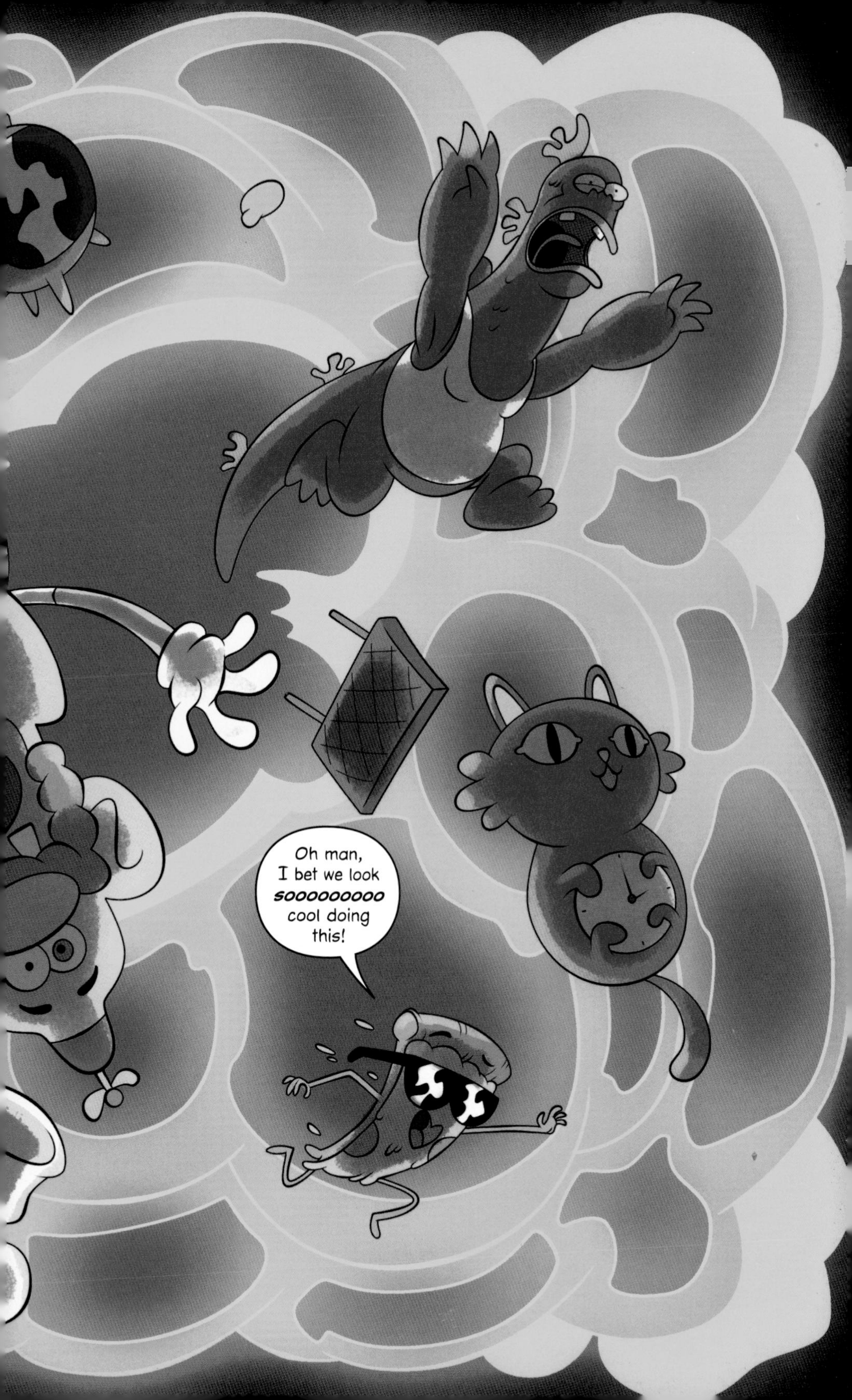
Oh man, I bet we look SOOOOOOOOO cool doing this!

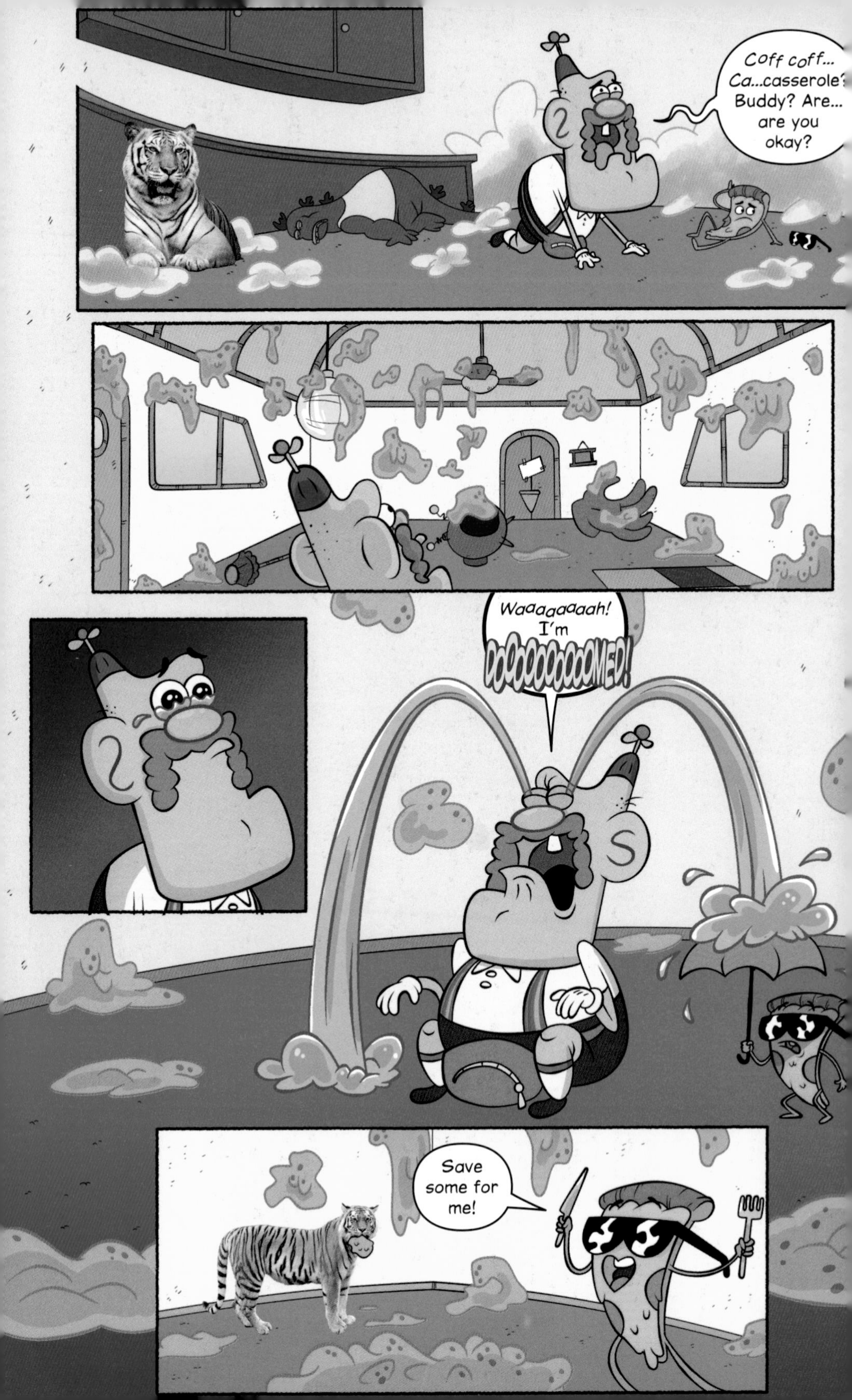
Coff coff...
Ca...casserole? Buddy? Are... are you okay?
Waaaaaaaah! I'm DOOOOOOOOOMED!
Save some for me!

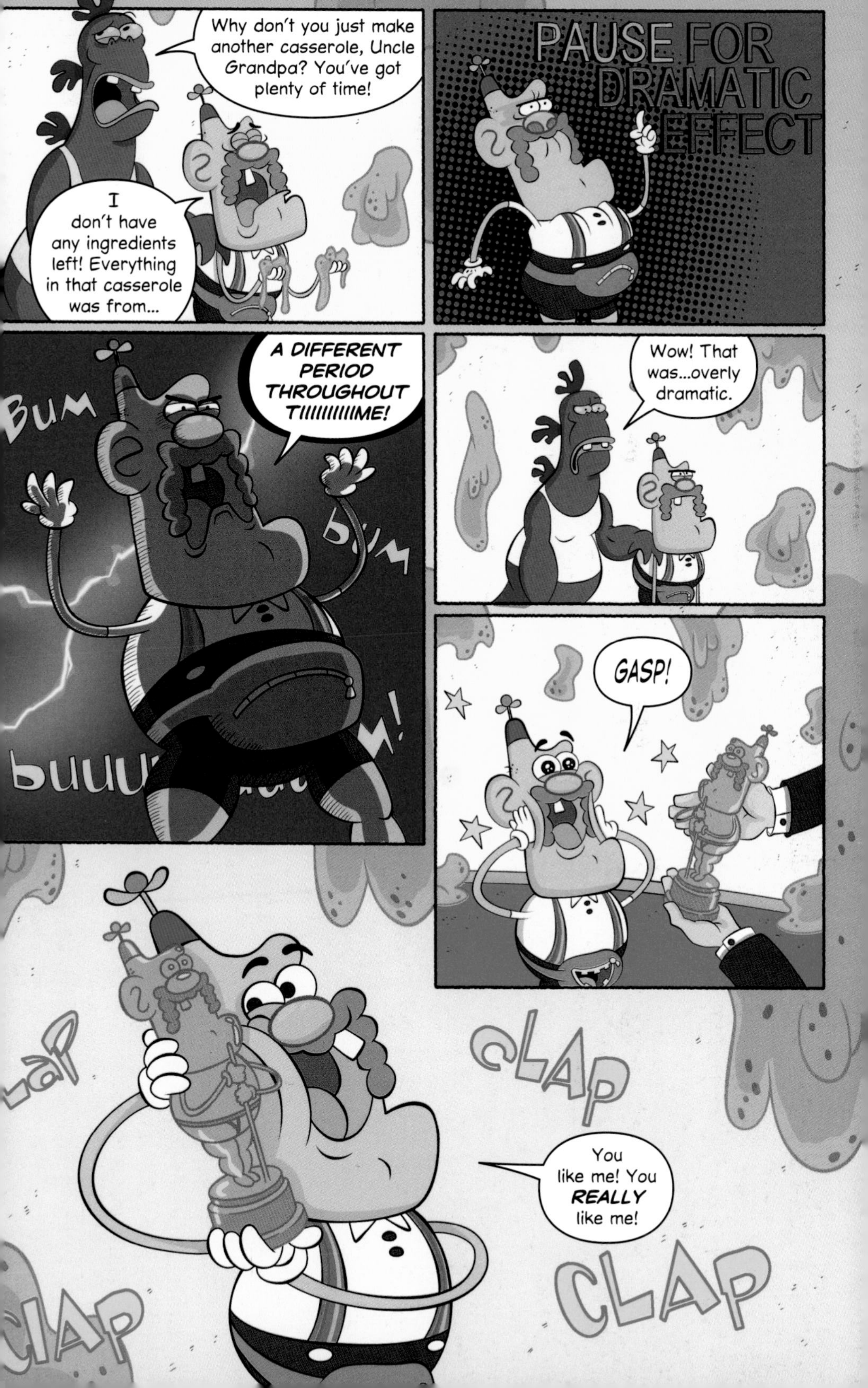

Why don't you just make another casserole, Uncle Grandpa? You've got plenty of time!
I don't have any ingredients left! Everything in that casserole was from...
PAUSE FOR DRAMATIC EFFECT
A DIFFERENT PERIOD THROUGHOUT TIIIIIIIIIME!
Bum
bum
Wow! That was...overly dramatic.
GASP!
CLAP
CLAP
You like me! You *REALLY* like me!

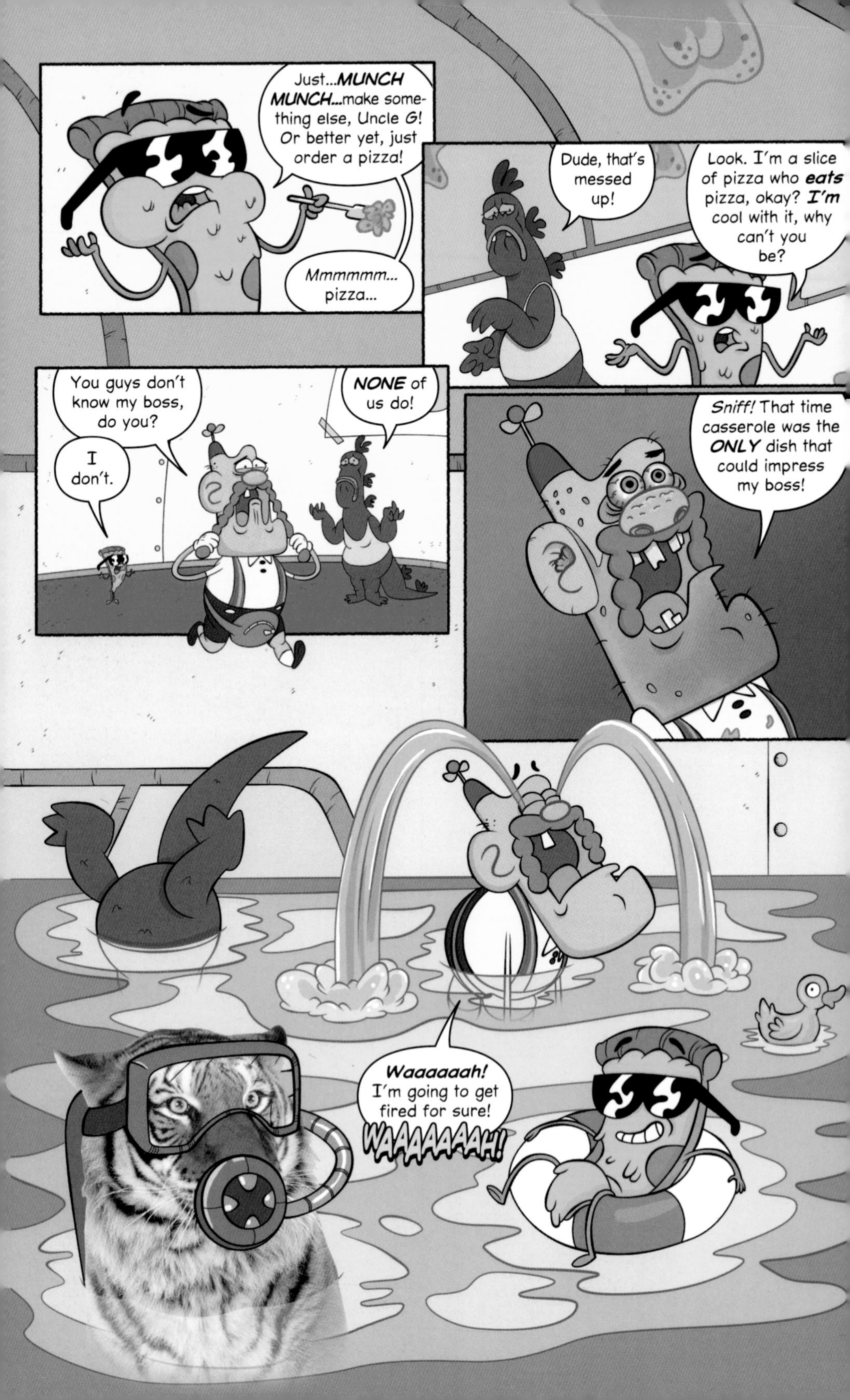

Just...MUNCH MUNCH...make something else, Uncle G! Or better yet, just order a pizza!
Mmmmmm... pizza...
Dude, that's messed up!
Look. I'm a slice of pizza who eats pizza, okay? I'm cool with it, why can't you be?
You guys don't know my boss, do you?
I don't.
NONE of us do!
Sniff! That time casserole was the ONLY dish that could impress my boss!
Waaaaaah! I'm going to get fired for sure!
WAAAAAAAH!

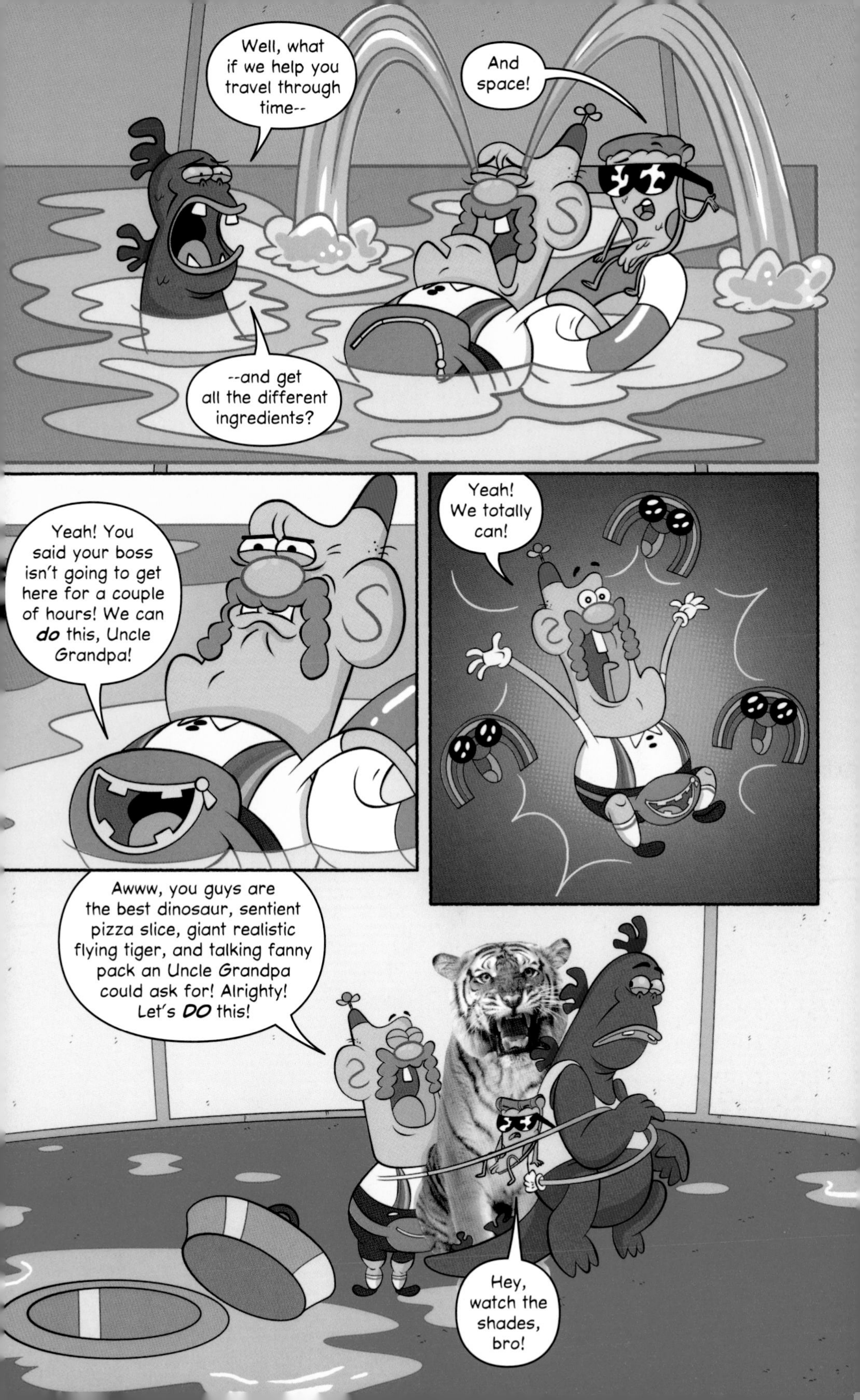
Well, what if we help you travel through time--
And space!
--and get all the different ingredients?
Yeah! You said your boss isn't going to get here for a couple of hours! We can *do* this, Uncle Grandpa!
Yeah! We totally can!
Awww, you guys are the best dinosaur, sentient pizza slice, giant realistic flying tiger, and talking fanny pack an Uncle Grandpa could ask for! Alrighty! Let's *DO* this!
Hey, watch the shades, bro!

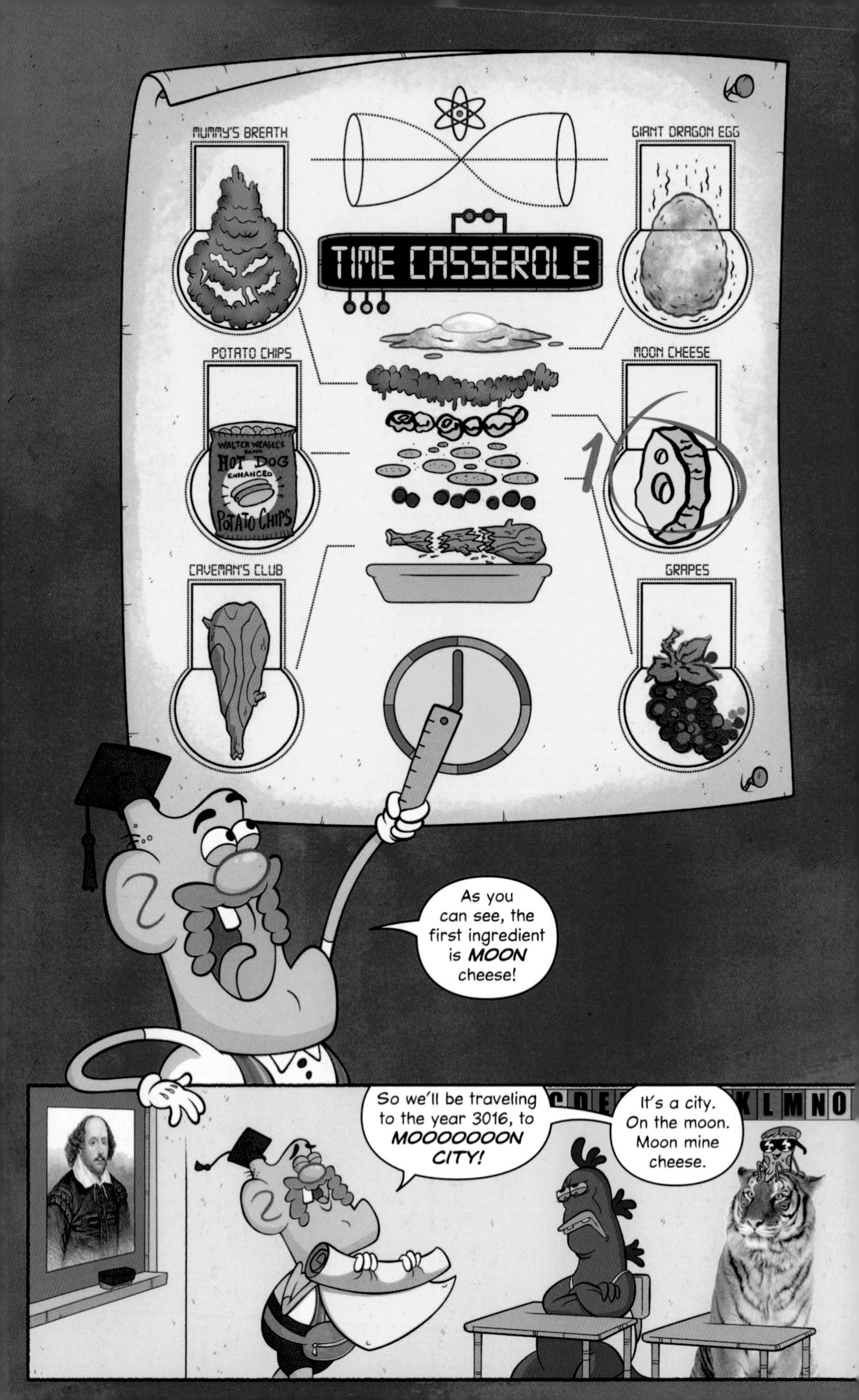
MUMMY'S BREATH
GIANT DRAGON EGG
TIME CASSEROLE
POTATO CHIPS
WALTER WEASEL'S
HOT DOG
ENHANCED
POTATO CHIPS
MOON CHEESE
CAVEMAN'S CLUB
GRAPES
As you can see, the first ingredient is ***MOON*** cheese!
So we'll be traveling to the year 3016, to ***MOOOOOOON CITY!***
It's a city. On the moon. Moon mine cheese.

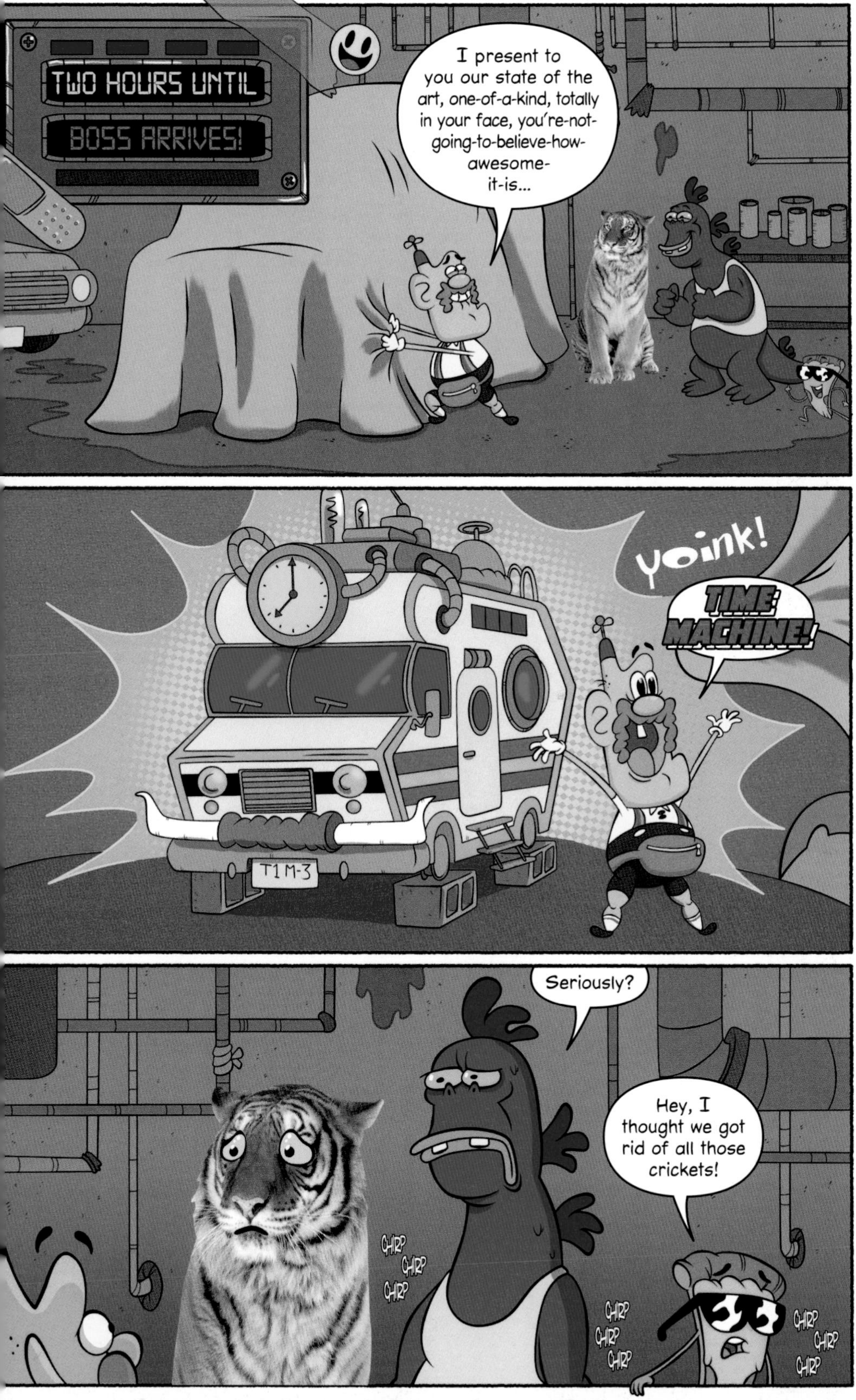
TWO HOURS UNTIL
BOSS ARRIVES!
I present to you our state of the art, one-of-a-kind, totally in your face, you're-not-going-to-believe-how-awesome-it-is...
yoink!
TIME MACHINE!
T1M-3
Seriously?
Hey, I thought we got rid of all those crickets!
CHIRP CHIRP CHIRP
CHIRP CHIRP CHIRP
CHIRP CHIRP CHIRP

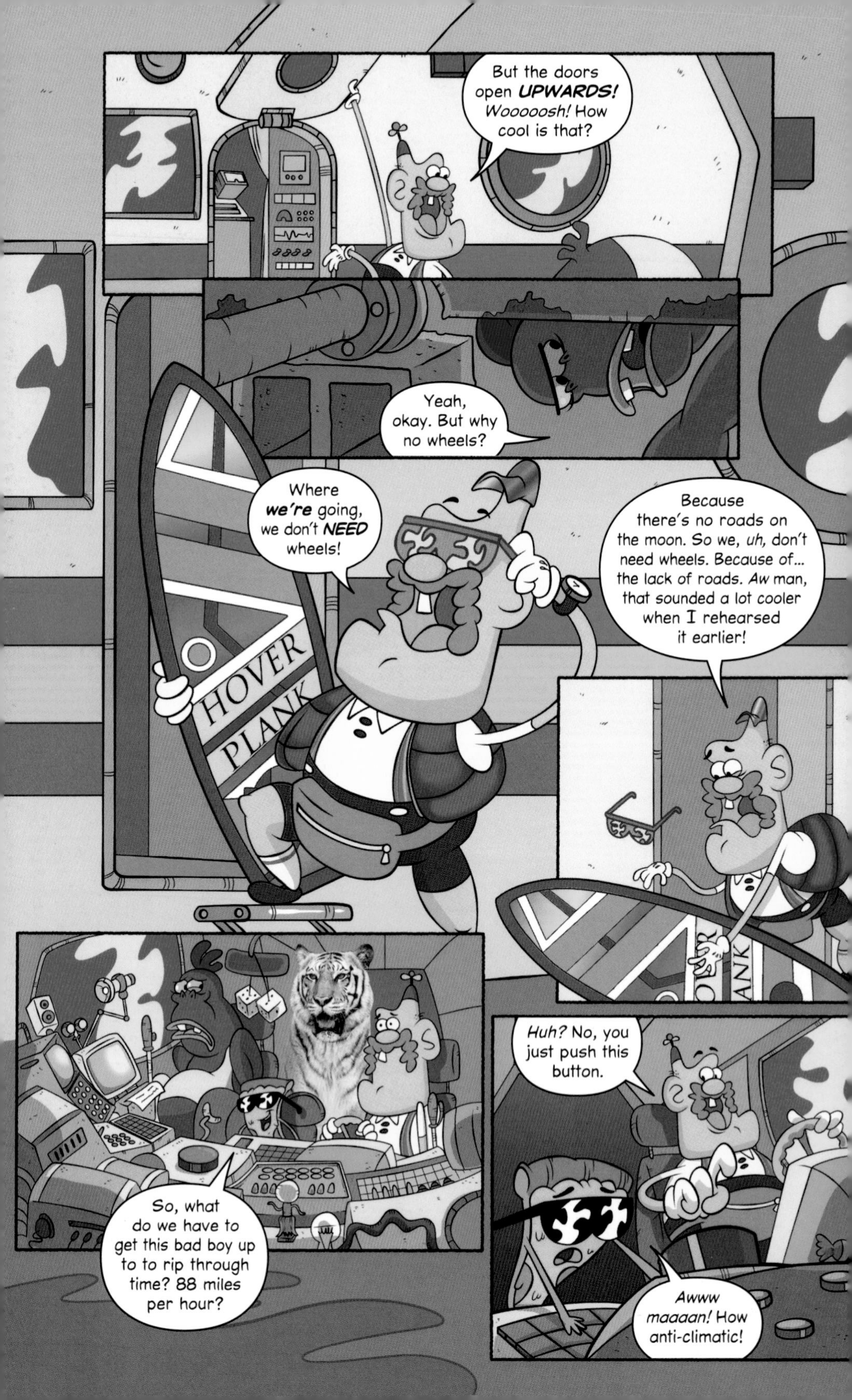
But the doors open **UPWARDS!** *Woooosh!* How cool is that?
Yeah, okay. But why no wheels?
Where ***we're*** going, we don't ***NEED*** wheels!
Because there's no roads on the moon. So we, *uh,* don't need wheels. Because of... the lack of roads. *Aw* man, that sounded a lot cooler when I rehearsed it earlier!
HOVER PLANK
So, what do we have to get this bad boy up to to rip through time? 88 miles per hour?
Huh? No, you just push this button.
Awww maaaan! How anti-climatic!

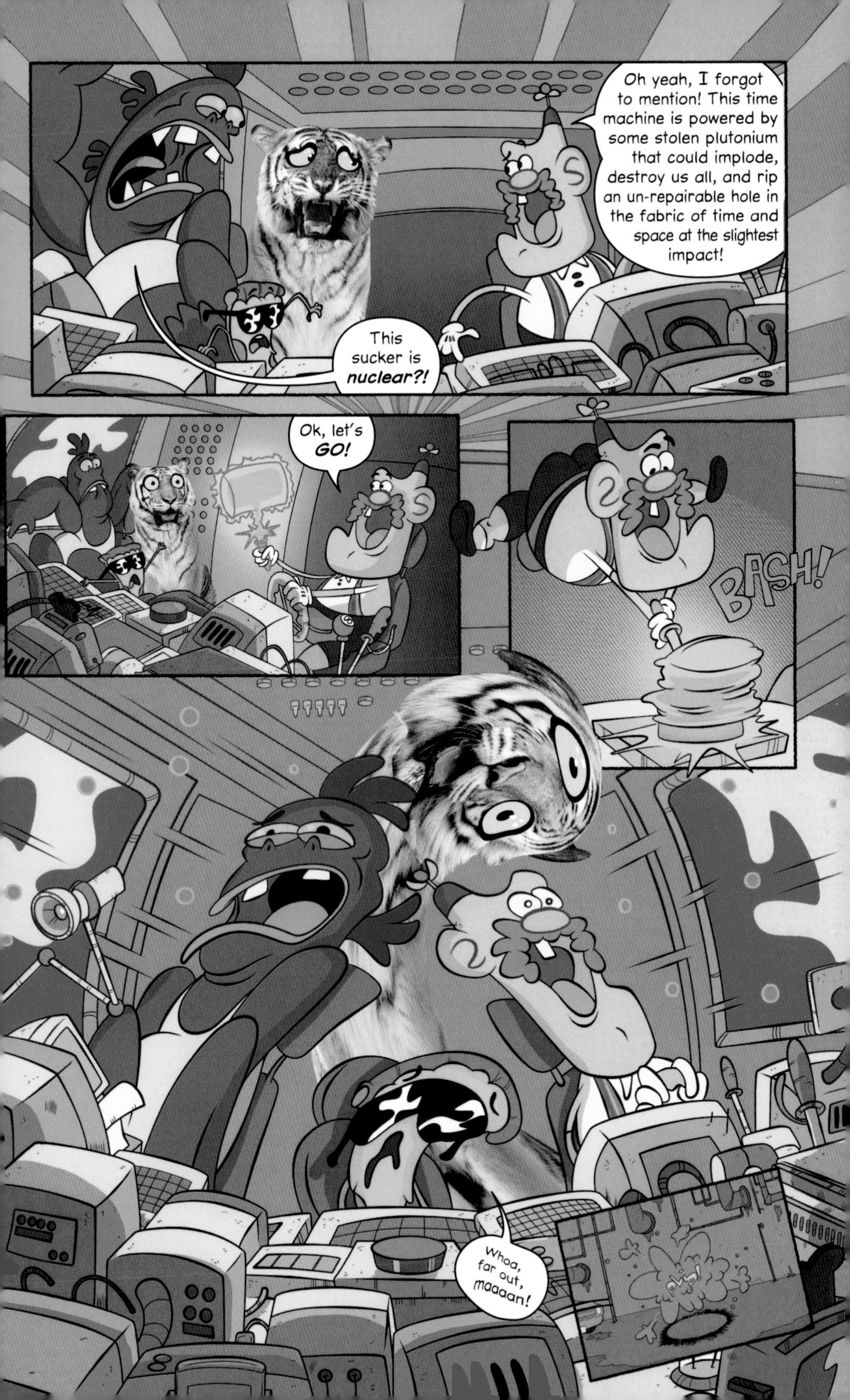
Oh yeah, I forgot to mention! This time machine is powered by some stolen plutonium that could implode, destroy us all, and rip an un-repairable hole in the fabric of time and space at the slightest impact!
This sucker is **nuclear?!**
Ok, let's **GO!**
BASH!
Whoa, far out, maaaan!

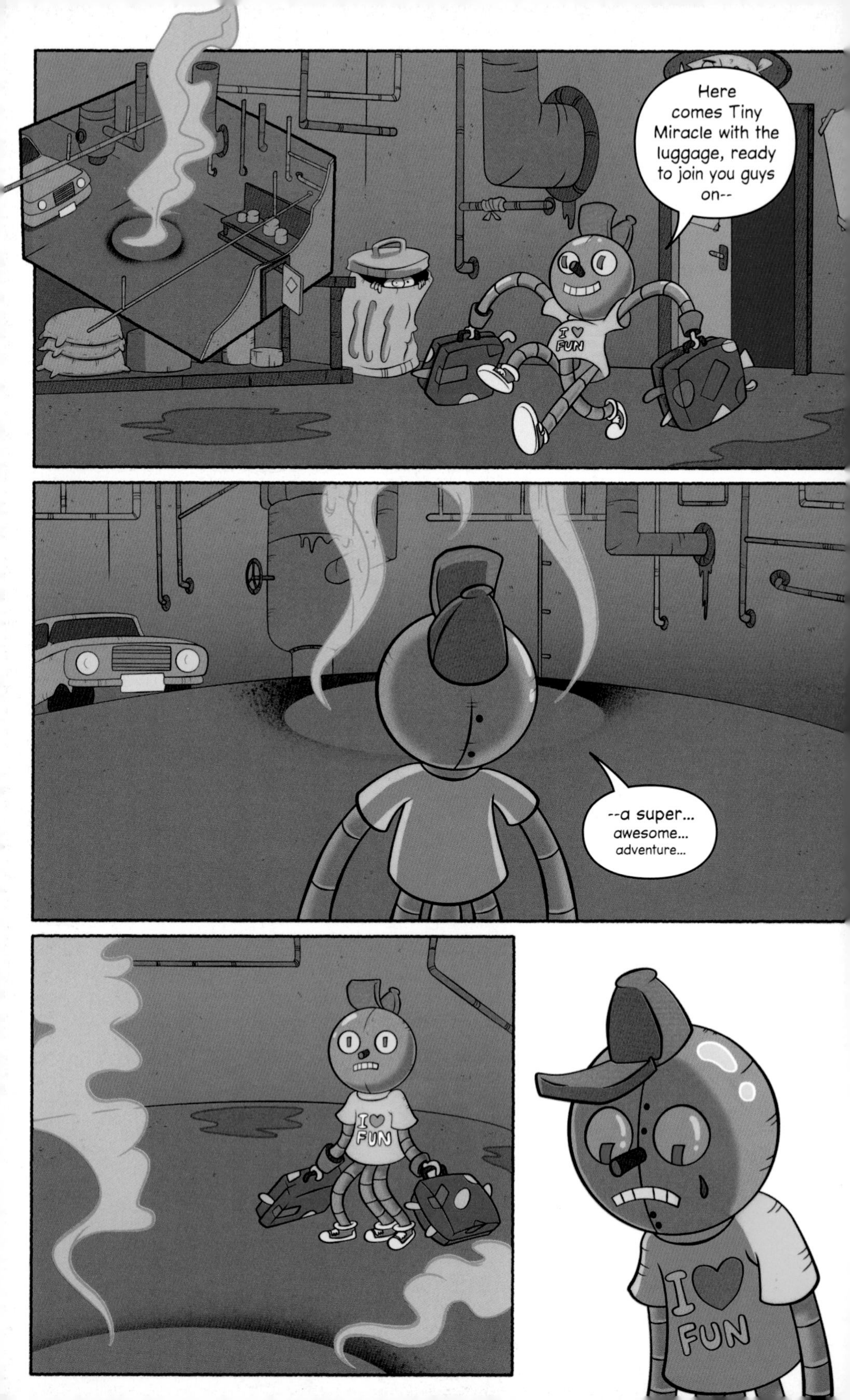
Here comes Tiny Miracle with the luggage, ready to join you guys on--
I ♥ FUN
--a super... awesome... adventure...
I ♥ FUN
I ♥ FUN

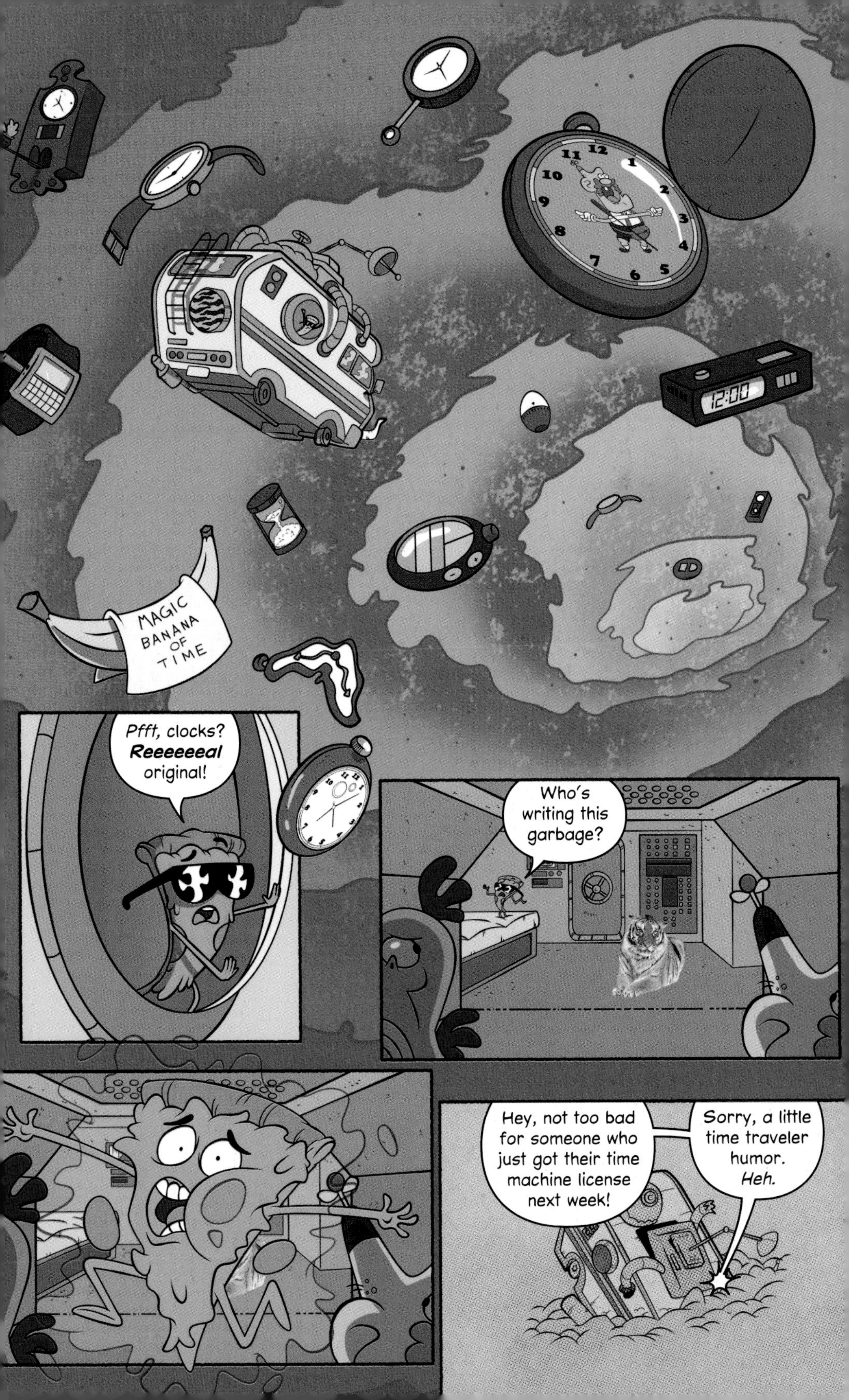

12
11
1
10
2
9
3
8
4
7
5
6
12:00
MAGIC BANANA OF TIME
Pfft, clocks? **Reeeeeeal** original!
Who's writing this garbage?
Hey, not too bad for someone who just got their time machine license next week!
Sorry, a little time traveler humor. *Heh.*

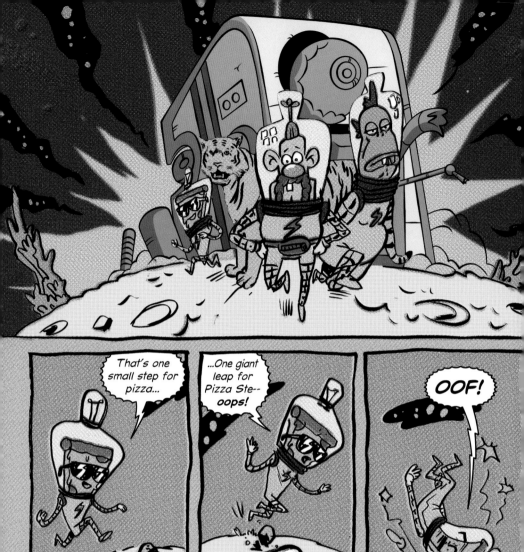

That's one small step for pizza...

...One giant leap for Pizza Ste-- oops!

OOF!

THOOMP! SPLORT!

Why have I been the butt of all the slapstick jokes so far? Why?!

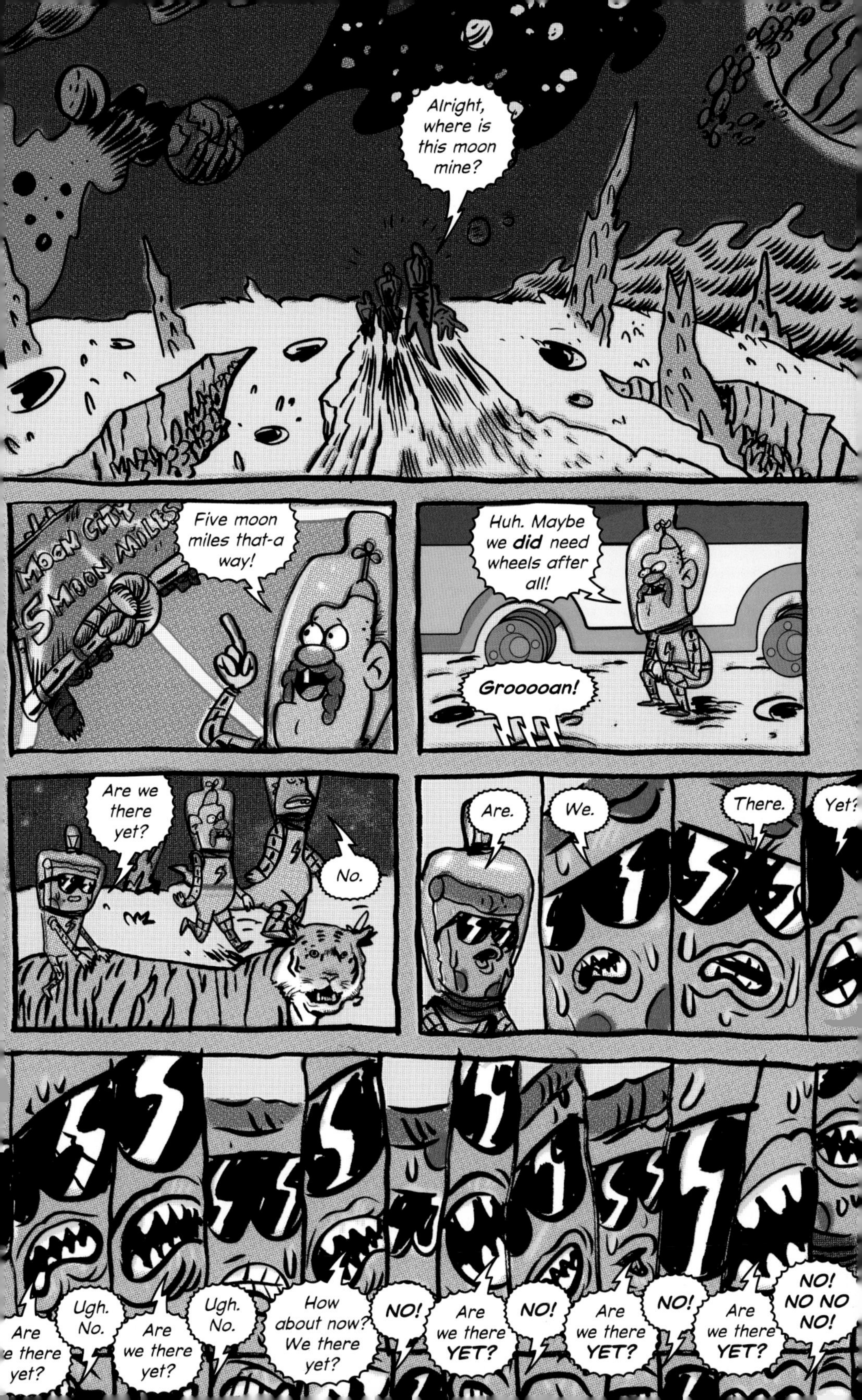

Alright, where is this moon mine?
MOON CITY 5 MOON MILES
Five moon miles that-a way!
Huh. Maybe we **did** need wheels after all!
Grooooan!
Are we there yet?
No.
Are.
We.
There.
Yet?
Are we there yet?
Ugh. No.
Are we there yet?
Ugh. No.
How about now? We there yet?
NO!
Are we there YET?
NO!
Are we there YET?
NO!
Are we there YET?
NO! NO NO NO!

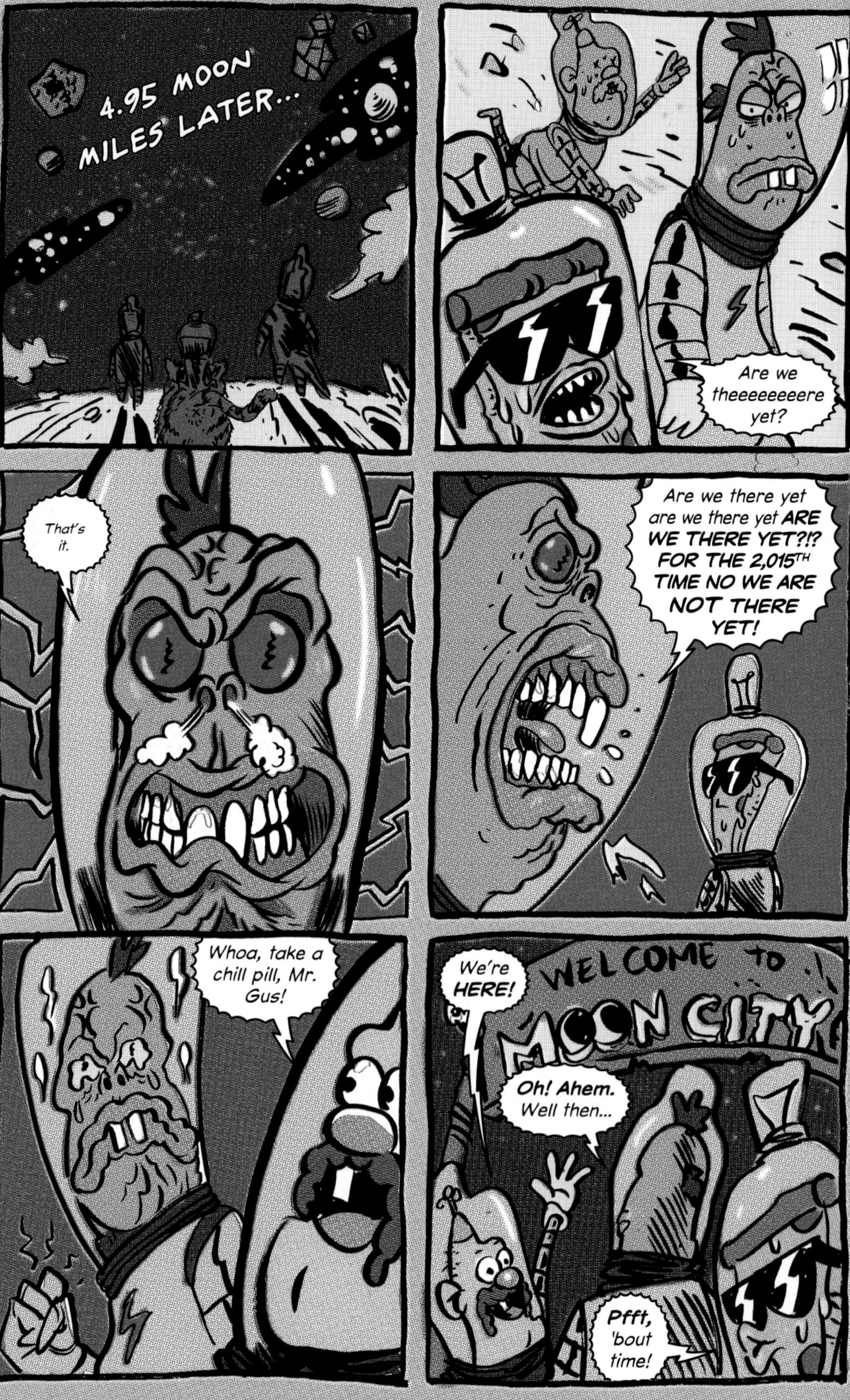
4.95 MOON MILES LATER...
Are we theeeeeeeere yet?
That's it.
Are we there yet are we there yet ARE WE THERE YET?!? FOR THE 2,015TH TIME NO WE ARE NOT THERE YET!
Whoa, take a chill pill, Mr. Gus!
We're HERE!
WELCOME TO MOON CITY
Oh! Ahem. Well then...
Pfft, 'bout time!

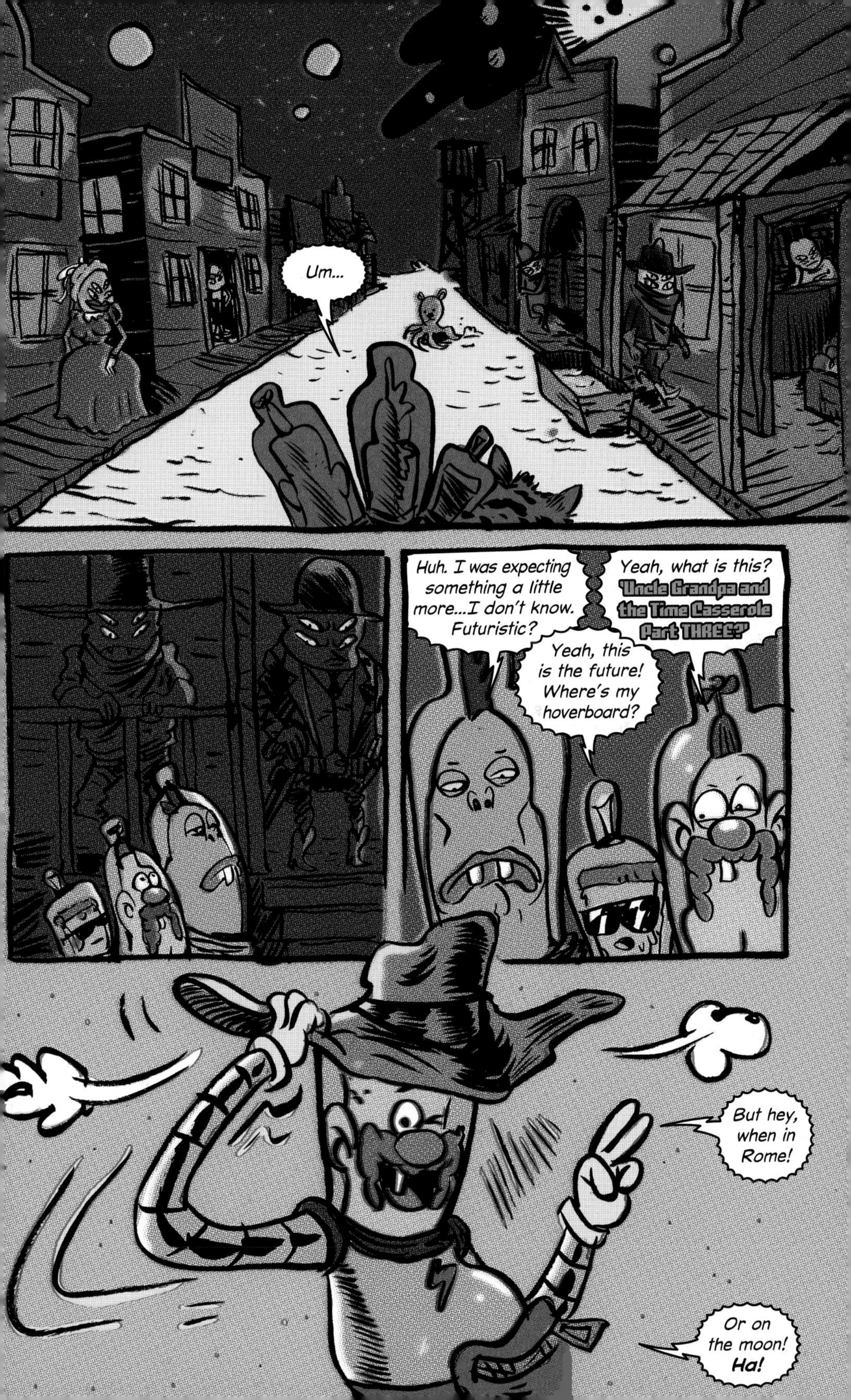

Um...
Huh. I was expecting something a little more...I don't know. Futuristic?
Yeah, this is the future! Where's my hoverboard?
Yeah, what is this? 'Uncle Grandpa and the Time Casserole Part THREE?'
But hey, when in Rome!
Or on the moon! **Ha!**

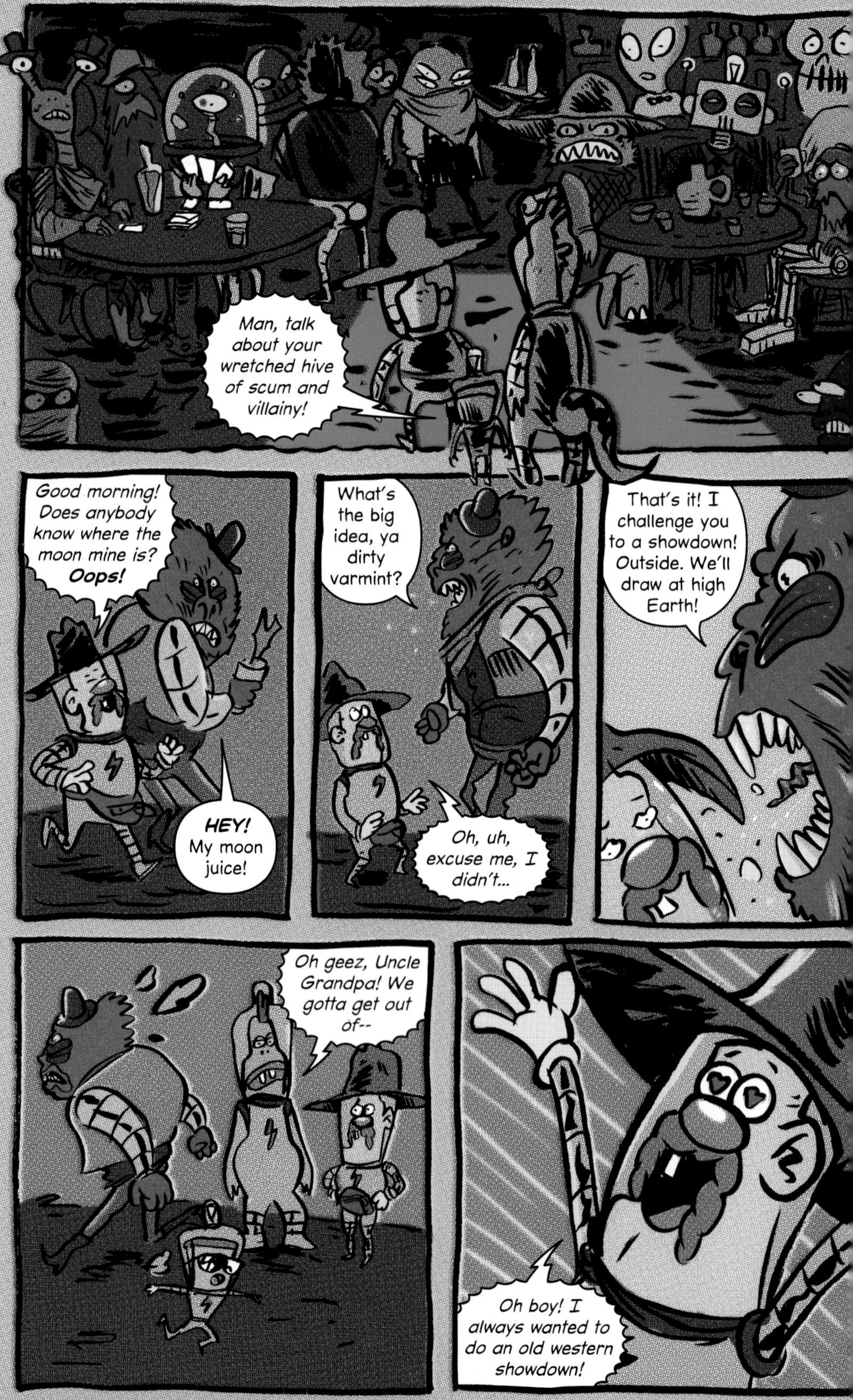
Man, talk about your wretched hive of scum and villainy!
Good morning! Does anybody know where the moon mine is? Oops!
HEY! My moon juice!
What's the big idea, ya dirty varmint?
Oh, uh, excuse me, I didn't...
That's it! I challenge you to a showdown! Outside. We'll draw at high Earth!
Oh geez, Uncle Grandpa! We gotta get out of--
Oh boy! I always wanted to do an old western showdown!

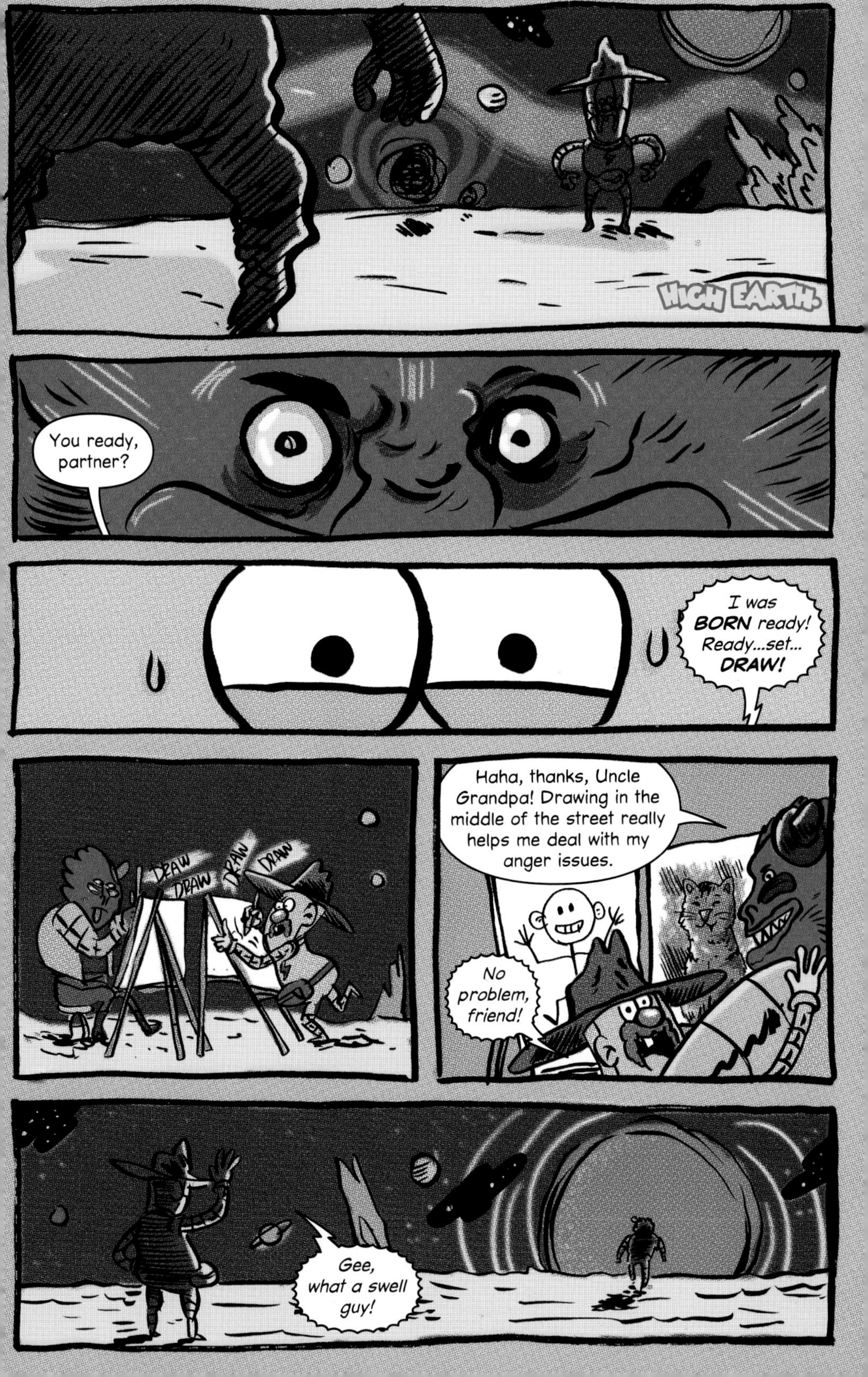
HIGH EARTH.
You ready, partner?
I was BORN ready! Ready...set... DRAW!
DRAW
DRAW
DRAW
DRAW
Haha, thanks, Uncle Grandpa! Drawing in the middle of the street really helps me deal with my anger issues.
No problem, friend!
Gee, what a swell guy!

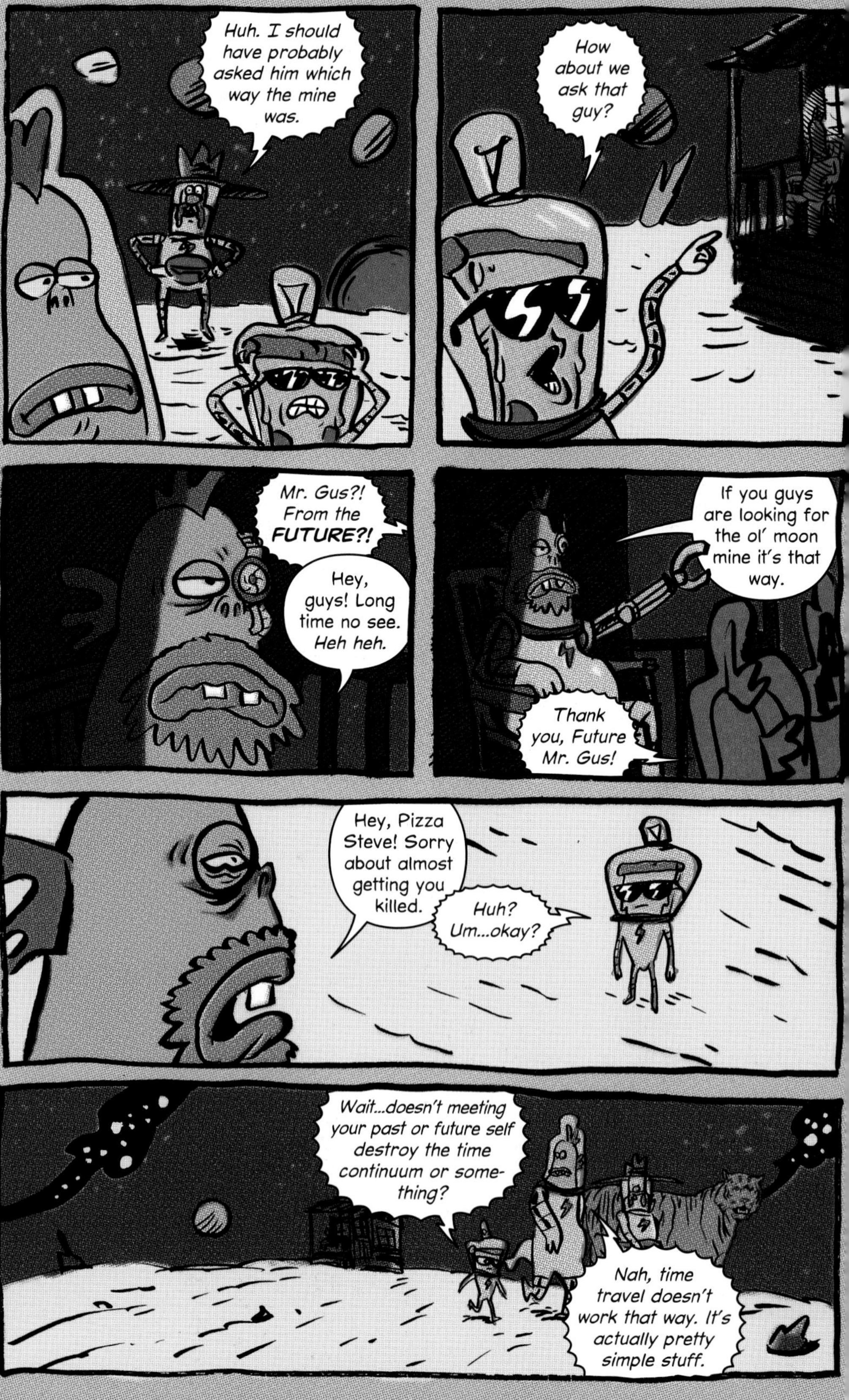
Huh. I should have probably asked him which way the mine was.
How about we ask that guy?
Mr. Gus?! From the FUTURE?!
Hey, guys! Long time no see. Heh heh.
If you guys are looking for the ol' moon mine it's that way.
Thank you, Future Mr. Gus!
Hey, Pizza Steve! Sorry about almost getting you killed.
Huh? Um...okay?
Wait...doesn't meeting your past or future self destroy the time continuum or something?
Nah, time travel doesn't work that way. It's actually pretty simple stuff.

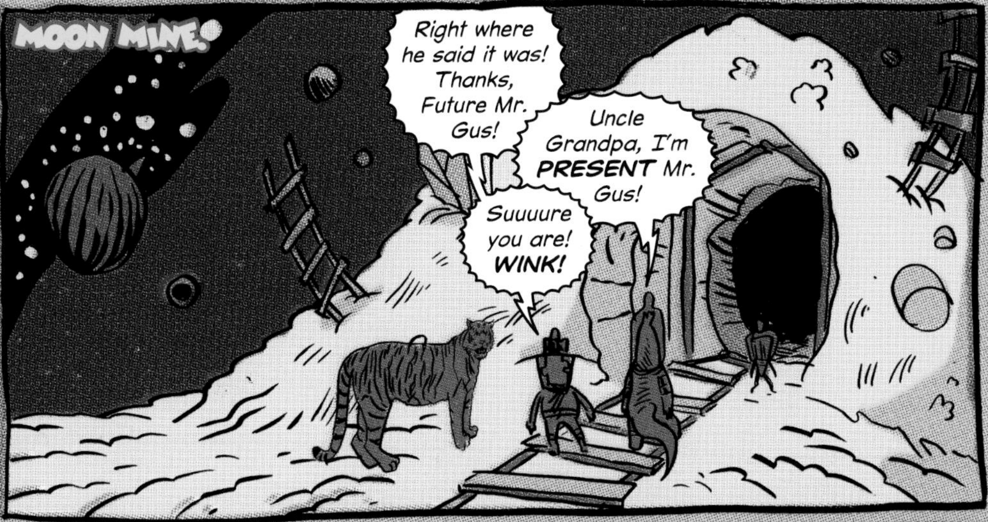
MOON MINE!
Right where he said it was! Thanks, Future Mr. Gus!
Uncle Grandpa, I'm PRESENT Mr. Gus!
Suuuure you are! WINK!

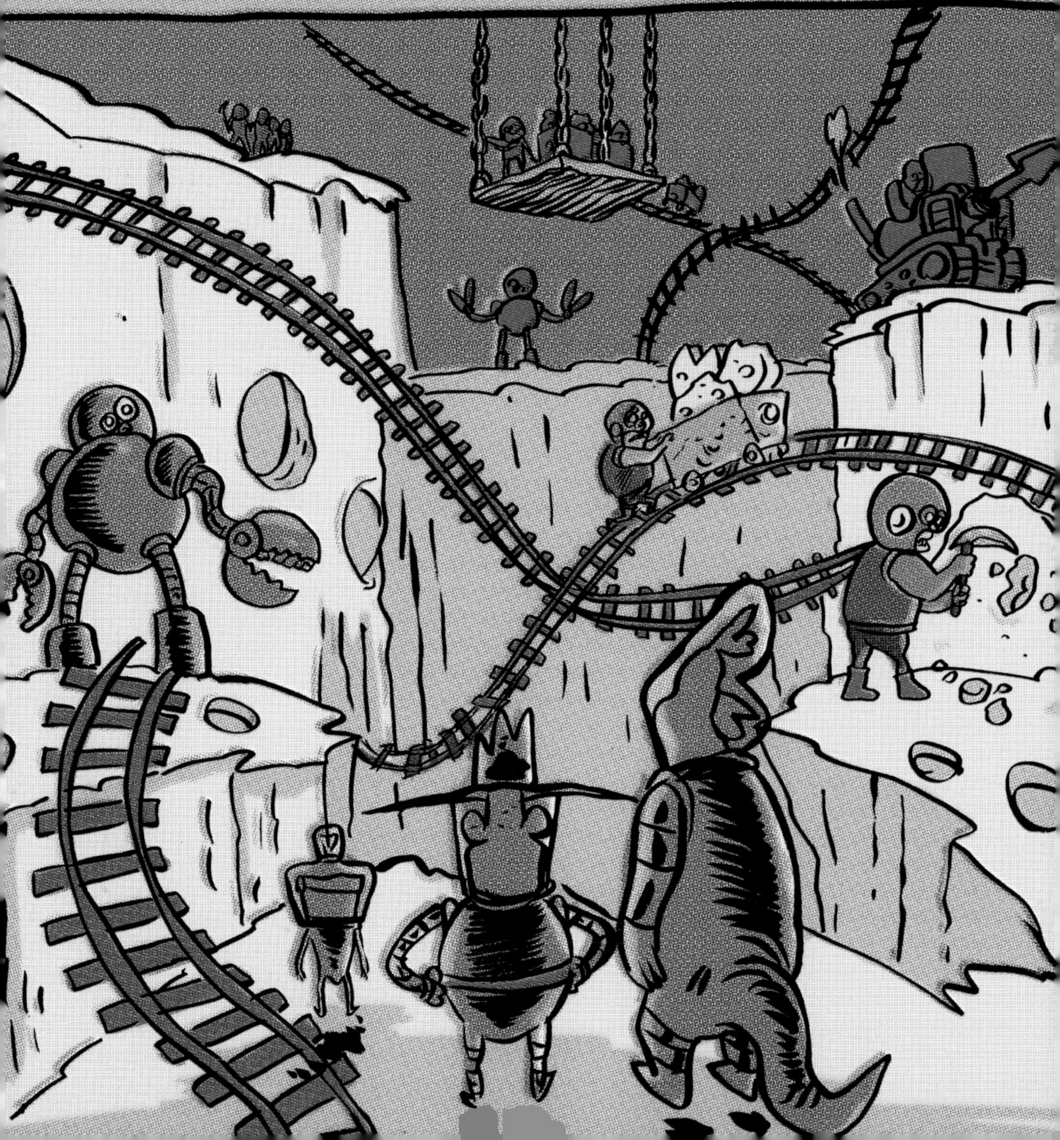

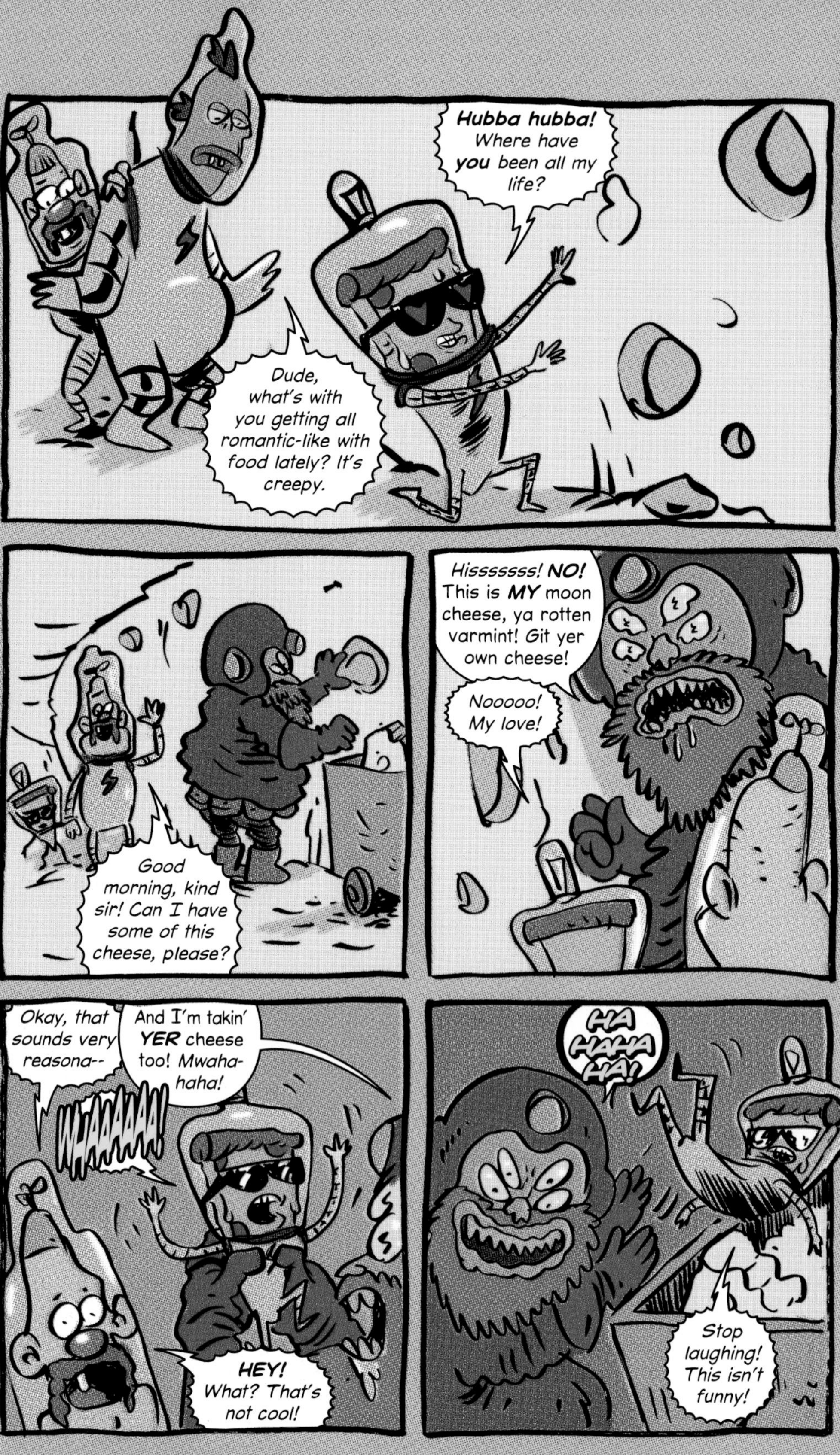
Hubba hubba! Where have you been all my life?
Dude, what's with you getting all romantic-like with food lately? It's creepy.
Good morning, kind sir! Can I have some of this cheese, please?
Hisssssss! NO! This is MY moon cheese, ya rotten varmint! Git yer own cheese!
Nooooo! My love!
Okay, that sounds very reasona--
And I'm takin' YER cheese too! Mwaha-haha!
WHAAAAAA!
HEY! What? That's not cool!
HA HAHA HA!
Stop laughing! This isn't funny!

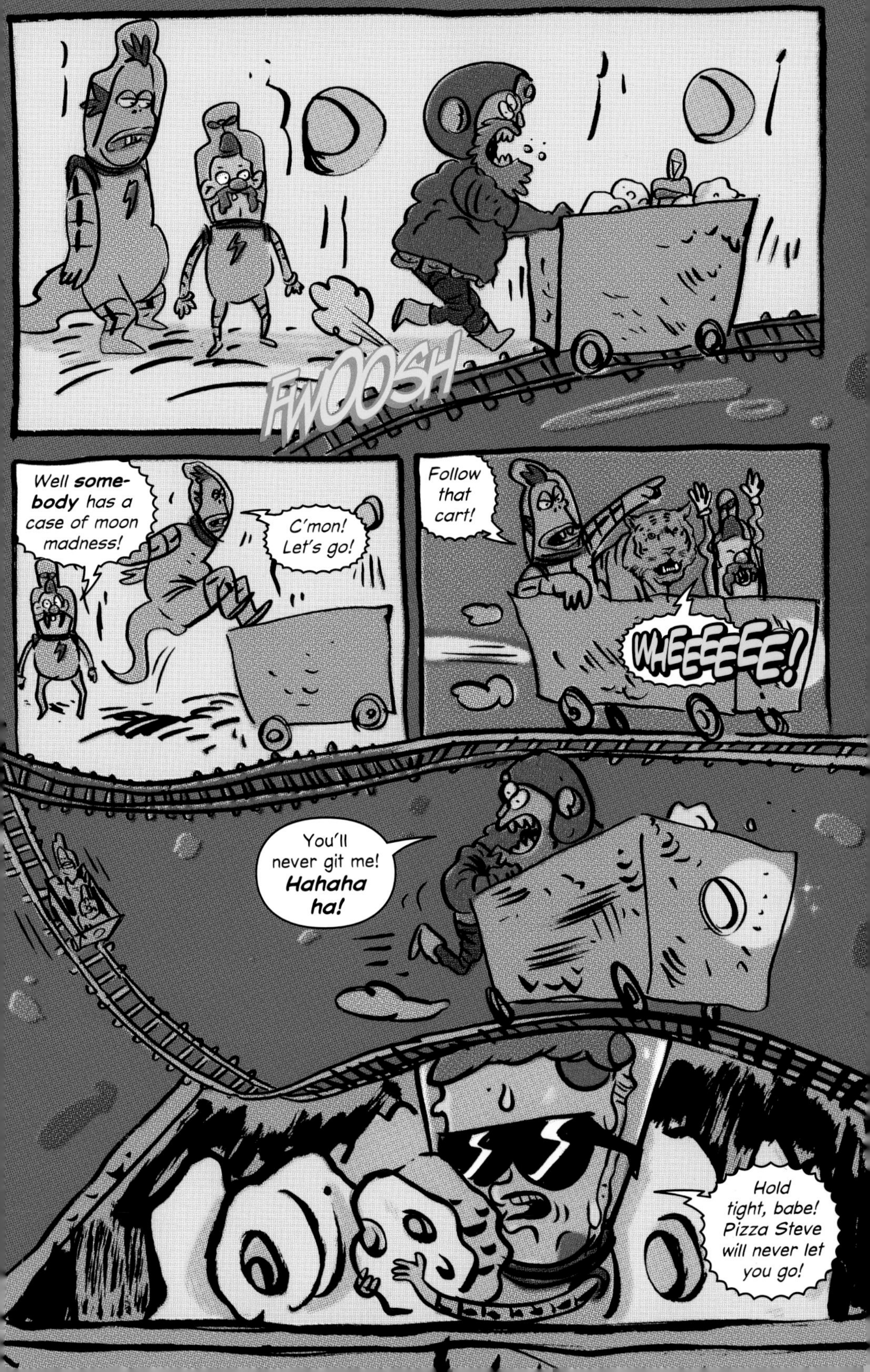
FWOOSH
Well somebody has a case of moon madness!
C'mon! Let's go!
Follow that cart!
WHEEEEEE!
You'll never git me! Hahaha ha!
Hold tight, babe! Pizza Steve will never let you go!

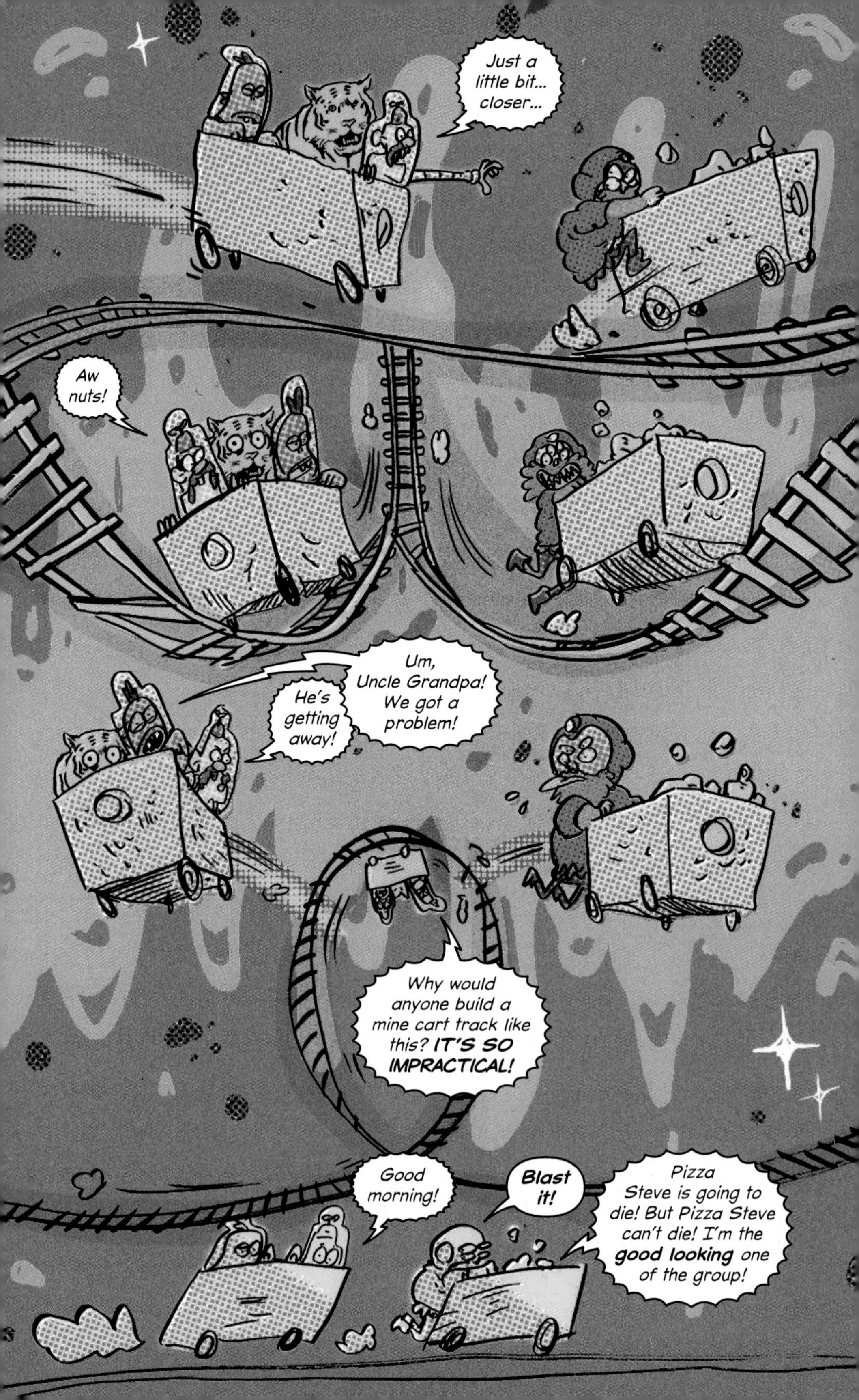

Just a little bit... closer...
Aw nuts!
Um, Uncle Grandpa! We got a problem!
He's getting away!
Why would anyone build a mine cart track like this? **IT'S SO IMPRACTICAL!**
Good morning!
Blast it!
Pizza Steve is going to die! But Pizza Steve can't die! I'm the **good looking** one of the group!

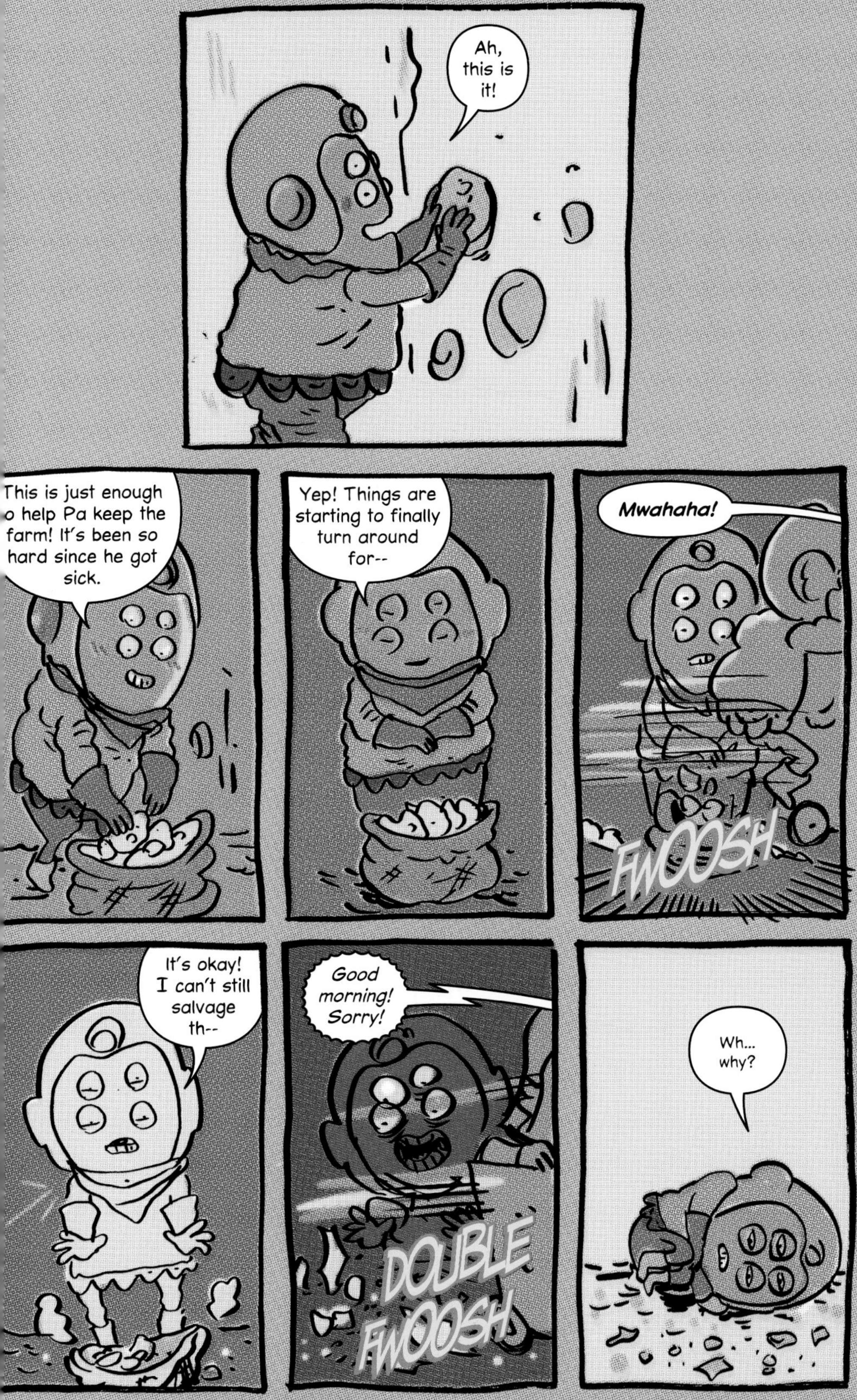
Ah, this is it!
This is just enough o help Pa keep the farm! It's been so hard since he got sick.
Yep! Things are starting to finally turn around for--
Mwahaha!
FWOOSH
It's okay! I can't still salvage th--
Good morning! Sorry!
DOUBLE FWOOSH
Wh... why?

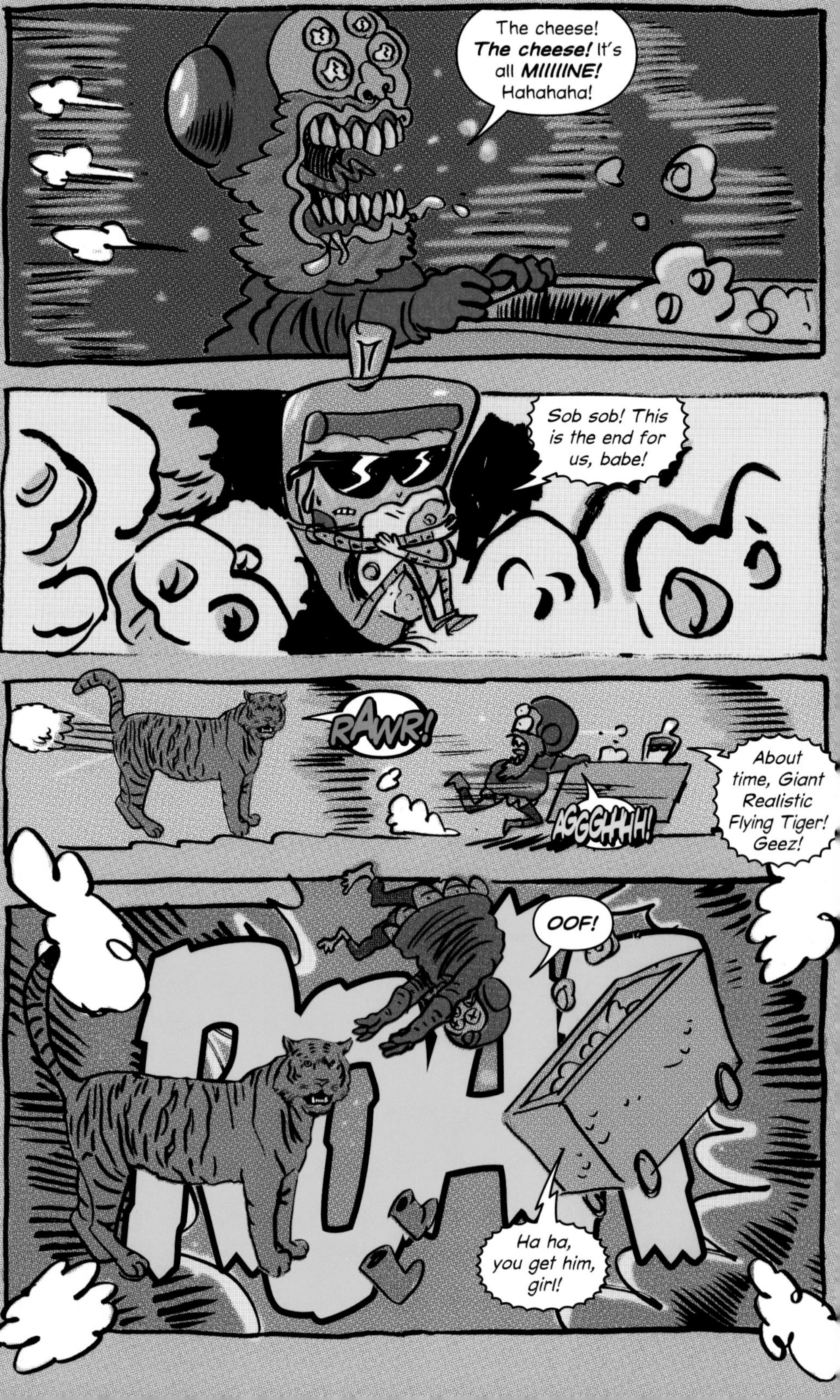
The cheese! **The cheese!** It's all **MIIIIINE!** Hahahaha!
Sob sob! This is the end for us, babe!
RAWR!
AGGGHHH!
About time, Giant Realistic Flying Tiger! Geez!
OOF!
Ha ha, you get him, girl!

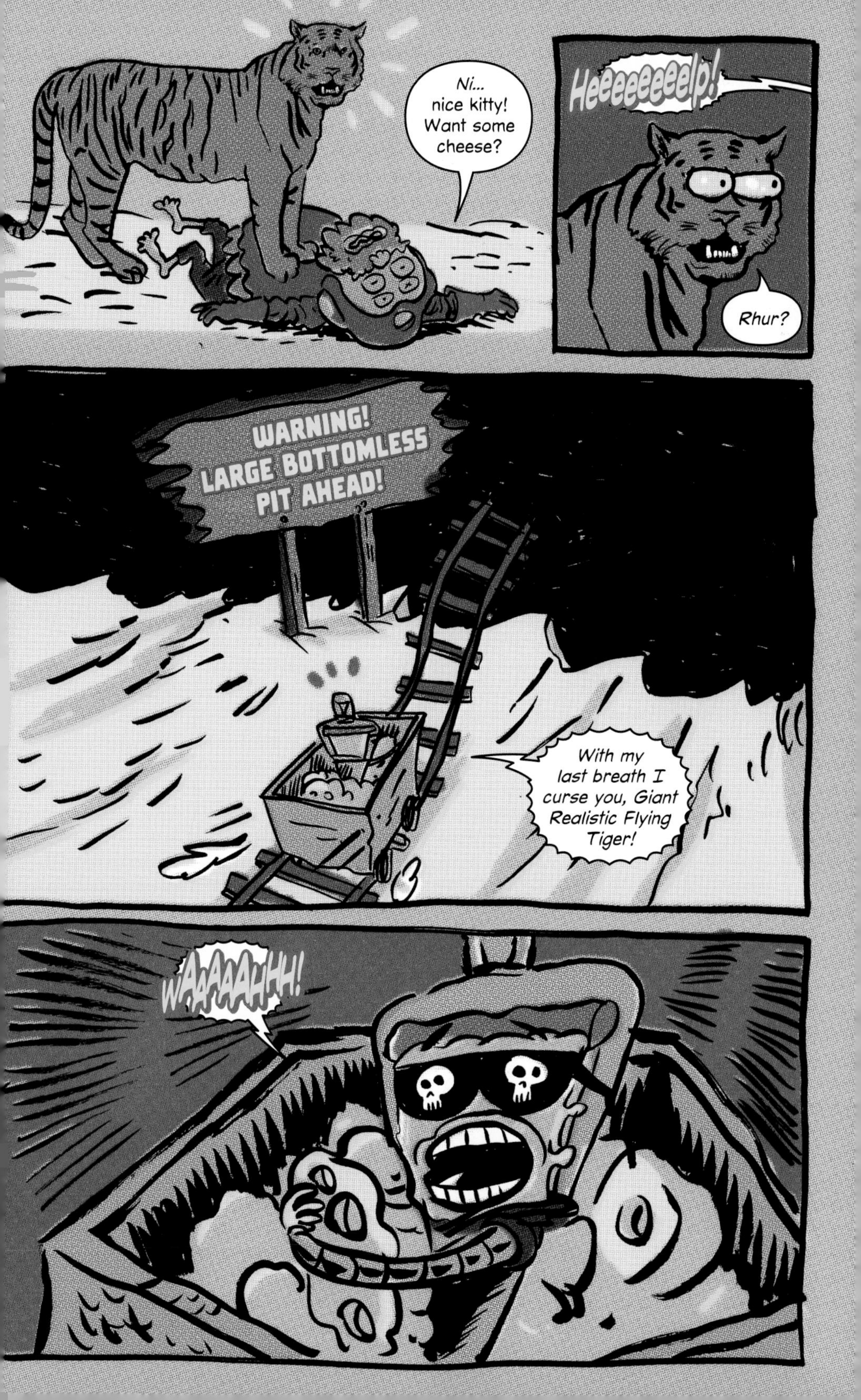
Ni...
nice kitty!
Want some
cheese?
Heeeeeeeelp!
Rhur?
WARNING!
LARGE BOTTOMLESS
PIT AHEAD!
With my last breath I curse you, Giant Realistic Flying Tiger!
WAAAAAHH!

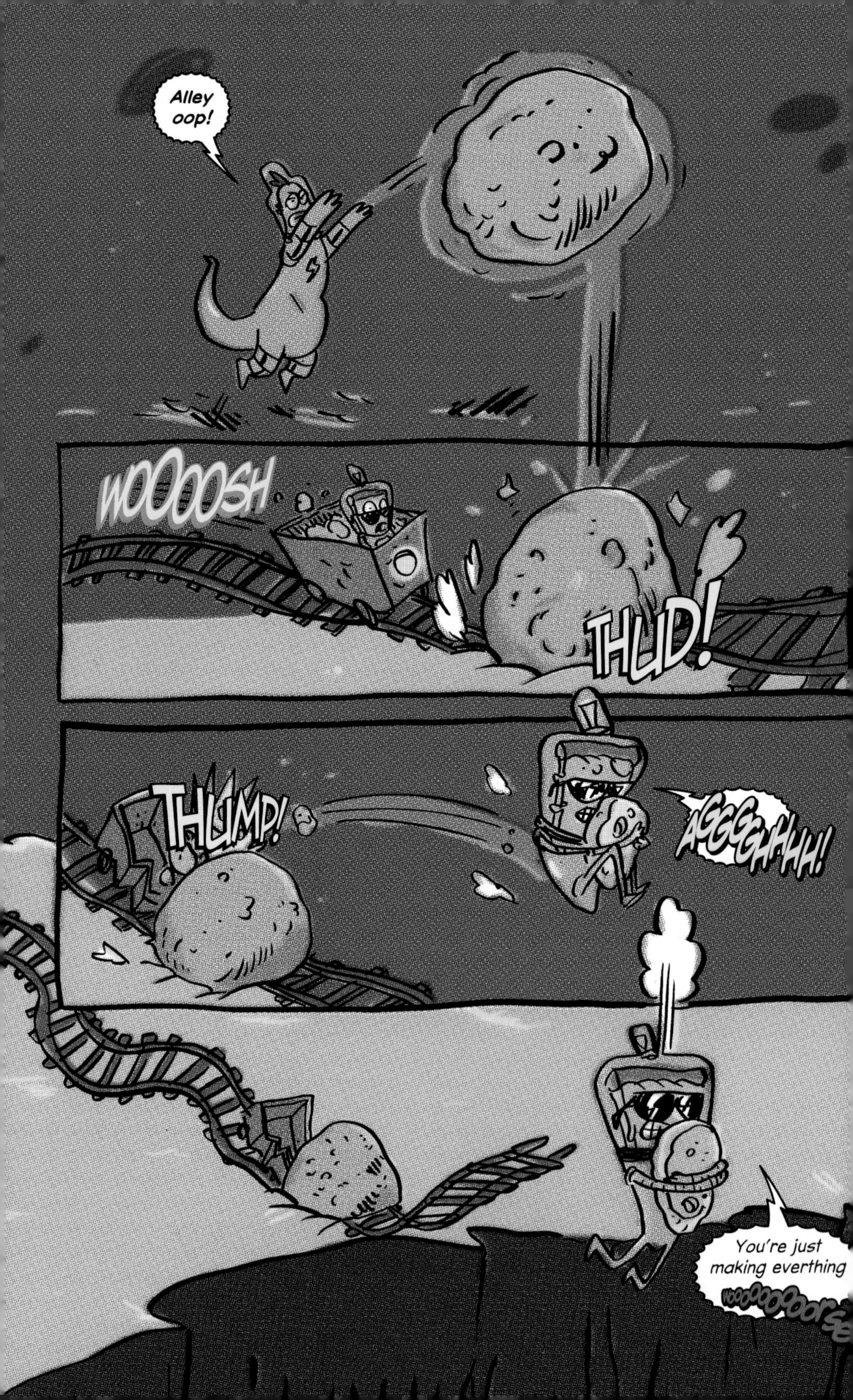
Alley oop!
WOOOOSH
THUD!
THUMP!
AGGGGHHHH!
You're just making everthing
wooooooooorse

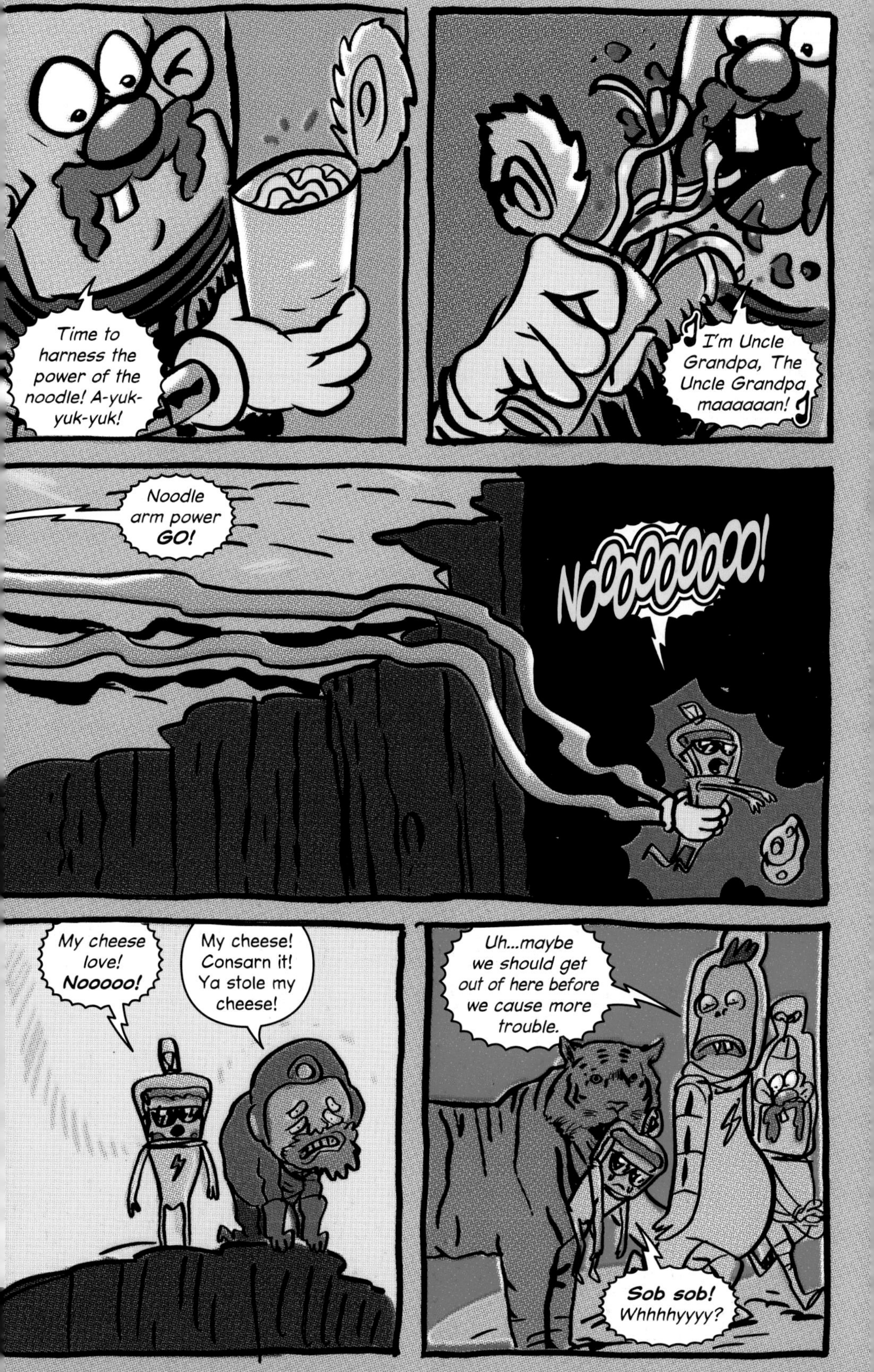

Time to harness the power of the noodle! A-yuk-yuk-yuk!
I'm Uncle Grandpa, The Uncle Grandpa maaaaaan!
Noodle arm power GO!
NOOOOOOOOOO!
My cheese love! Nooooo!
My cheese! Consarn it! Ya stole my cheese!
Uh...maybe we should get out of here before we cause more trouble.
Sob sob! Whhhhyyyy?

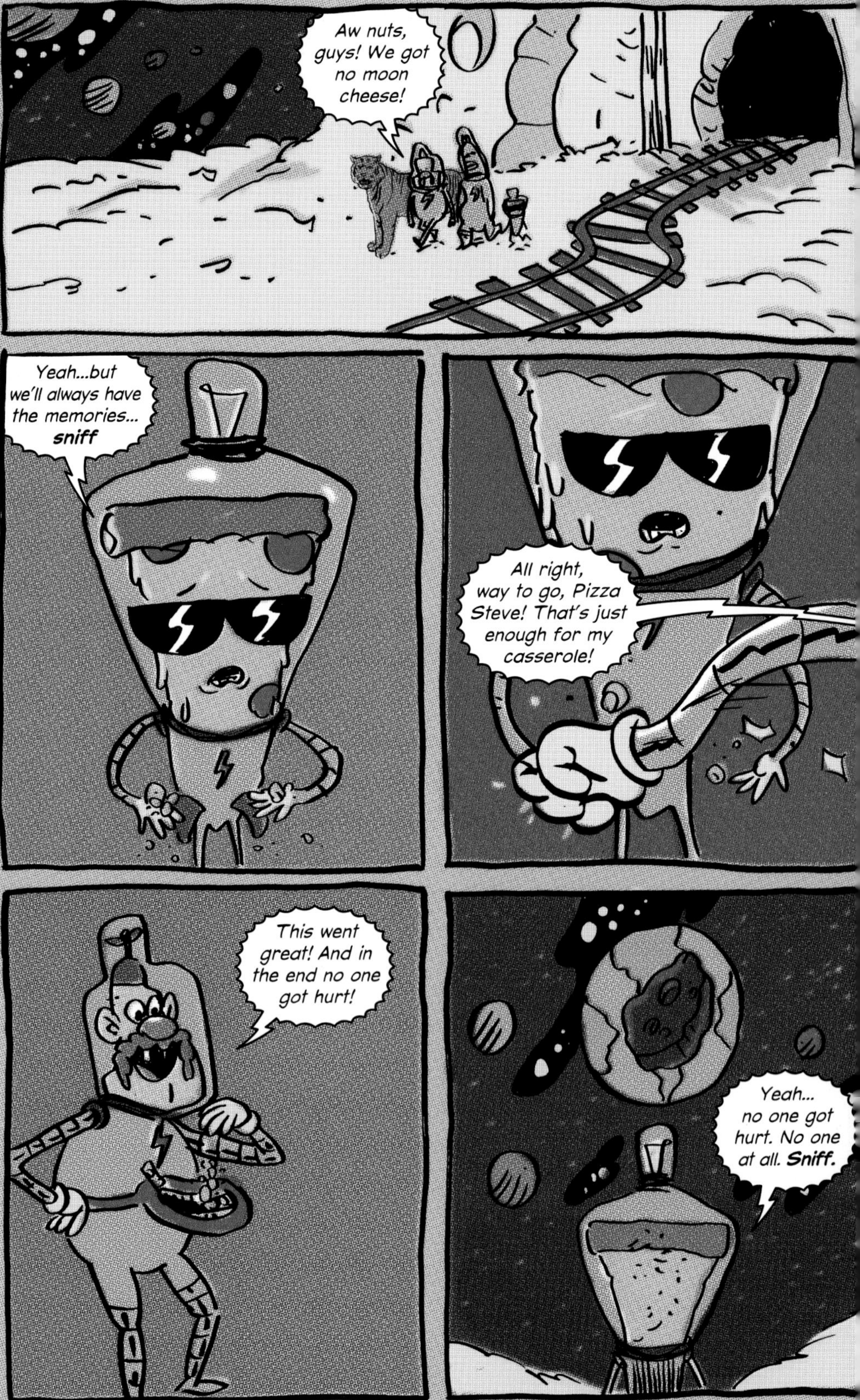
Aw nuts, guys! We got no moon cheese!
Yeah...but we'll always have the memories... **sniff**
All right, way to go, Pizza Steve! That's just enough for my casserole!
This went great! And in the end no one got hurt!
Yeah... no one got hurt. No one at all. **Sniff.**

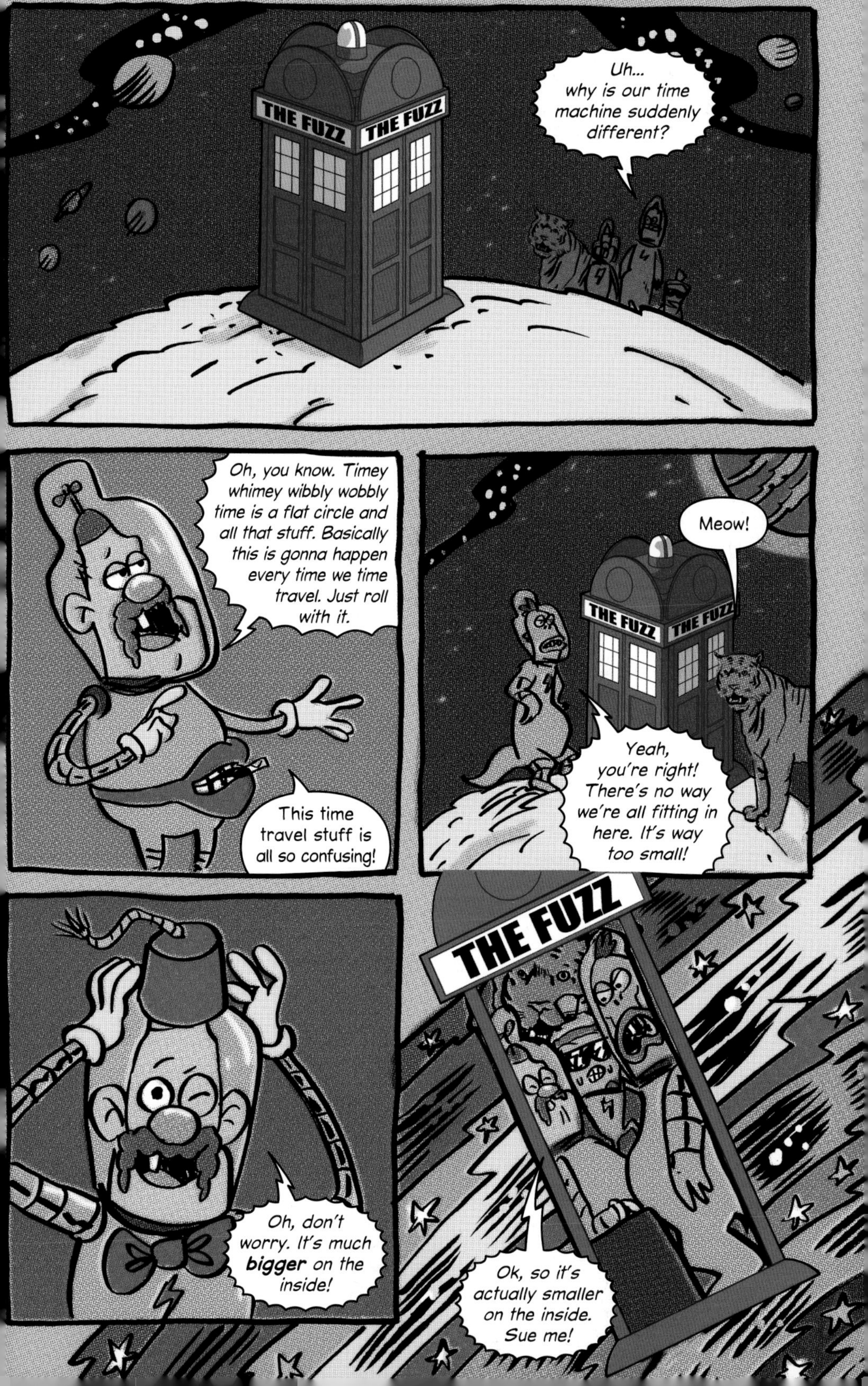
Uh... why is our time machine suddenly different?
THE FUZZ
THE FUZZ
Oh, you know. Timey whimey wibbly wobbly time is a flat circle and all that stuff. Basically this is gonna happen every time we time travel. Just roll with it.
This time travel stuff is all so confusing!
Meow!
THE FUZZ
THE FUZZ
Yeah, you're right! There's no way we're all fitting in here. It's way too small!
Oh, don't worry. It's much **bigger** on the inside!
THE FUZZ
Ok, so it's actually smaller on the inside. Sue me!

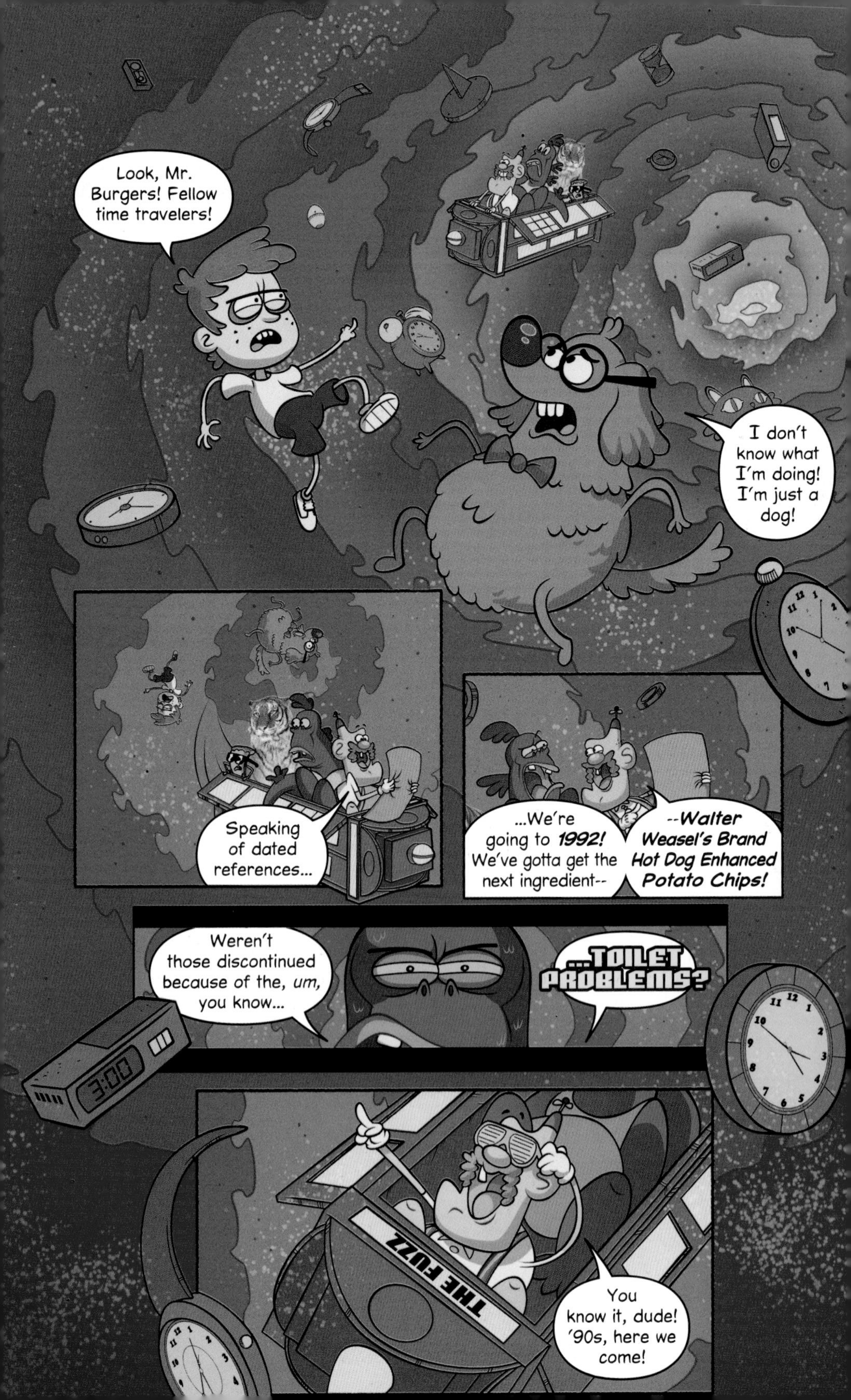
Look, Mr. Burgers! Fellow time travelers!
I don't know what I'm doing! I'm just a dog!
Speaking of dated references...
...We're going to *1992!* We've gotta get the next ingredient--
--***Walter Weasel's Brand Hot Dog Enhanced Potato Chips!***
Weren't those discontinued because of the, *um,* you know...
...TOILET PROBLEMS?
THE FUZZ
You know it, dude! '90s, here we come!

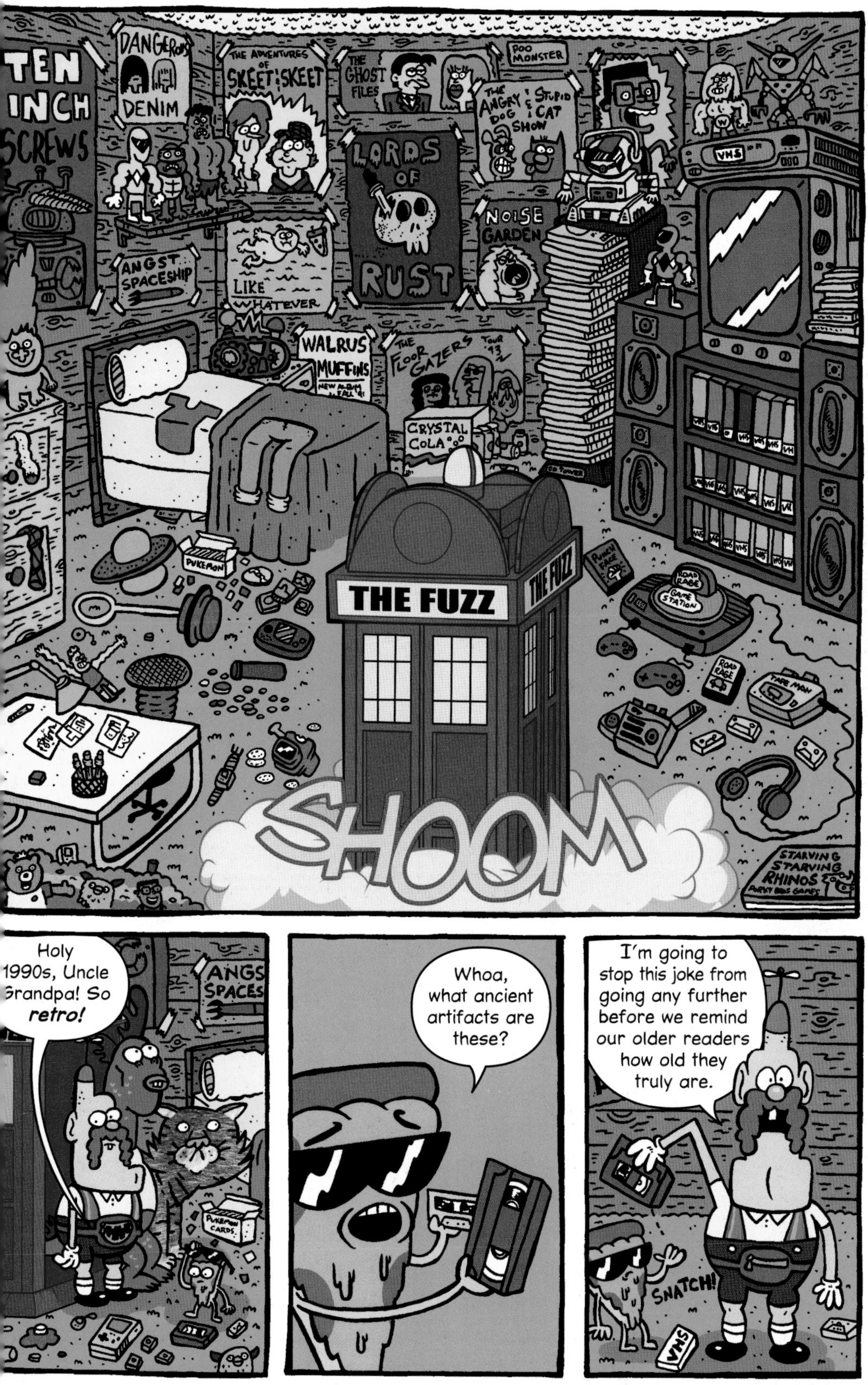
TEN INCH SCREWS
DANGEROUS DENIM
THE ADVENTURES OF SKEET & SKEET
THE GHOST FILES
POO MONSTER
THE ANGRY DOG & STUPID CAT SHOW
LORDS OF RUST
NOISE GARDEN
ANGST SPACESHIP
LIKE WHATEVER
WALRUS MUFFINS
THE FLOOR GAZERS
CRYSTAL COLA
VHS
PUKEMON
ROAD RAGE
GAME STATION
TAPE MAN
THE FUZZ
SHOOM
STARVING STARVING RHINOS
Holy 1990s, Uncle Grandpa! So *retro!*
PUKEMON CARDS
Whoa, what ancient artifacts are these?
I'm going to stop this joke from going any further before we remind our older readers how old they truly are.
SNATCH!
VHS

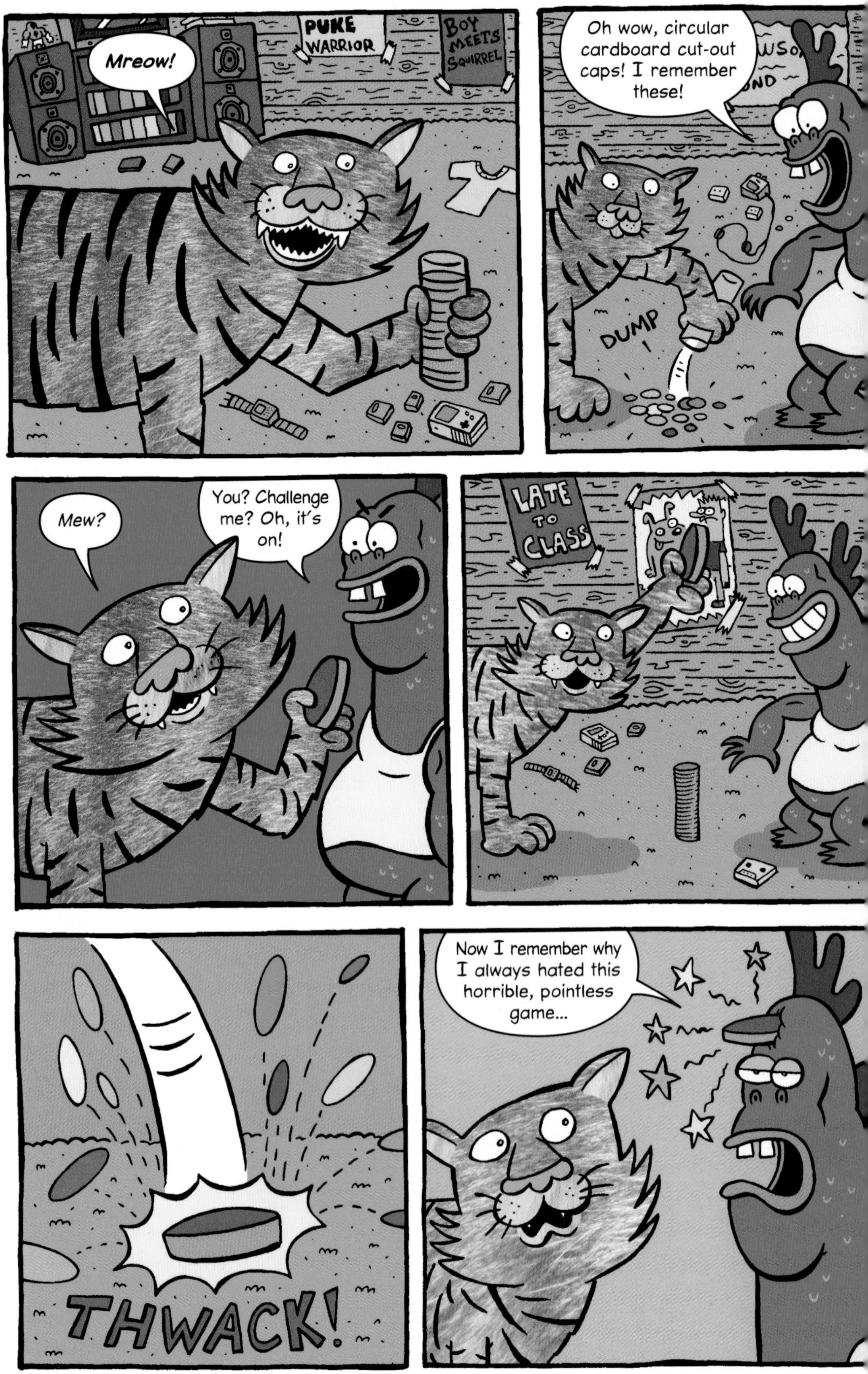
PUKE WARRIOR
BOY MEETS SQUIRREL
Mreow!
Oh wow, circular cardboard cut-out caps! I remember these!
DUMP
Mew?
You? Challenge me? Oh, it's on!
LATE TO CLASS
THWACK!
Now I remember why I always hated this horrible, pointless game...

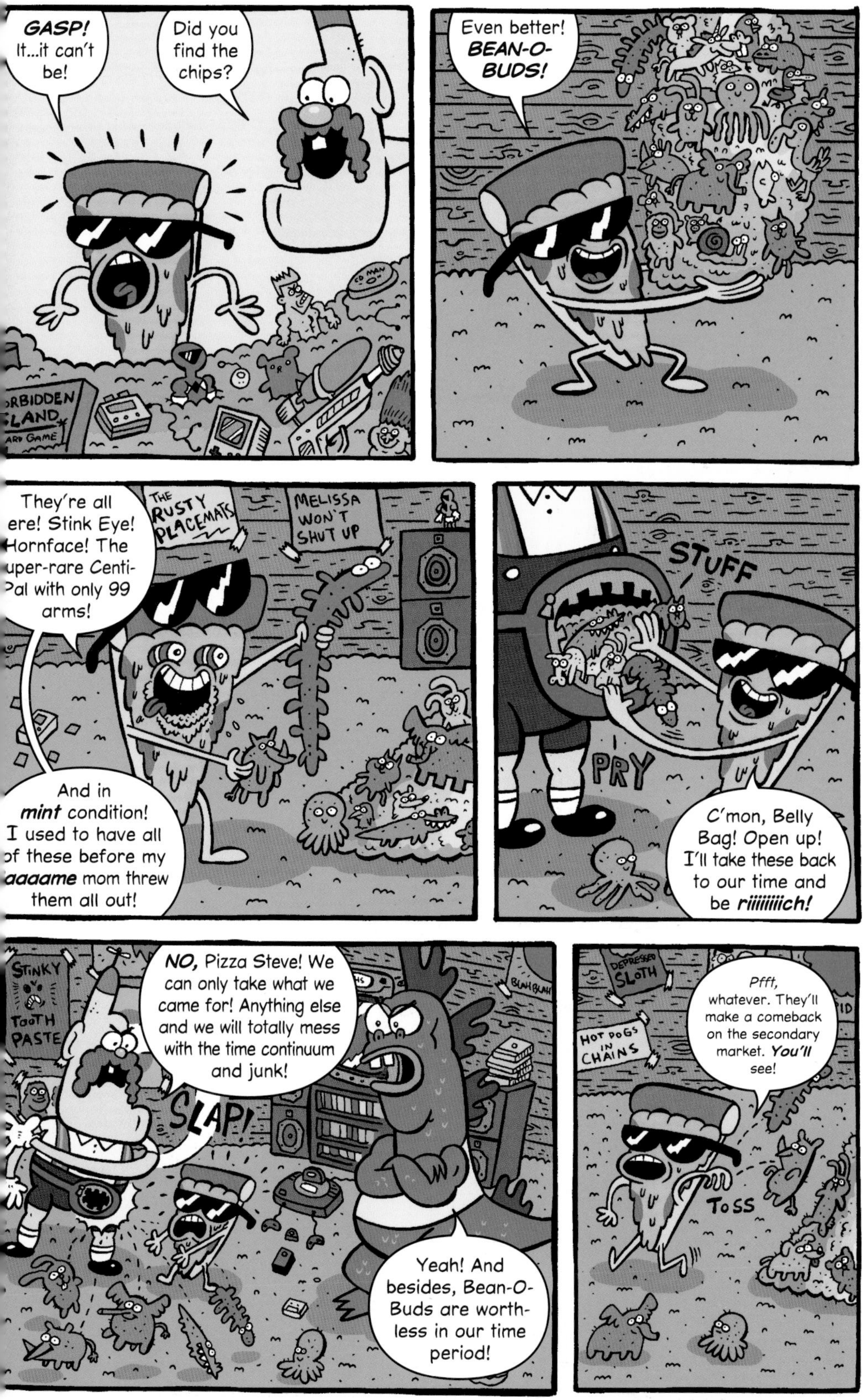
GASP! It...it can't be!
Did you find the chips?
Even better! BEAN-O-BUDS!
They're all ere! Stink Eye! Hornface! The uper-rare Centi-Pal with only 99 arms!
THE RUSTY PLACEMATS
MELISSA WON'T SHUT UP
And in mint condition! I used to have all of these before my aaaame mom threw them all out!
STUFF
PRY
C'mon, Belly Bag! Open up! I'll take these back to our time and be riiiiiiich!
STINKY TOOTH PASTE
NO, Pizza Steve! We can only take what we came for! Anything else and we will totally mess with the time continuum and junk!
SLAP!
BLAH BLAH
Yeah! And besides, Bean-O-Buds are worthless in our time period!
DEPRESSED SLOTH
HOT DOGS IN CHAINS
Pfft, whatever. They'll make a comeback on the secondary market. You'll see!
TOSS

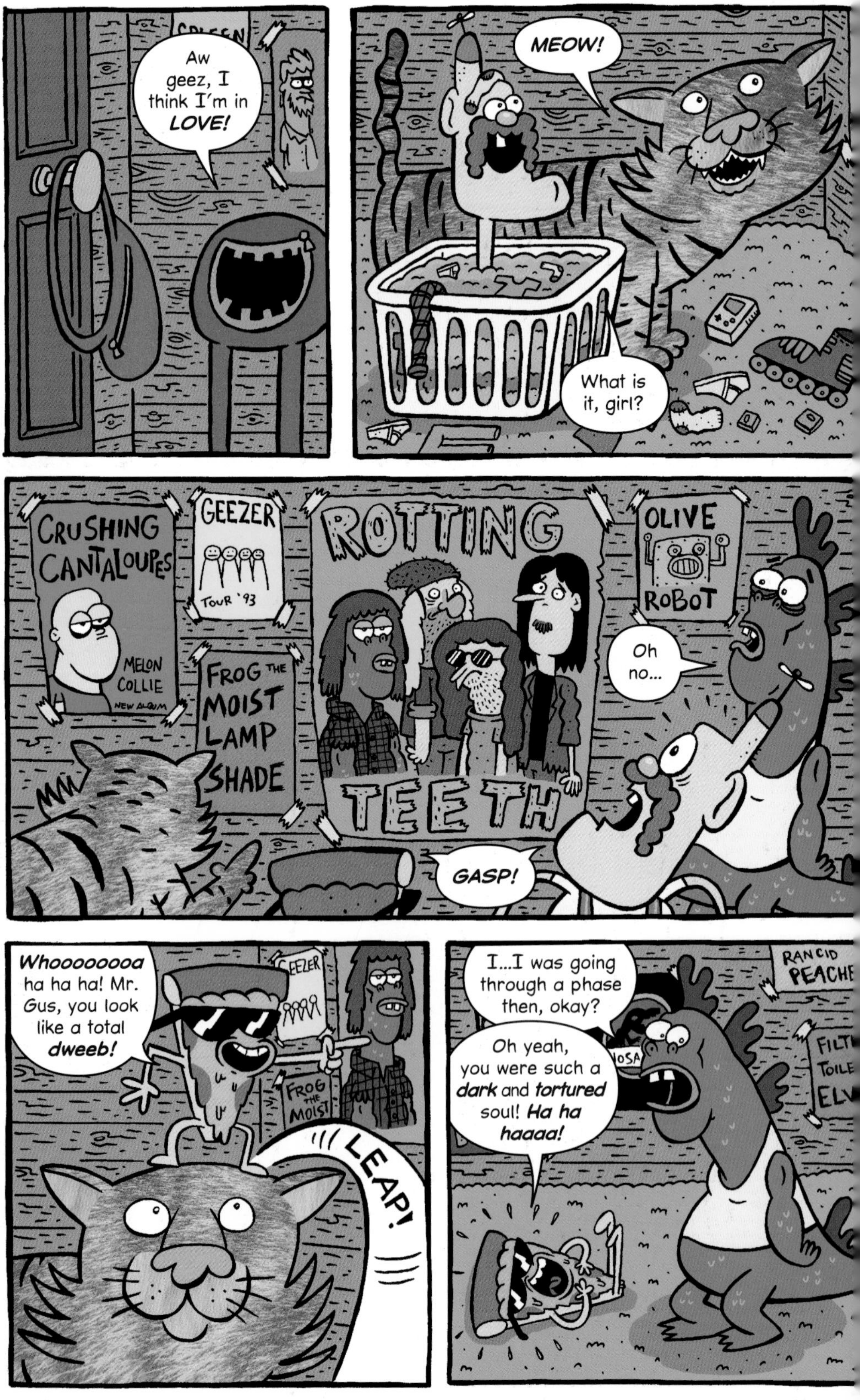
Aw geez, I think I'm in **LOVE!**
MEOW!
What is it, girl?
CRUSHING CANTALOUPES
MELON COLLIE
NEW ALBUM
GEEZER
TOUR '93
ROTTING TEETH
OLIVE ROBOT
FROG THE MOIST LAMP SHADE
Oh no...
GASP!
Whoooooooa ha ha ha! Mr. Gus, you look like a total ***dweeb!***
LEAP!
I...I was going through a phase then, okay?
Oh yeah, you were such a ***dark*** and ***tortured*** soul! ***Ha ha haaaa!***
RANCID PEACHE

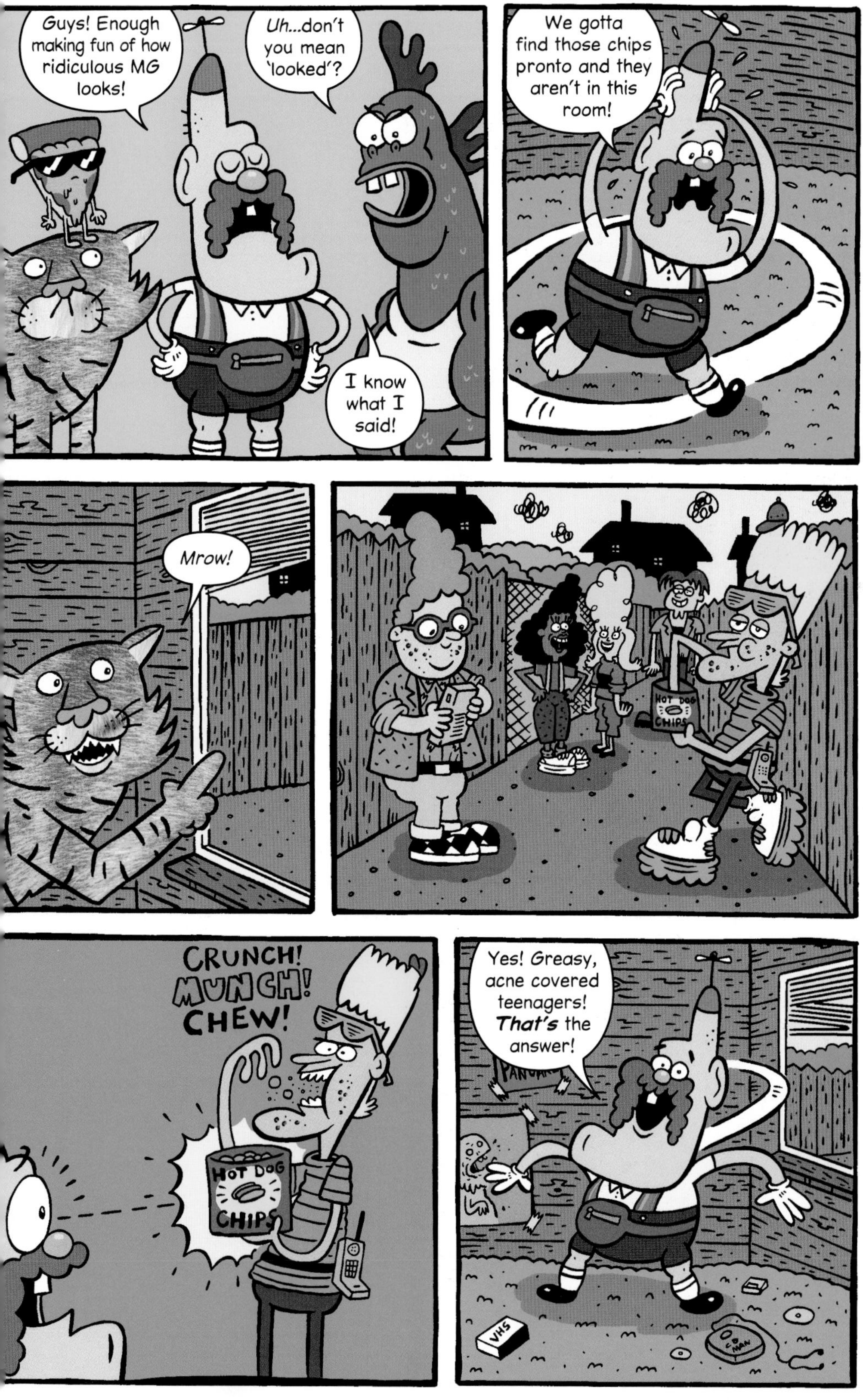
Guys! Enough making fun of how ridiculous MG looks!
Uh...don't you mean 'looked'?
I know what I said!
We gotta find those chips pronto and they aren't in this room!
Mrow!
HOT DOG CHIPS
CRUNCH!
MUNCH!
CHEW!
HOT DOG CHIPS
Yes! Greasy, acne covered teenagers! That's the answer!
VHS

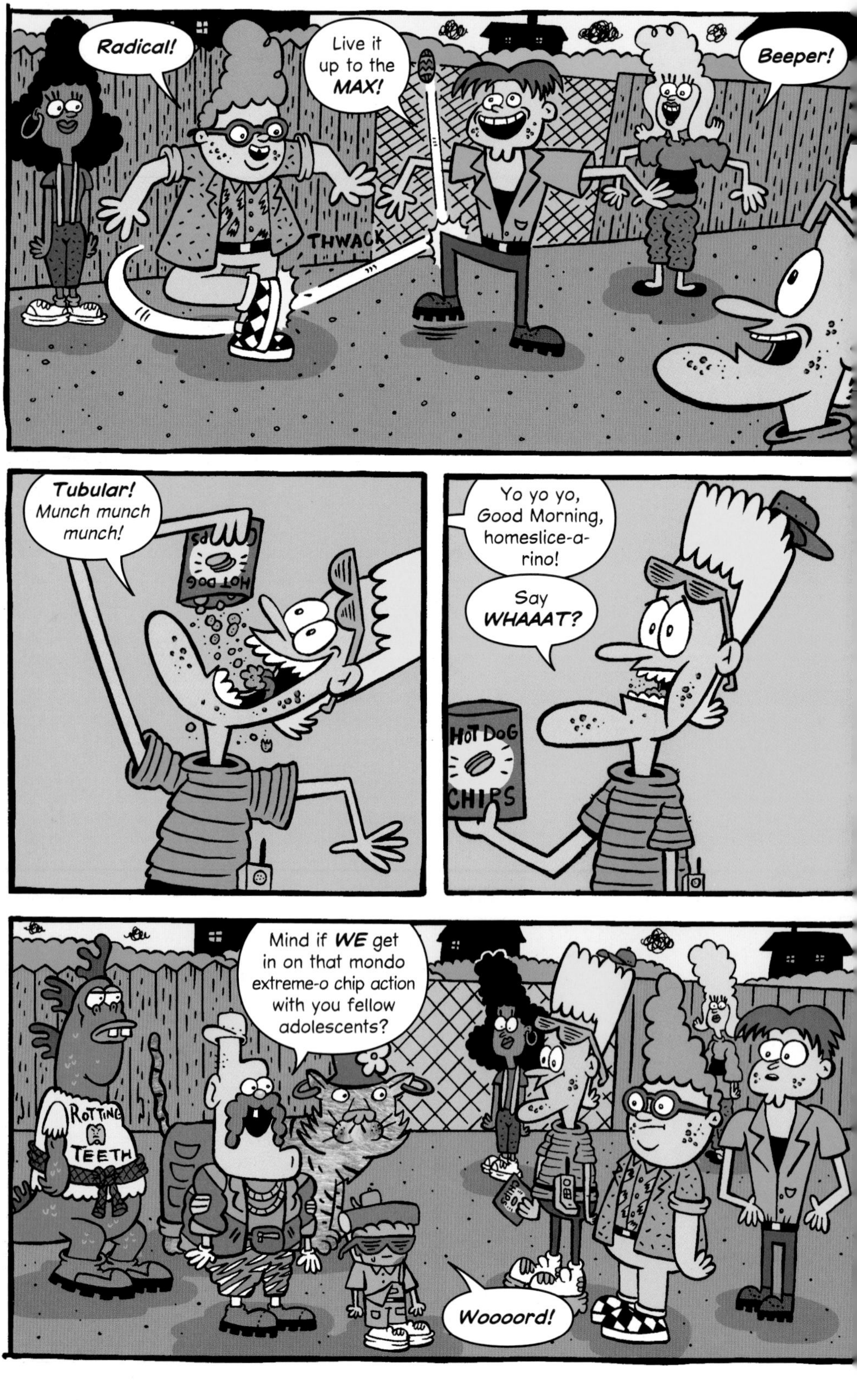
Radical!
Live it up to the MAX!
Beeper!
THWACK
Tubular! Munch munch munch!
HOT DOG CHIPS
Yo yo yo, Good Morning, homeslice-a-rino!
Say WHAAAT?
HOT DOG CHIPS
Mind if WE get in on that mondo extreme-o chip action with you fellow adolescents?
ROTTING TEETH
Woooord!

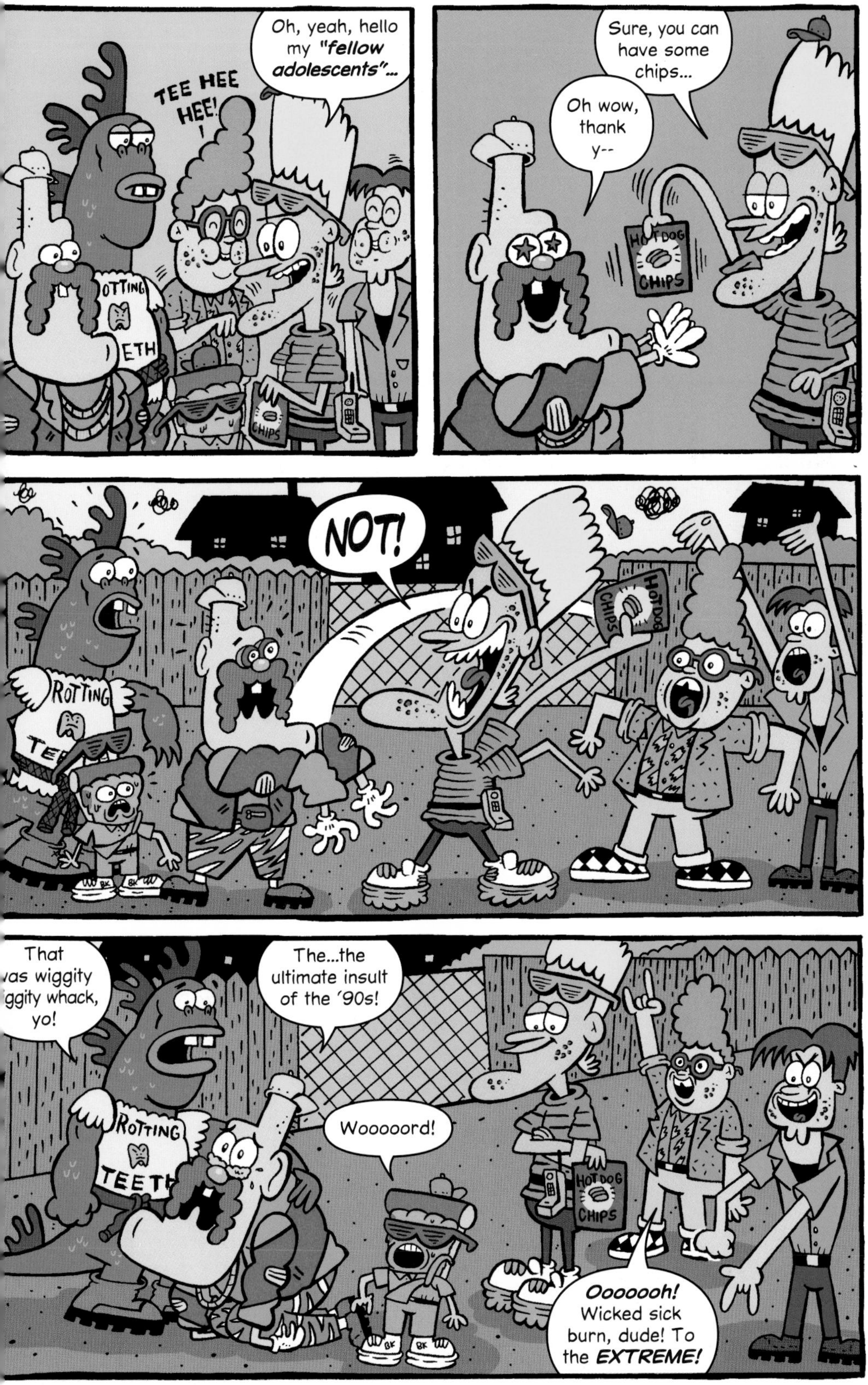
TEE HEE HEE!
Oh, yeah, hello my **"fellow adolescents"...**
Sure, you can have some chips...
Oh wow, thank y--
HOT DOG CHIPS
NOT!
That …as wiggity …iggity whack, yo!
The...the ultimate insult of the '90s!
Wooooord!
Ooooooh! Wicked sick burn, dude! To the **EXTREME!**

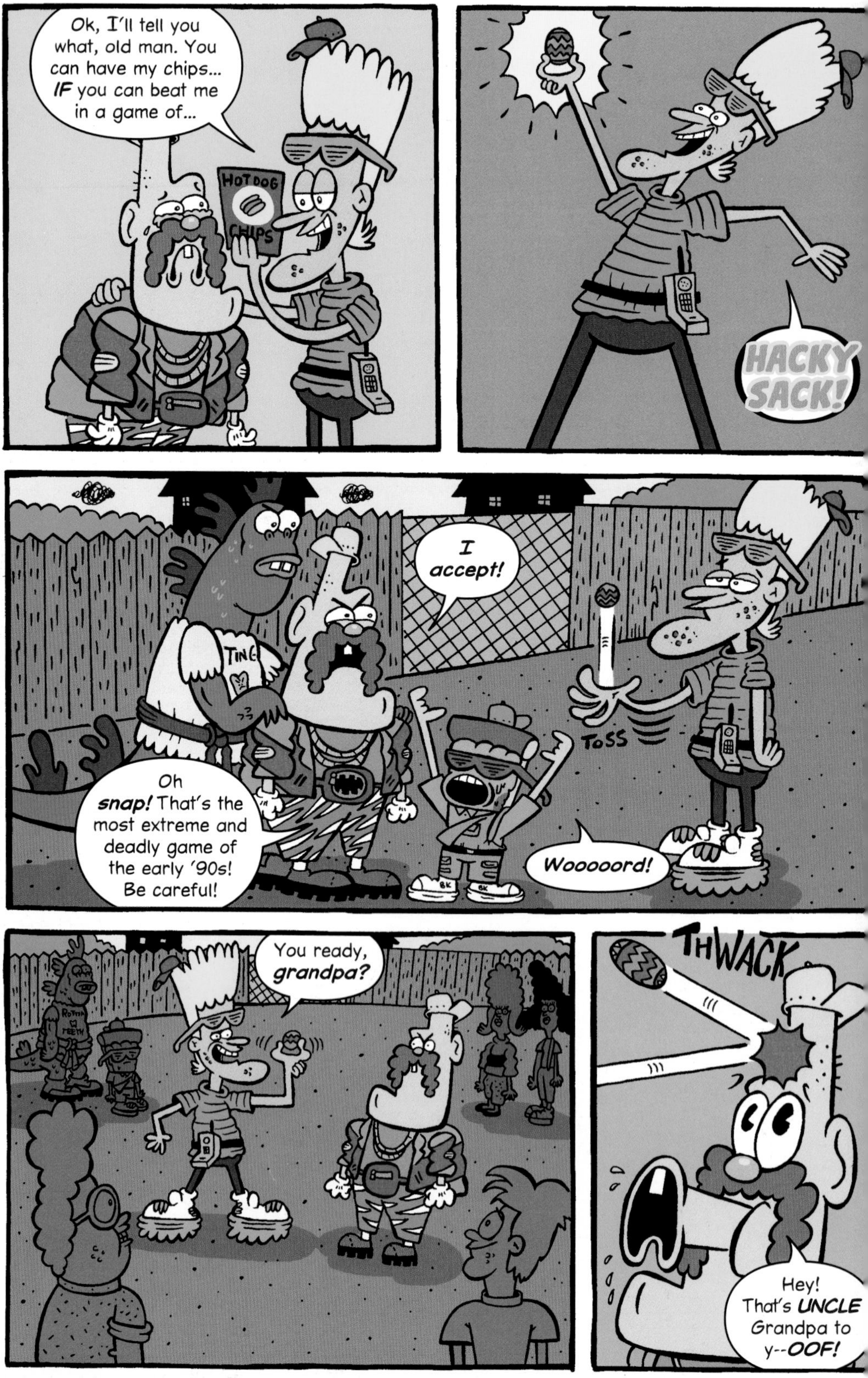
Ok, I'll tell you what, old man. You can have my chips... IF you can beat me in a game of...
HOT DOG CHIPS
HACKY SACK!
I accept!
TING
TOSS
Oh snap! That's the most extreme and deadly game of the early '90s! Be careful!
Wooooord!
BK
BK
You ready, grandpa?
THWACK
Hey! That's UNCLE Grandpa to y--OOF!

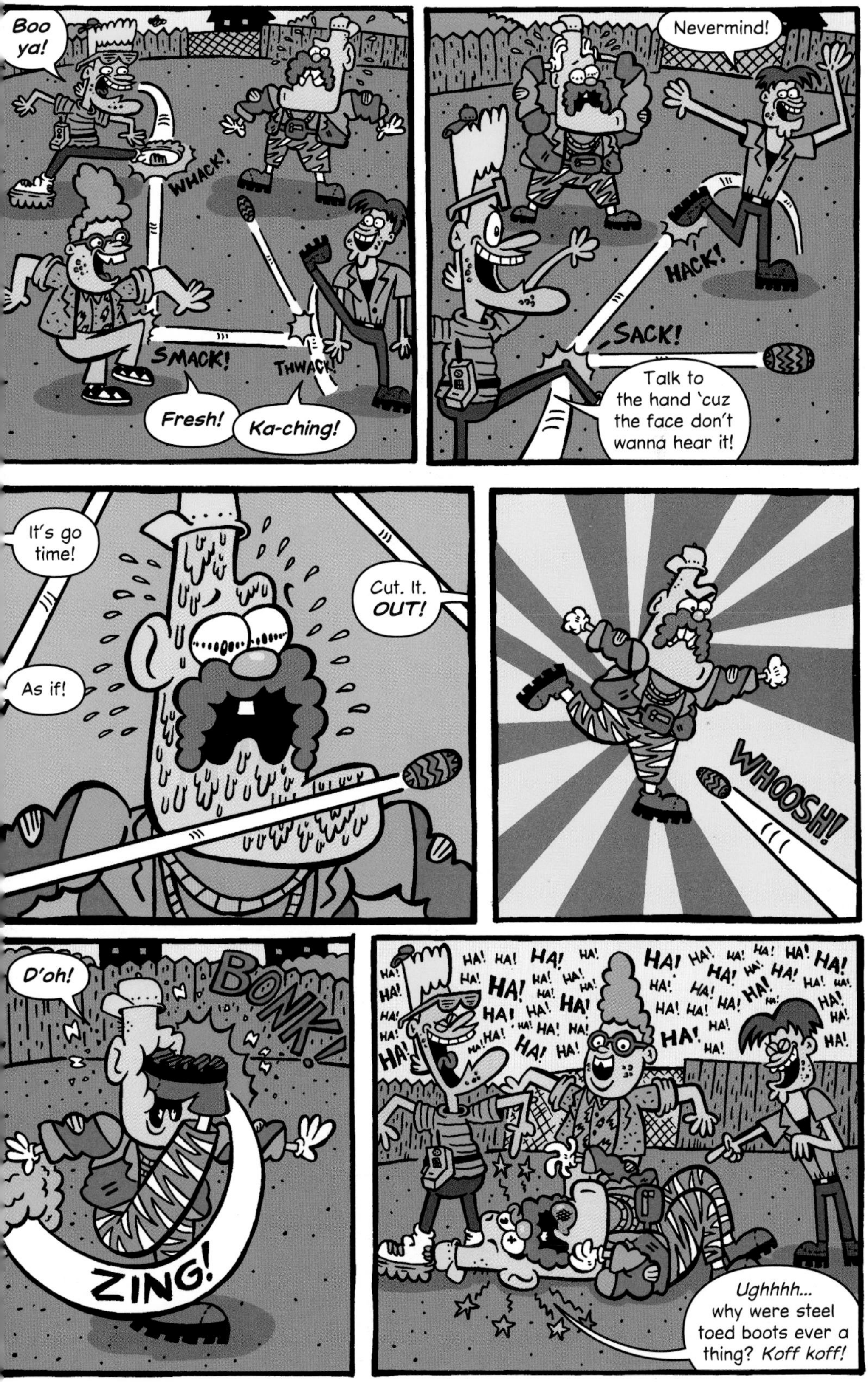
Boo ya!
WHACK!
SMACK!
THWACK!
Fresh!
Ka-ching!
Nevermind!
HACK!
SACK!
Talk to the hand 'cuz the face don't wanna hear it!
It's go time!
Cut. It. OUT!
As if!
WHOOSH!
D'oh!
BONK!
ZING!
HA! HA! HA! HA! HA! HA! HA! HA!
Ughhhh... why were steel toed boots ever a thing? Koff koff!

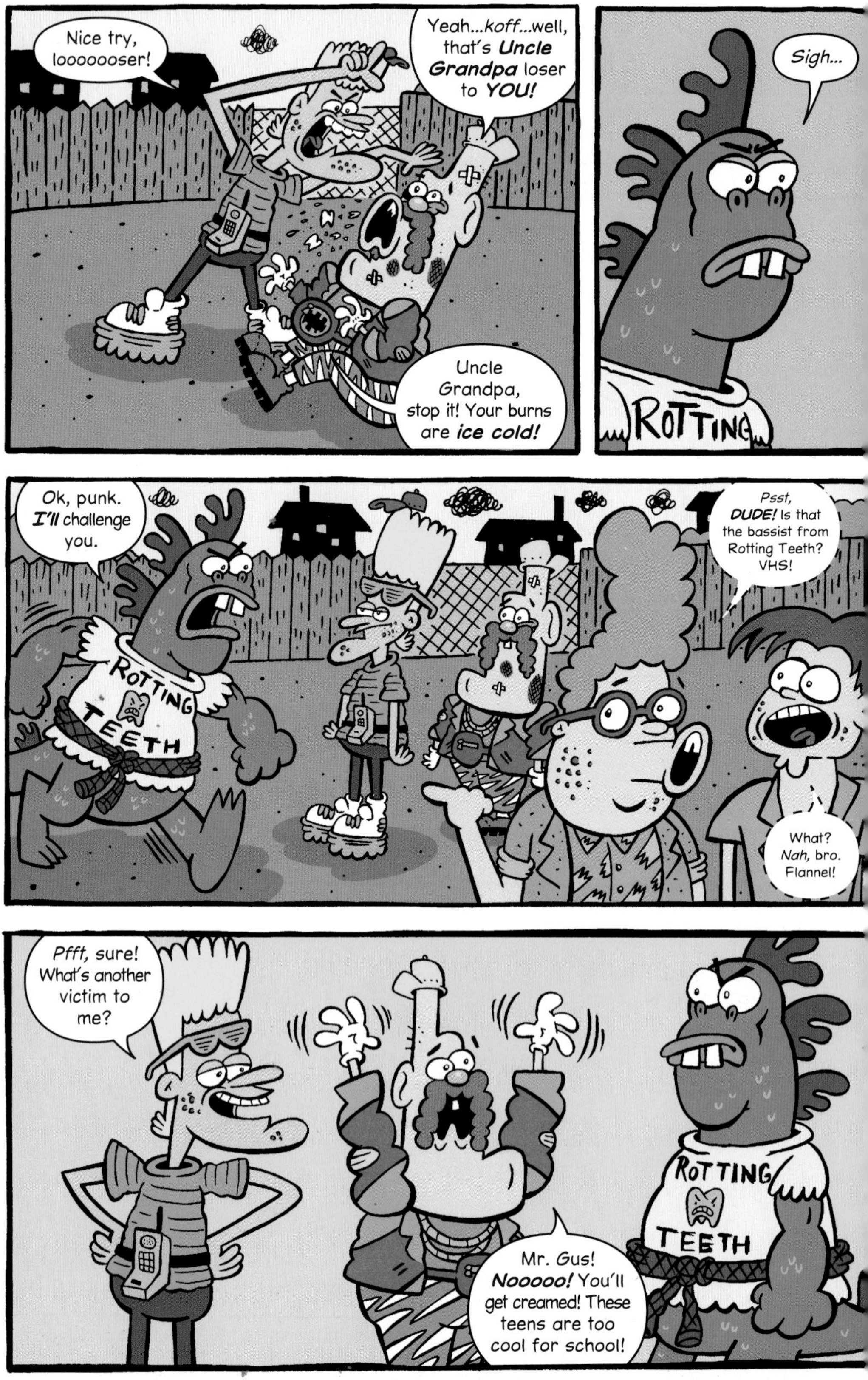
Nice try, looooooser!
Yeah...koff...well, that's Uncle Grandpa loser to YOU!
Uncle Grandpa, stop it! Your burns are ice cold!
Sigh...
ROTTING
Ok, punk. I'll challenge you.
ROTTING TEETH
Psst, DUDE! Is that the bassist from Rotting Teeth? VHS!
What? Nah, bro. Flannel!
Pfft, sure! What's another victim to me?
ROTTING TEETH
Mr. Gus! Nooooo! You'll get creamed! These teens are too cool for school!

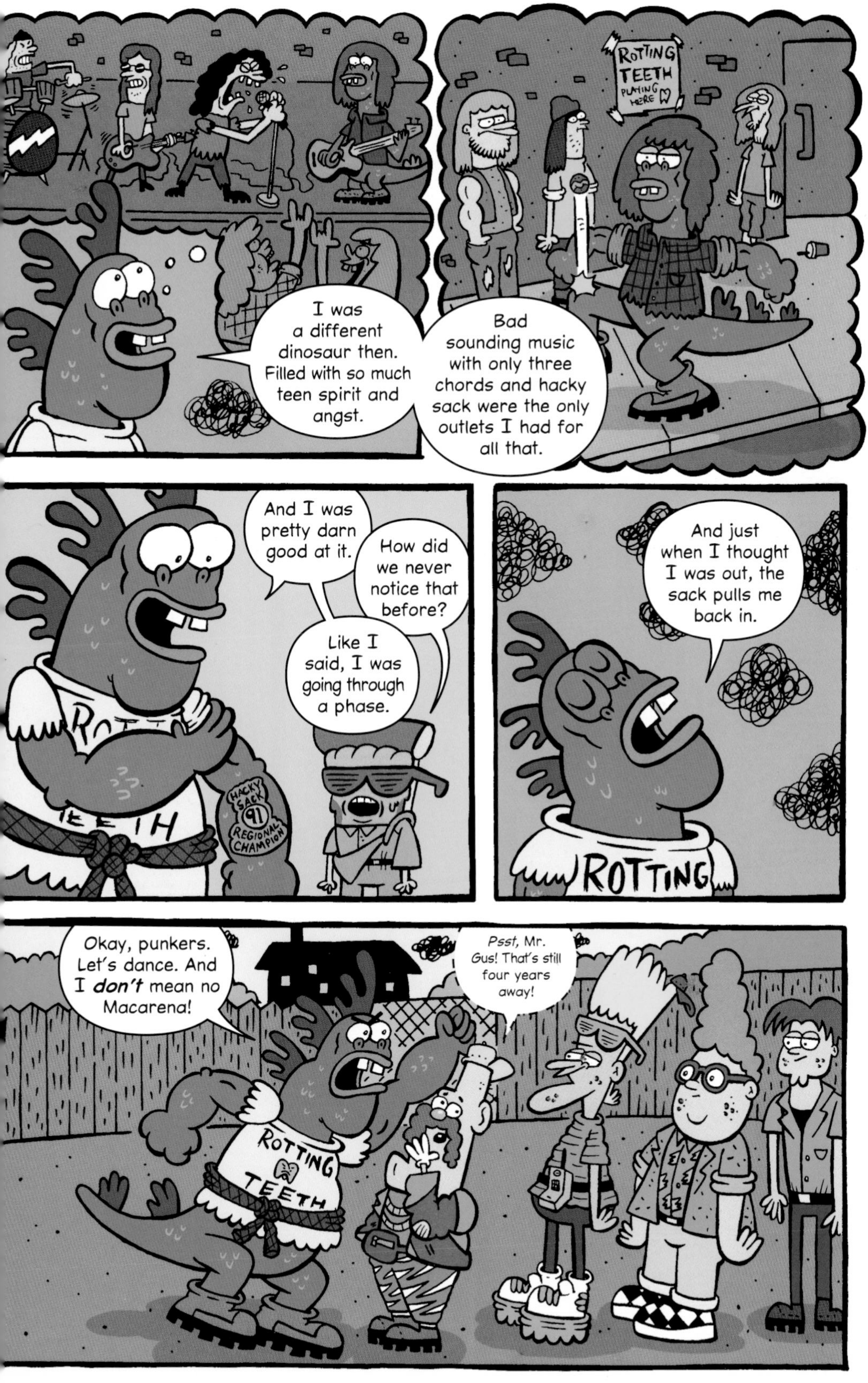

ROTTING TEETH PLAYING HERE
I was a different dinosaur then. Filled with so much teen spirit and angst.
Bad sounding music with only three chords and hacky sack were the only outlets I had for all that.
And I was pretty darn good at it.
How did we never notice that before?
Like I said, I was going through a phase.
HACKY SACK 91 REGIONAL CHAMPION
And just when I thought I was out, the sack pulls me back in.
ROTTING
Okay, punkers. Let's dance. And I ***don't*** mean no Macarena!
Psst, Mr. Gus! That's still four years away!
ROTTING TEETH

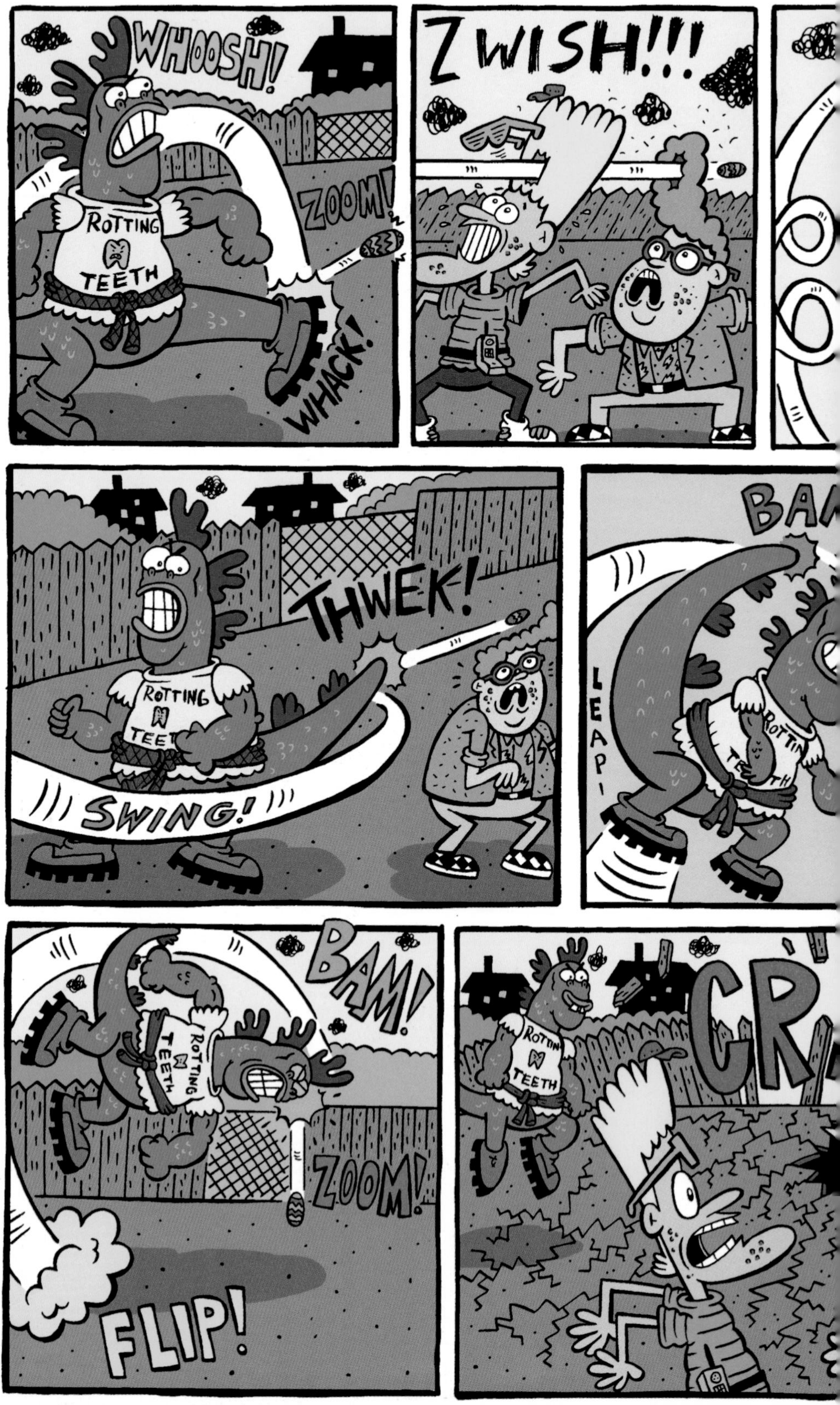

WHOOSH!
ROTTING TEETH
ZOOM!
WHACK!
ZWISH!!!
THWEK!
SWING!
LEAP!
BAM!
ROTTING TEETH
ZOOM!
FLIP!

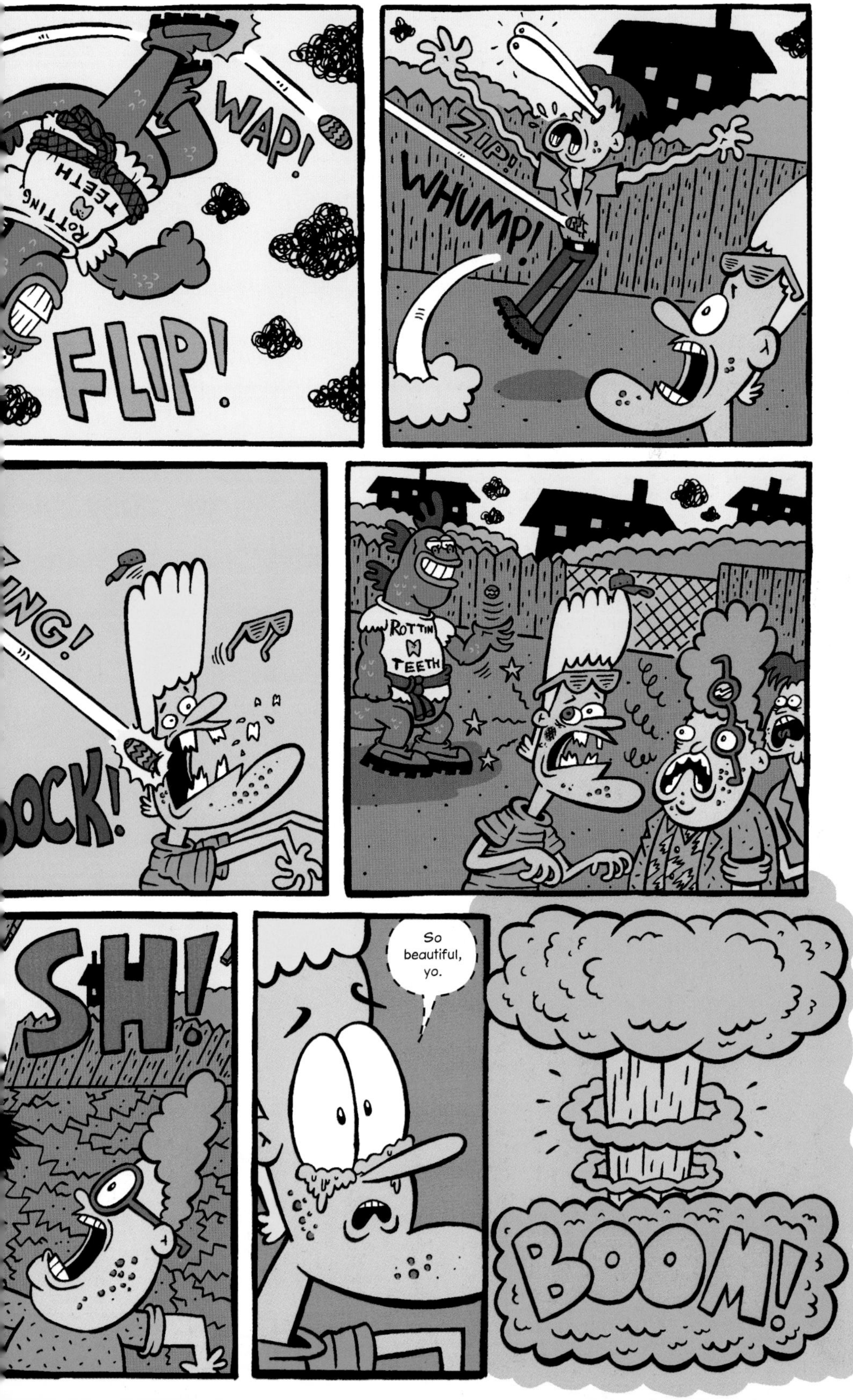
WAP!
ROTTING TEETH
FLIP!
ZIP!
WHUMP!
NG!
OCK!
ROTTIN TEETH
SH!
So beautiful, yo.
BOOM!

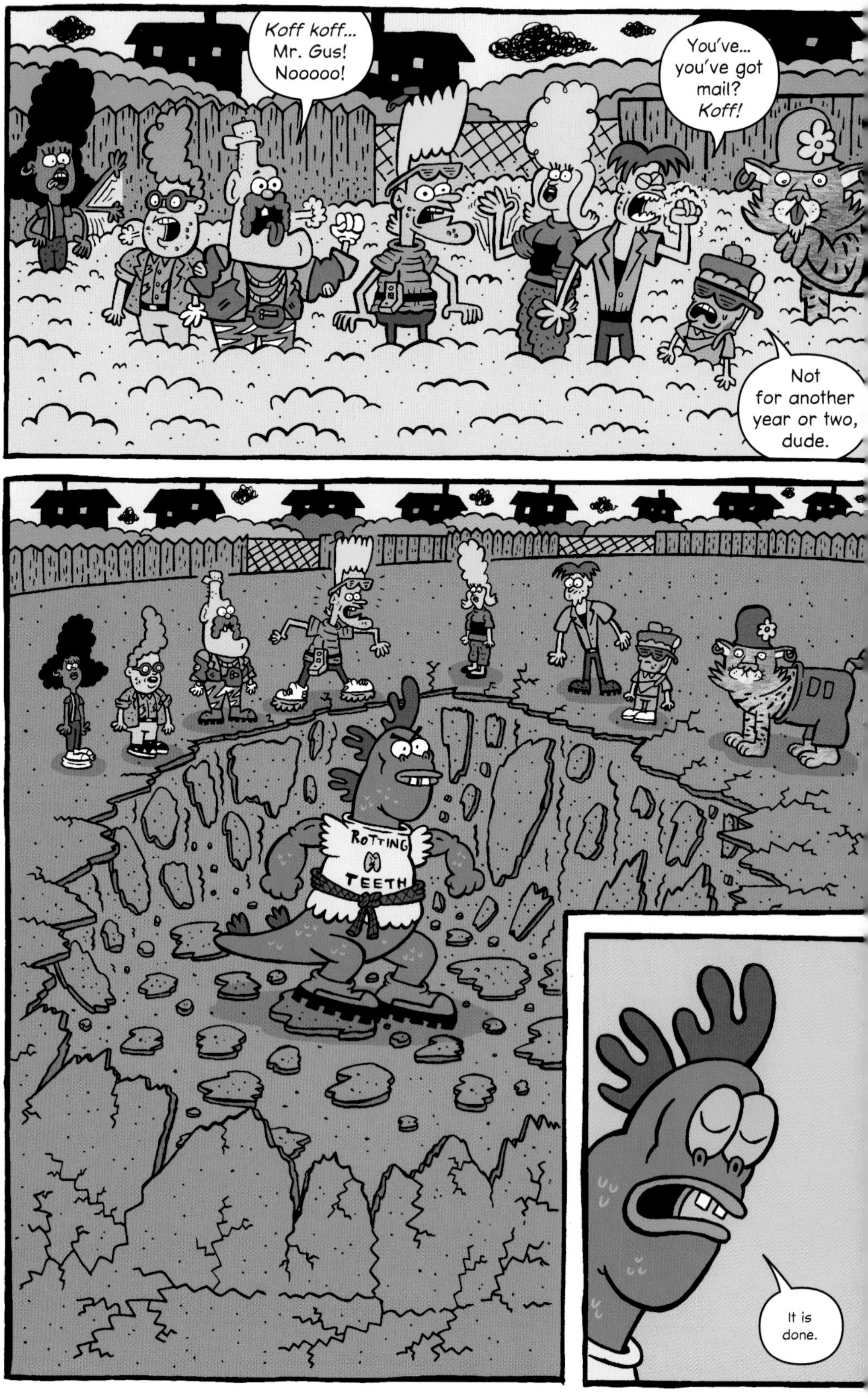
Koff koff... Mr. Gus! Nooooo!
You've... you've got mail? Koff!
Not for another year or two, dude.
ROTTING TEETH
It is done.

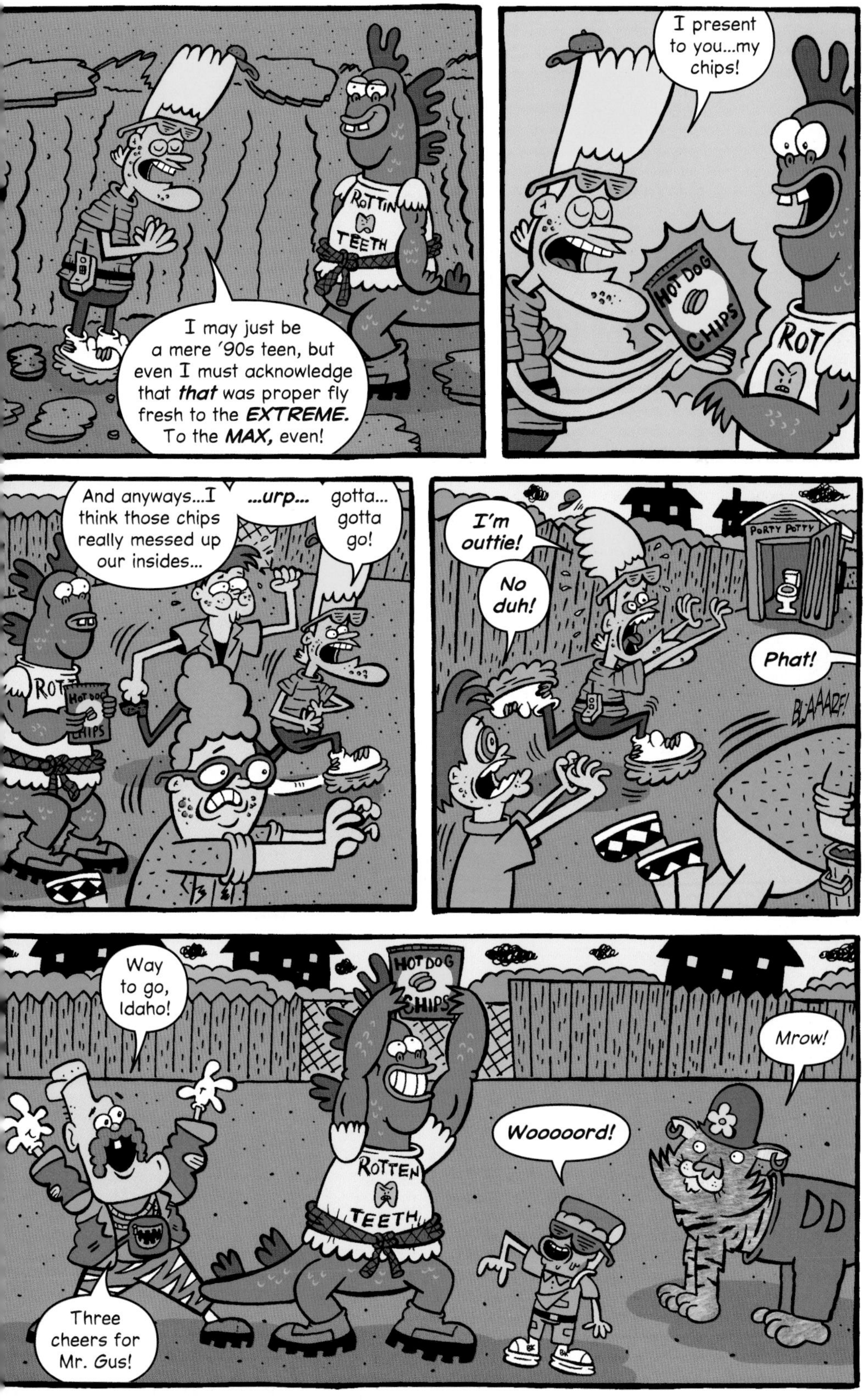
ROTTIN TEETH
I may just be a mere '90s teen, but even I must acknowledge that *that* was proper fly fresh to the ***EXTREME.*** To the ***MAX,*** even!
I present to you...my chips!
HOT DOG CHIPS
ROT
And anyways...I think those chips really messed up our insides...
...urp...
gotta... gotta go!
ROT
HOT DOG CHIPS
I'm outtie!
No duh!
PORTY POTTY
Phat!
BLAAARF!
Way to go, Idaho!
HOT DOG CHIPS
ROTTEN TEETH
Three cheers for Mr. Gus!
Wooooord!
Mrow!

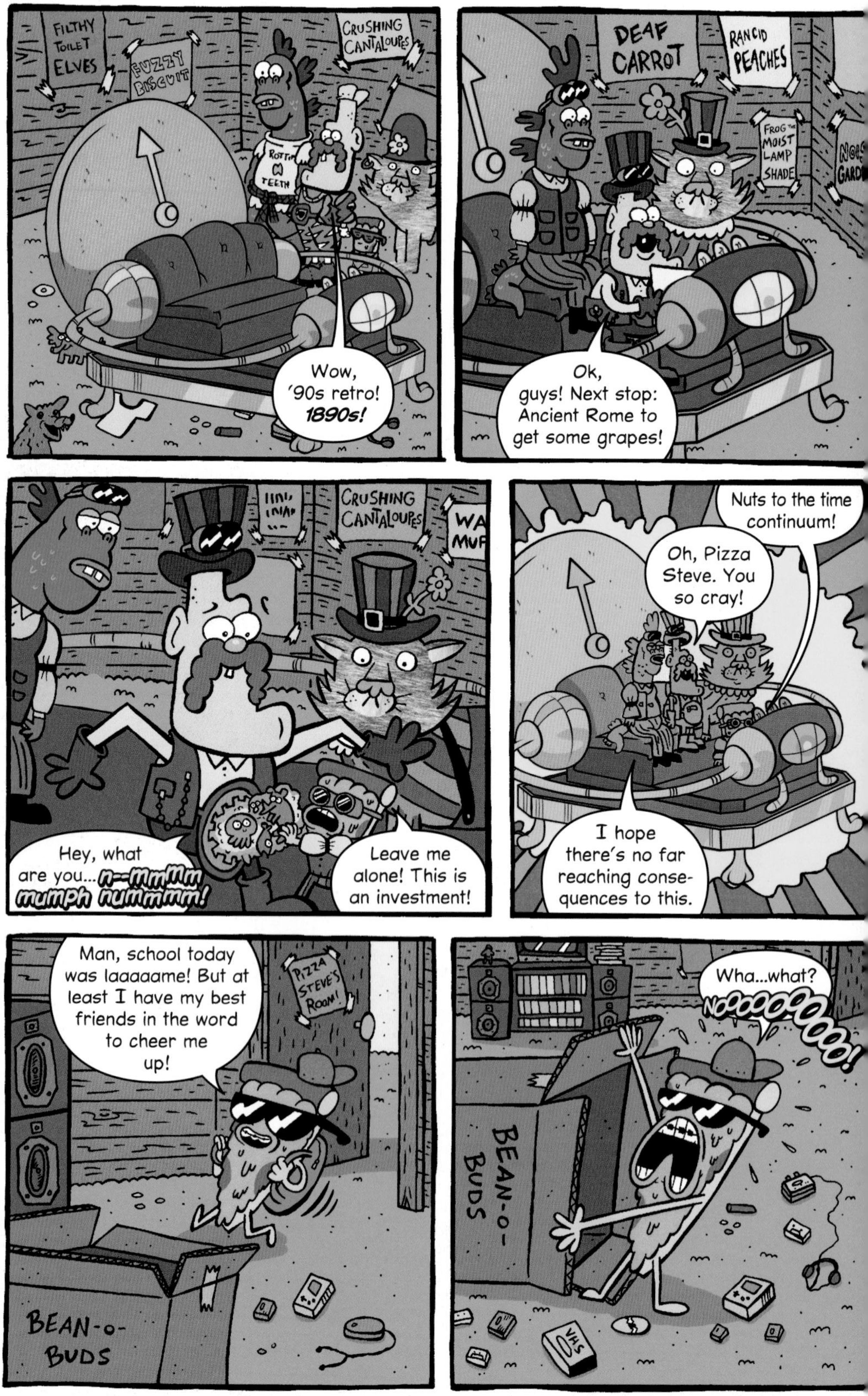
FILTHY TOILET ELVES
FUZZY BISCUIT
CRUSHING CANTALOUPES
ROTTEN TEETH
Wow, '90s retro! *1890s!*
DEAF CARROT
RANCID PEACHES
FROG THE MOIST LAMP SHADE
Ok, guys! Next stop: Ancient Rome to get some grapes!
CRUSHING CANTALOUPES
Hey, what are you... n--mmMm mumph nummmm!
Leave me alone! This is an investment!
Nuts to the time continuum!
Oh, Pizza Steve. You so cray!
I hope there's no far reaching conse-quences to this.
Man, school today was laaaaame! But at least I have my best friends in the word to cheer me up!
PIZZA STEVE'S ROOM!
BEAN-o-BUDS
Wha...what?
NOOOOOOOOOOO!
BEAN-o-BUDS
VHS

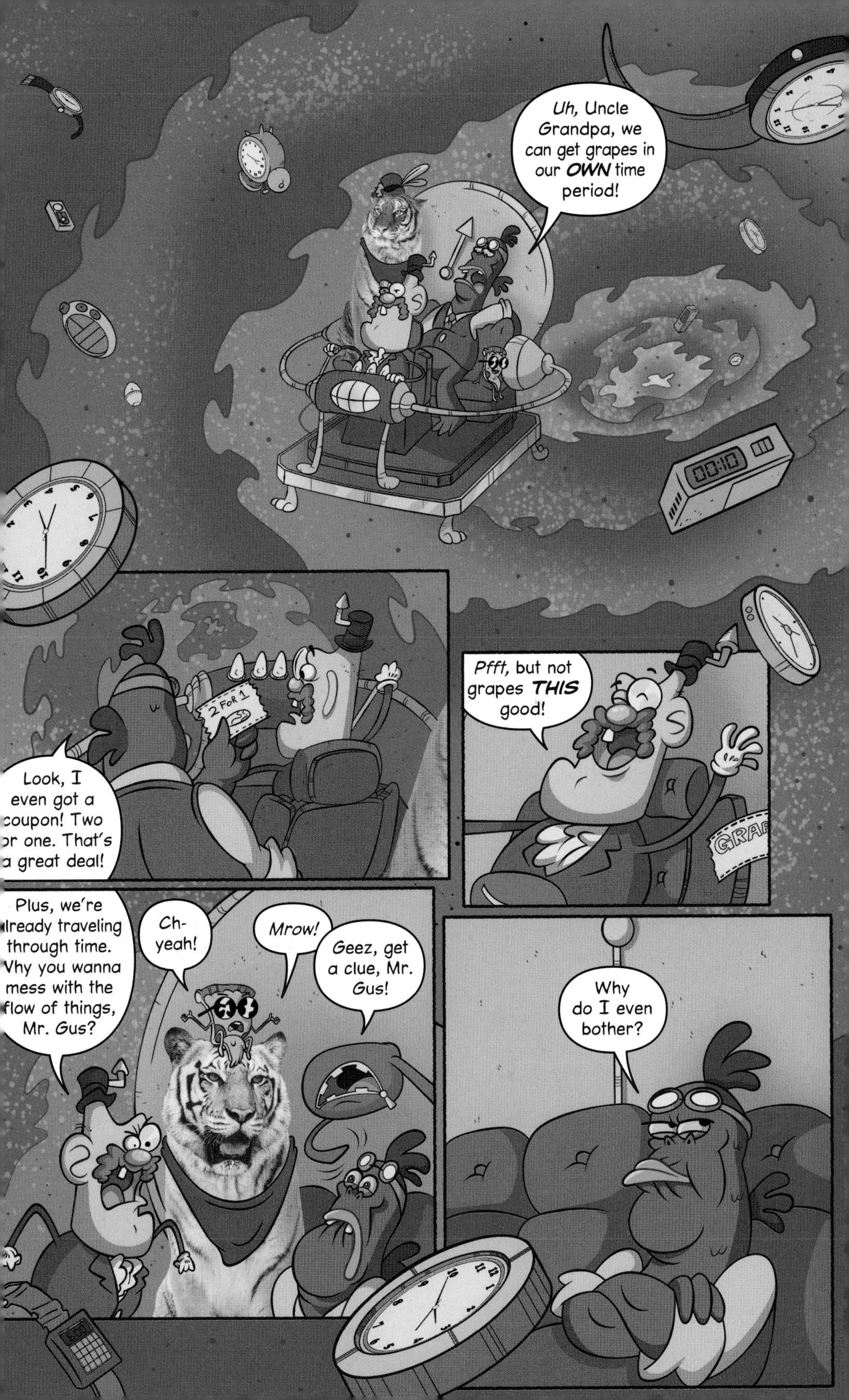

Uh, Uncle Grandpa, we can get grapes in our ***OWN*** time period!
00:10
2 FOR 1
Look, I even got a coupon! Two or one. That's a great deal!
Pfft, but not grapes ***THIS*** good!
GRAP
Plus, we're lready traveling through time. Vhy you wanna mess with the flow of things, Mr. Gus?
Ch-yeah!
Mrow!
Geez, get a clue, Mr. Gus!
Why do I even bother?

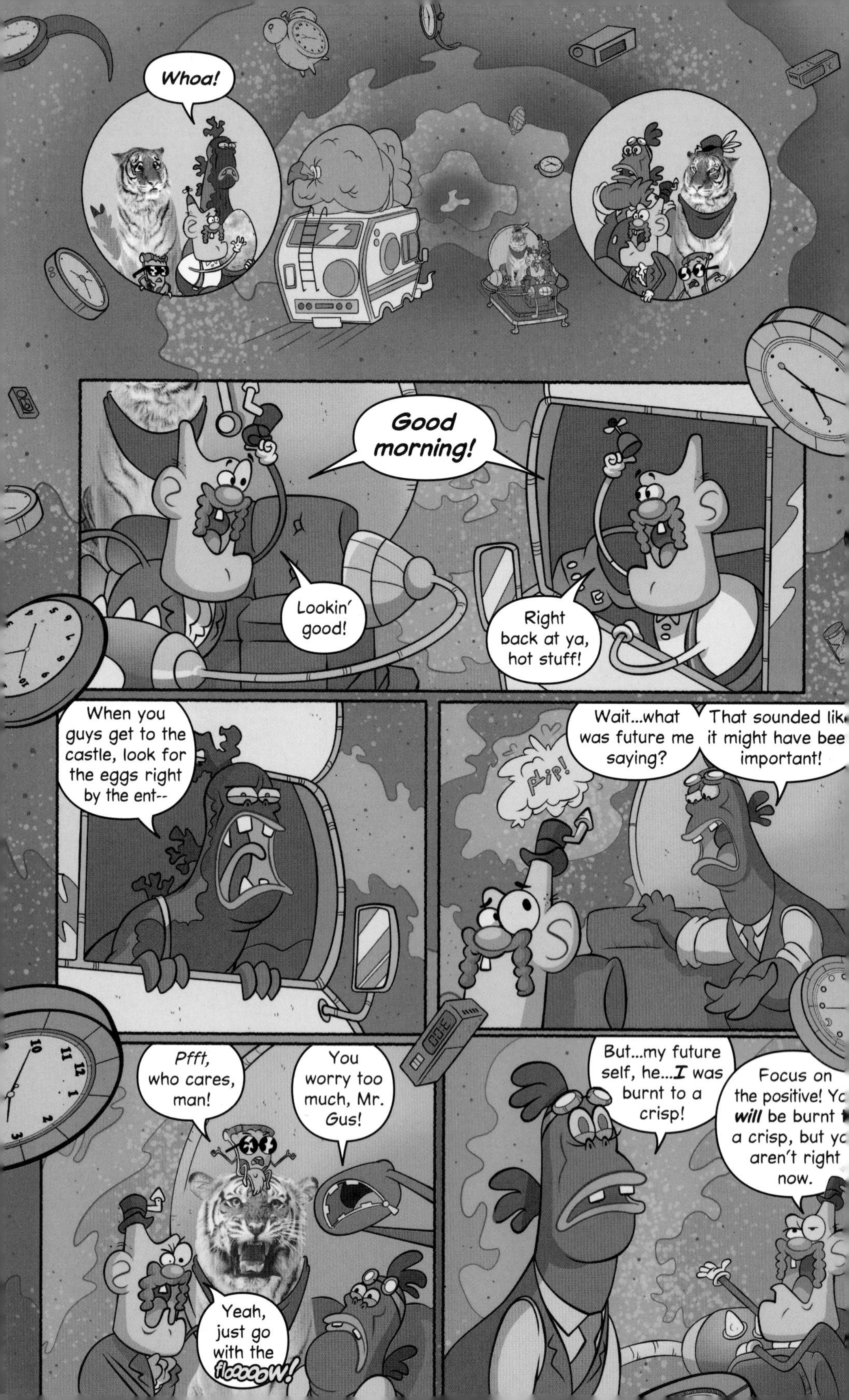

Whoa!
Good morning!
Lookin' good!
Right back at ya, hot stuff!
When you guys get to the castle, look for the eggs right by the ent--
plip!
Wait...what was future me saying?
That sounded lik it might have bee important!
Pfft, who cares, man!
You worry too much, Mr. Gus!
Yeah, just go with the flooooow!
But...my future self, he...I was burnt to a crisp!
Focus on the positive! Yo will be burnt t a crisp, but yo aren't right now.

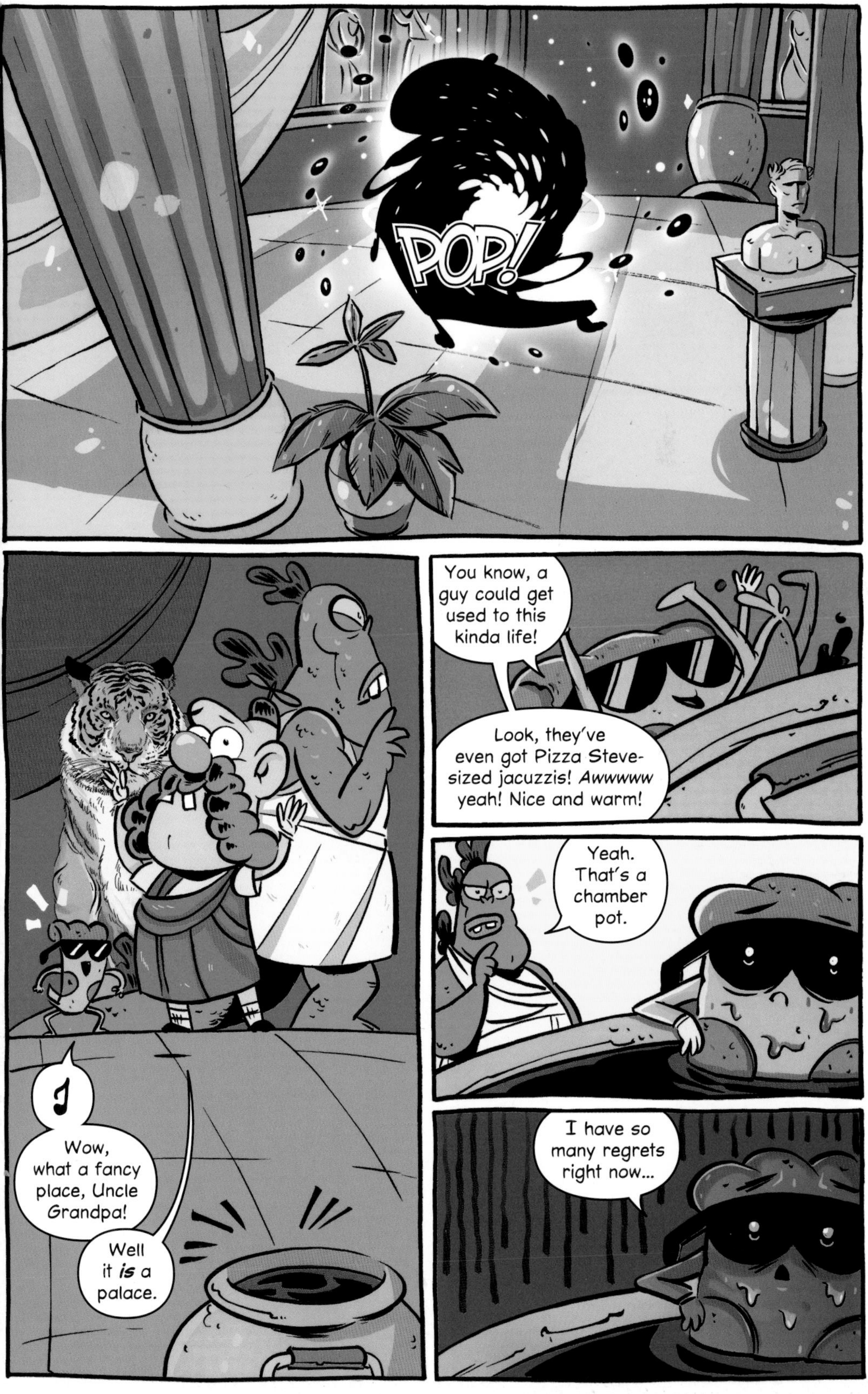
POP!
You know, a guy could get used to this kinda life!
Look, they've even got Pizza Steve-sized jacuzzis! *Awwwww* yeah! Nice and warm!
Wow, what a fancy place, Uncle Grandpa!
Well it ***is*** a palace.
Yeah. That's a chamber pot.
I have so many regrets right now...

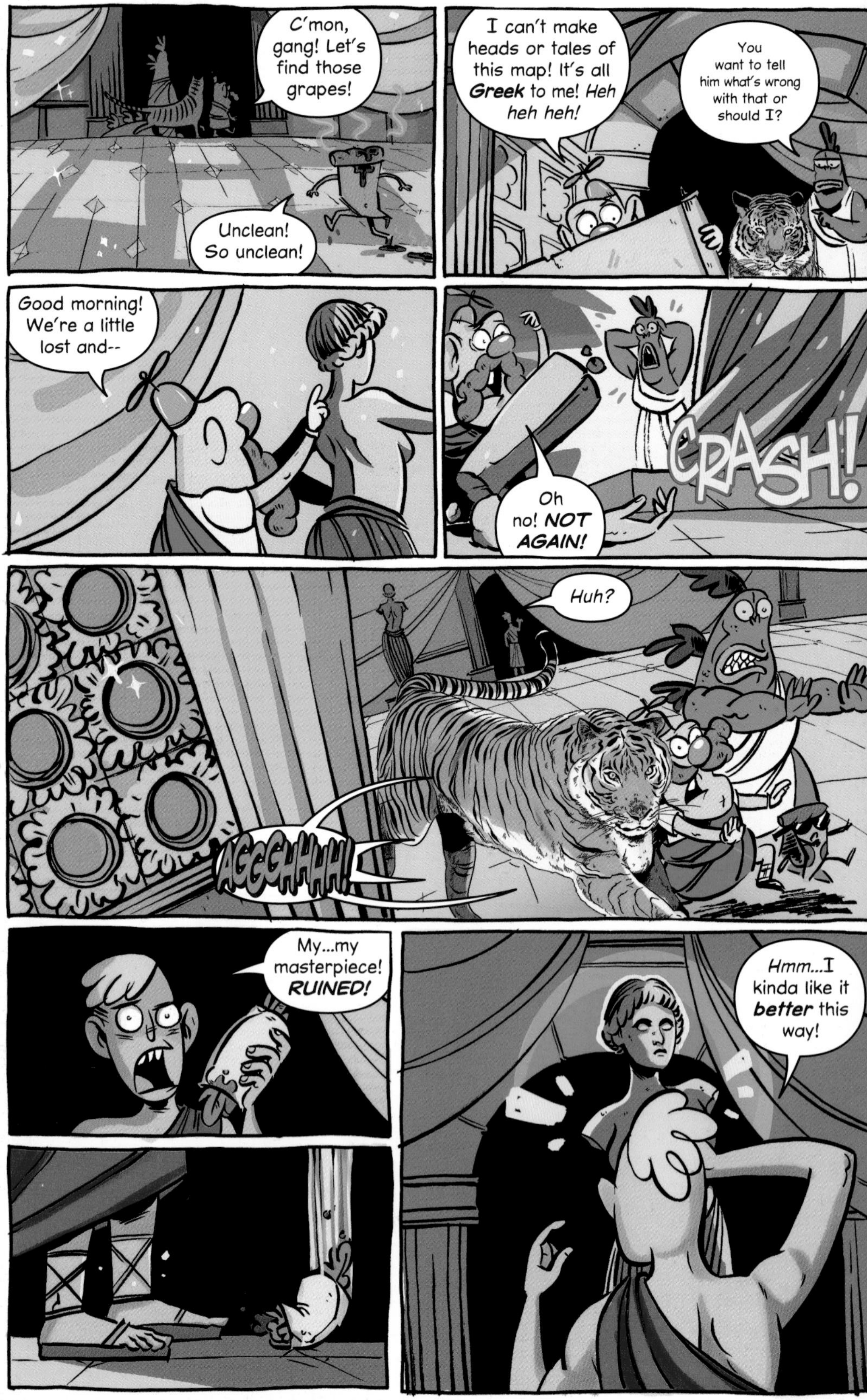

C'mon, gang! Let's find those grapes!
Unclean! So unclean!
I can't make heads or tales of this map! It's all **Greek** to me! *Heh heh heh!*
You want to tell him what's wrong with that or should I?
Good morning! We're a little lost and--
Oh no! ***NOT AGAIN!***
CRASH!
Huh?
AGGGHHHH!
My...my masterpiece! ***RUINED!***
*Hmm...*I kinda like it ***better*** this way!

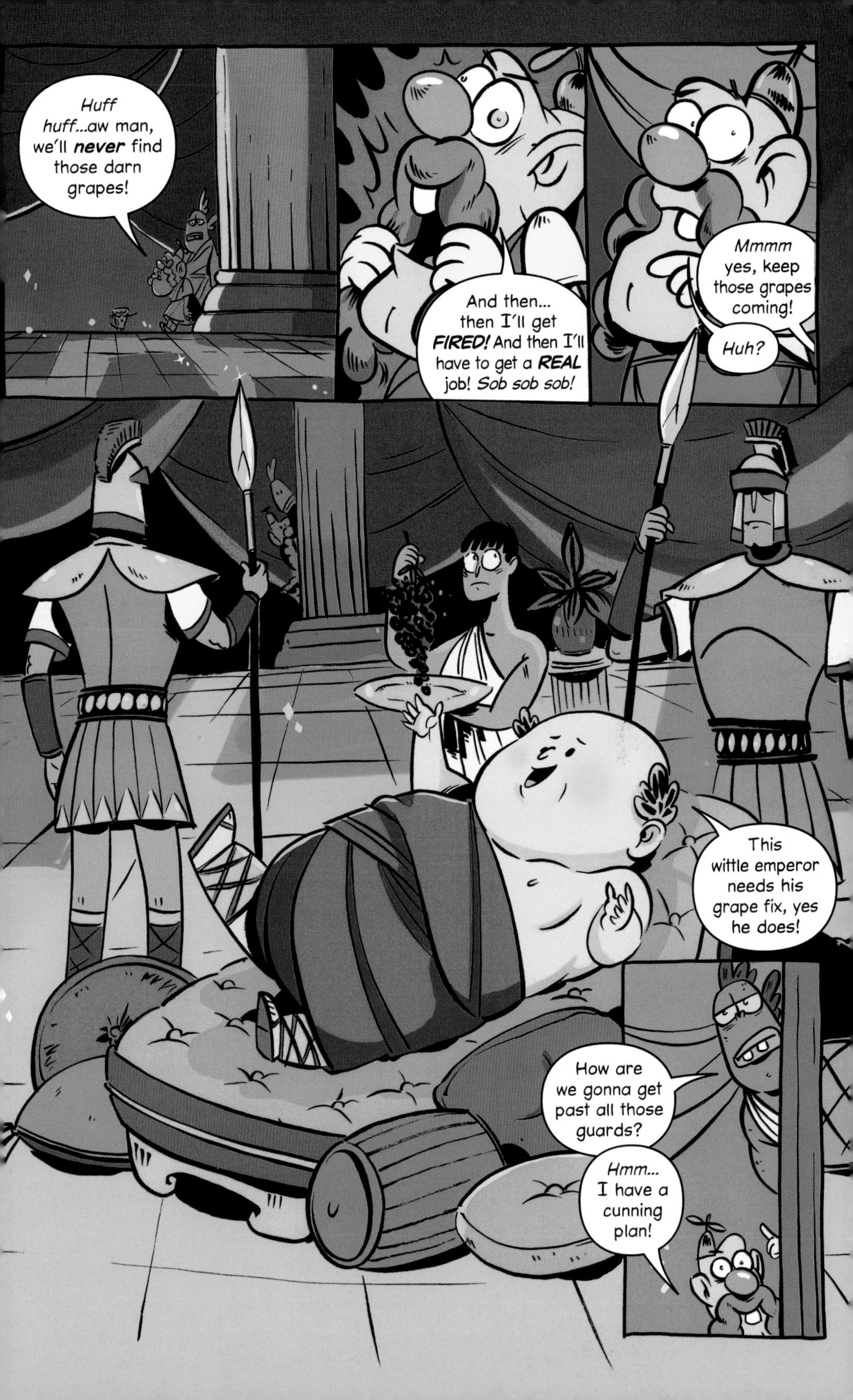
Huff huff...aw man, we'll **never** find those darn grapes!
And then... then I'll get **FIRED!** And then I'll have to get a **REAL** job! *Sob sob sob!*
Mmmm yes, keep those grapes coming!
Huh?
This wittle emperor needs his grape fix, yes he does!
How are we gonna get past all those guards?
Hmm... I have a cunning plan!

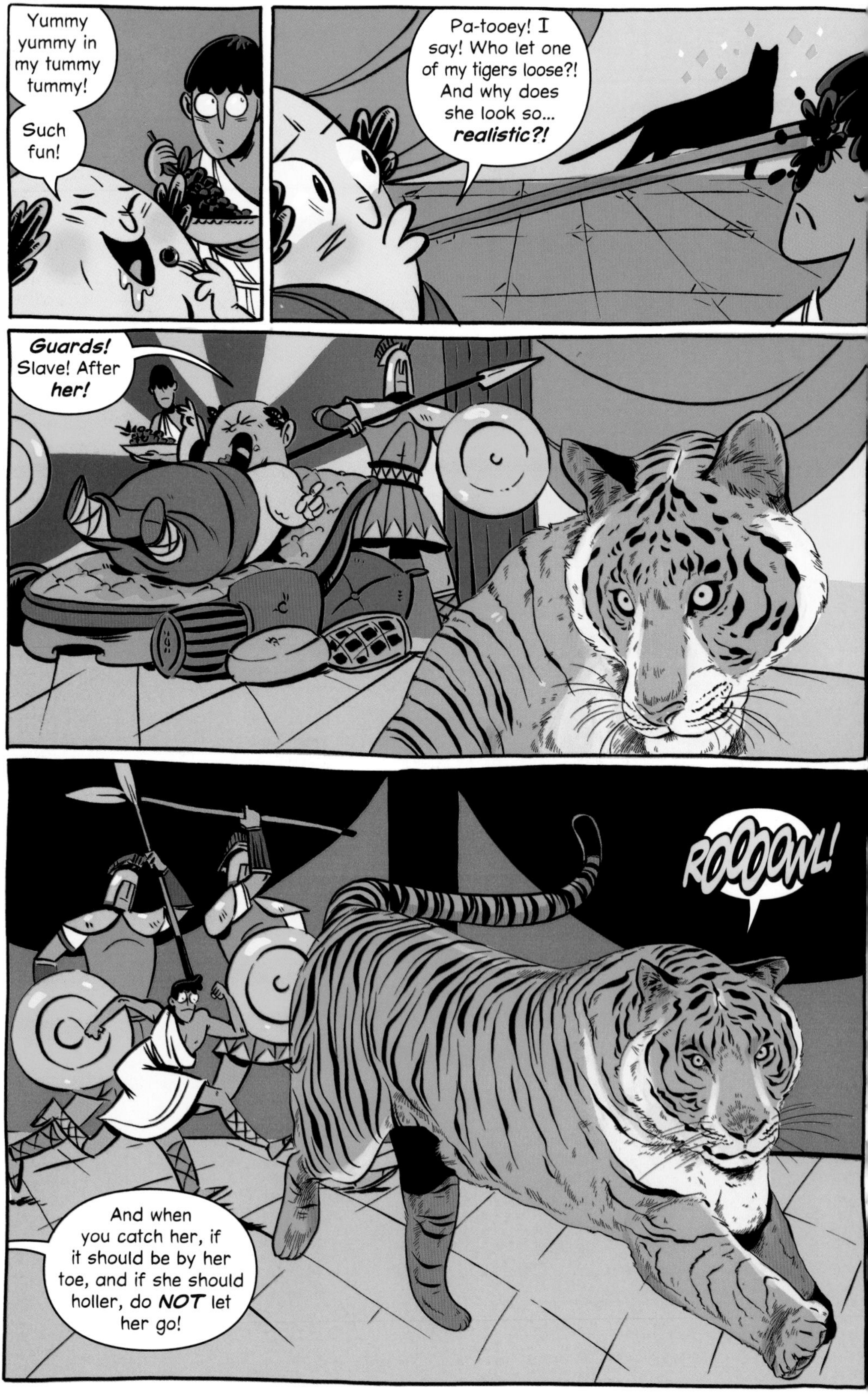
Yummy yummy in my tummy tummy!
Such fun!
Pa-tooey! I say! Who let one of my tigers loose?! And why does she look so... ***realistic?!***
Guards! Slave! After ***her!***
ROOOOWL!
And when you catch her, if it should be by her toe, and if she should holler, do **NOT** let her go!

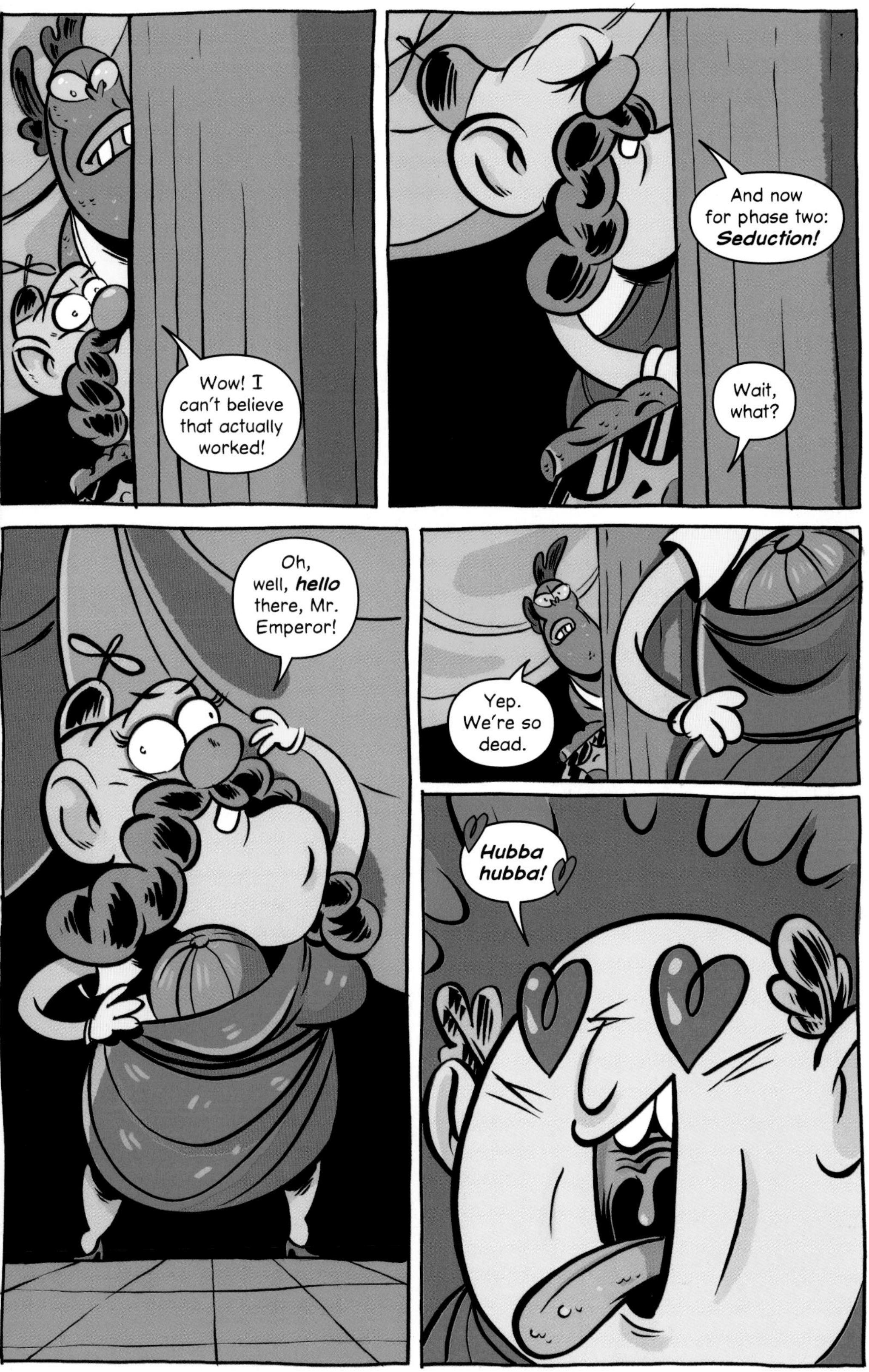
Wow! I can't believe that actually worked!
And now for phase two: **Seduction!**
Wait, what?
Oh, well, ***hello*** there, Mr. Emperor!
Yep. We're so dead.
Hubba hubba!

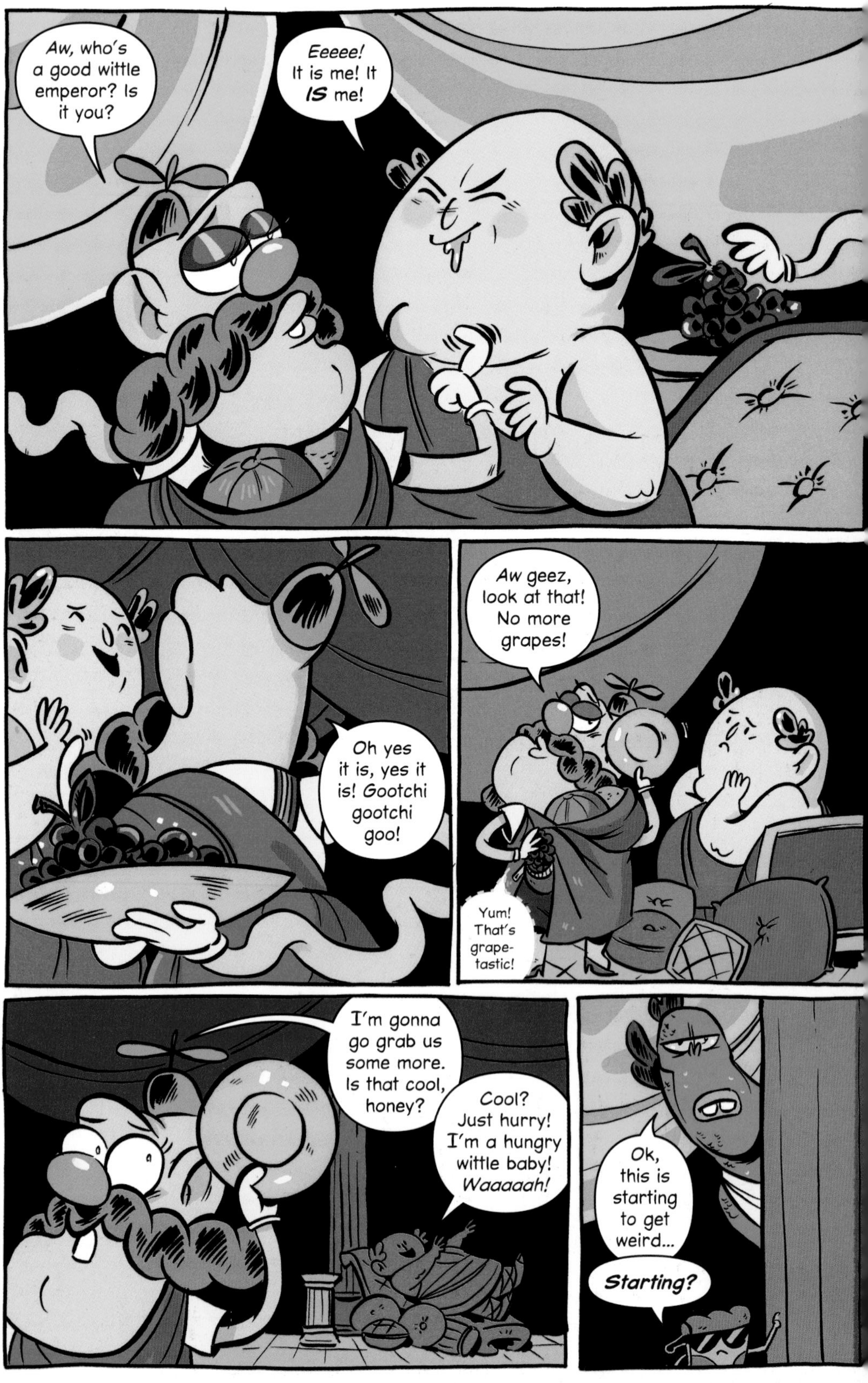
Aw, who's a good wittle emperor? Is it you?
Eeeee! It is me! It *IS* me!
Oh yes it is, yes it is! Gootchi gootchi goo!
Aw geez, look at that! No more grapes!
Yum! That's grape-tastic!
I'm gonna go grab us some more. Is that cool, honey?
Cool? Just hurry! I'm a hungry wittle baby! *Waaaaah!*
Ok, this is starting to get weird...
Starting?

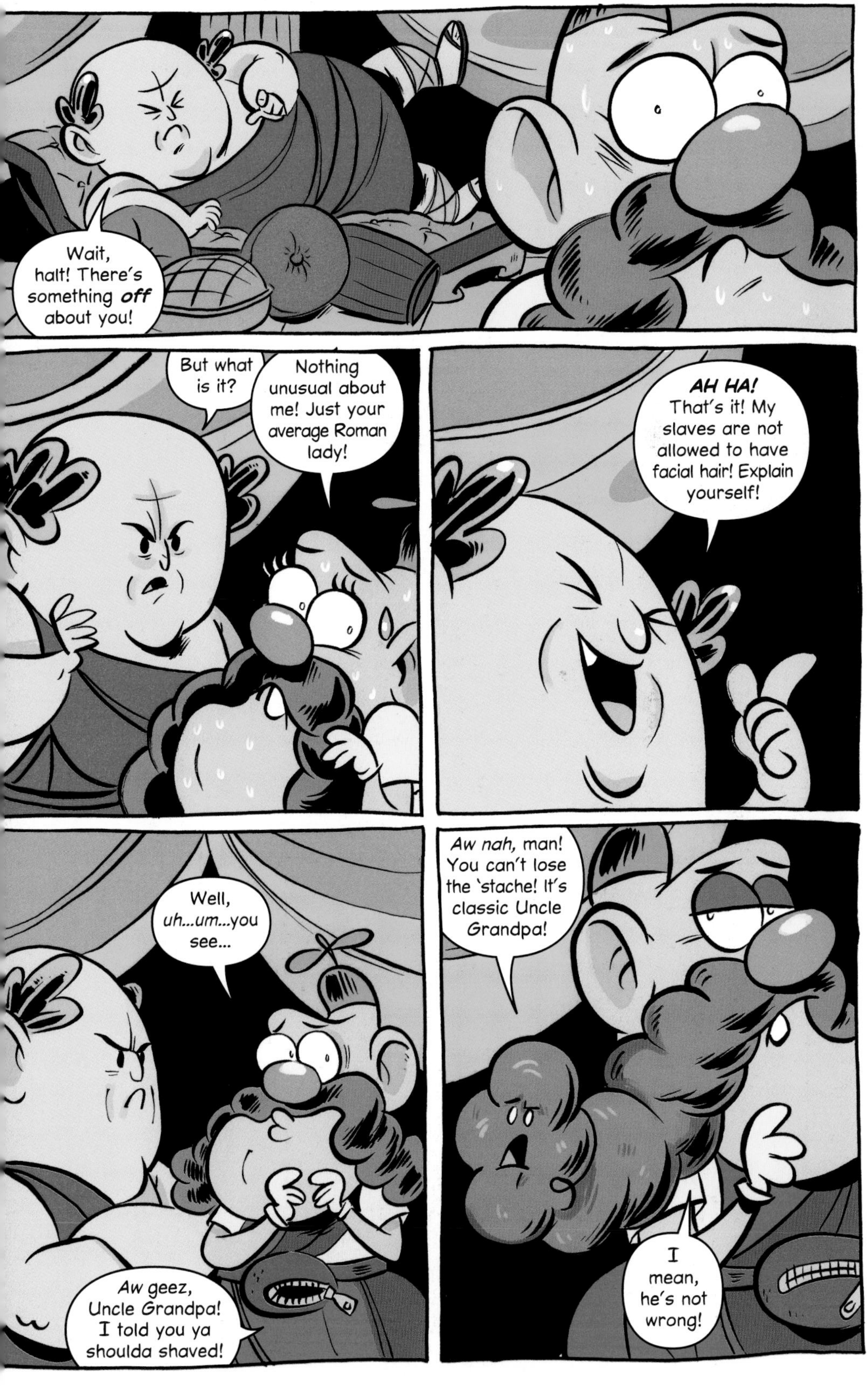

Wait, halt! There's something ***off*** about you!
But what is it?
Nothing unusual about me! Just your average Roman lady!
AH HA! That's it! My slaves are not allowed to have facial hair! Explain yourself!
Well, *uh...um...*you see...
Aw geez, Uncle Grandpa! I told you ya shoulda shaved!
Aw nah, man! You can't lose the 'stache! It's classic Uncle Grandpa!
I mean, he's not wrong!

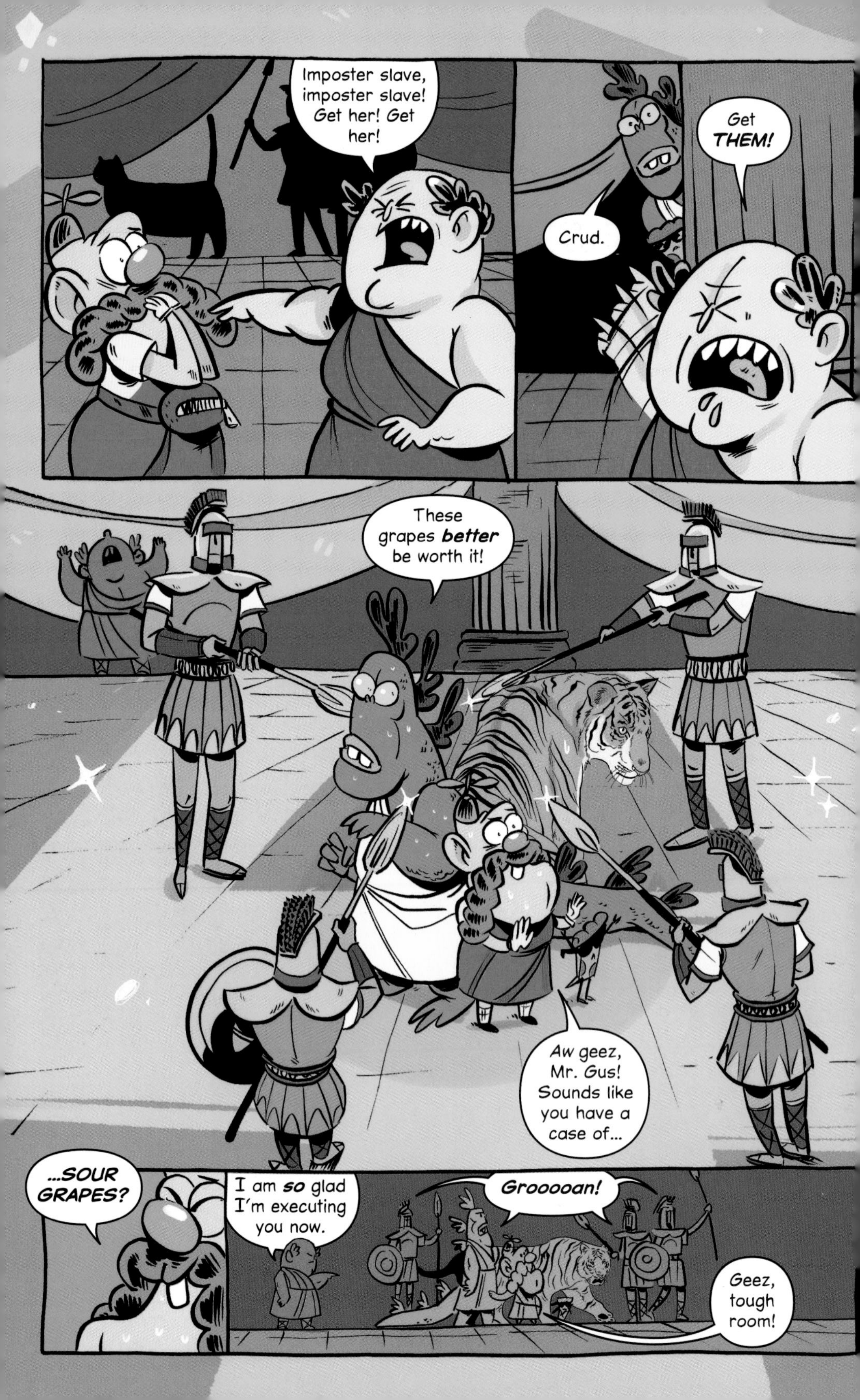
Imposter slave, imposter slave! Get her! Get her!
Crud.
Get THEM!
These grapes better be worth it!
Aw geez, Mr. Gus! Sounds like you have a case of...
...SOUR GRAPES?
I am so glad I'm executing you now.
Groooan!
Geez, tough room!

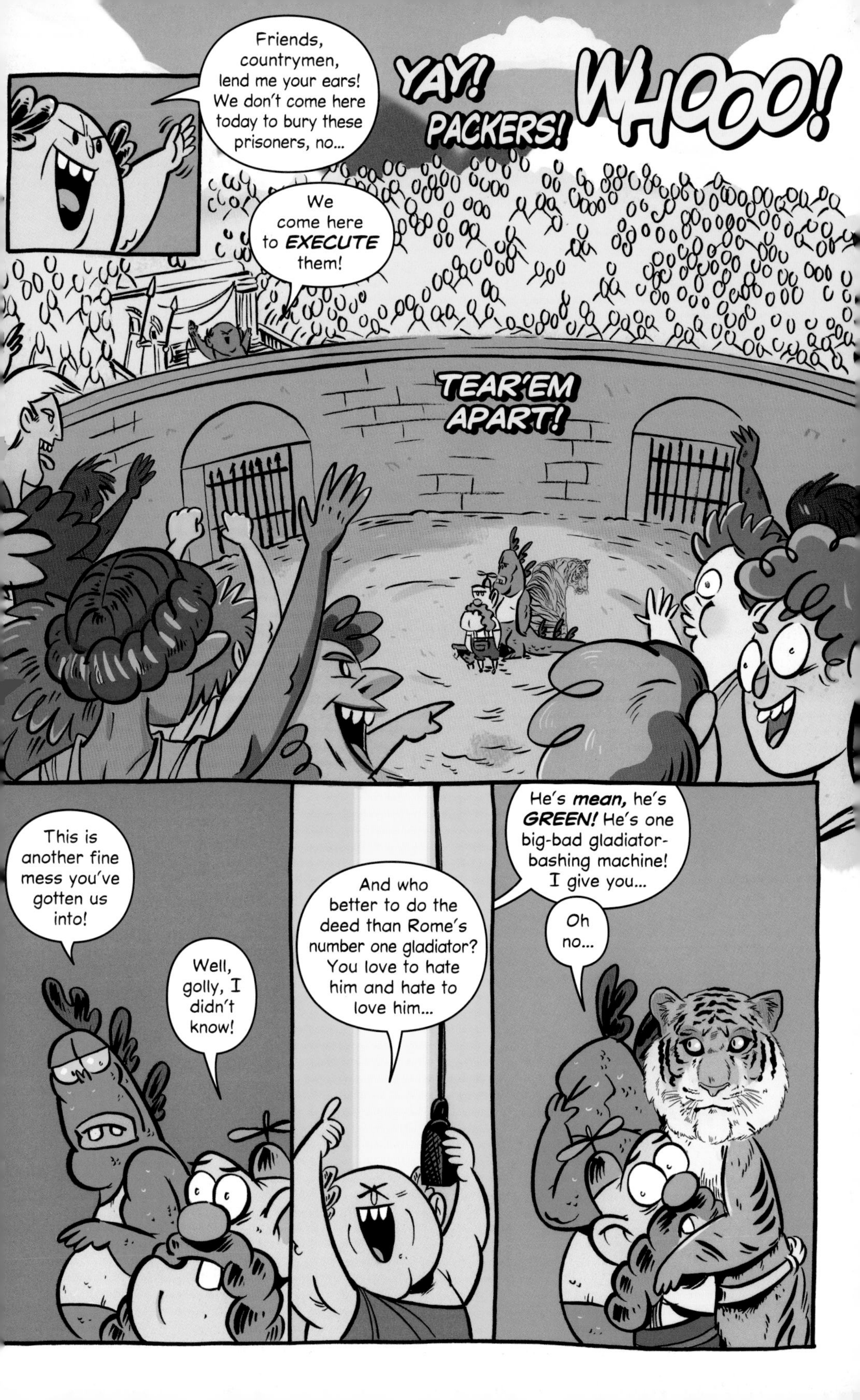

Friends, countrymen, lend me your ears! We don't come here today to bury these prisoners, no...
YAY!
PACKERS!
WHOOOO!
We come here to EXECUTE them!
TEAR'EM APART!
This is another fine mess you've gotten us into!
Well, golly, I didn't know!
And who better to do the deed than Rome's number one gladiator? You love to hate him and hate to love him...
He's mean, he's GREEN! He's one big-bad gladiator-bashing machine! I give you...
Oh no...

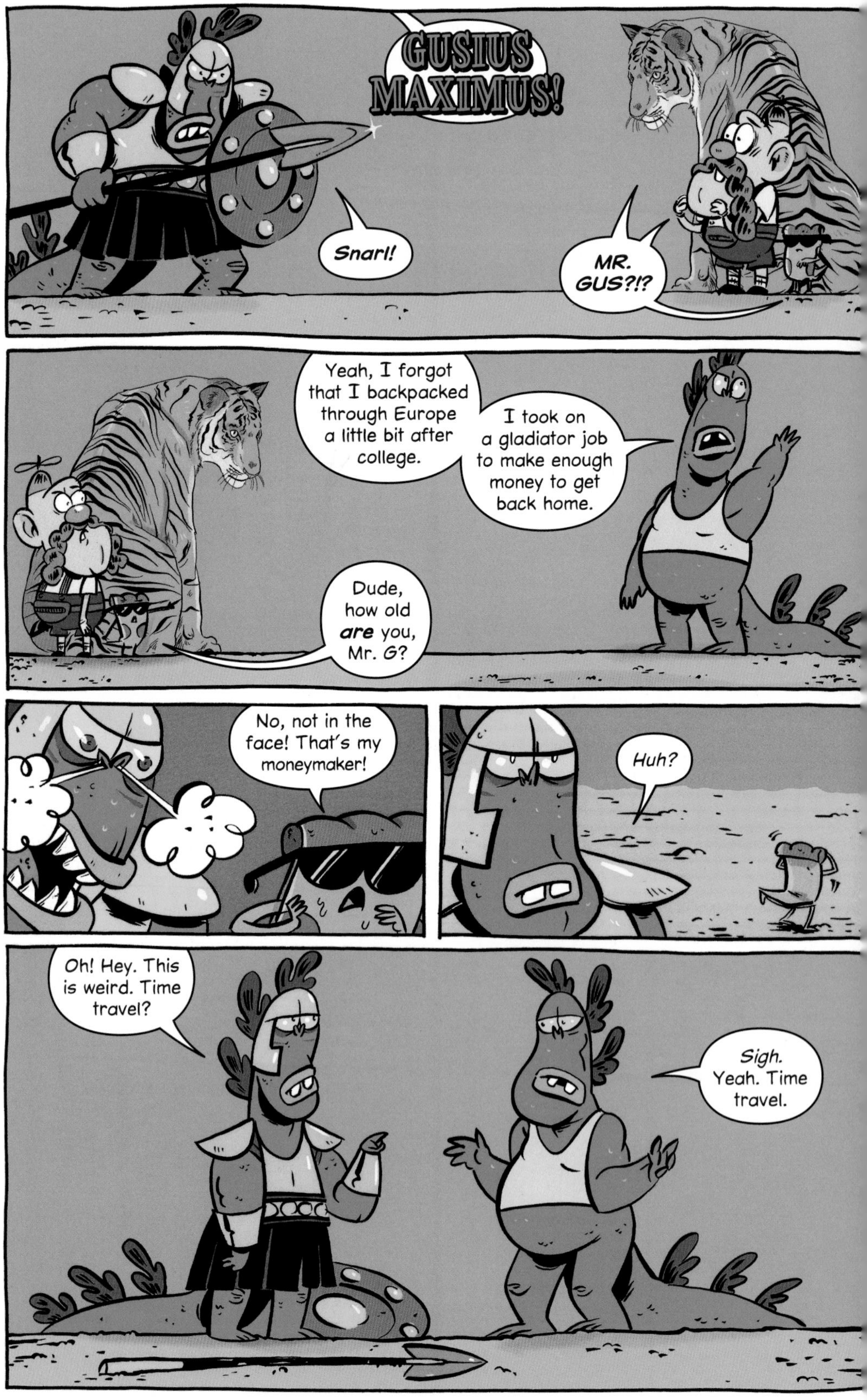
GUSIUS MAXIMUS!
Snarl!
MR. GUS?!?
Yeah, I forgot that I backpacked through Europe a little bit after college.
I took on a gladiator job to make enough money to get back home.
Dude, how old *are* you, Mr. G?
No, not in the face! That's my moneymaker!
Huh?
Oh! Hey. This is weird. Time travel?
Sigh. Yeah. Time travel.

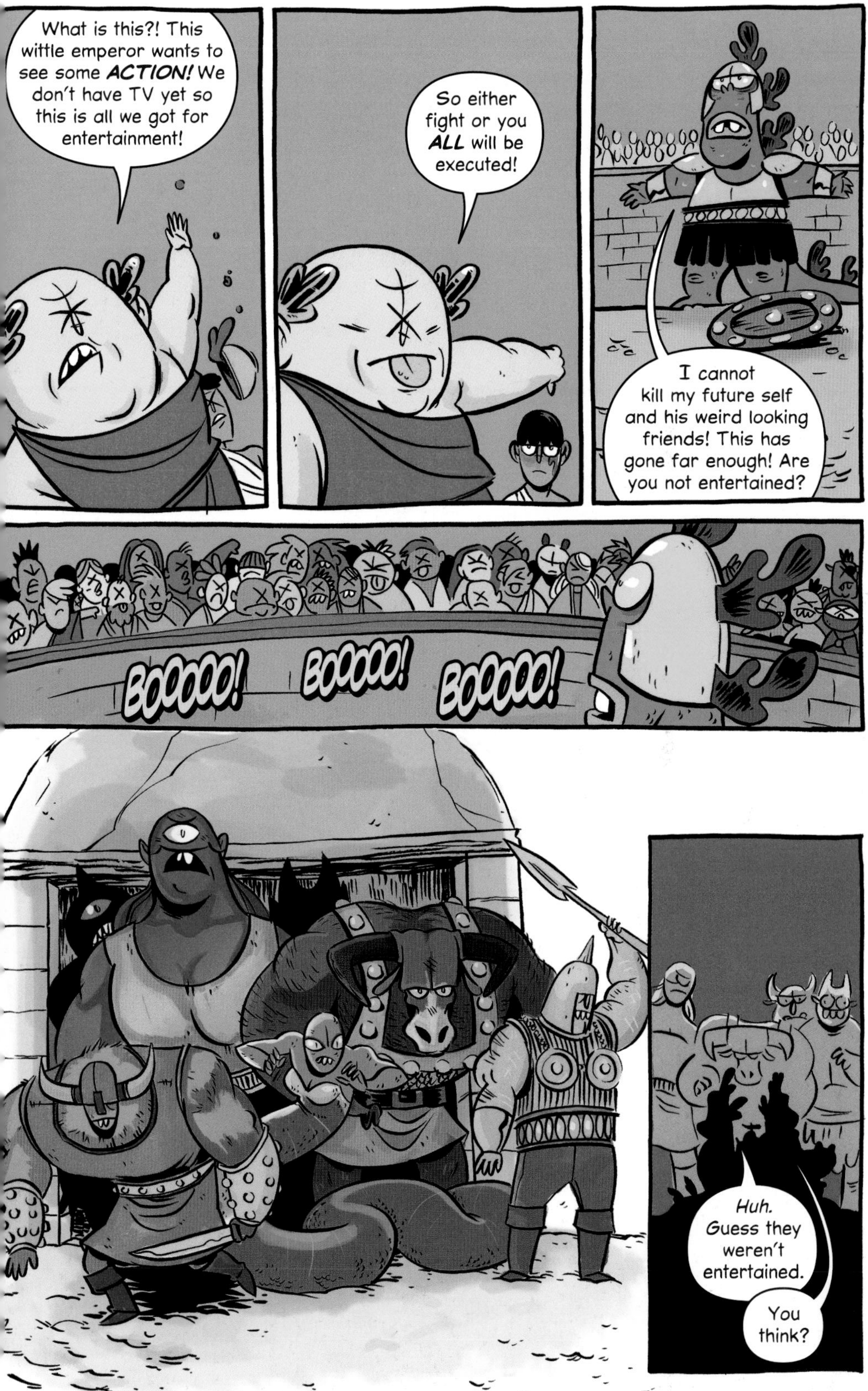
What is this?! This wittle emperor wants to see some ACTION! We don't have TV yet so this is all we got for entertainment!
So either fight or you ALL will be executed!
I cannot kill my future self and his weird looking friends! This has gone far enough! Are you not entertained?
BOOOOO! BOOOOO! BOOOOO!
Huh. Guess they weren't entertained.
You think?

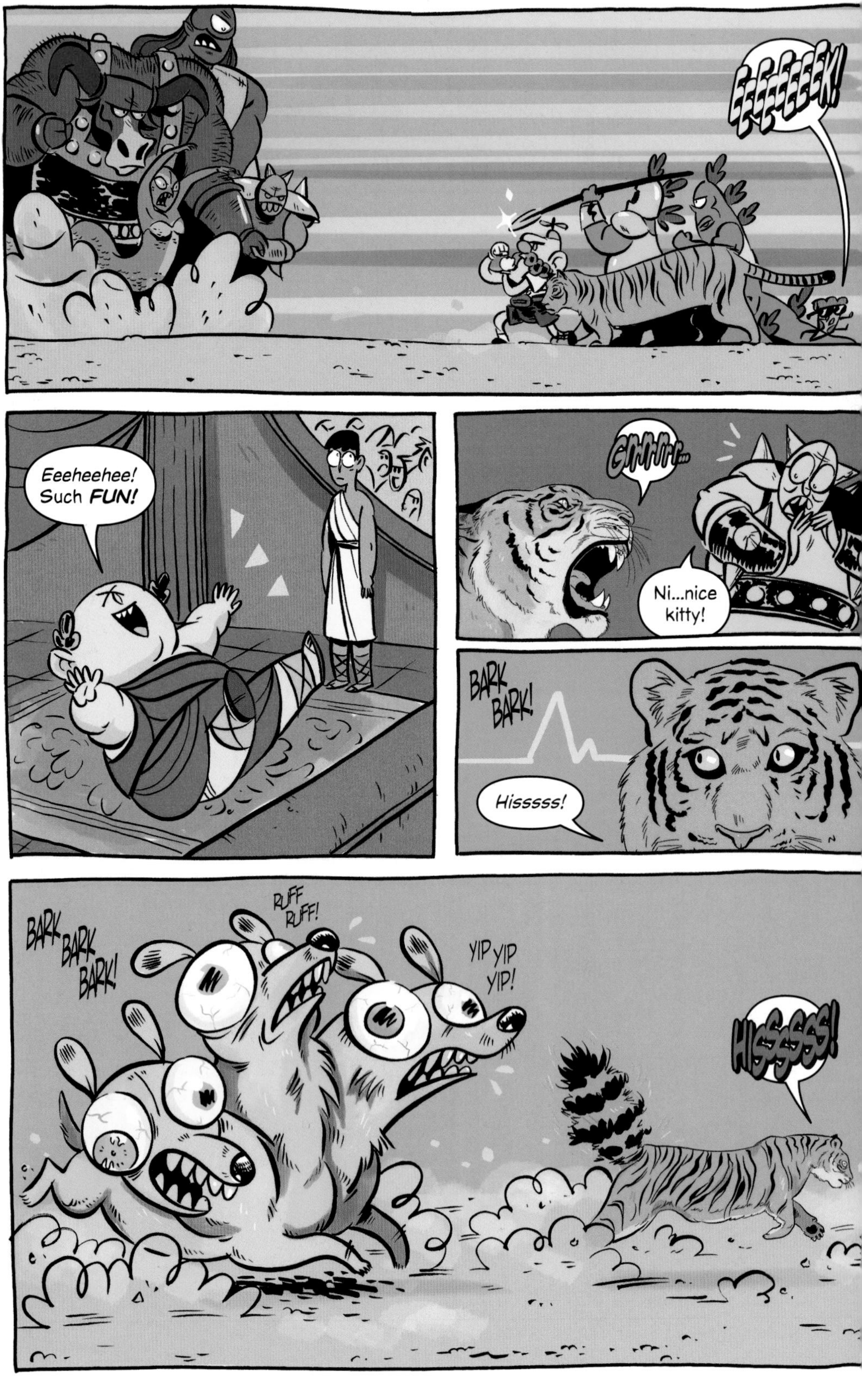
EEEEEEEEEK!
Eeeheehee! Such FUN!
Grrrrrr...
Ni...nice kitty!
BARK BARK!
Hisssss!
BARK BARK BARK!
RUFF RUFF!
YIP YIP YIP!
HISSSSS!

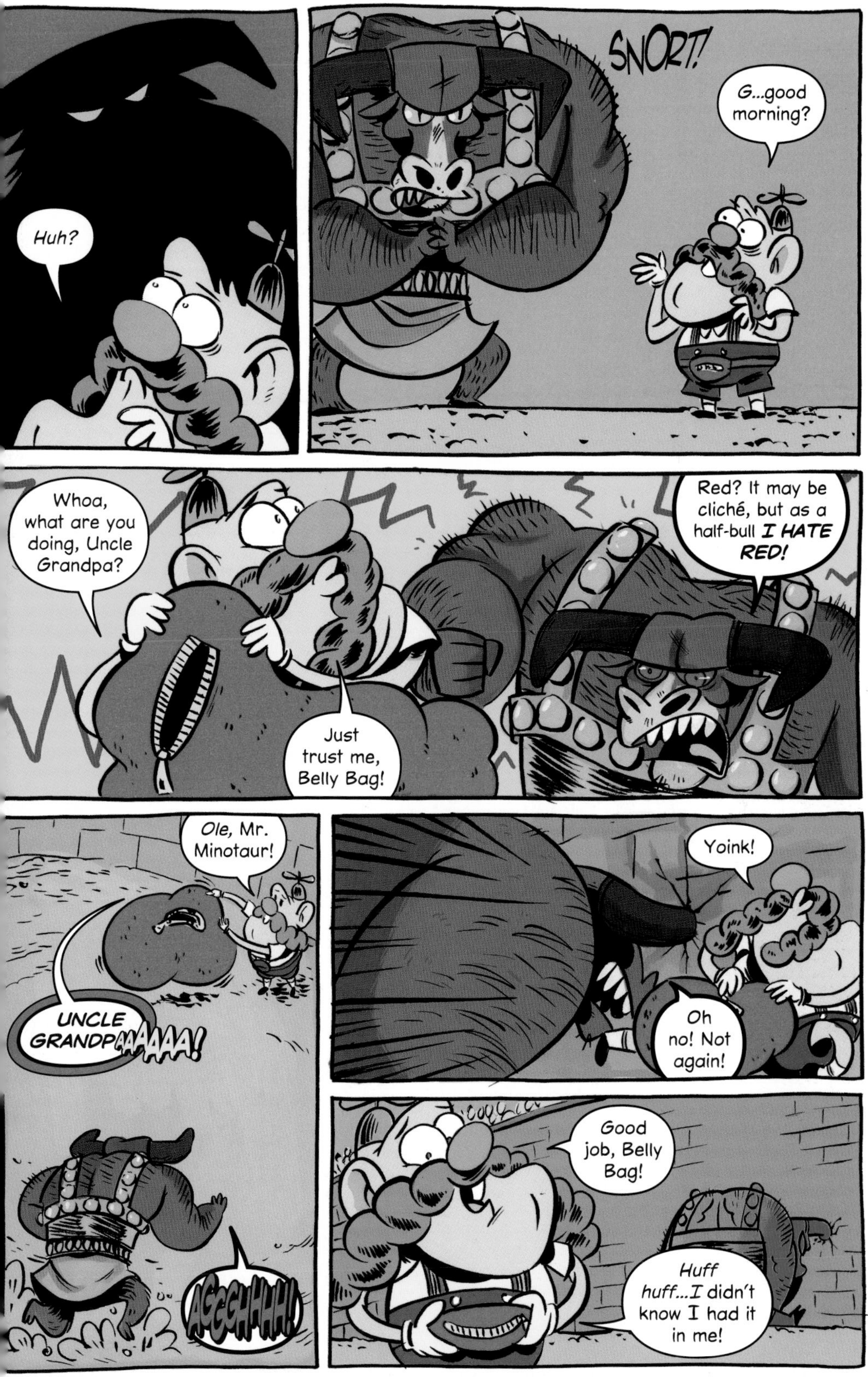

Huh?
SNORT!
G...good morning?
Whoa, what are you doing, Uncle Grandpa?
Just trust me, Belly Bag!
Red? It may be cliché, but as a half-bull I HATE RED!
Ole, Mr. Minotaur!
UNCLE GRANDPAAAAAA!
Yoink!
Oh no! Not again!
AGGGHHHH!
Good job, Belly Bag!
Huff huff...I didn't know I had it in me!

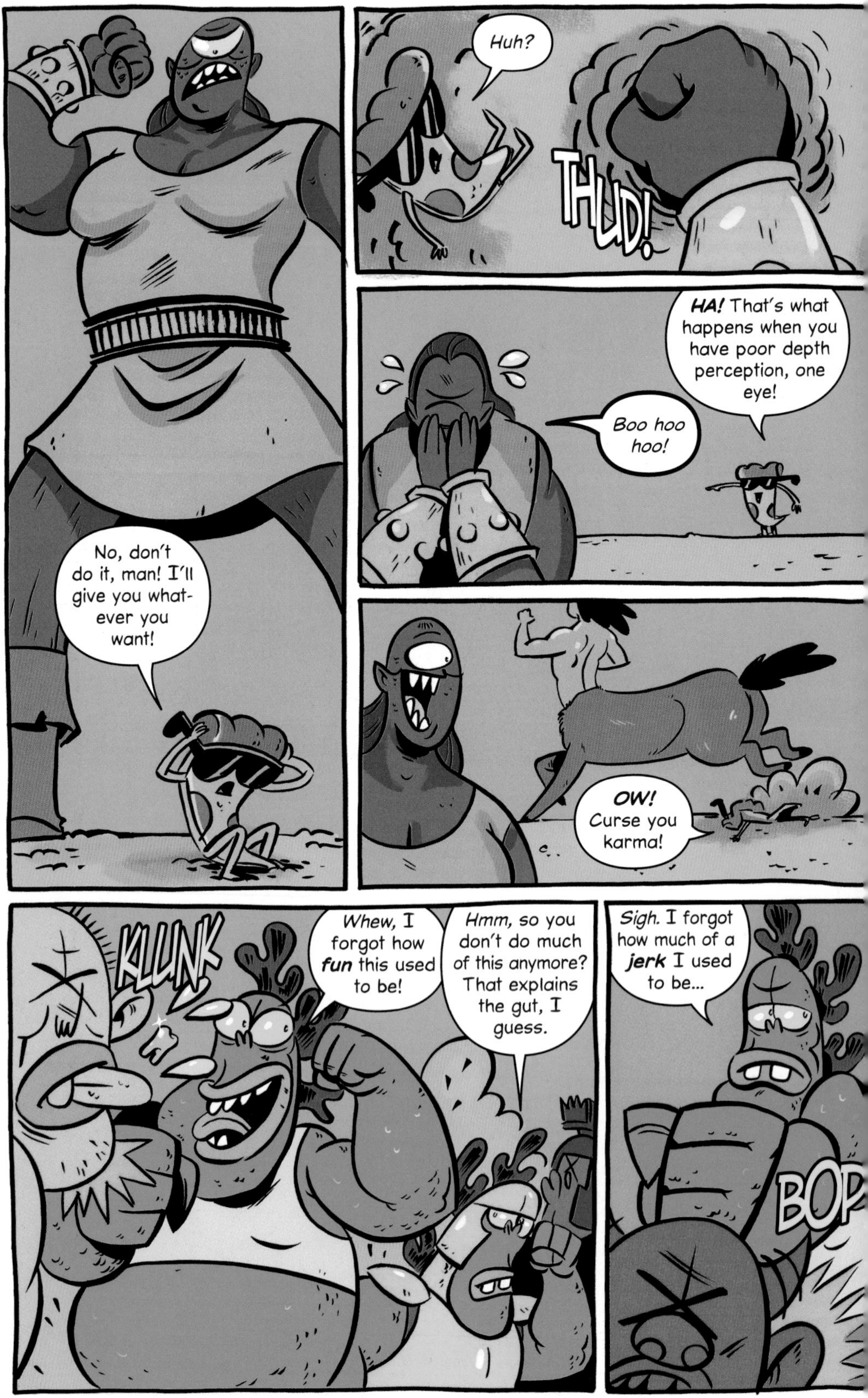
No, don't do it, man! I'll give you whatever you want!
Huh?
THUD!
HA! That's what happens when you have poor depth perception, one eye!
Boo hoo hoo!
OW! Curse you karma!
KLUNK
Whew, I forgot how fun this used to be!
Hmm, so you don't do much of this anymore? That explains the gut, I guess.
Sigh. I forgot how much of a jerk I used to be...
BOP

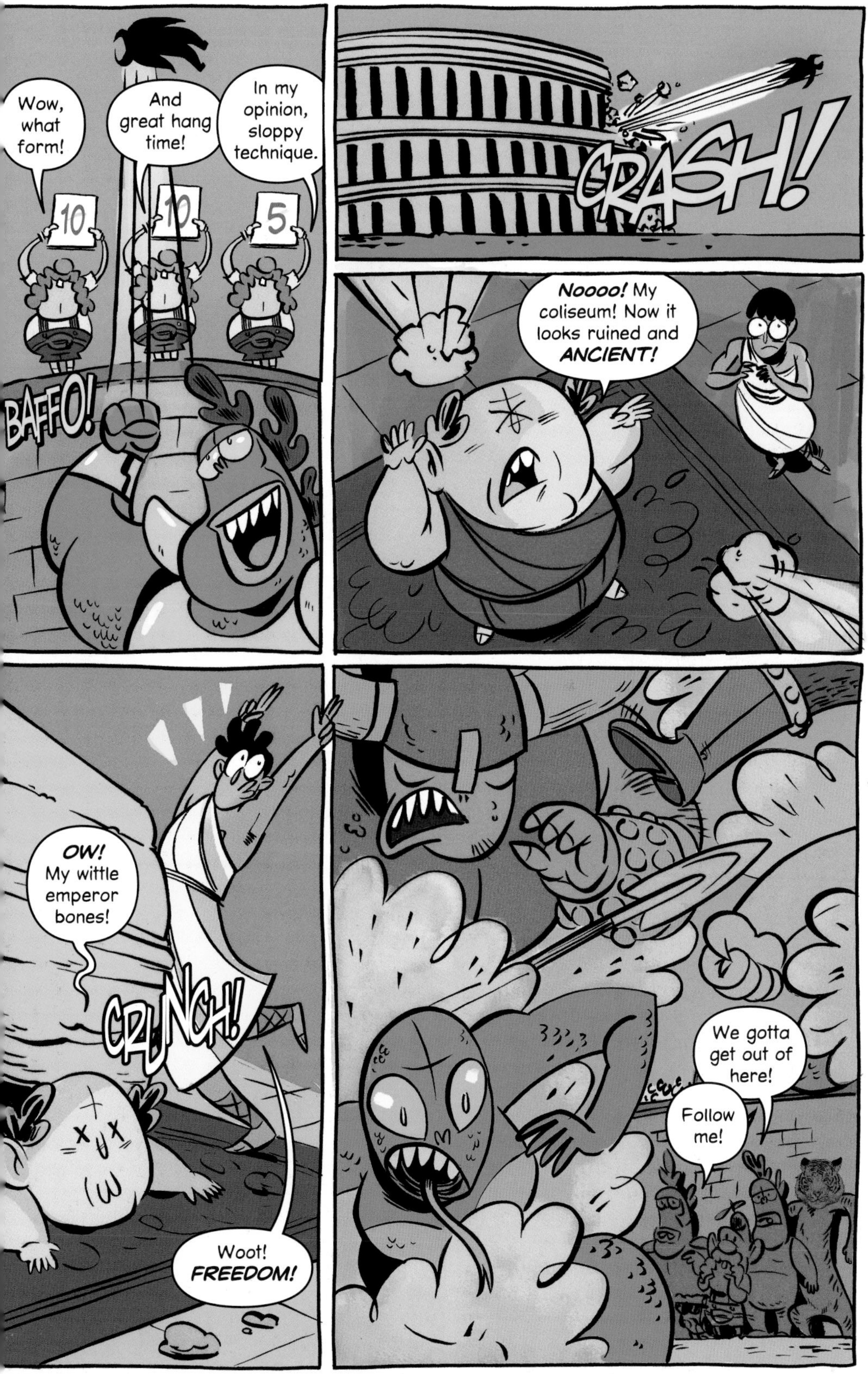
Wow, what form!
And great hang time!
In my opinion, sloppy technique.
10
10
5
BAFFO!
CRASH!
Noooo! My coliseum! Now it looks ruined and ANCIENT!
OW! My wittle emperor bones!
CRUNCH!
Woot! FREEDOM!
We gotta get out of here!
Follow me!

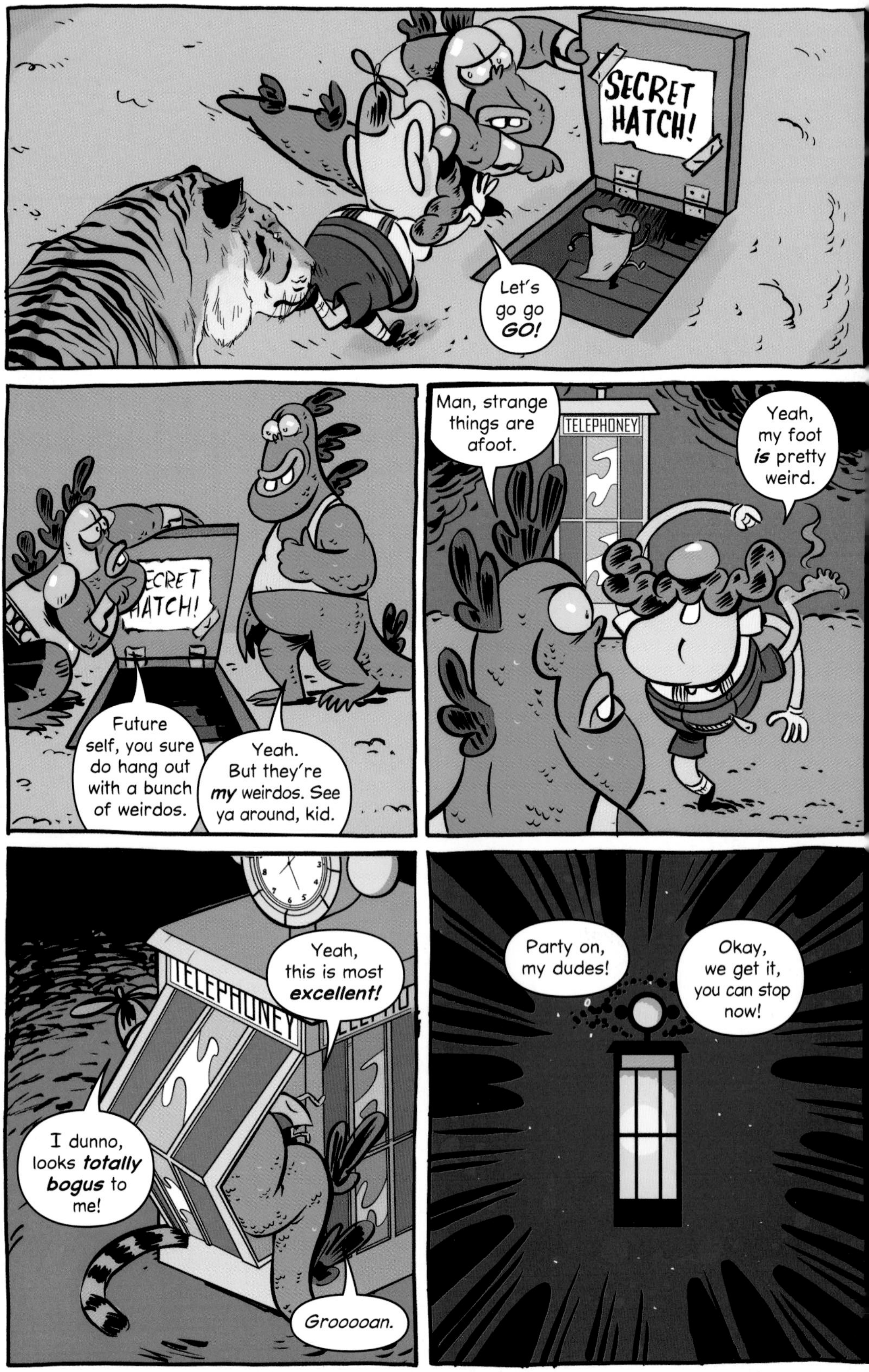
SECRET HATCH!
Let's go go GO!
SECRET HATCH!
Future self, you sure do hang out with a bunch of weirdos.
Yeah. But they're my weirdos. See ya around, kid.
Man, strange things are afoot.
TELEPHONEY
Yeah, my foot is pretty weird.
TELEPHONEY
Yeah, this is most excellent!
I dunno, looks totally bogus to me!
Groooooan.
Party on, my dudes!
Okay, we get it, you can stop now!

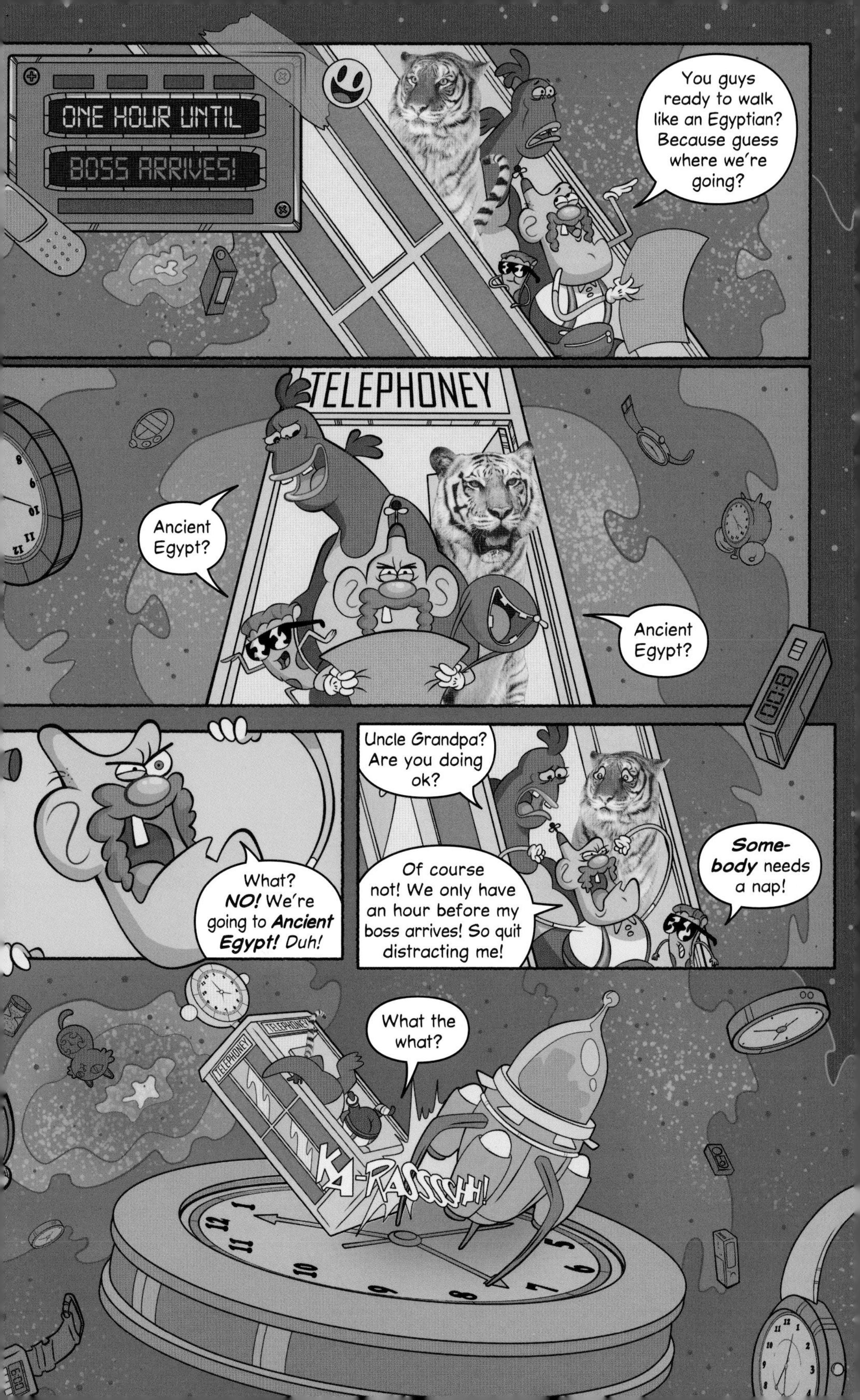
ONE HOUR UNTIL
BOSS ARRIVES!
You guys ready to walk like an Egyptian? Because guess where we're going?
TELEPHONEY
Ancient Egypt?
Ancient Egypt?
What? NO! We're going to Ancient Egypt! Duh!
Uncle Grandpa? Are you doing ok?
Of course not! We only have an hour before my boss arrives! So quit distracting me!
Some-body needs a nap!
What the what?
TELEPHONEY
TELEPHONEY
KA-RASSSSHH!

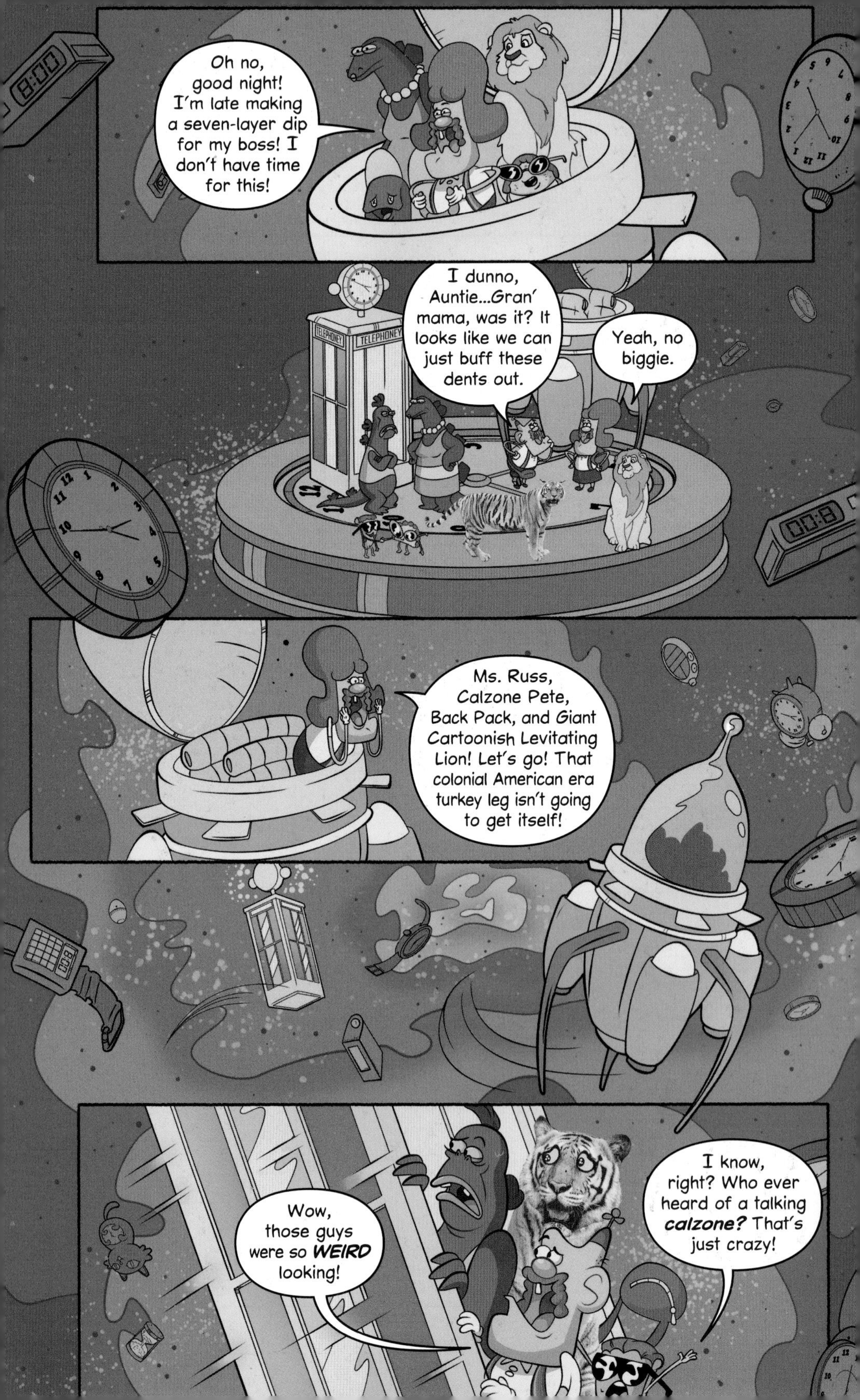
Oh no, good night! I'm late making a seven-layer dip for my boss! I don't have time for this!
TELEPHONEY
TELEPHONEY
I dunno, Auntie...Gran' mama, was it? It looks like we can just buff these dents out.
Yeah, no biggie.
Ms. Russ, Calzone Pete, Back Pack, and Giant Cartoonish Levitating Lion! Let's go! That colonial American era turkey leg isn't going to get itself!
Wow, those guys were so *WEIRD* looking!
I know, right? Who ever heard of a talking ***calzone?*** That's just crazy!

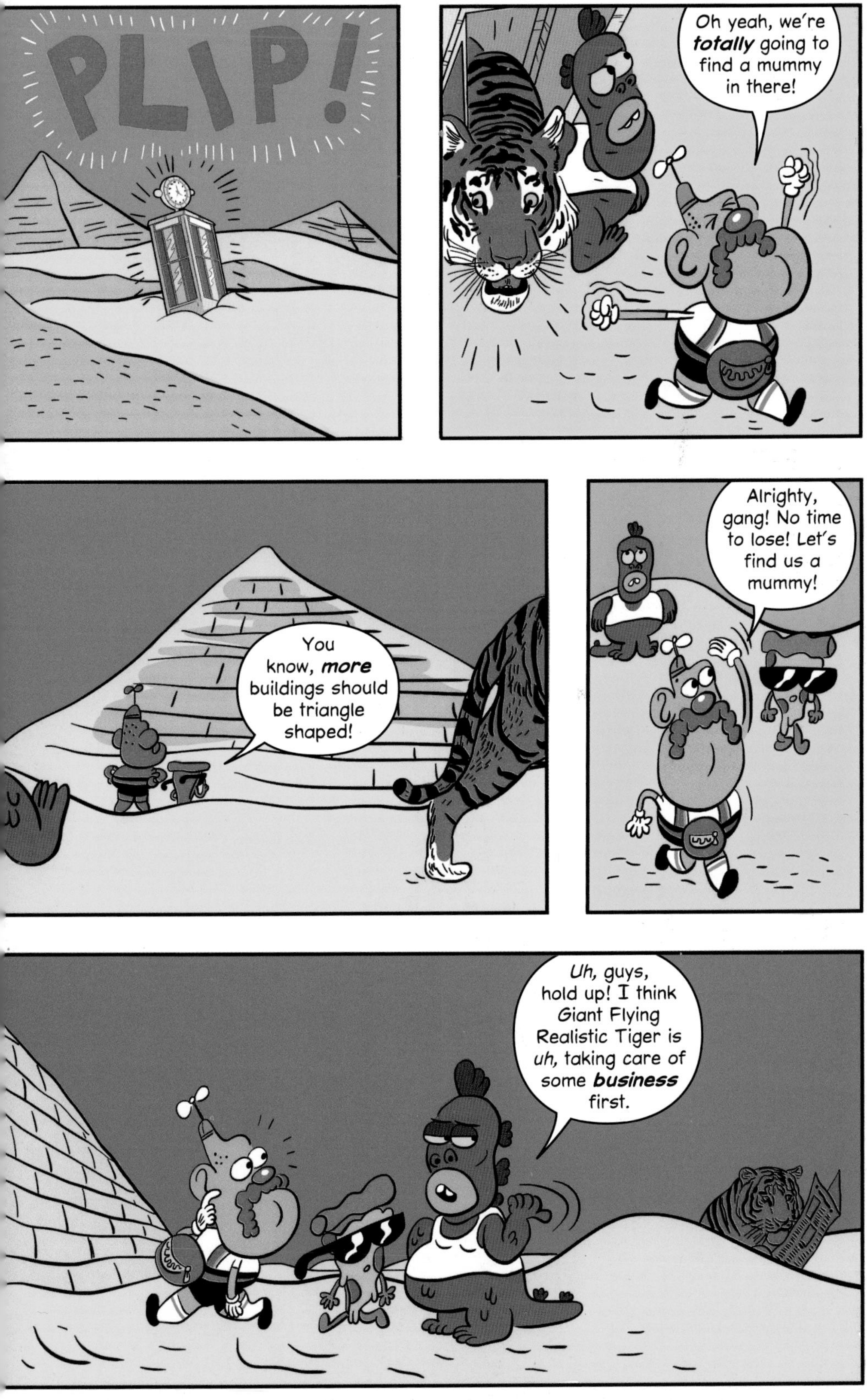
PLIP!
Oh yeah, we're *totally* going to find a mummy in there!
You know, *more* buildings should be triangle shaped!
Alrighty, gang! No time to lose! Let's find us a mummy!
Uh, guys, hold up! I think Giant Flying Realistic Tiger is *uh,* taking care of some *business* first.

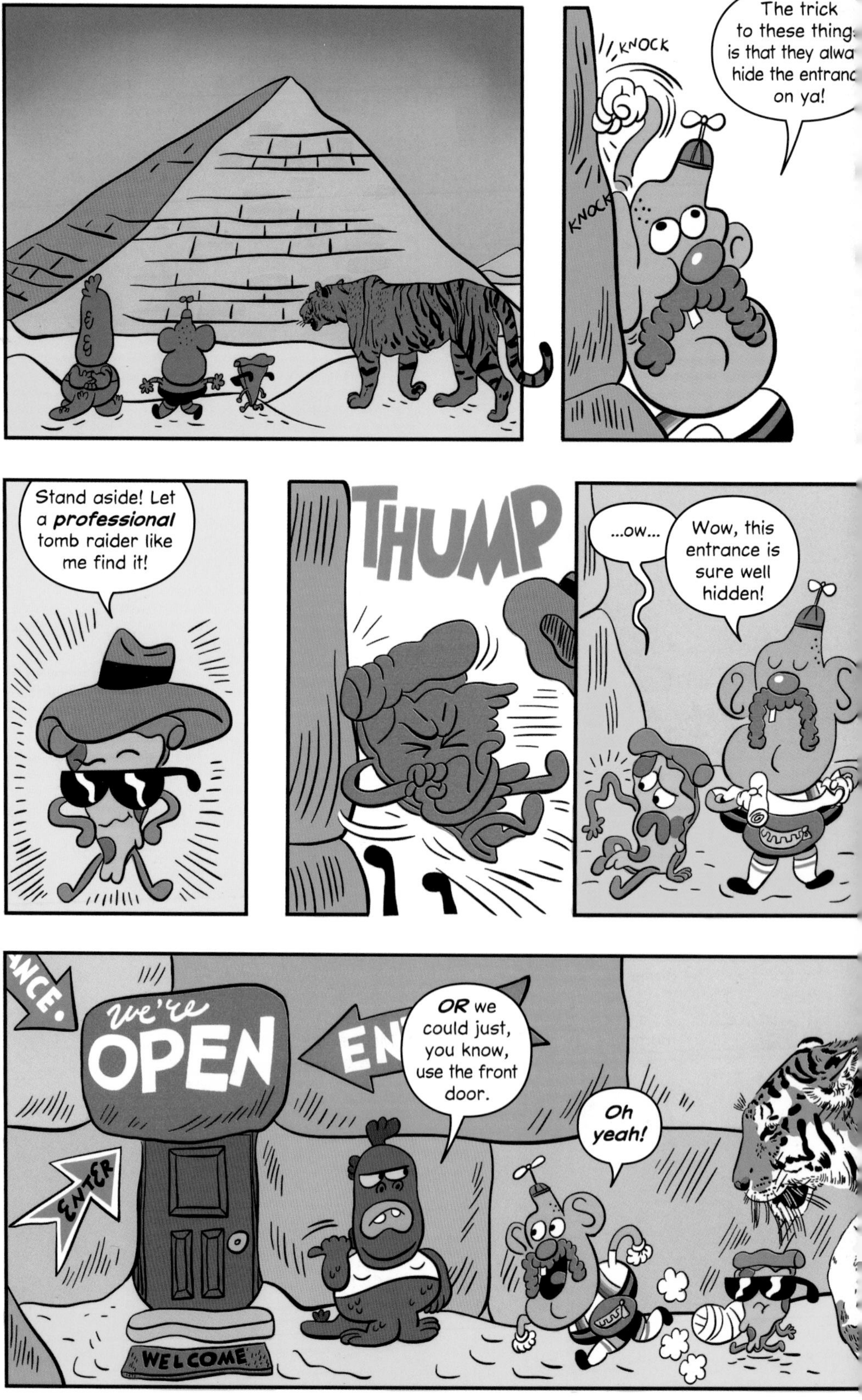

KNOCK
KNOCK
The trick to these thing is that they alwa hide the entranc on ya!
Stand aside! Let a ***professional*** tomb raider like me find it!
THUMP
...ow...
Wow, this entrance is sure well hidden!
ANCE.
We're OPEN
EN
ENTER
OR we could just, you know, use the front door.
Oh yeah!
WELCOME

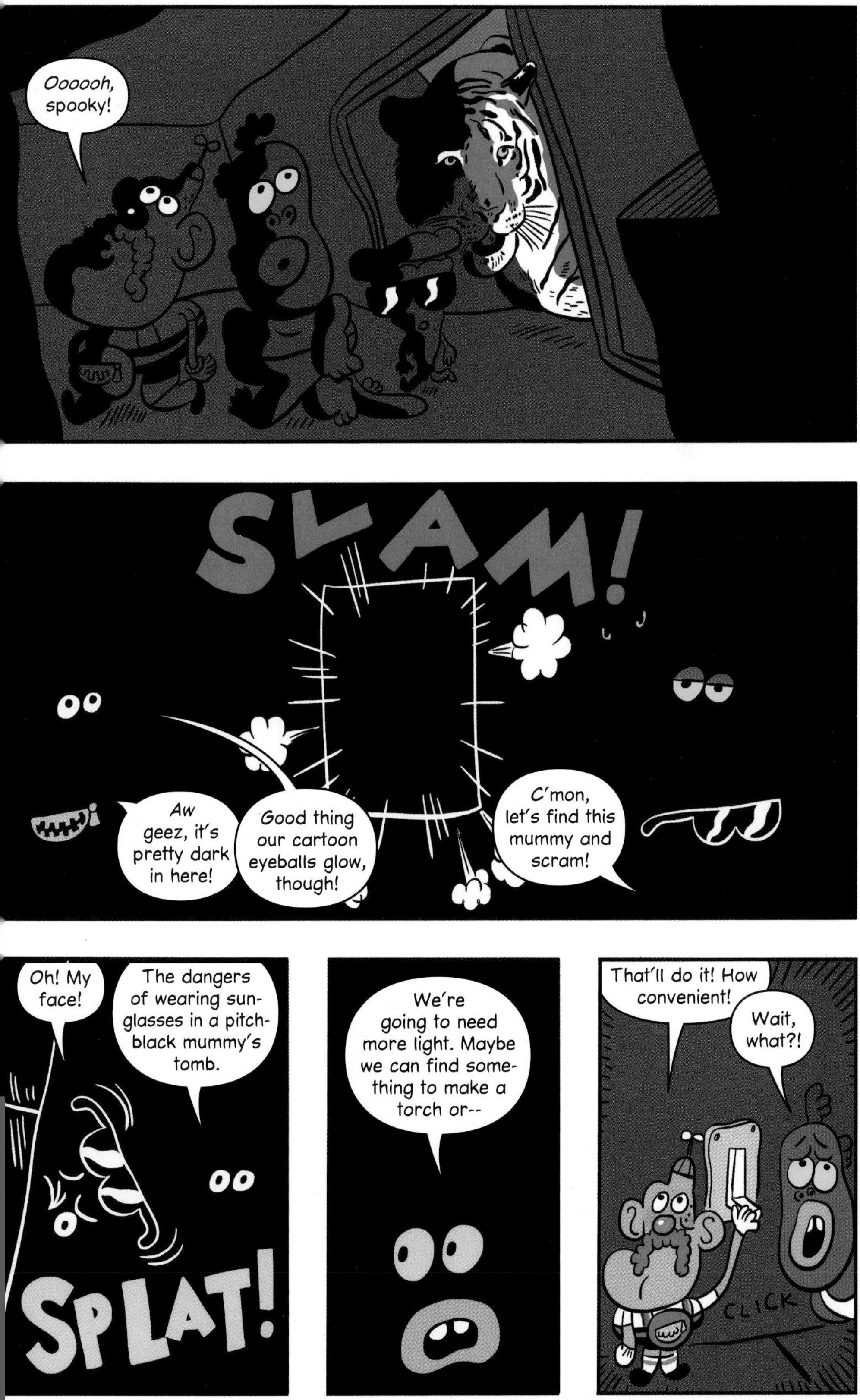
Oooooh, spooky!
SLAM!
Aw geez, it's pretty dark in here!
Good thing our cartoon eyeballs glow, though!
C'mon, let's find this mummy and scram!
Oh! My face!
The dangers of wearing sunglasses in a pitch-black mummy's tomb.
SPLAT!
We're going to need more light. Maybe we can find something to make a torch or--
That'll do it! How convenient!
Wait, what?!
CLICK

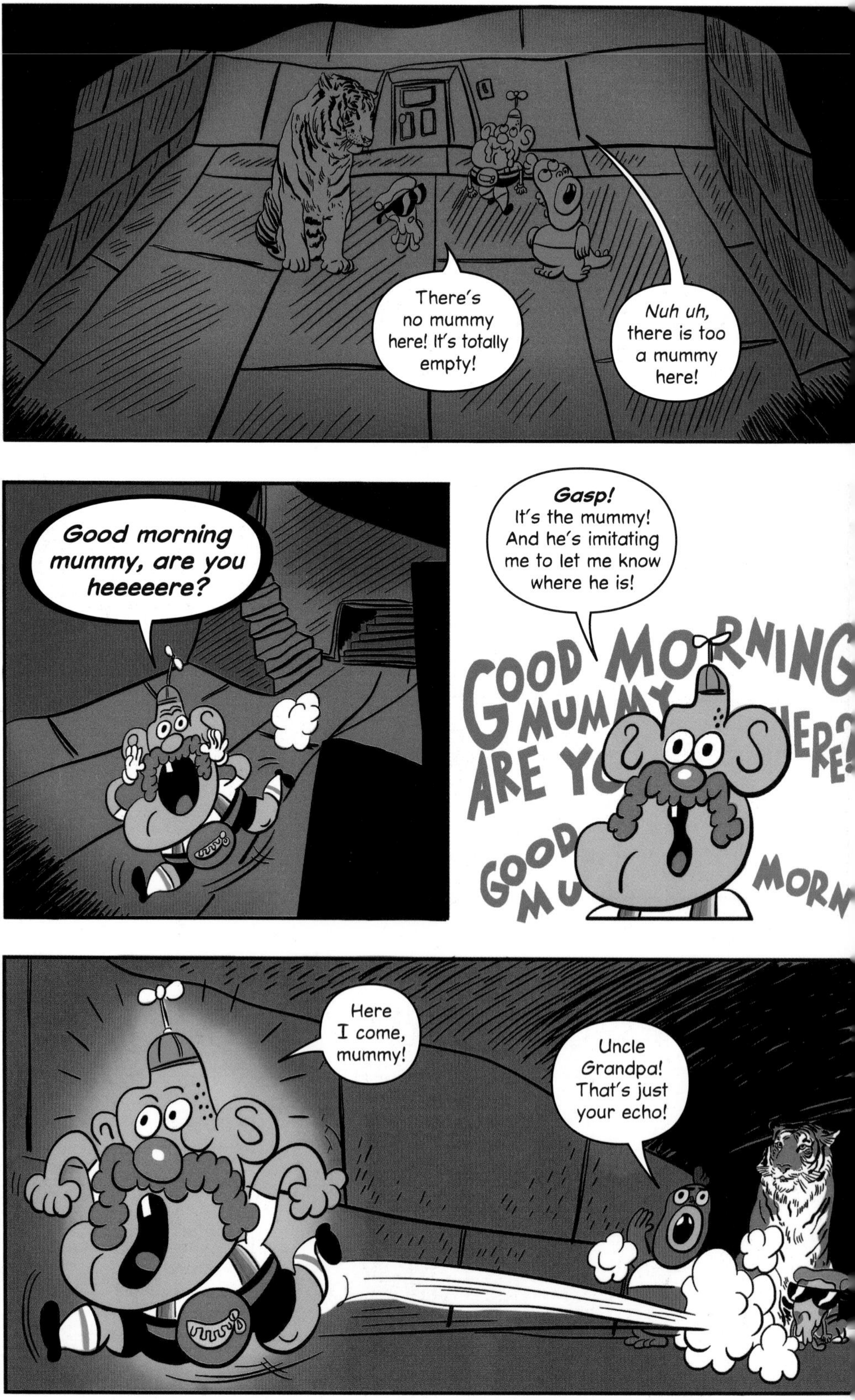
There's no mummy here! It's totally empty!
Nuh uh, there is too a mummy here!
Good morning mummy, are you heeeeere?
Gasp! It's the mummy! And he's imitating me to let me know where he is!
GOOD MORNING
MUMM
ARE YO
ERE?
GOOD
MU
MORN
Here I come, mummy!
Uncle Grandpa! That's just your echo!

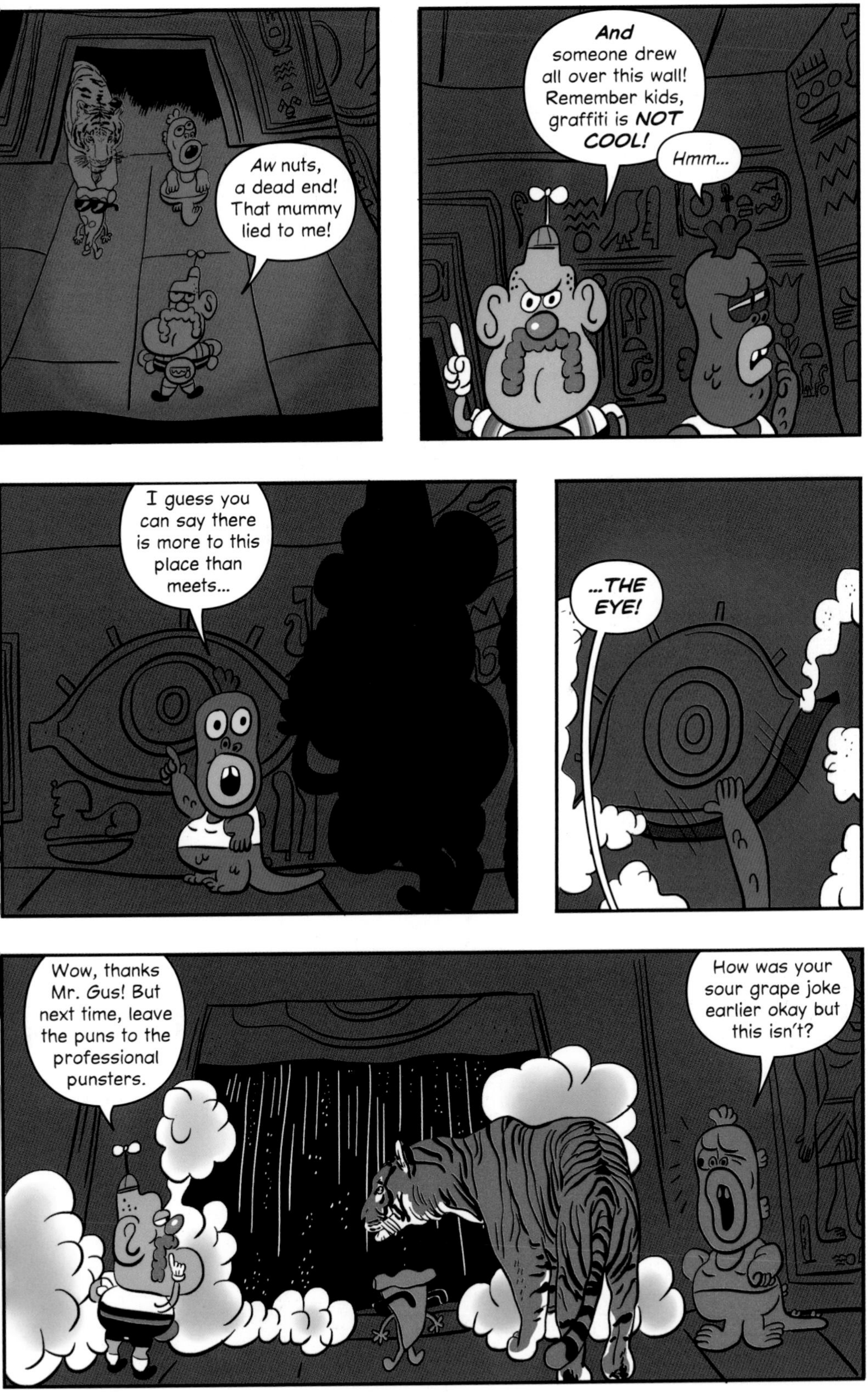
Aw nuts, a dead end! That mummy lied to me!
And someone drew all over this wall! Remember kids, graffiti is NOT COOL!
Hmm...
I guess you can say there is more to this place than meets...
...THE EYE!
Wow, thanks Mr. Gus! But next time, leave the puns to the professional punsters.
How was your sour grape joke earlier okay but this isn't?

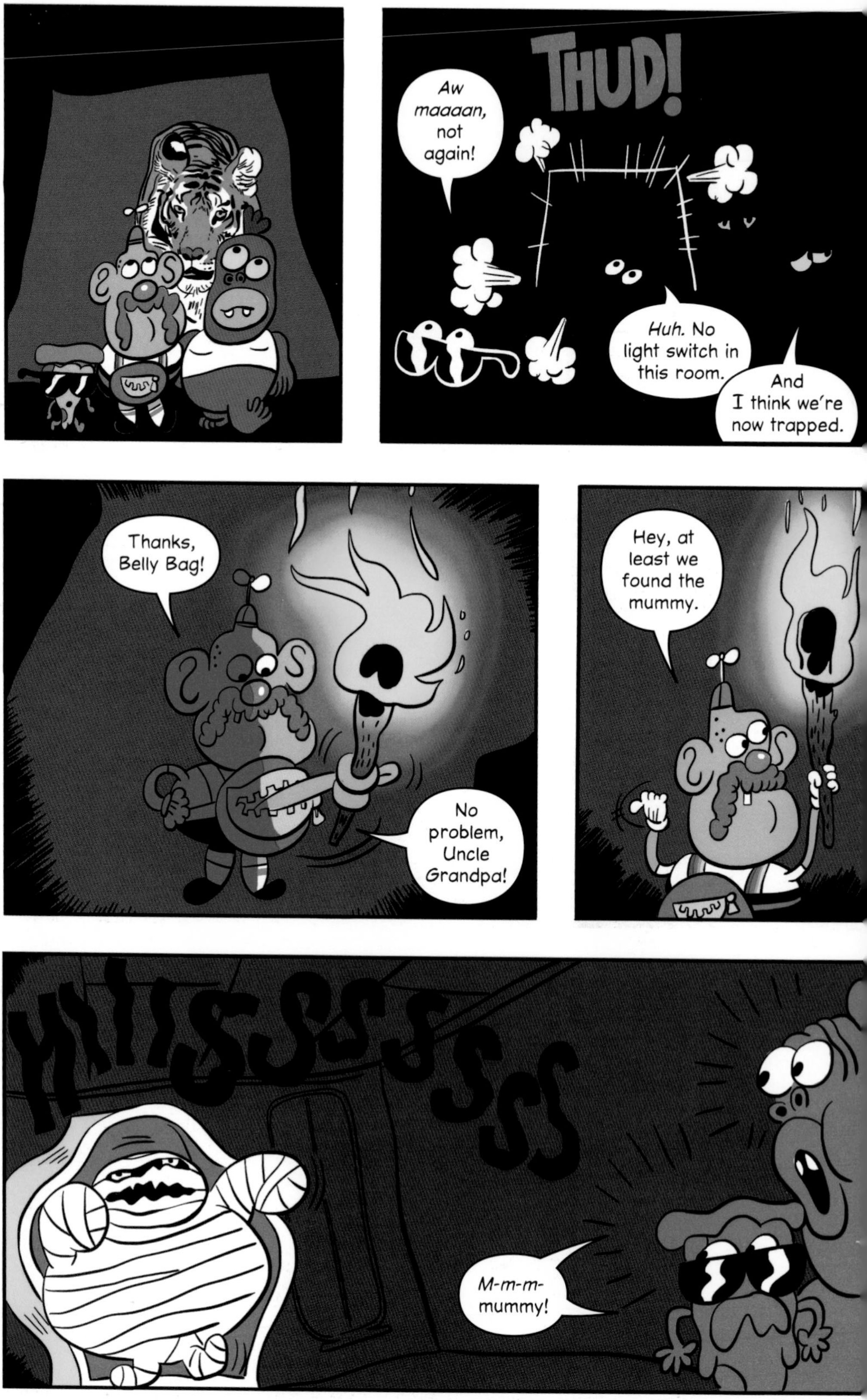
THUD!
Aw maaaan, not again!
Huh. No light switch in this room.
And I think we're now trapped.
Thanks, Belly Bag!
No problem, Uncle Grandpa!
Hey, at least we found the mummy.
HHISSSSSSS
M-m-m-mummy!

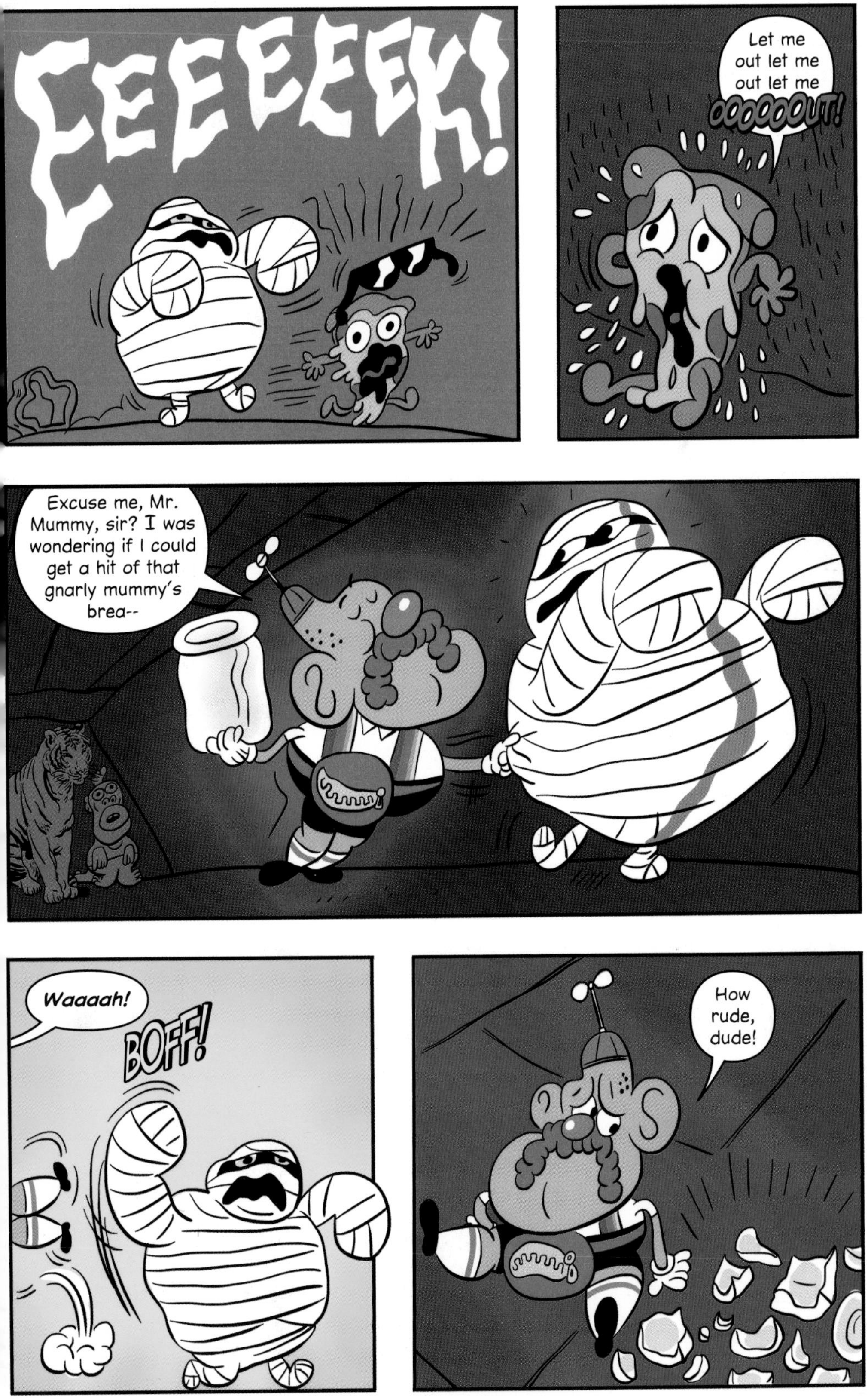
EEEEEEK!
Let me out let me out let me OOOOOOUT!
Excuse me, Mr. Mummy, sir? I was wondering if I could get a hit of that gnarly mummy's brea--
Waaaah!
BOFF!
How rude, dude!

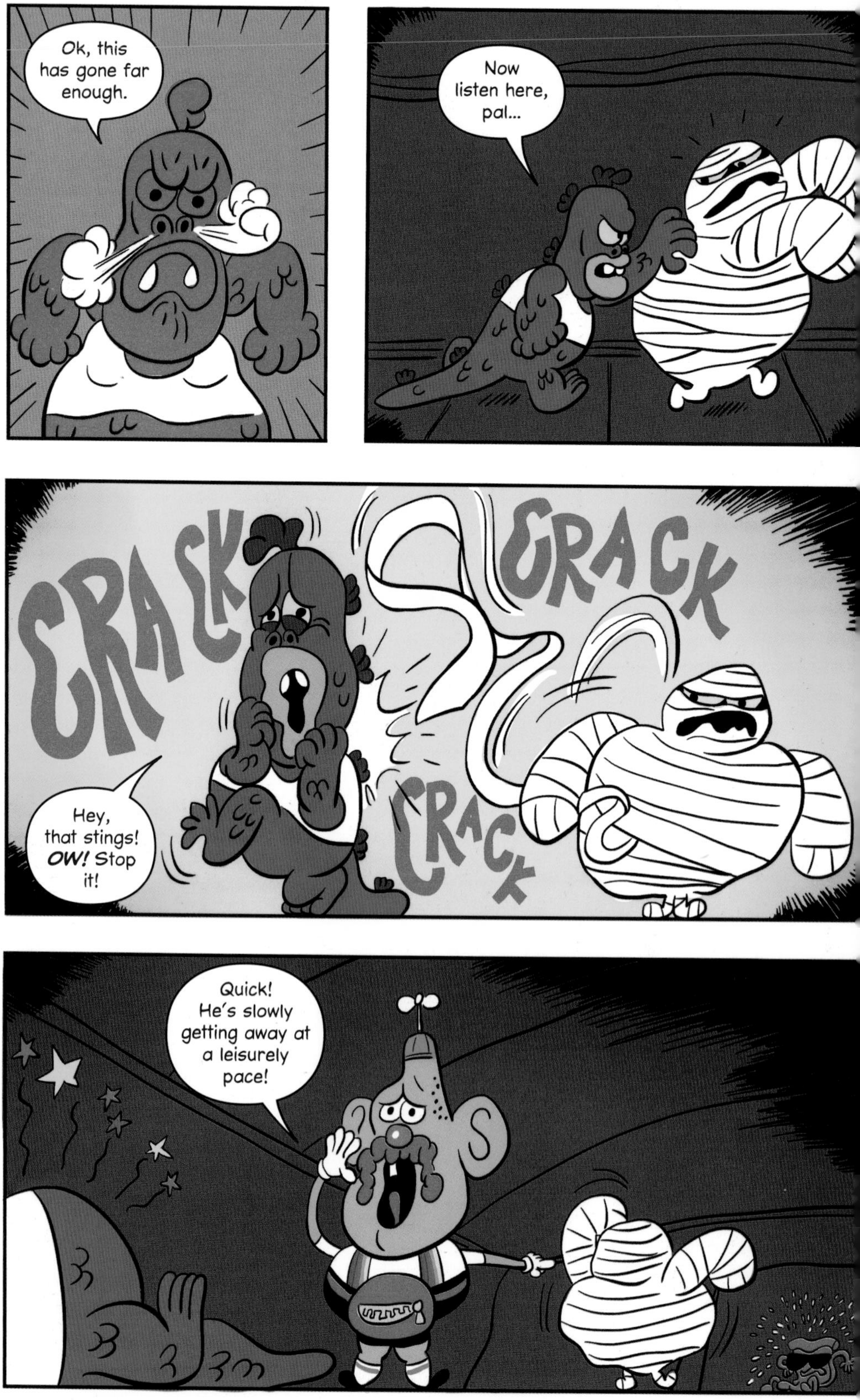
Ok, this has gone far enough.
Now listen here, pal...
CRACK
CRACK
CRACK
Hey, that stings! ***OW!*** Stop it!
Quick! He's slowly getting away at a leisurely pace!

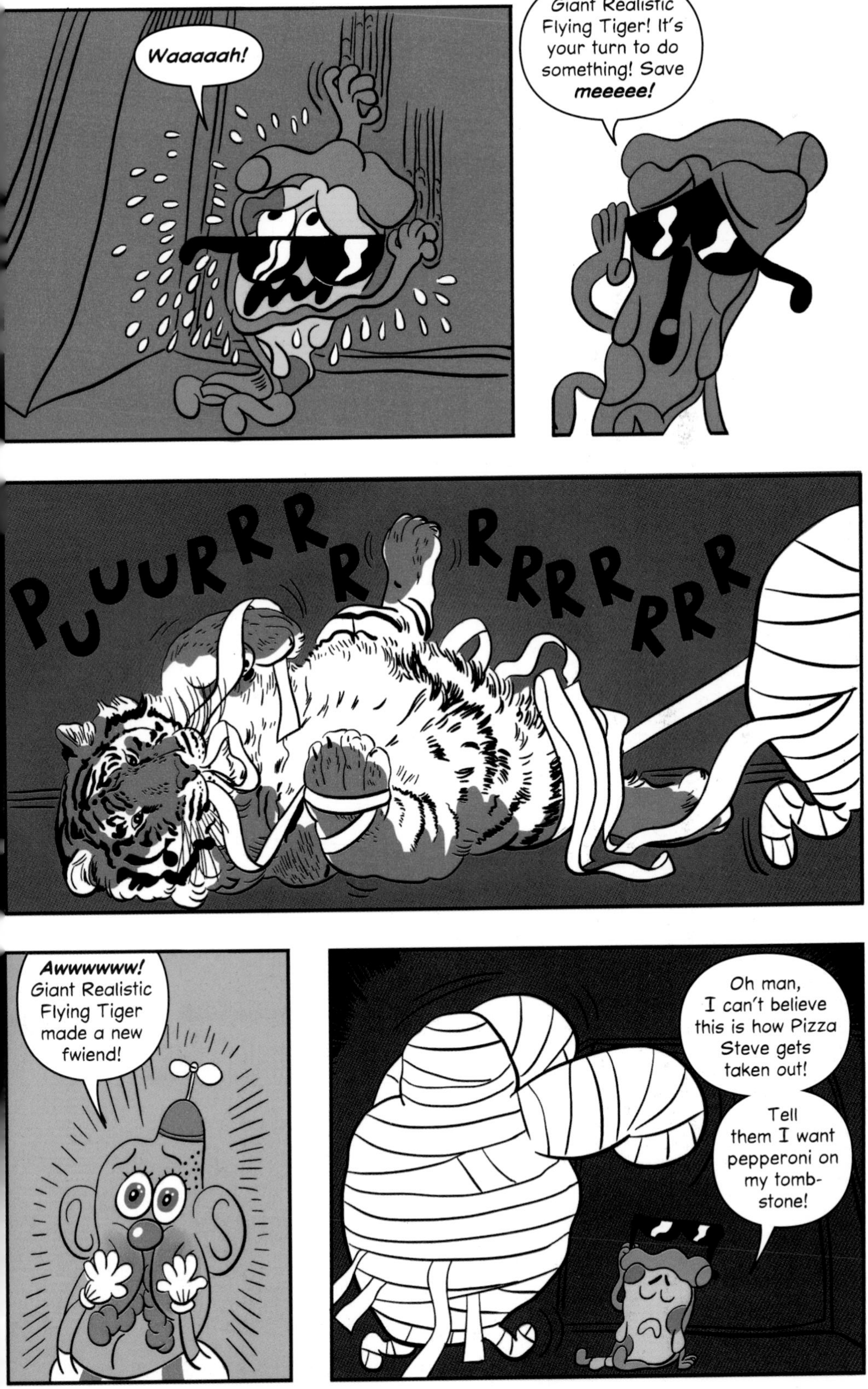
Waaaaah!
Giant Realistic Flying Tiger! It's your turn to do something! Save **meeeee!**
PUURRRRRRRRRRRR
Awwwwww! Giant Realistic Flying Tiger made a new fwiend!
Oh man, I can't believe this is how Pizza Steve gets taken out!
Tell them I want pepperoni on my tomb-stone!

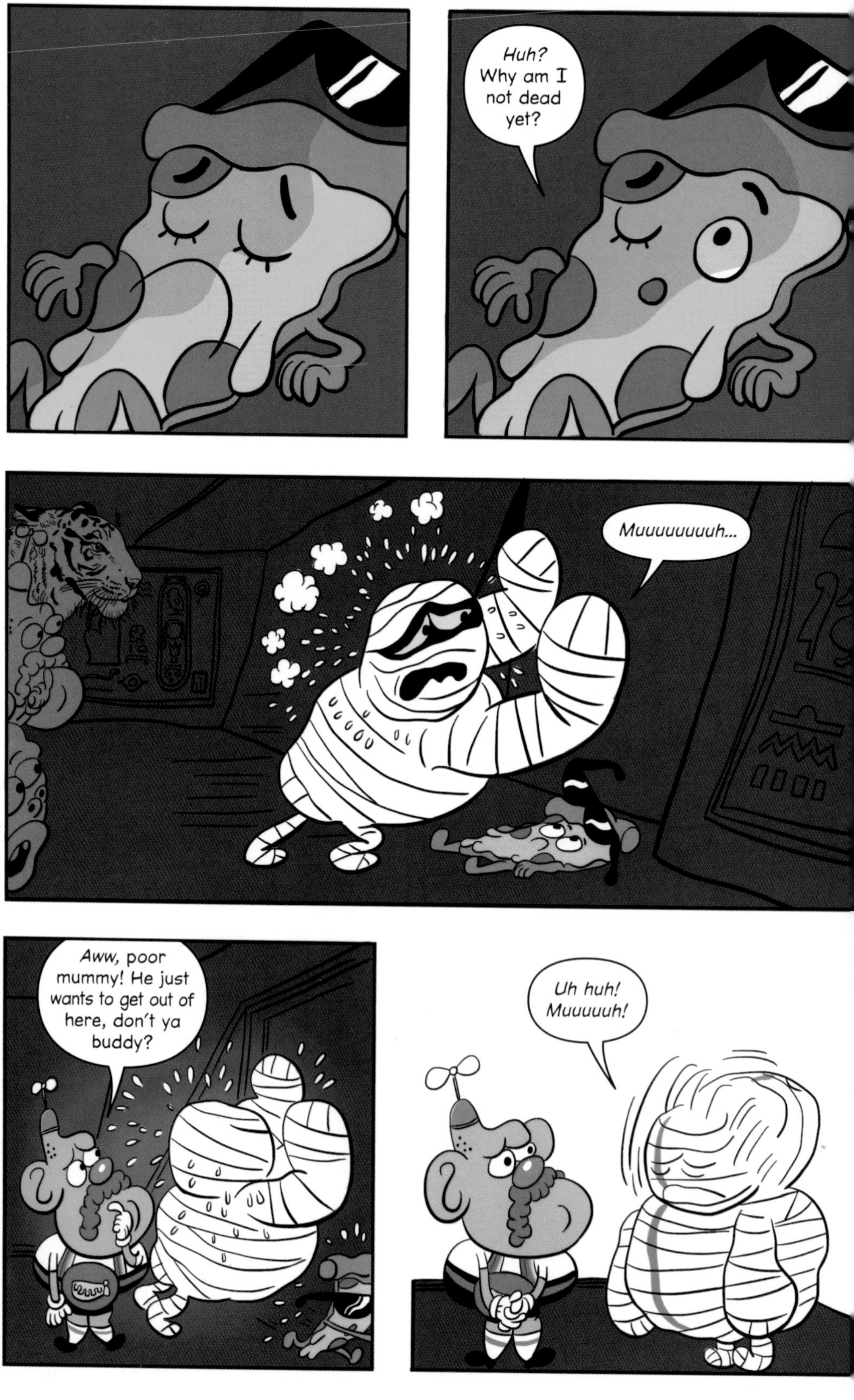
Huh? Why am I not dead yet?
Muuuuuuuuh...
Aww, poor mummy! He just wants to get out of here, don't ya buddy?
Uh huh! Muuuuuh!

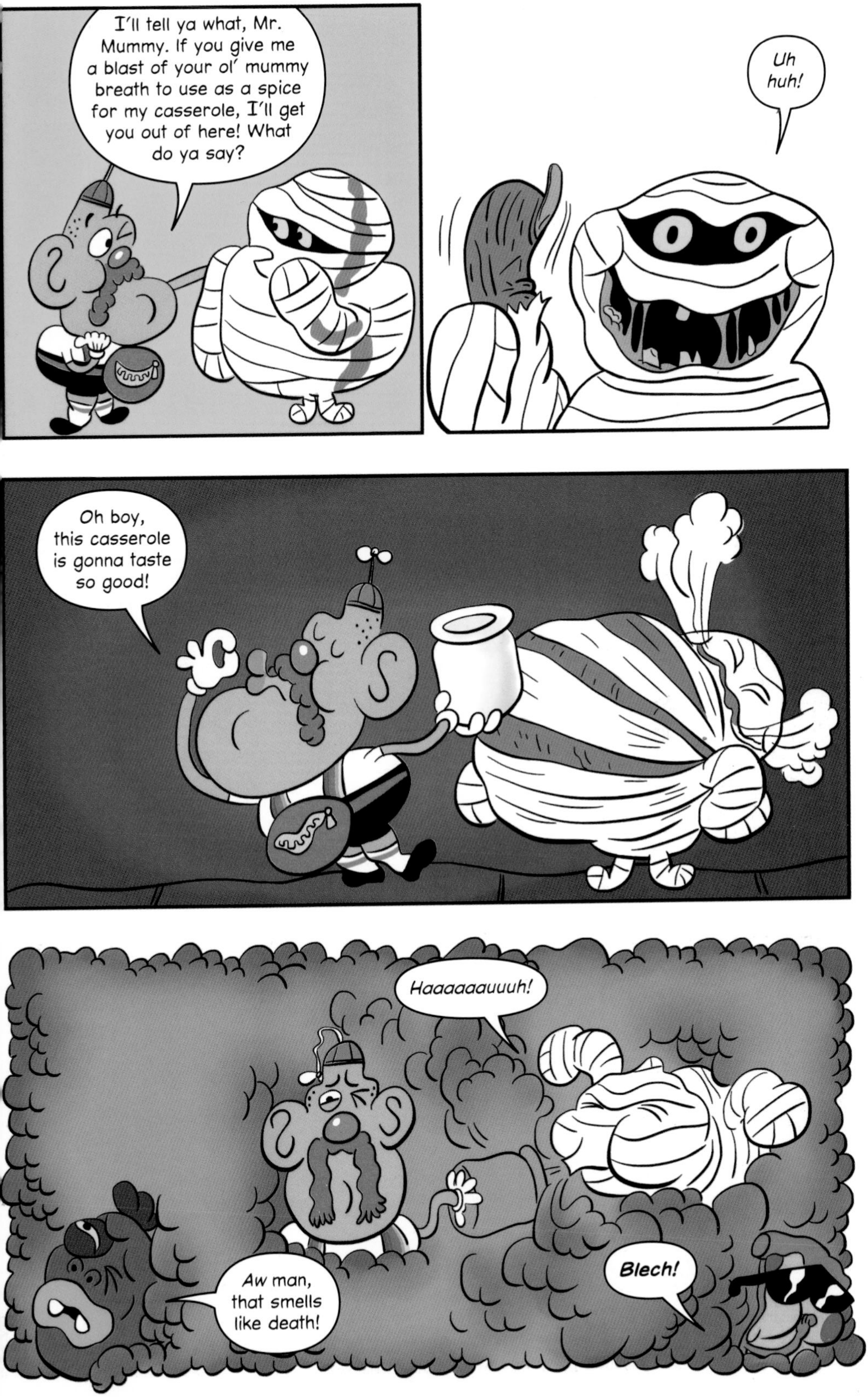
I'll tell ya what, Mr. Mummy. If you give me a blast of your ol' mummy breath to use as a spice for my casserole, I'll get you out of here! What do ya say?
Uh huh!
Oh boy, this casserole is gonna taste so good!
Haaaaaauuuh!
Aw man, that smells like death!
Blech!

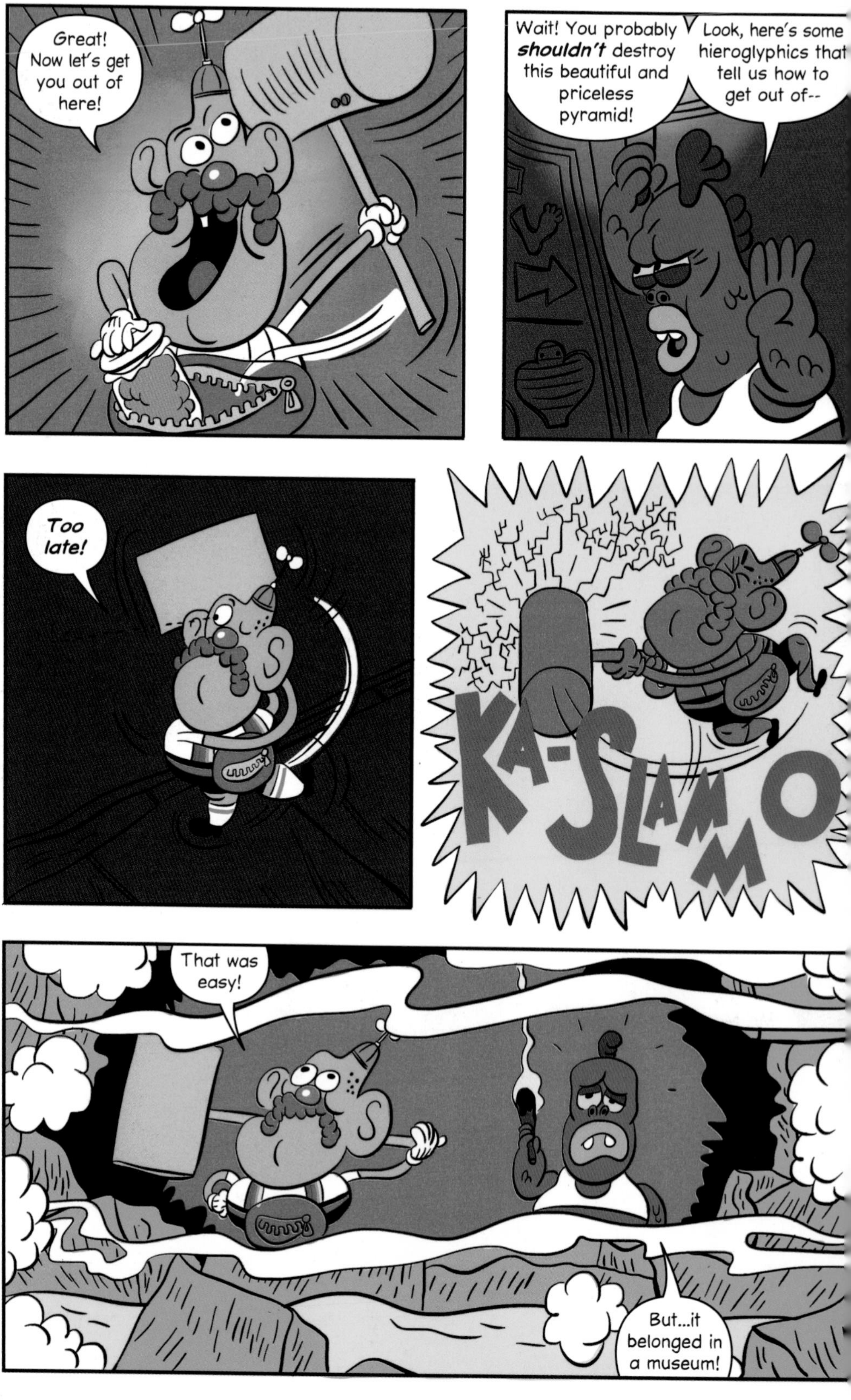
Great! Now let's get you out of here!
Wait! You probably *shouldn't* destroy this beautiful and priceless pyramid!
Look, here's some hieroglyphics that tell us how to get out of--
Too late!
KA-SLAMM
That was easy!
But...it belonged in a museum!

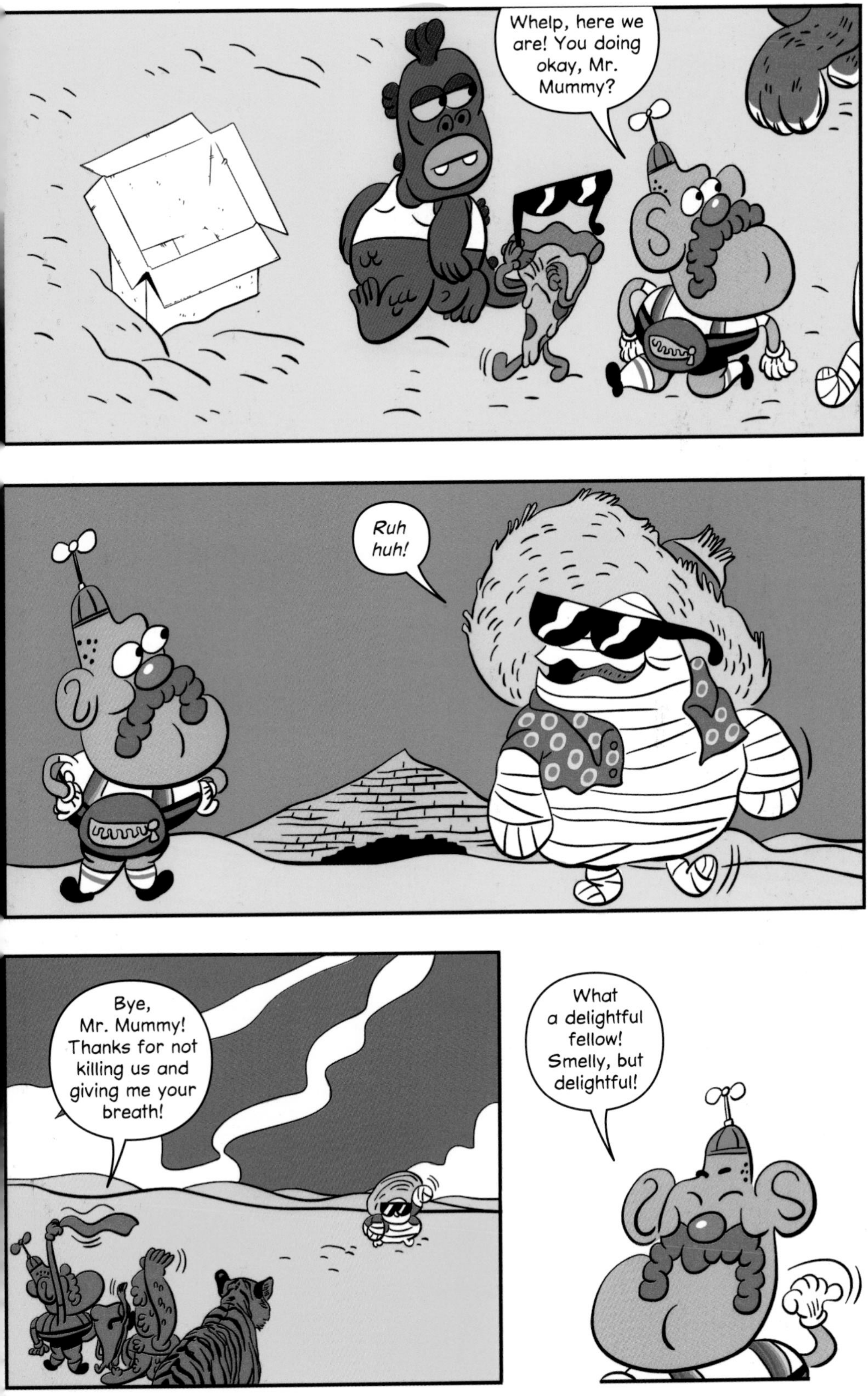
Whelp, here we are! You doing okay, Mr. Mummy?
Ruh huh!
Bye, Mr. Mummy! Thanks for not killing us and giving me your breath!
What a delightful fellow! Smelly, but delightful!

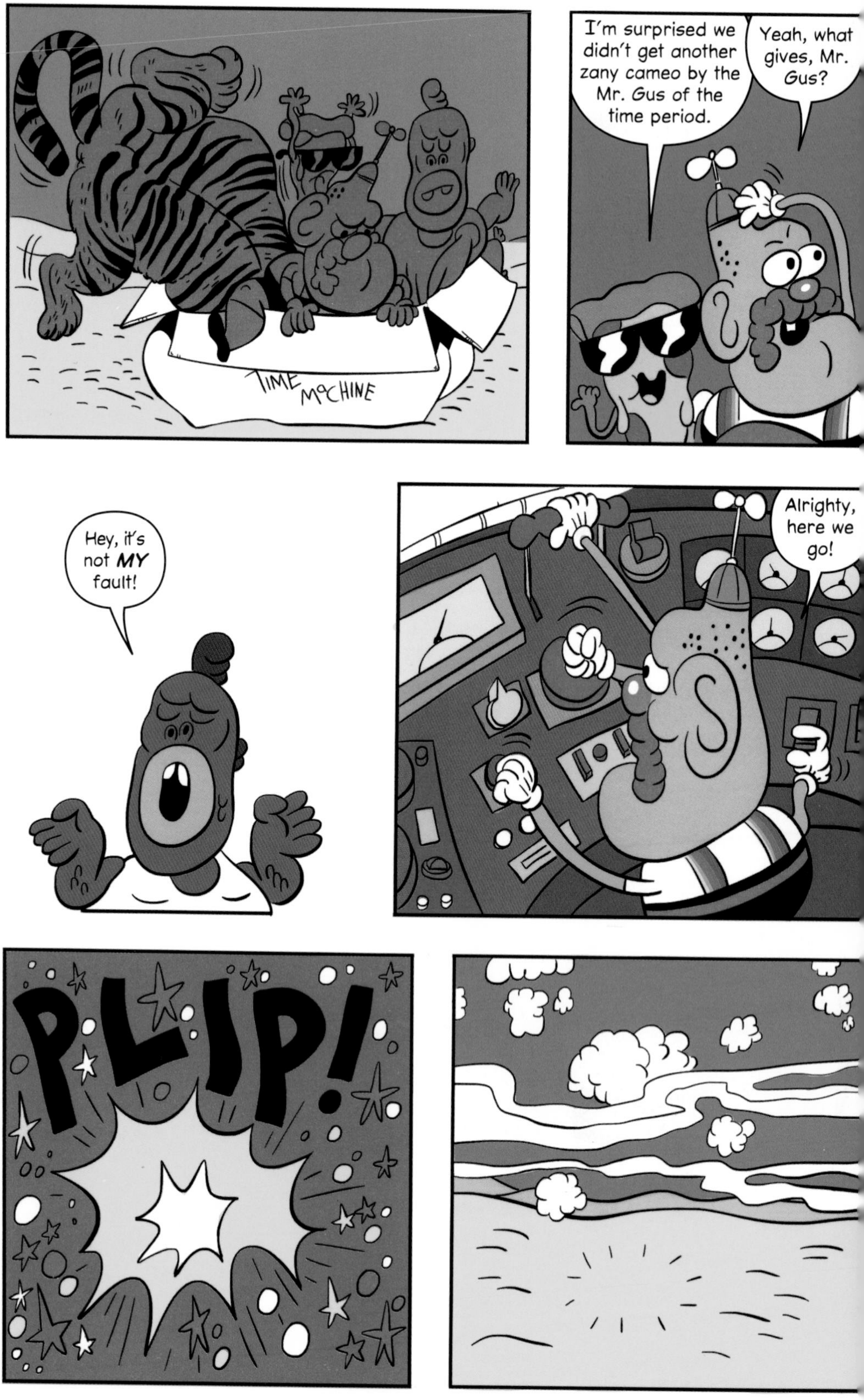
TIME MACHINE
I'm surprised we didn't get another zany cameo by the Mr. Gus of the time period.
Yeah, what gives, Mr. Gus?
Hey, it's not ***MY*** fault!
Alrighty, here we go!
PLIP!

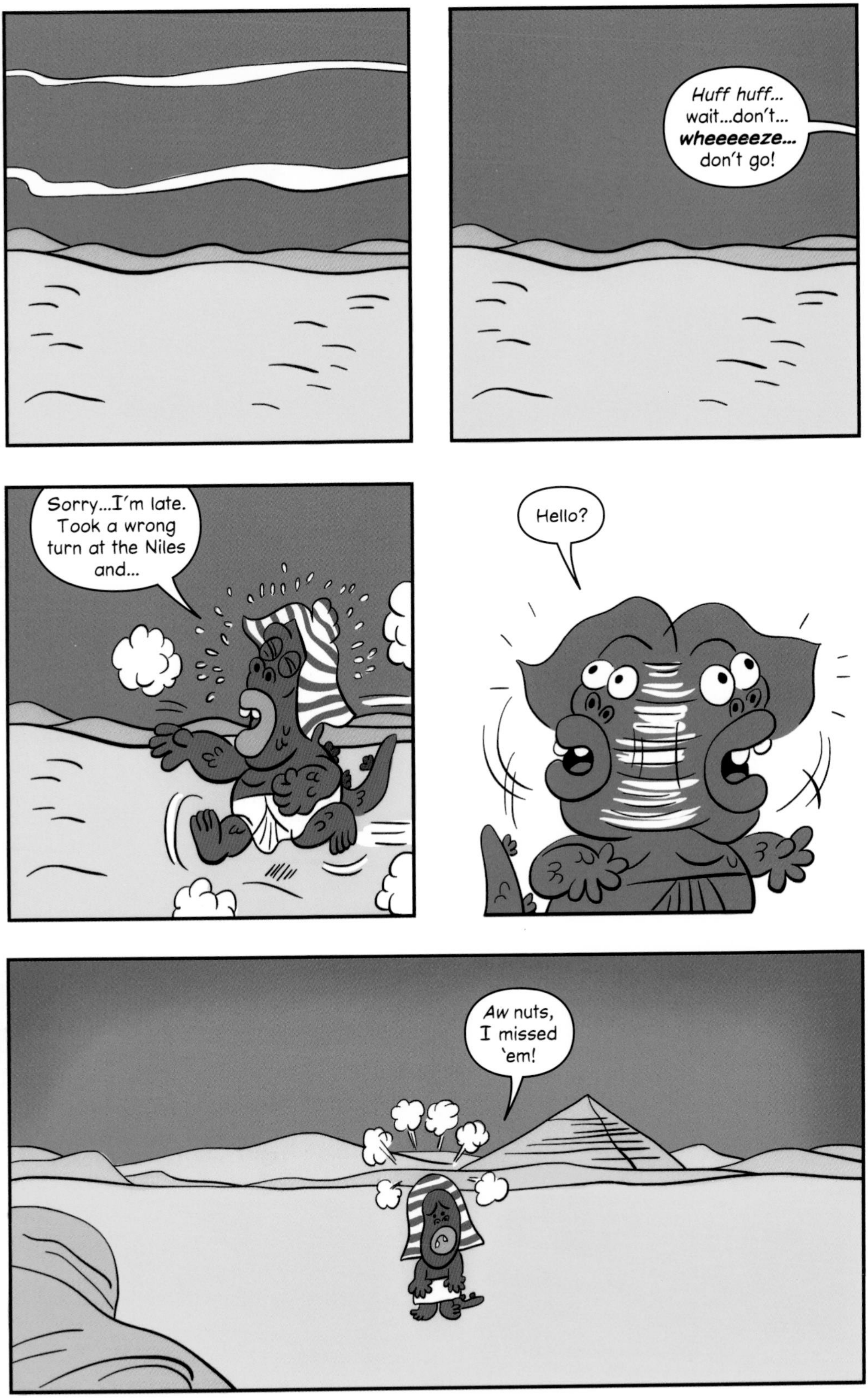
Huff huff... wait...don't... **wheeeeeze...** don't go!
Sorry...I'm late. Took a wrong turn at the Niles and...
Hello?
Aw nuts, I missed 'em!

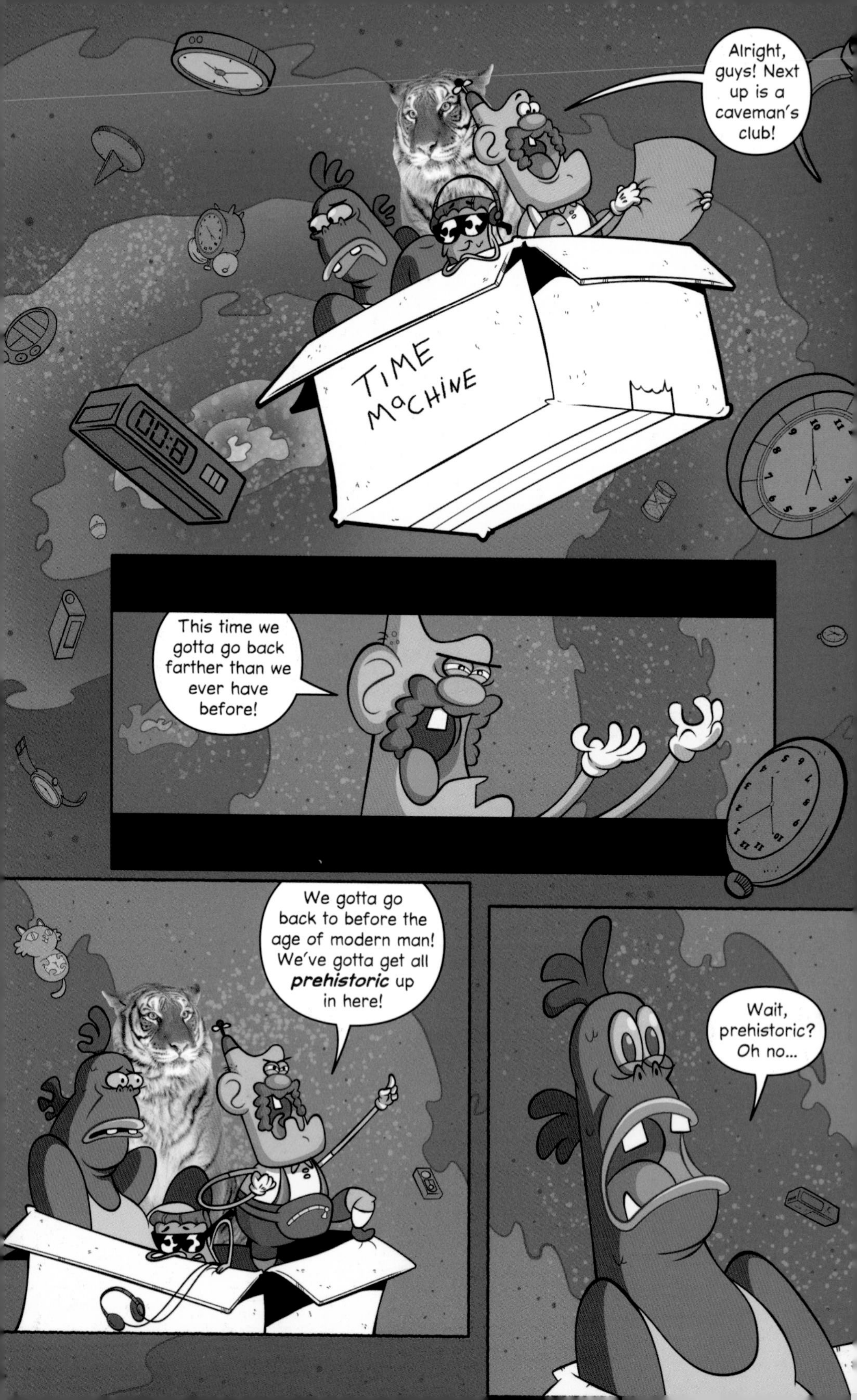
Alright, guys! Next up is a caveman's club!
TIME MaCHINE
This time we gotta go back farther than we ever have before!
We gotta go back to before the age of modern man! We've gotta get all ***prehistoric*** up in here!
Wait, prehistoric? Oh no...

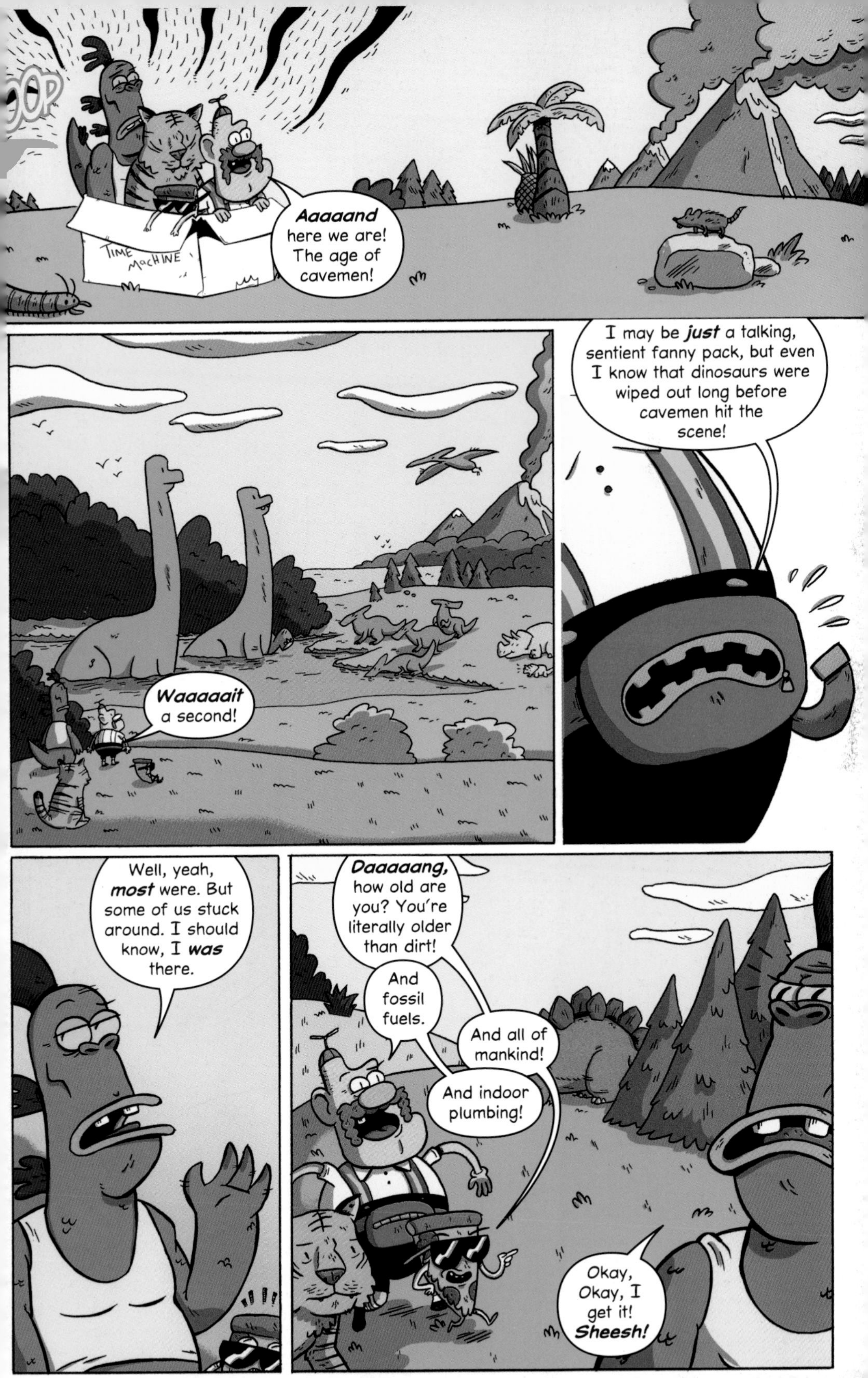
OOP
TIME MACHINE
Aaaaand here we are! The age of cavemen!
Waaaaait a second!
I may be just a talking, sentient fanny pack, but even I know that dinosaurs were wiped out long before cavemen hit the scene!
Well, yeah, most were. But some of us stuck around. I should know, I was there.
Daaaaang, how old are you? You're literally older than dirt!
And fossil fuels.
And all of mankind!
And indoor plumbing!
Okay, Okay, I get it! Sheesh!

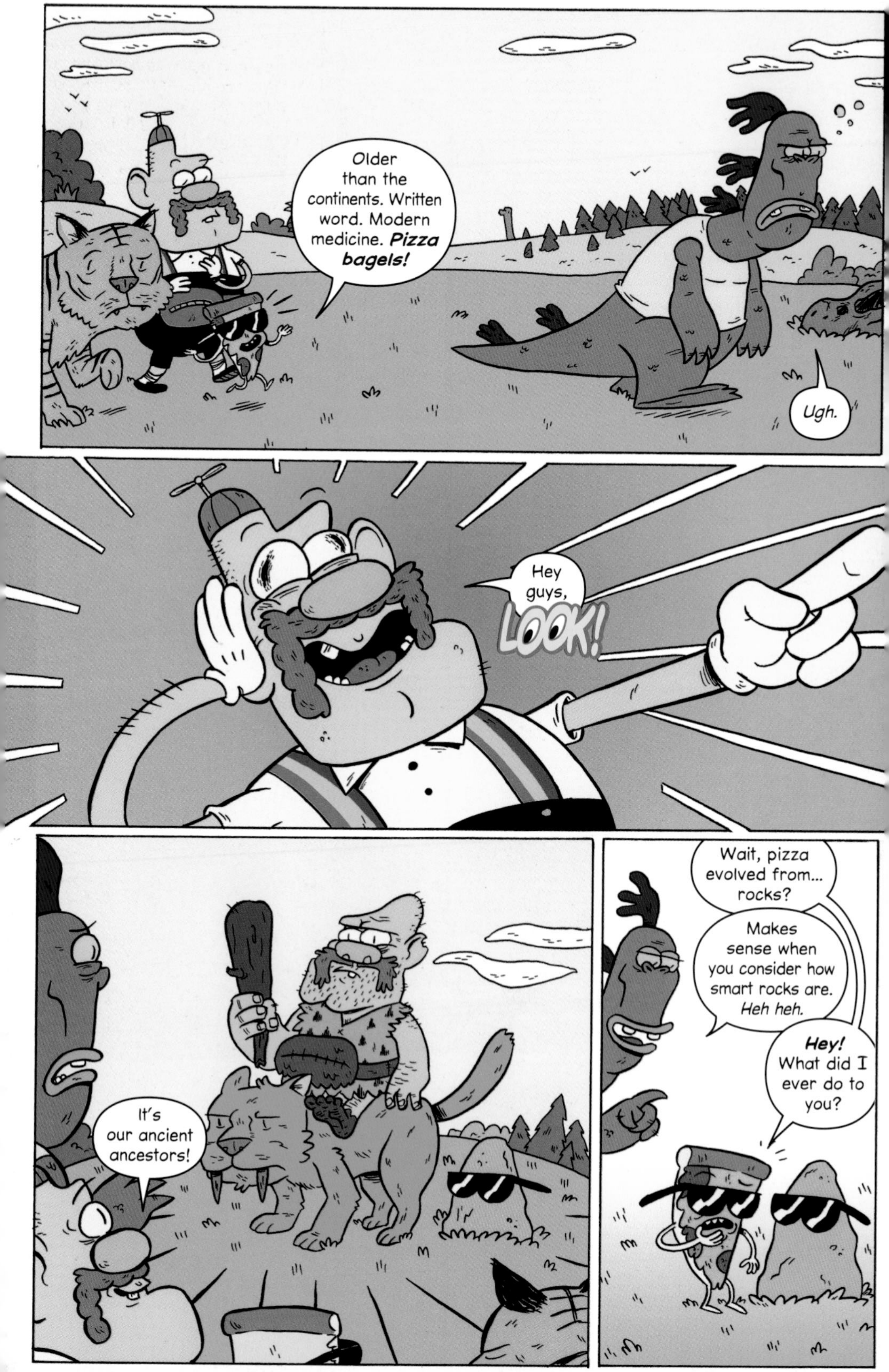

Older than the continents. Written word. Modern medicine. **Pizza bagels!**
Ugh.
Hey guys, LOOK!
It's our ancient ancestors!
Wait, pizza evolved from... rocks?
Makes sense when you consider how smart rocks are. *Heh heh.*
Hey! What did I ever do to you?

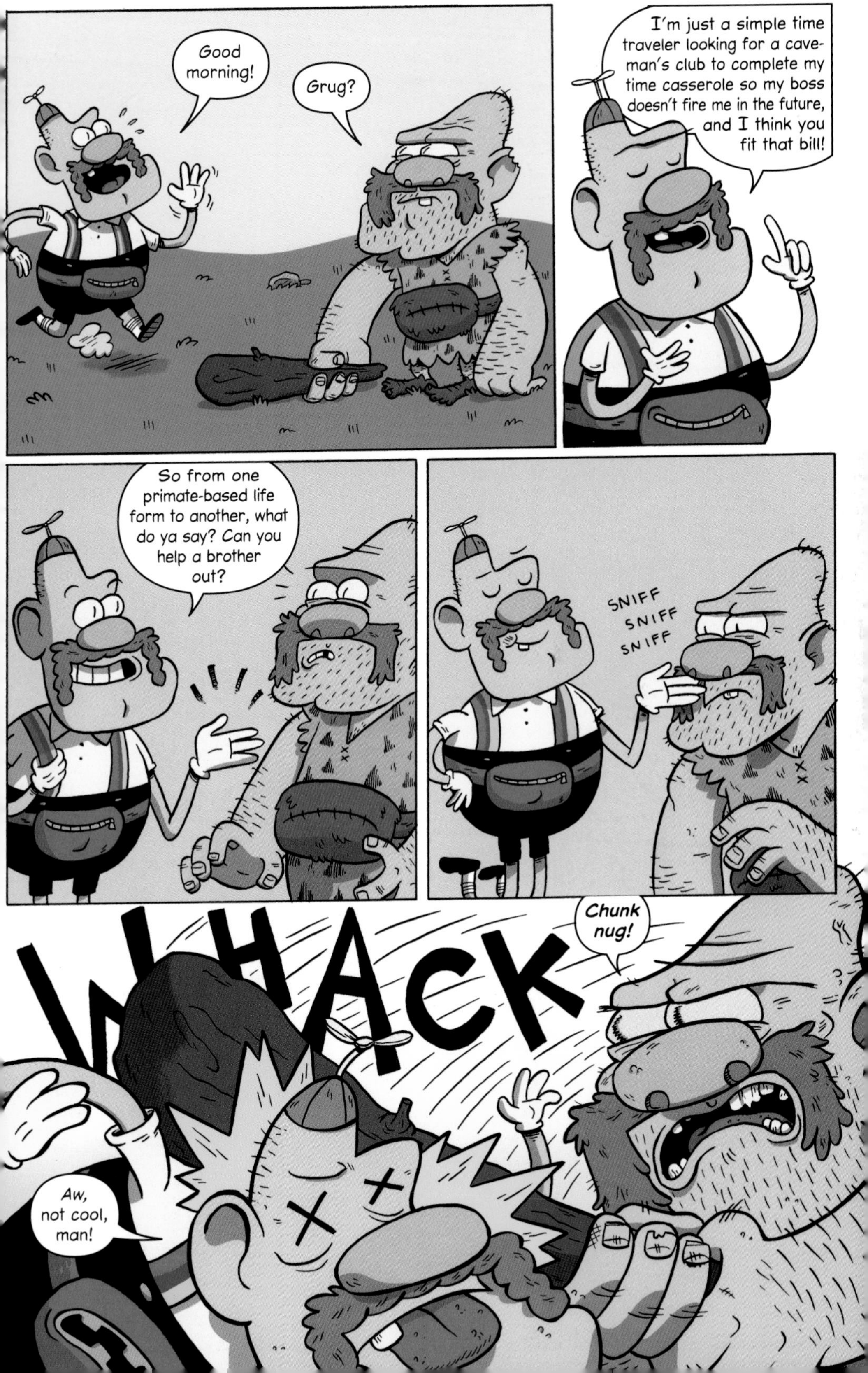
Good morning!
Grug?
I'm just a simple time traveler looking for a caveman's club to complete my time casserole so my boss doesn't fire me in the future, and I think you fit that bill!
So from one primate-based life form to another, what do ya say? Can you help a brother out?
SNIFF SNIFF SNIFF
WHACK
Chunk nug!
Aw, not cool, man!

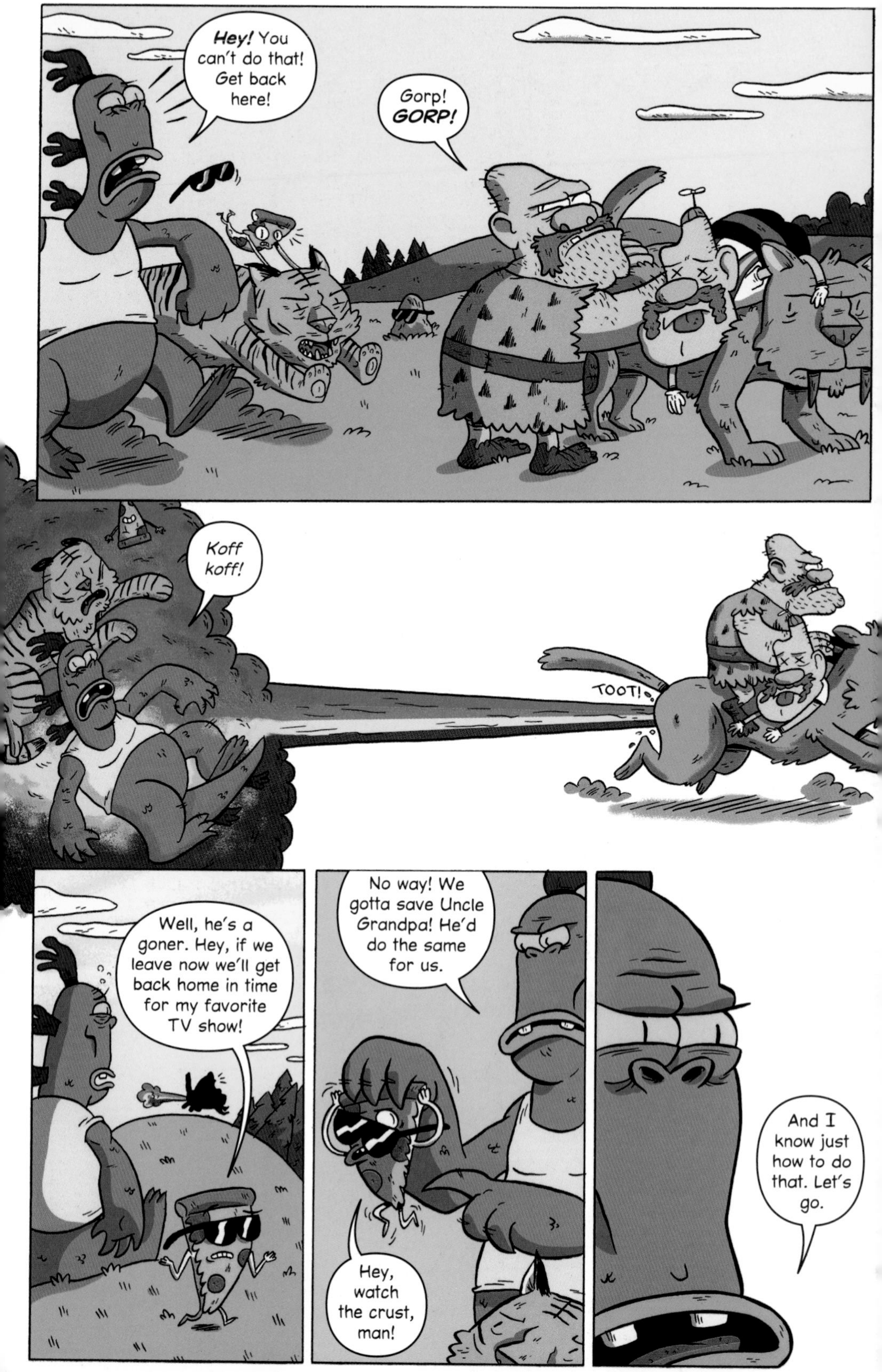

Hey! You can't do that! Get back here!
Gorp! GORP!
Koff koff!
TOOT!
Well, he's a goner. Hey, if we leave now we'll get back home in time for my favorite TV show!
No way! We gotta save Uncle Grandpa! He'd do the same for us.
Hey, watch the crust, man!
And I know just how to do that. Let's go.

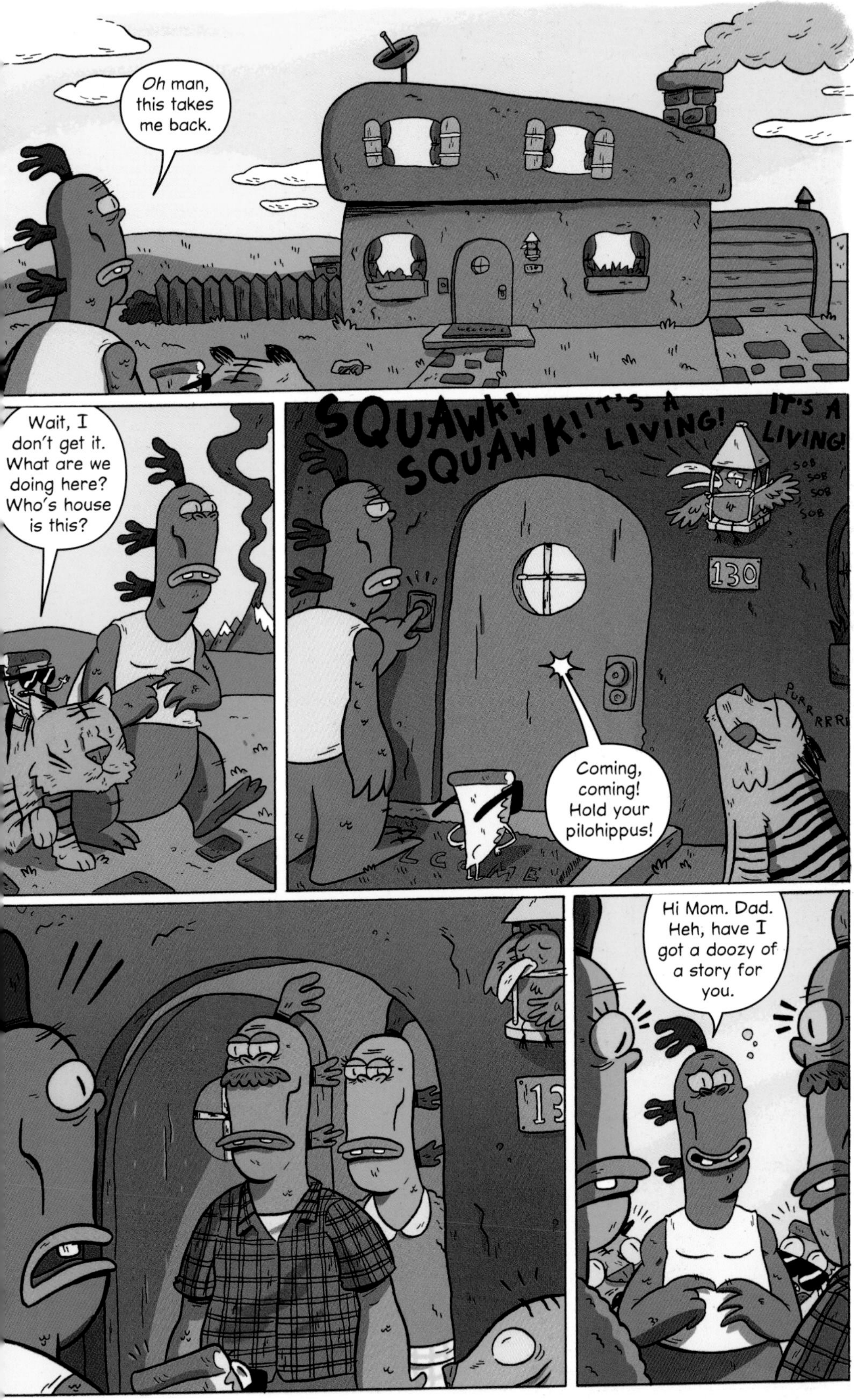
Oh man, this takes me back.
Wait, I don't get it. What are we doing here? Who's house is this?
SQUAWK! SQUAWK!
IT'S A LIVING! IT'S A LIVING!
SOB SOB SOB SOB
130
PURRRRRR
Coming, coming! Hold your pilohippus!
Hi Mom. Dad. Heh, have I got a doozy of a story for you.

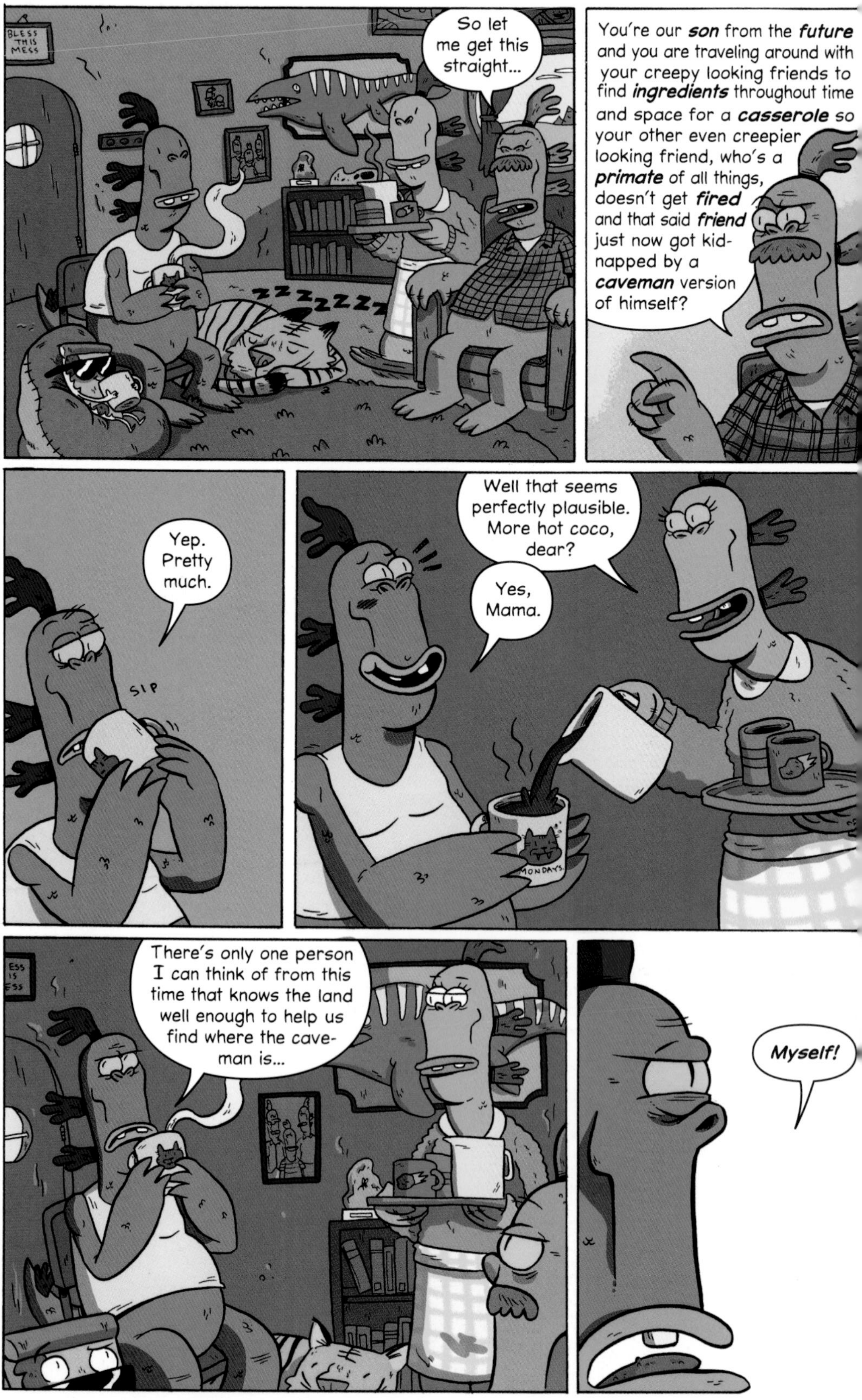
BLESS THIS MESS
So let me get this straight...
You're our son from the future and you are traveling around with your creepy looking friends to find ingredients throughout time and space for a casserole so your other even creepier looking friend, who's a primate of all things, doesn't get fired and that said friend just now got kid-napped by a caveman version of himself?
Yep. Pretty much.
SIP
Well that seems perfectly plausible. More hot coco, dear?
Yes, Mama.
MONDAYS
There's only one person I can think of from this time that knows the land well enough to help us find where the cave-man is...
Myself!

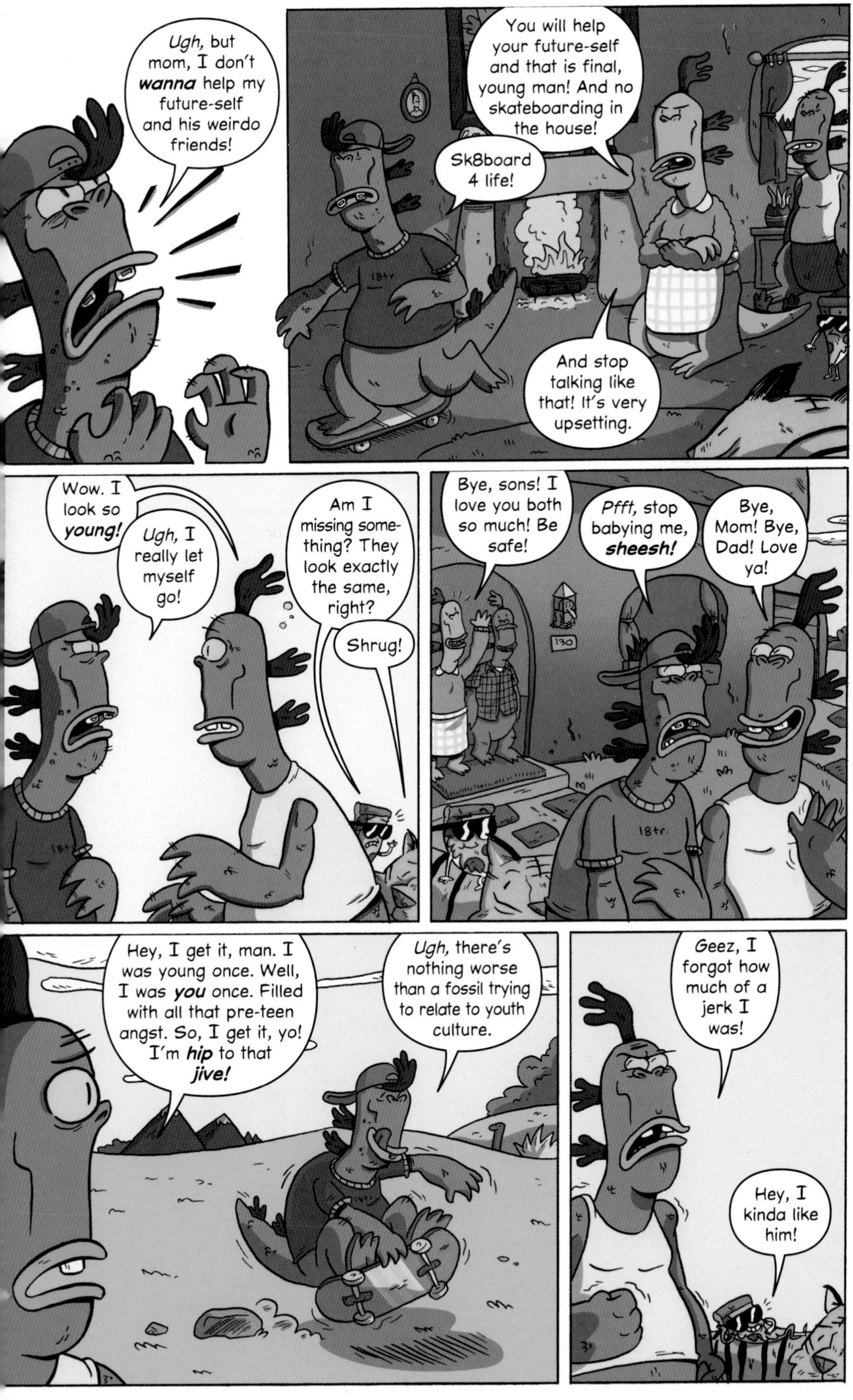
Ugh, but mom, I don't wanna help my future-self and his weirdo friends!
You will help your future-self and that is final, young man! And no skateboarding in the house!
Sk8board 4 life!
And stop talking like that! It's very upsetting.
Wow. I look so young!
Ugh, I really let myself go!
Am I missing something? They look exactly the same, right?
Shrug!
Bye, sons! I love you both so much! Be safe!
Pfft, stop babying me, sheesh!
Bye, Mom! Bye, Dad! Love ya!
Hey, I get it, man. I was young once. Well, I was you once. Filled with all that pre-teen angst. So, I get it, yo! I'm hip to that jive!
Ugh, there's nothing worse than a fossil trying to relate to youth culture.
Geez, I forgot how much of a jerk I was!
Hey, I kinda like him!

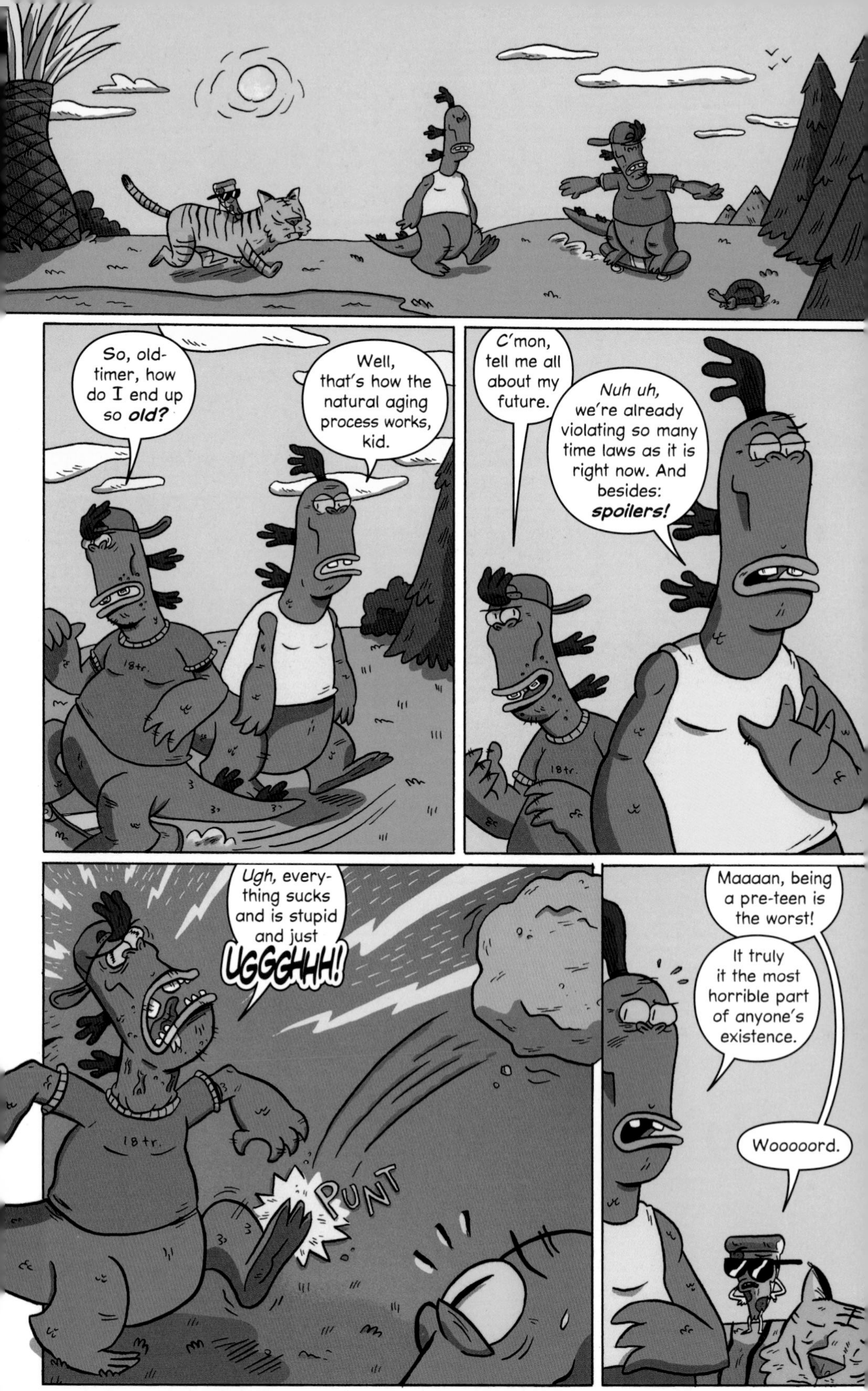
So, old-timer, how do I end up so ***old?***
Well, that's how the natural aging process works, kid.
C'mon, tell me all about my future.
Nuh uh, we're already violating so many time laws as it is right now. And besides: ***spoilers!***
Ugh, every-thing sucks and is stupid and just
UGGGHHH!
PUNT
Maaaan, being a pre-teen is the worst!
It truly it the most horrible part of anyone's existence.
Wooooord.
18tr.

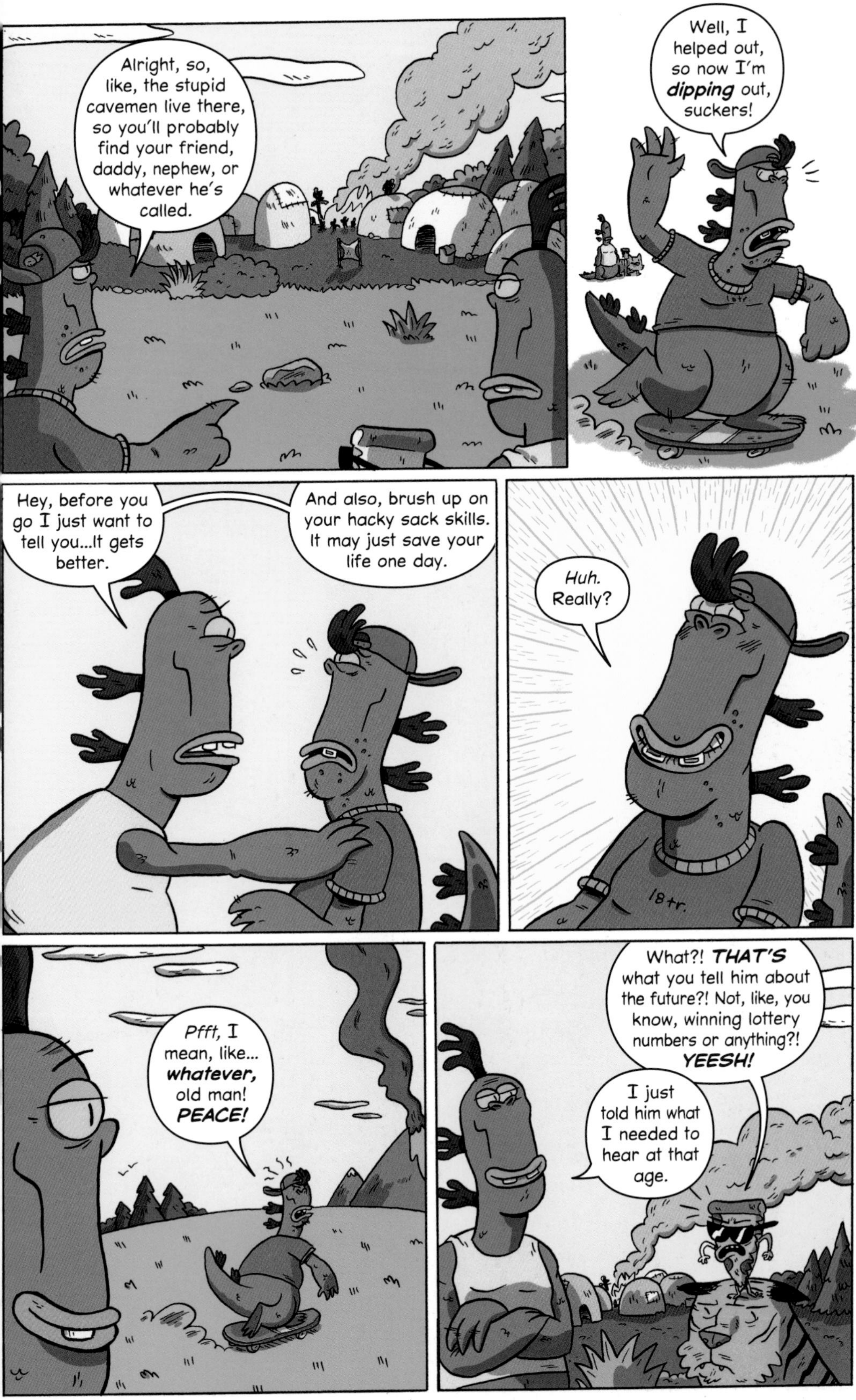
Alright, so, like, the stupid cavemen live there, so you'll probably find your friend, daddy, nephew, or whatever he's called.
Well, I helped out, so now I'm *dipping* out, suckers!
Hey, before you go I just want to tell you...It gets better.
And also, brush up on your hacky sack skills. It may just save your life one day.
Huh. Really?
18tr.
Pfft, I mean, like... ***whatever,*** old man! ***PEACE!***
What?! ***THAT'S*** what you tell him about the future?! Not, like, you know, winning lottery numbers or anything?! ***YEESH!***
I just told him what I needed to hear at that age.

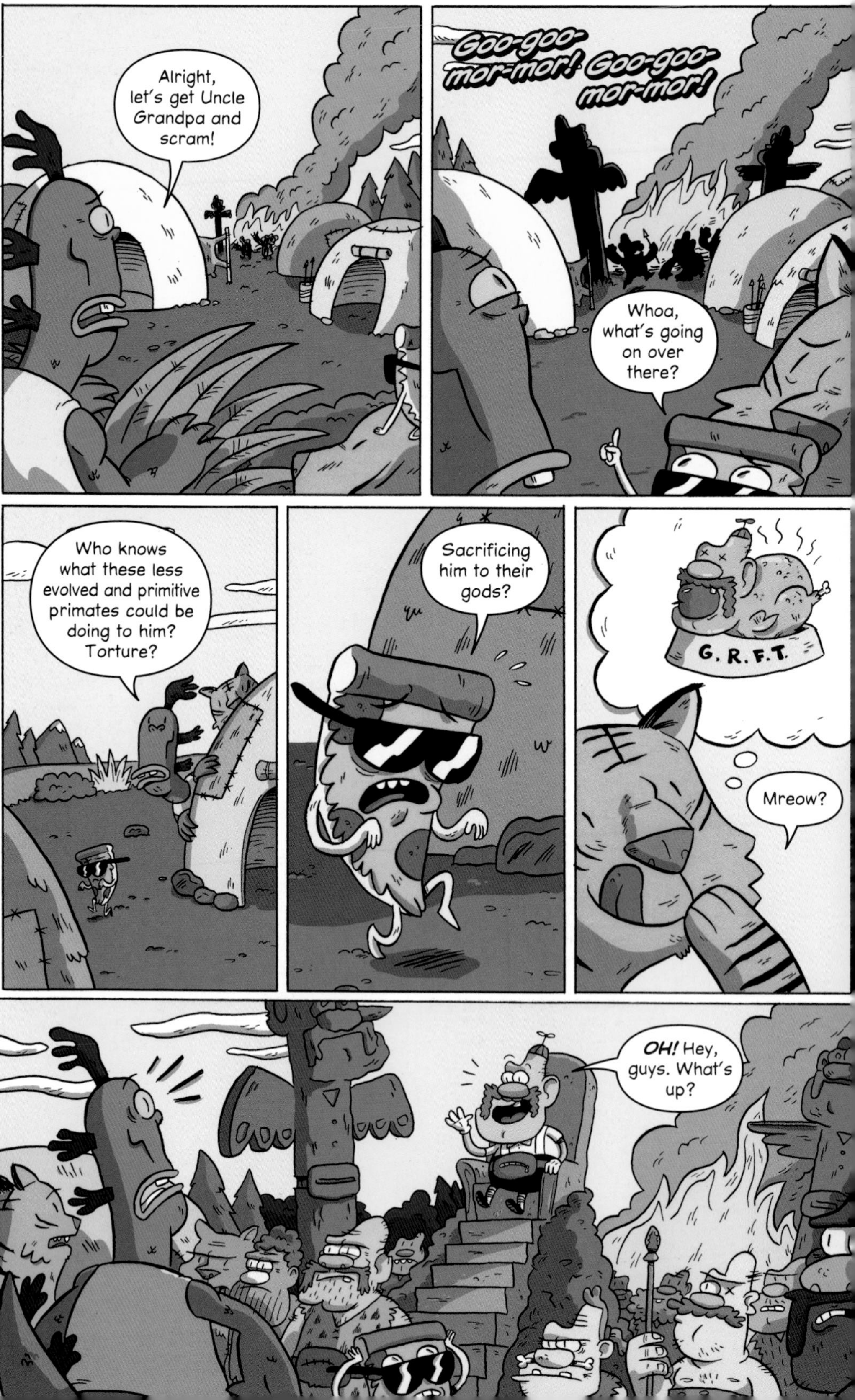

Alright, let's get Uncle Grandpa and scram!
Goo-goo-mor-mor! Goo-goo-mor-mor!
Whoa, what's going on over there?
Who knows what these less evolved and primitive primates could be doing to him? Torture?
Sacrificing him to their gods?
G.R.F.T.
Mreow?
OH! Hey, guys. What's up?

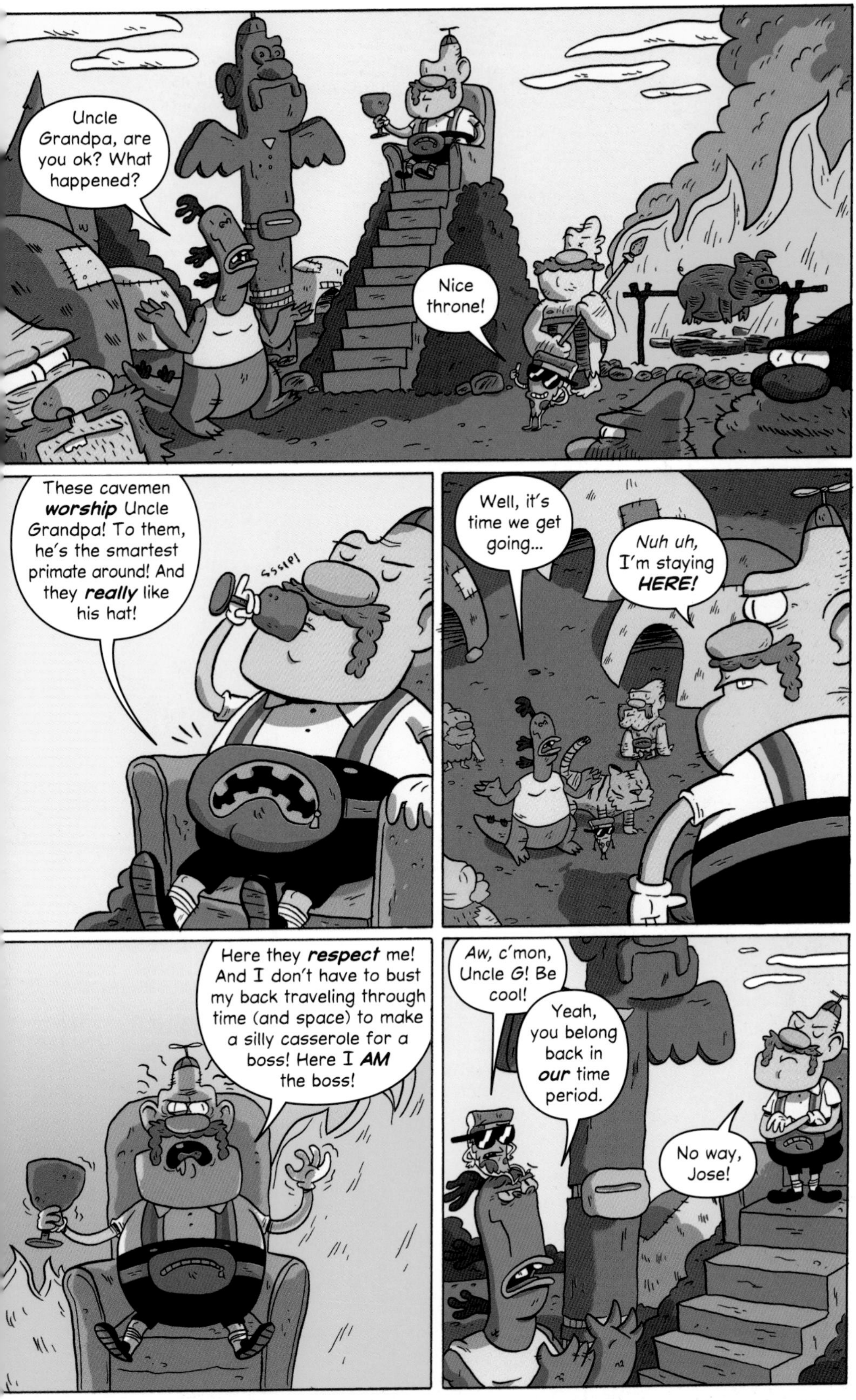
Uncle Grandpa, are you ok? What happened?
Nice throne!
These cavemen ***worship*** Uncle Grandpa! To them, he's the smartest primate around! And they ***really*** like his hat!
Well, it's time we get going...
Nuh uh, I'm staying ***HERE!***
Here they ***respect*** me! And I don't have to bust my back traveling through time (and space) to make a silly casserole for a boss! Here I ***AM*** the boss!
Aw, c'mon, Uncle *G*! Be cool!
Yeah, you belong back in ***our*** time period.
No way, Jose!

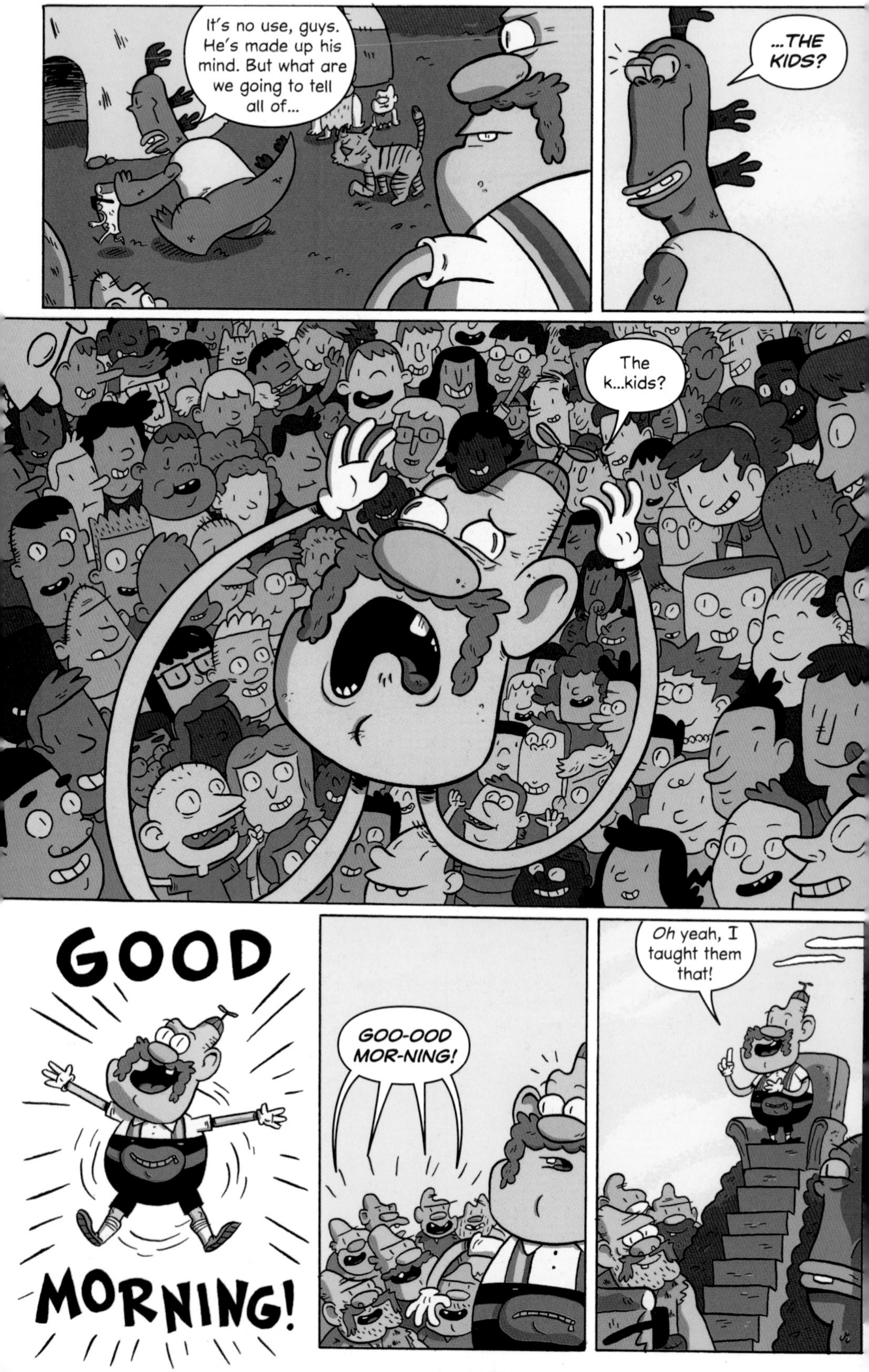
It's no use, guys. He's made up his mind. But what are we going to tell all of...
...THE KIDS?
The k...kids?
GOOD MORNING!
GOO-OOD MOR-NING!
Oh yeah, I taught them that!

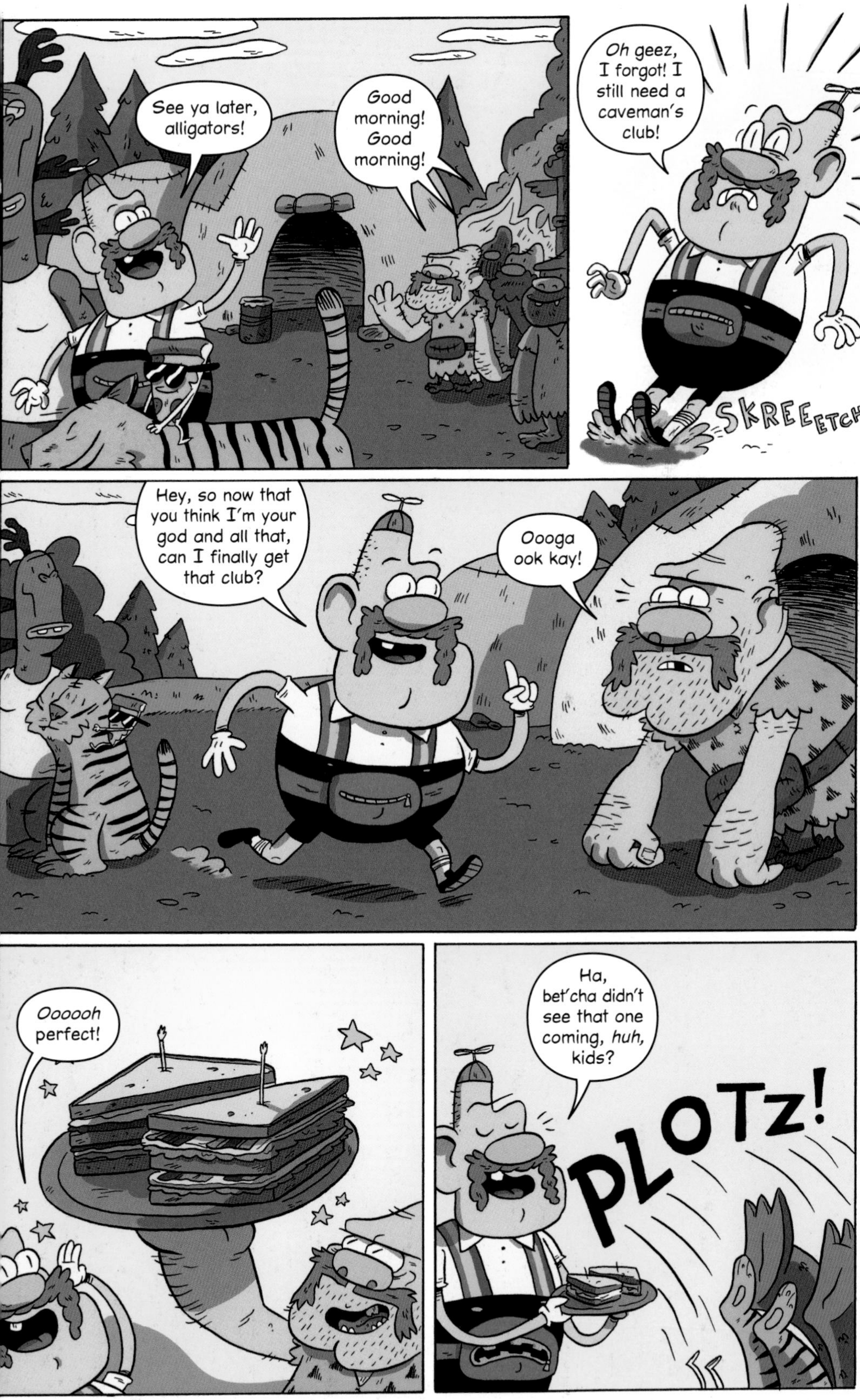
See ya later, alligators!
Good morning! Good morning!
Oh geez, I forgot! I still need a caveman's club!
SKREEETCH
Hey, so now that you think I'm your god and all that, can I finally get that club?
Oooga ook kay!
Oooooh perfect!
Ha, bet'cha didn't see that one coming, huh, kids?
PLOTz!

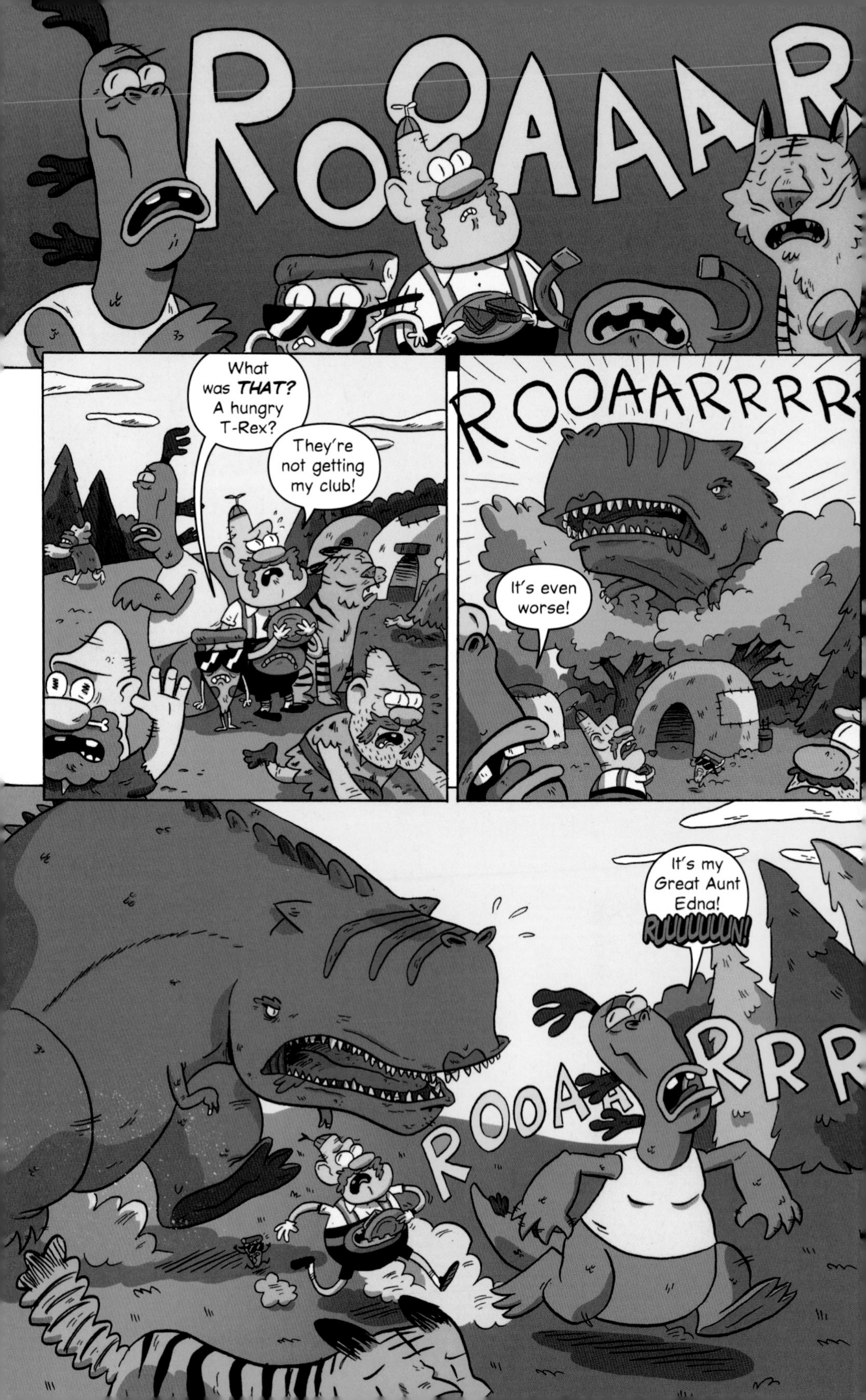
ROOAAAR
What was ***THAT?*** A hungry T-Rex?
They're not getting my club!
ROOAARRRR
It's even worse!
It's my Great Aunt Edna!
RUUUUUUN!
ROOAARRRR

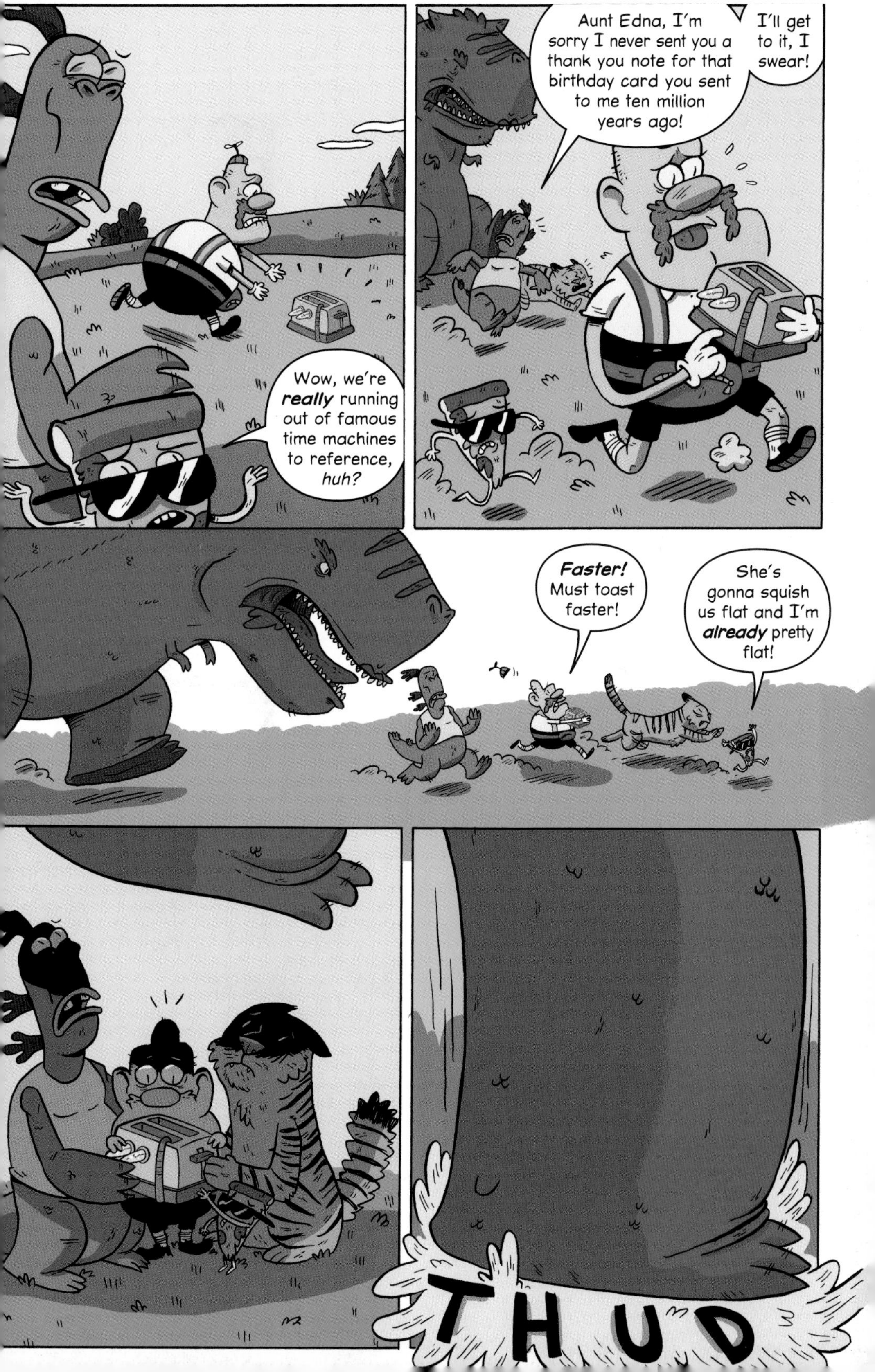
Wow, we're ***really*** running out of famous time machines to reference, *huh?*
Aunt Edna, I'm sorry I never sent you a thank you note for that birthday card you sent to me ten million years ago!
I'll get to it, I swear!
Faster! Must toast faster!
She's gonna squish us flat and I'm ***already*** pretty flat!
THUD

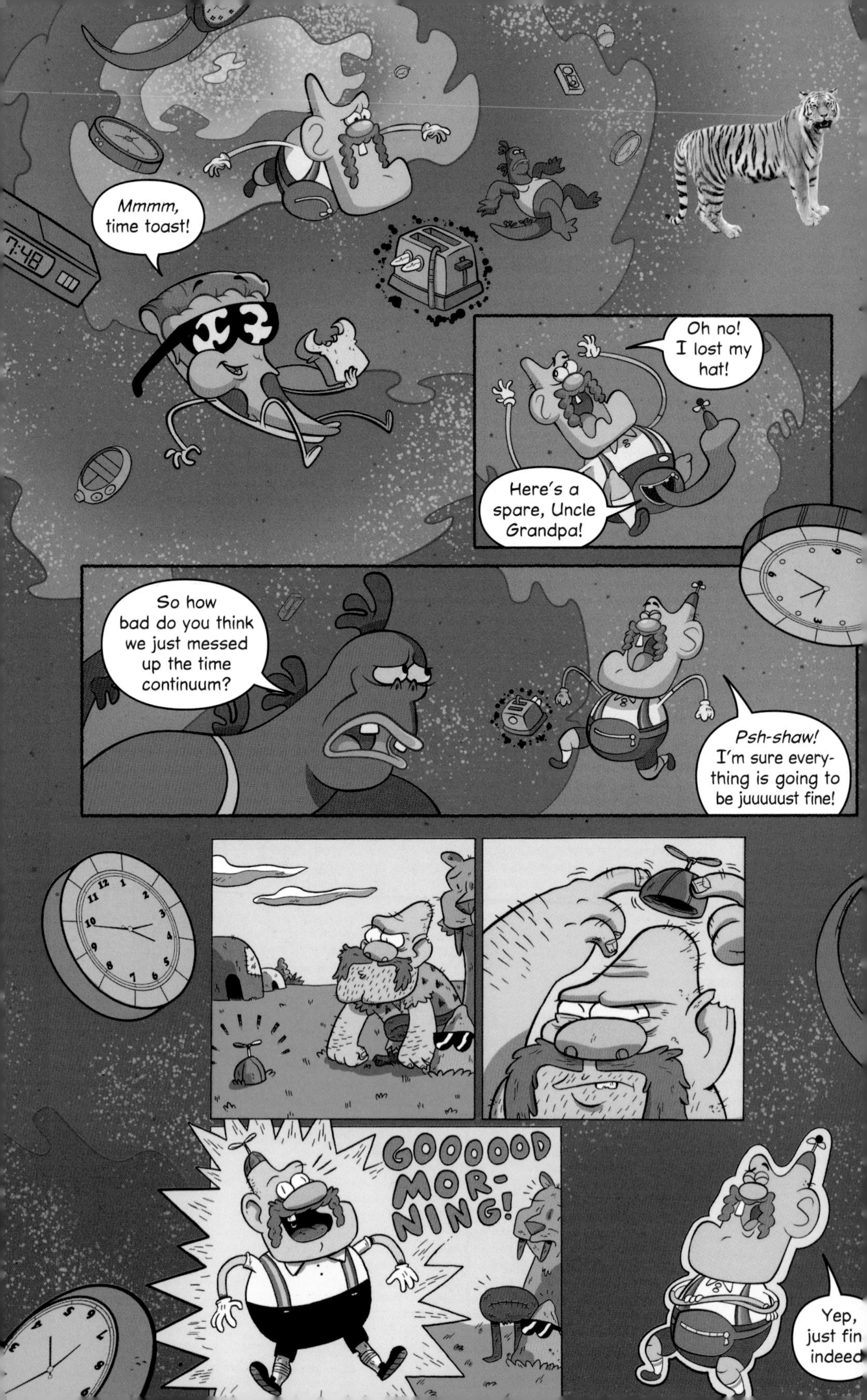

Mmmm, time toast!
Oh no! I lost my hat!
Here's a spare, Uncle Grandpa!
So how bad do you think we just messed up the time continuum?
Psh-shaw! I'm sure every-thing is going to be juuuuust fine!
GOOOOOD MOR-NING!
Yep, just fin indeed

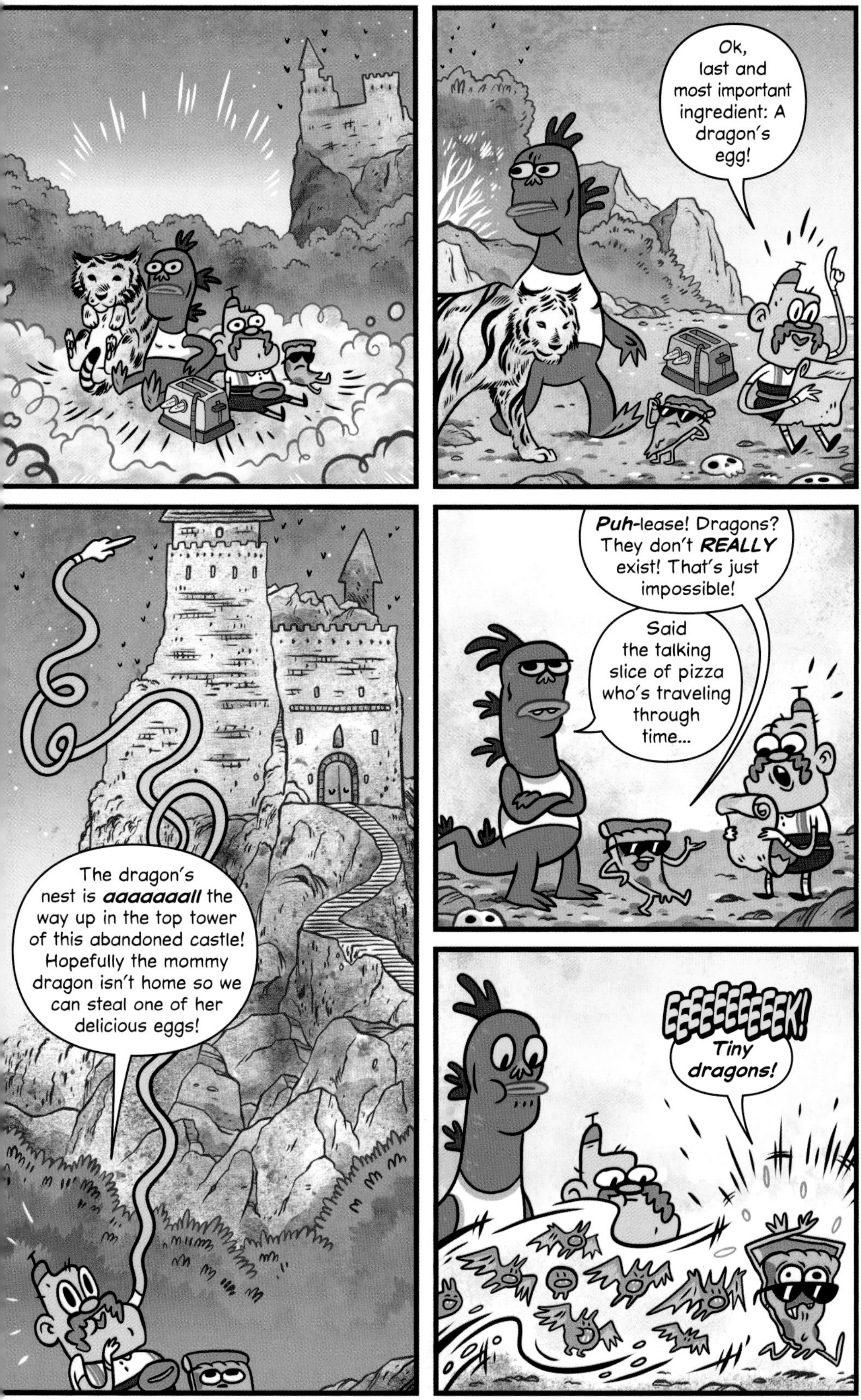
Ok, last and most important ingredient: A dragon's egg!
The dragon's nest is aaaaaaall the way up in the top tower of this abandoned castle! Hopefully the mommy dragon isn't home so we can steal one of her delicious eggs!
Puh-lease! Dragons? They don't REALLY exist! That's just impossible!
Said the talking slice of pizza who's traveling through time...
EEEEEEEEEEK!
Tiny dragons!

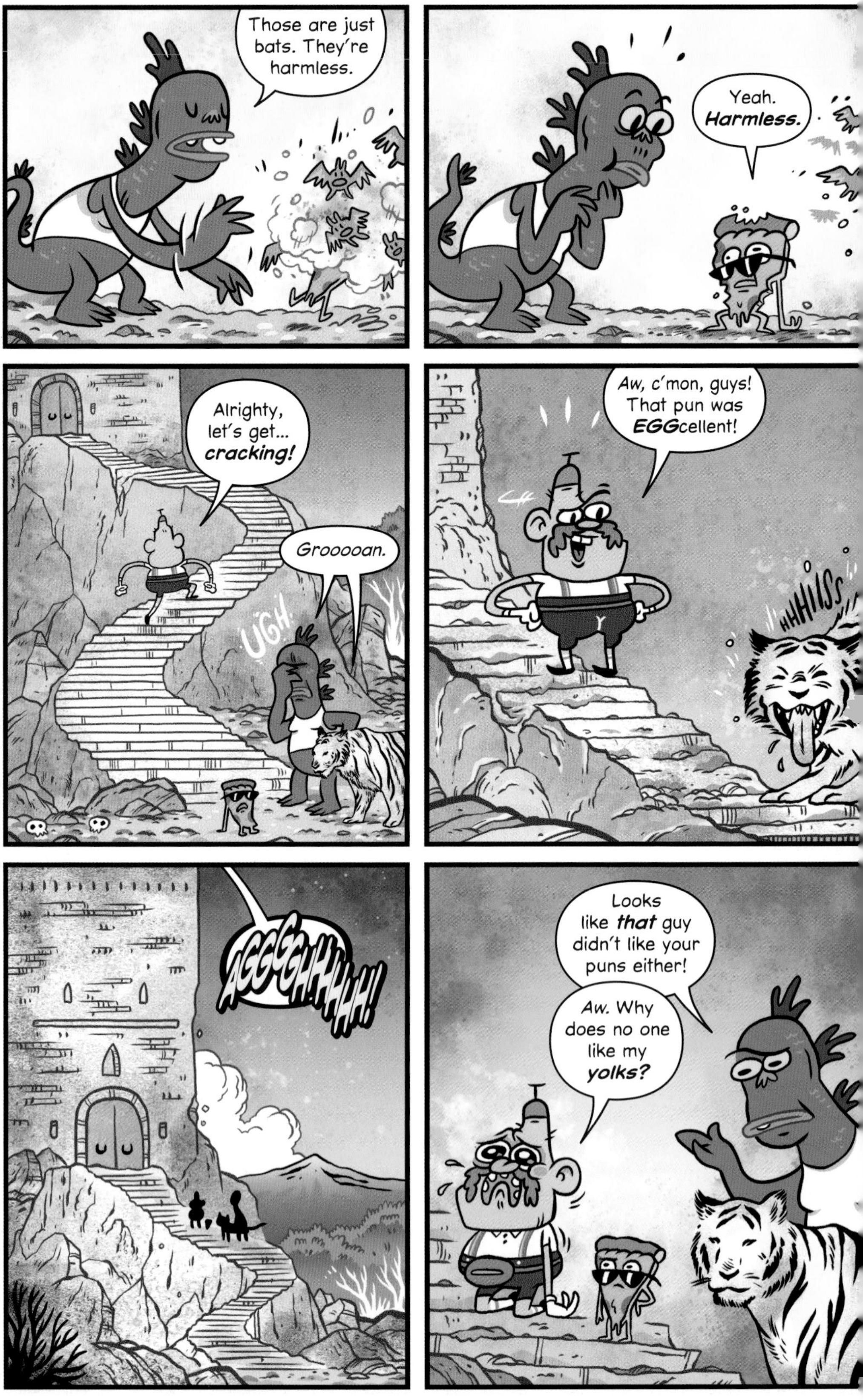
Those are just bats. They're harmless.
Yeah. **Harmless.**
Alrighty, let's get... ***cracking!***
Grooooan.
UGH
Aw, c'mon, guys! That pun was ***EGG***cellent!
HHHISS
AGGGGHHHHH!
Looks like ***that*** guy didn't like your puns either!
Aw. Why does no one like my ***yolks?***

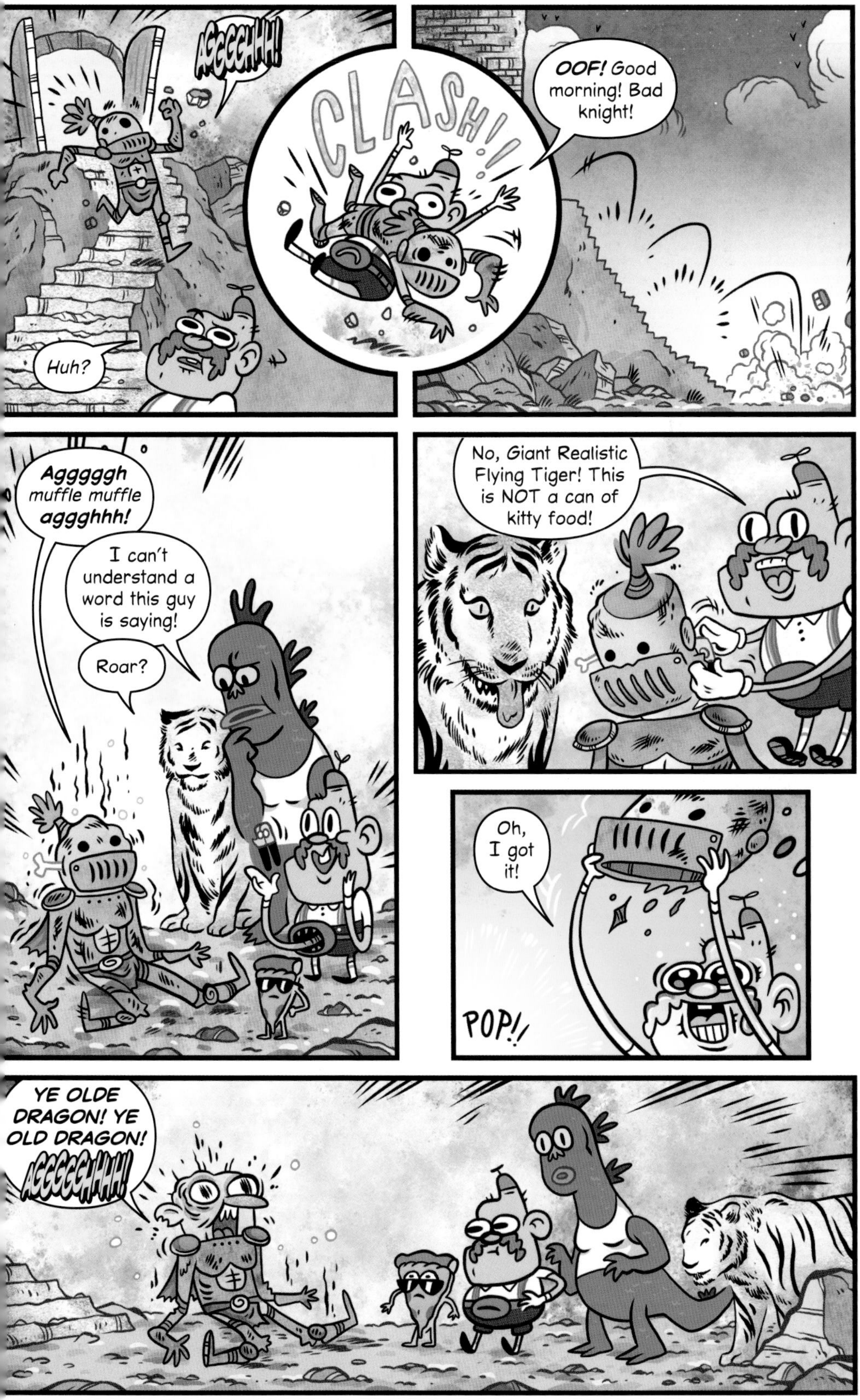
AGGGCHHH!
Huh?
CLASH!!!
OOF! Good morning! Bad knight!
Agggggh muffle muffle aggghhh!
I can't understand a word this guy is saying!
Roar?
No, Giant Realistic Flying Tiger! This is NOT a can of kitty food!
Oh, I got it!
POP!!
YE OLDE DRAGON! YE OLD DRAGON!
AGGGGGHHH!

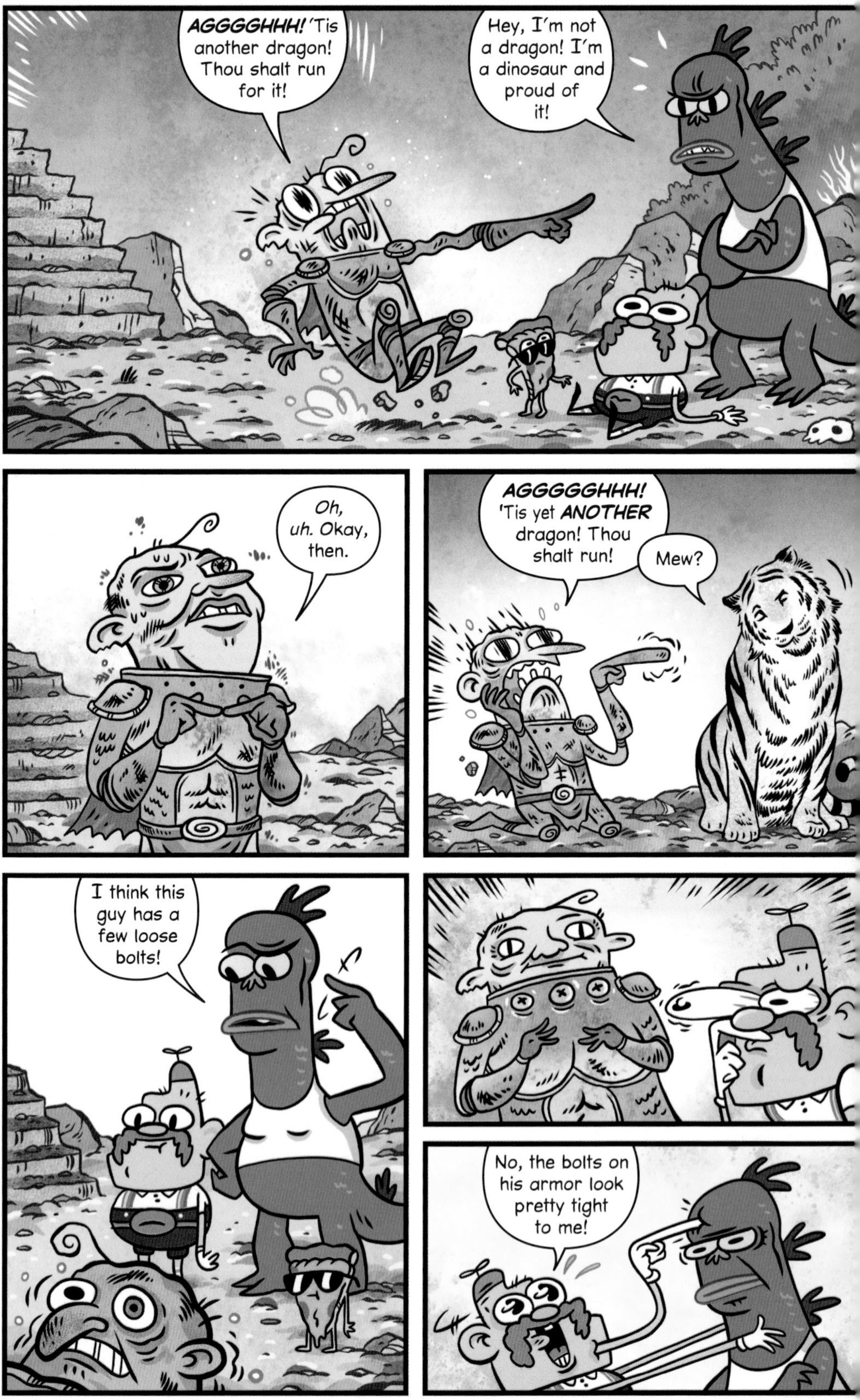
AGGGGHHH! 'Tis another dragon! Thou shalt run for it!
Hey, I'm not a dragon! I'm a dinosaur and proud of it!
Oh, uh. Okay, then.
AGGGGGHHH! 'Tis yet ANOTHER dragon! Thou shalt run!
Mew?
I think this guy has a few loose bolts!
No, the bolts on his armor look pretty tight to me!

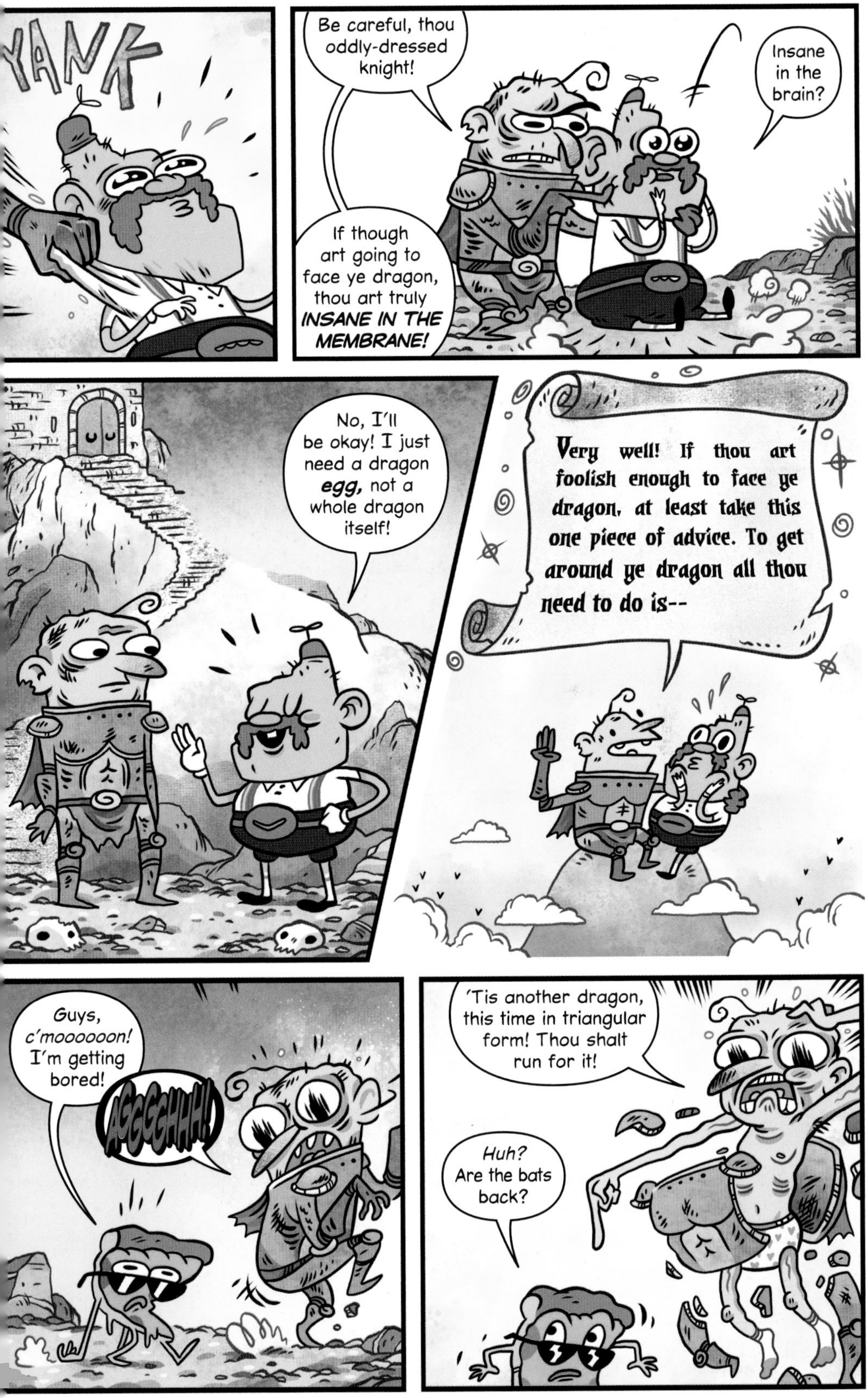
YANK
Be careful, thou oddly-dressed knight!
If though art going to face ye dragon, thou art truly INSANE IN THE MEMBRANE!
Insane in the brain?
No, I'll be okay! I just need a dragon egg, not a whole dragon itself!
Very well! If thou art foolish enough to face ye dragon, at least take this one piece of advice. To get around ye dragon all thou need to do is--
Guys, c'mooooon! I'm getting bored!
AGGGHHH!
'Tis another dragon, this time in triangular form! Thou shalt run for it!
Huh? Are the bats back?

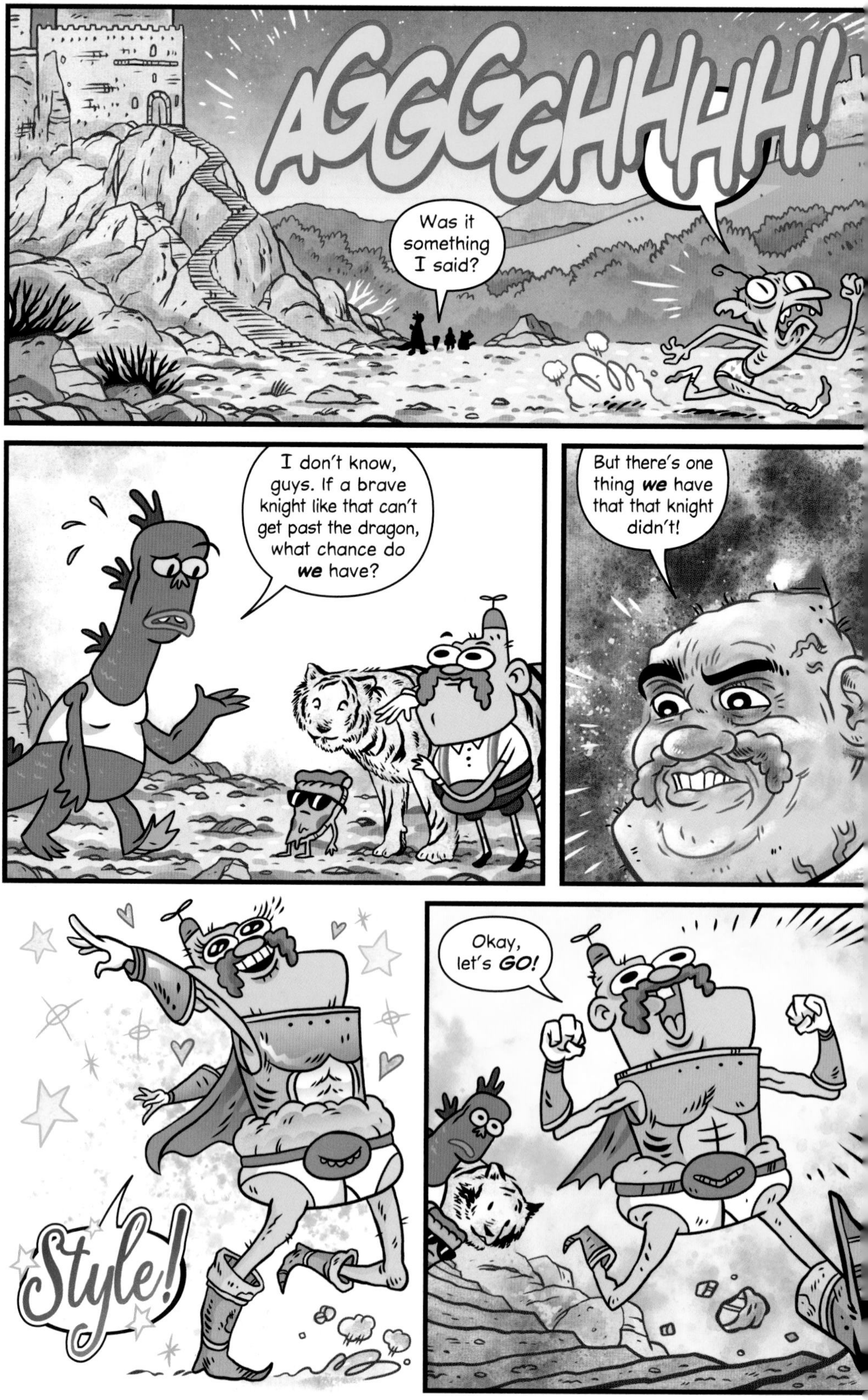
AGGGGHHHH!
Was it something I said?
I don't know, guys. If a brave knight like that can't get past the dragon, what chance do **we** have?
But there's one thing **we** have that that knight didn't!
Style!
Okay, let's **GO**!

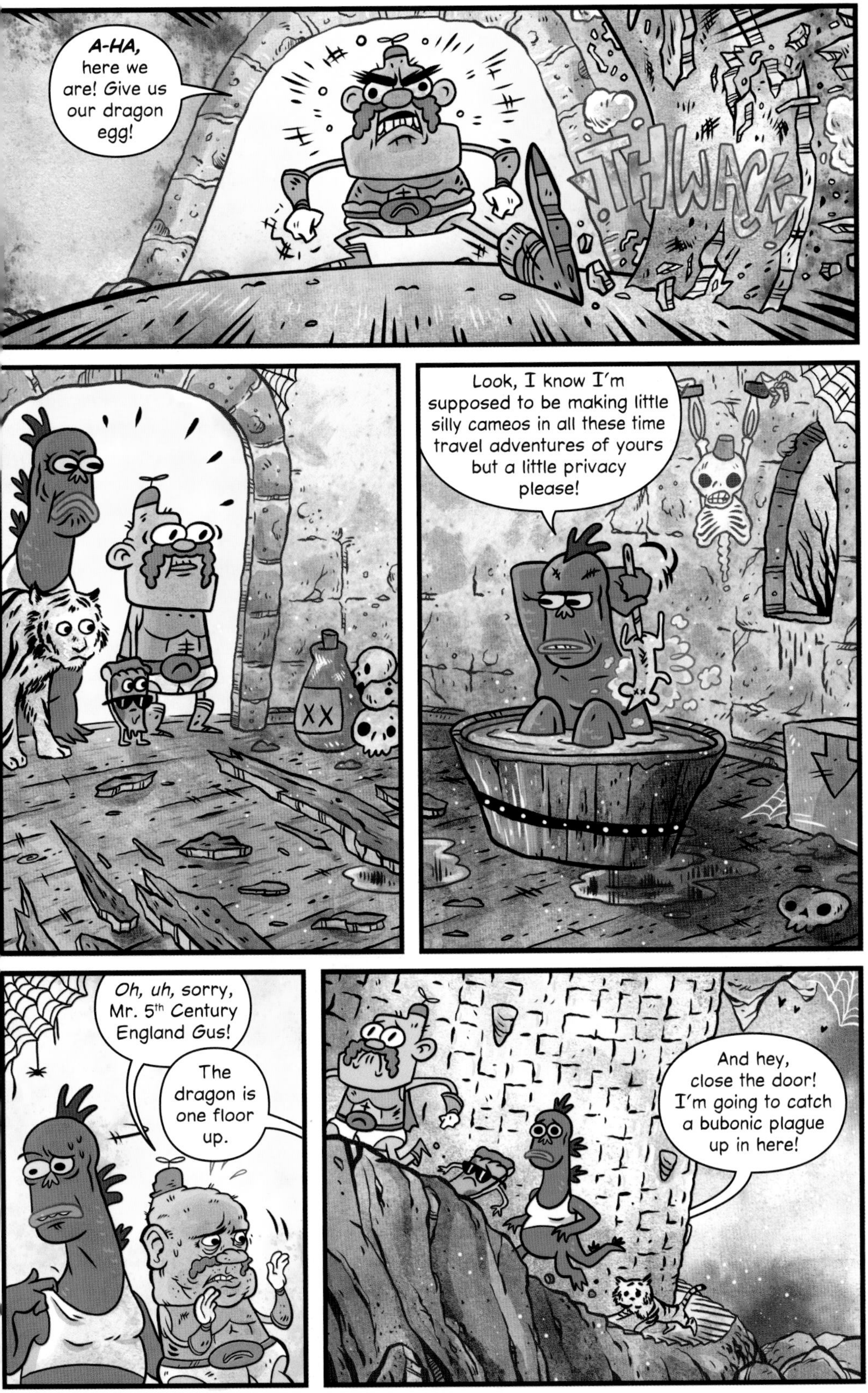
A-HA, here we are! Give us our dragon egg!
THWACK
Look, I know I'm supposed to be making little silly cameos in all these time travel adventures of yours but a little privacy please!
Oh, uh, sorry, Mr. 5th Century England Gus!
The dragon is one floor up.
And hey, close the door! I'm going to catch a bubonic plague up in here!

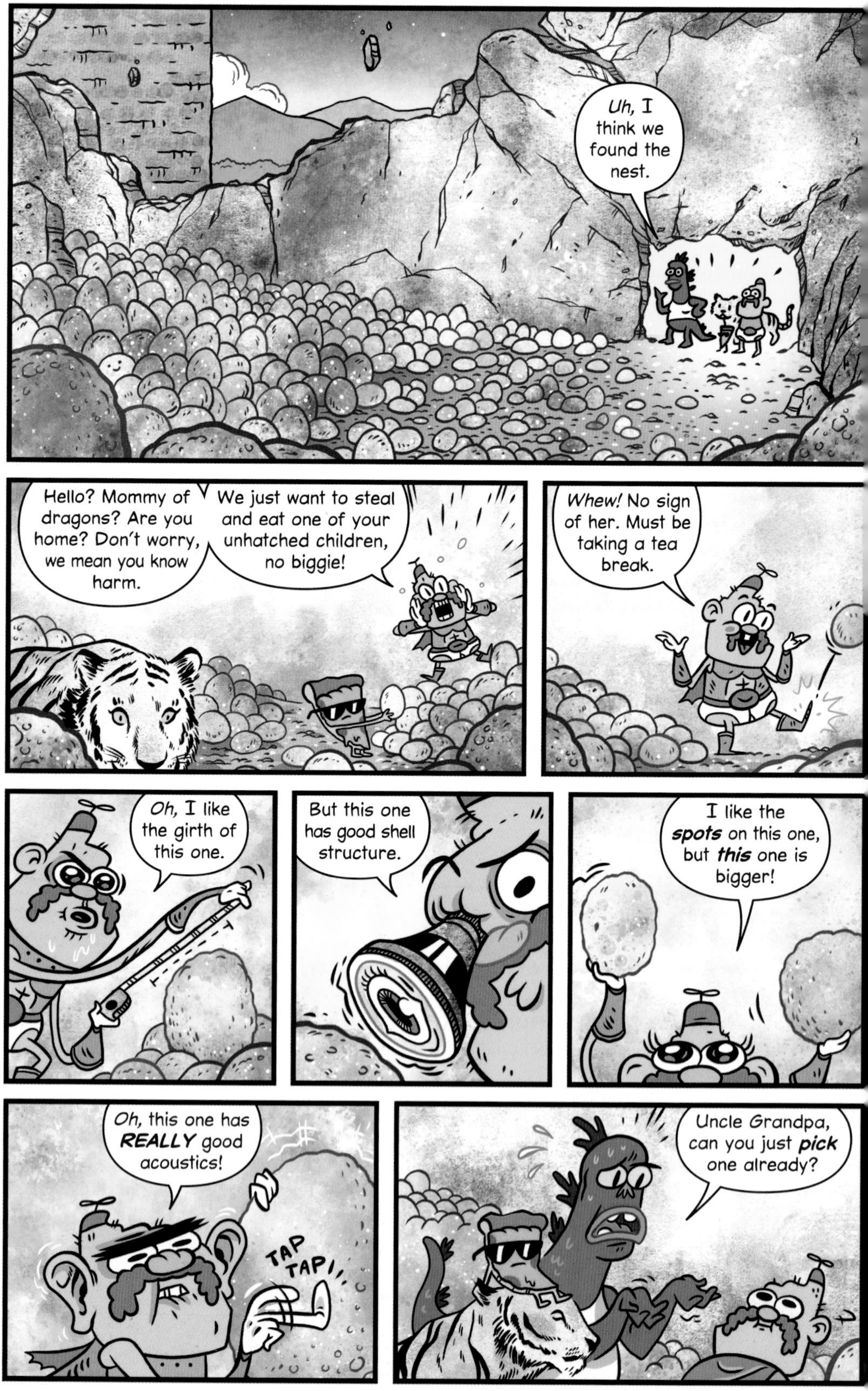
Uh, I think we found the nest.
Hello? Mommy of dragons? Are you home? Don't worry, we mean you know harm.
We just want to steal and eat one of your unhatched children, no biggie!
Whew! No sign of her. Must be taking a tea break.
Oh, I like the girth of this one.
But this one has good shell structure.
I like the spots on this one, but this one is bigger!
Oh, this one has REALLY good acoustics!
TAP TAP!
Uncle Grandpa, can you just pick one already?

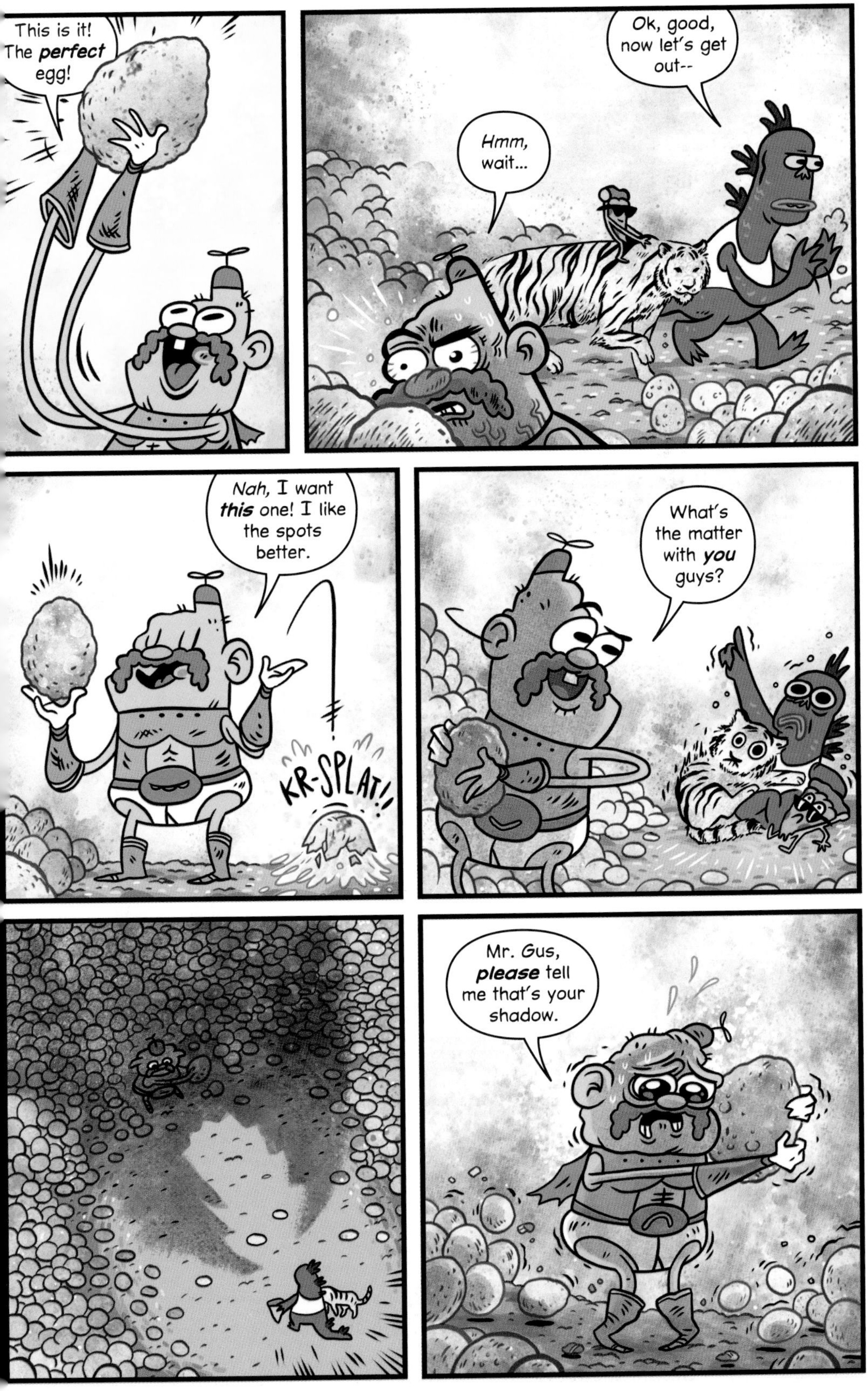
This is it! The *perfect* egg!
Ok, good, now let's get out--
Hmm, wait...
Nah, I want ***this*** one! I like the spots better.
KR-SPLAT!
What's the matter with ***you*** guys?
Mr. Gus, ***please*** tell me that's your shadow.

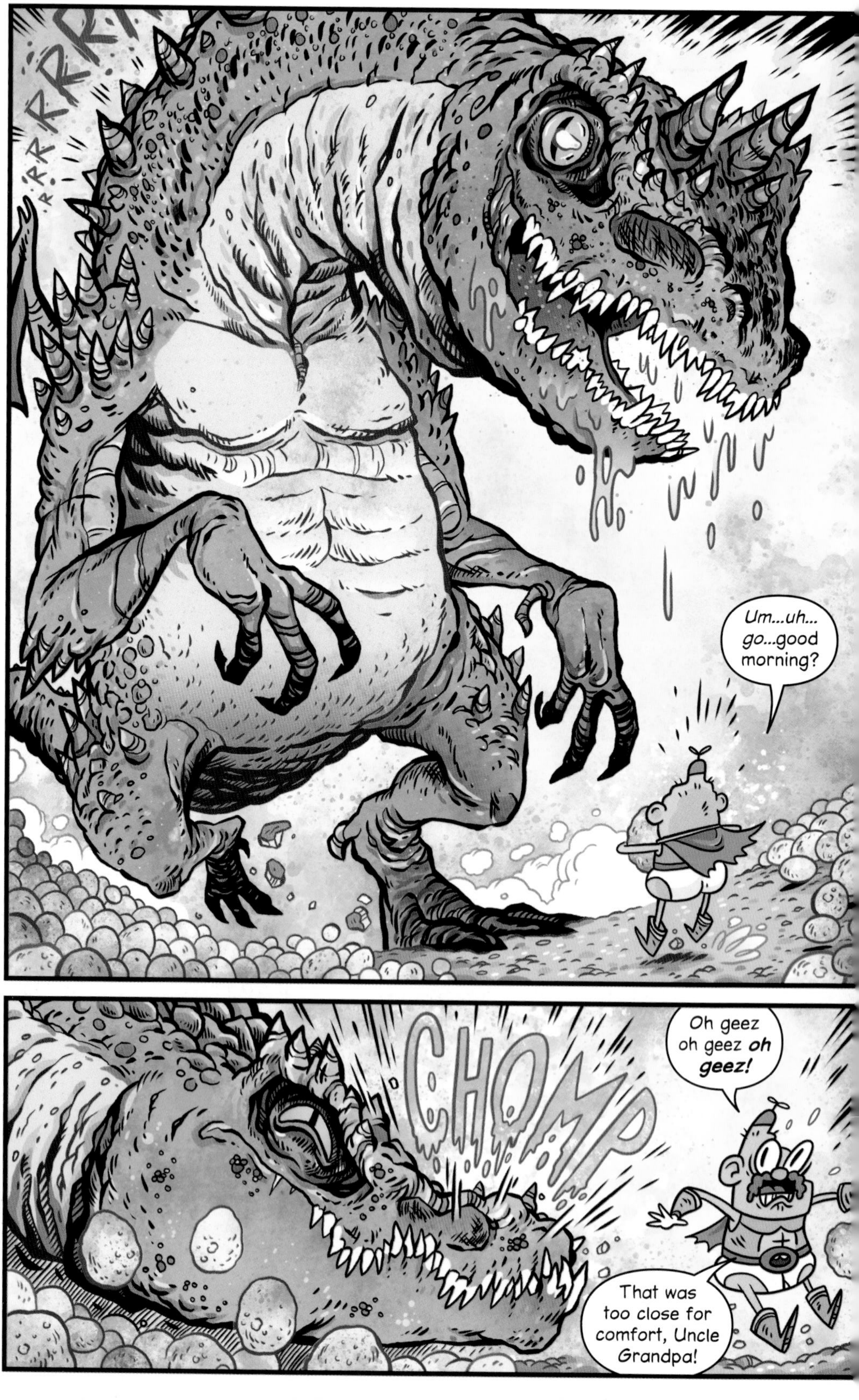

Um...uh... go...good morning?
CHOMP
Oh geez oh geez oh geez!
That was too close for comfort, Uncle Grandpa!

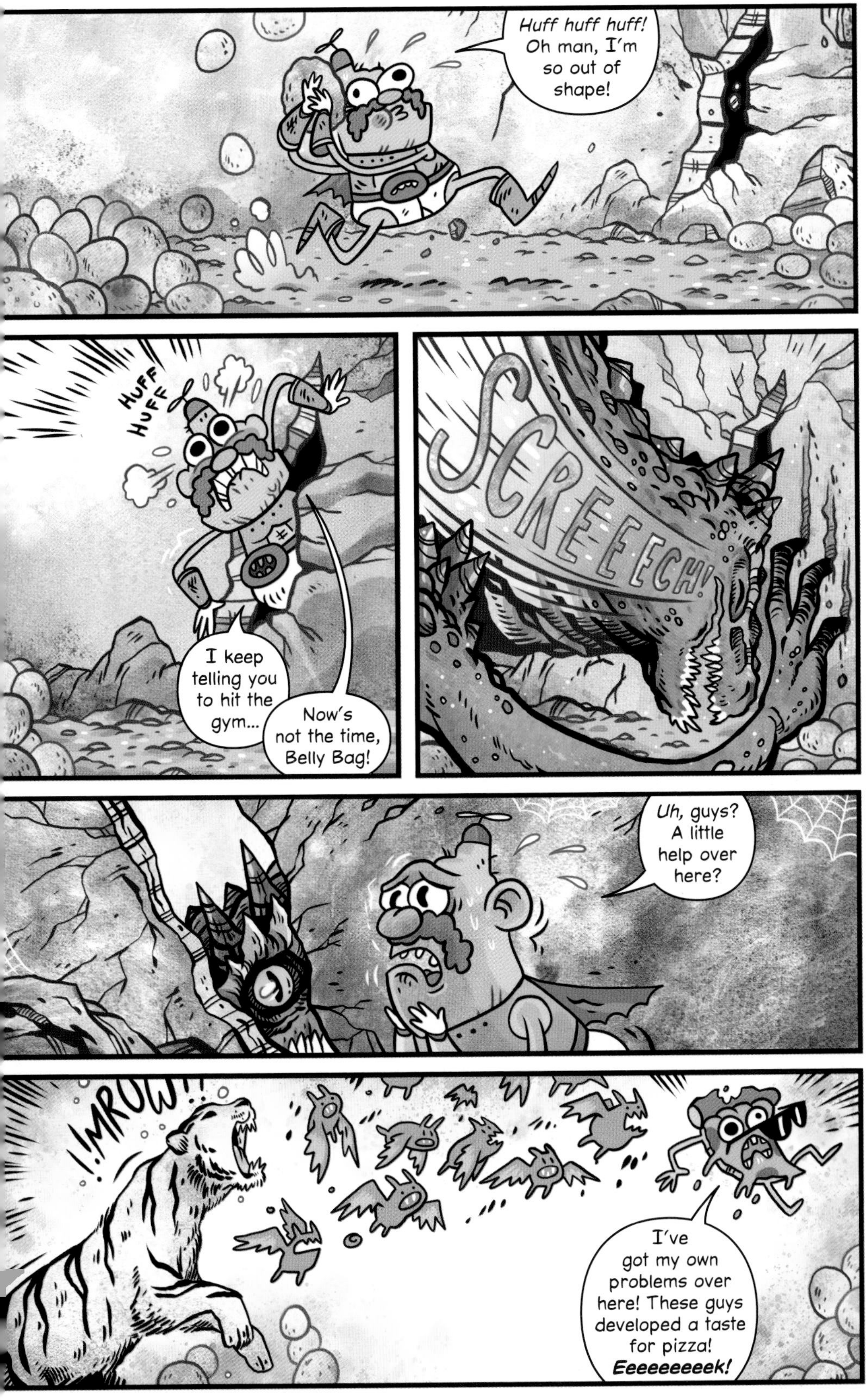

Huff huff huff! Oh man, I'm so out of shape!
HUFF HUFF
I keep telling you to hit the gym...
Now's not the time, Belly Bag!
SCREEECH!
Uh, guys? A little help over here?
MROW!!
I've got my own problems over here! These guys developed a taste for pizza! **Eeeeeeeeek!**

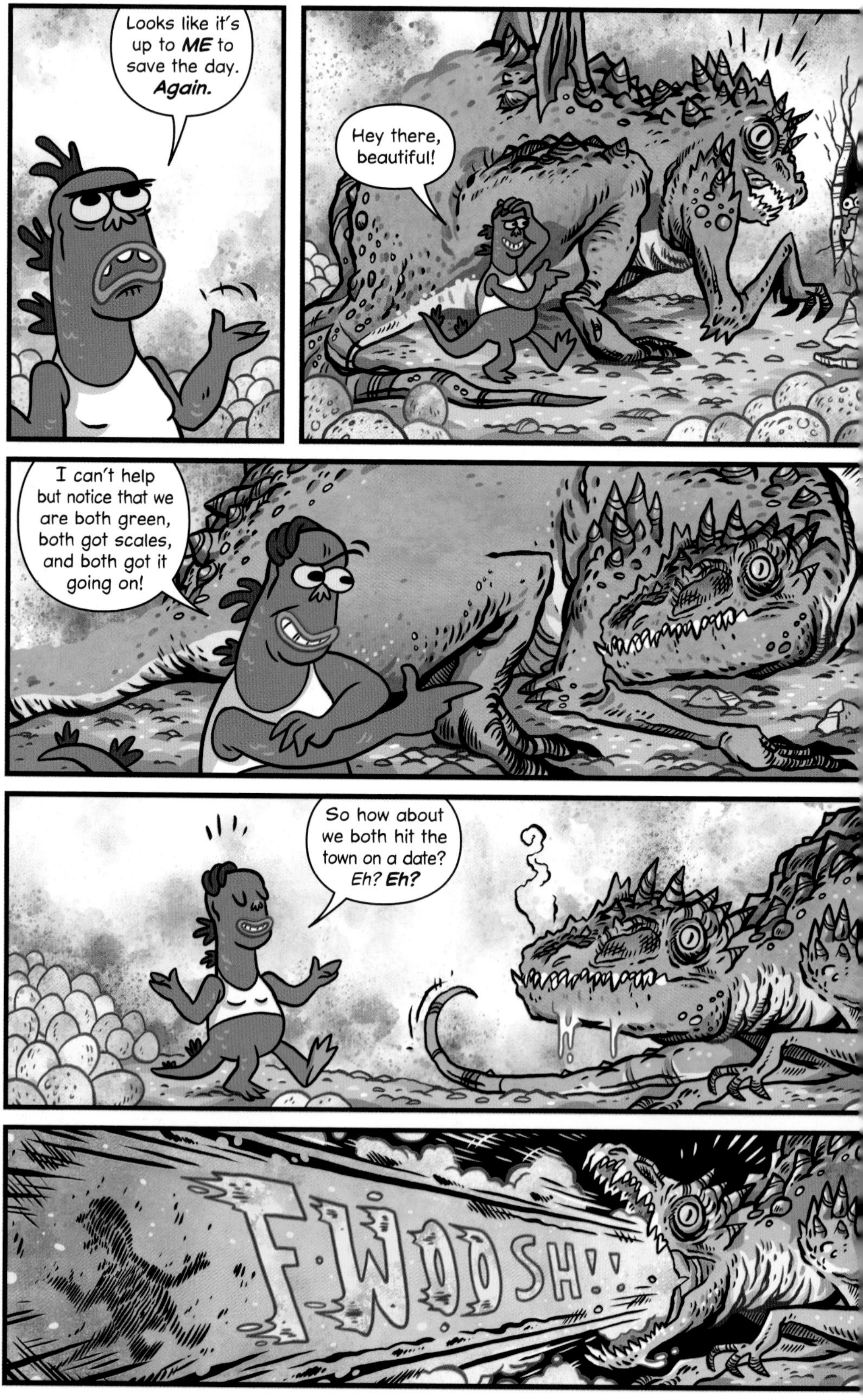
Looks like it's up to ME to save the day. Again.
Hey there, beautiful!
I can't help but notice that we are both green, both got scales, and both got it going on!
So how about we both hit the town on a date? Eh? Eh?
FWOOSH!!

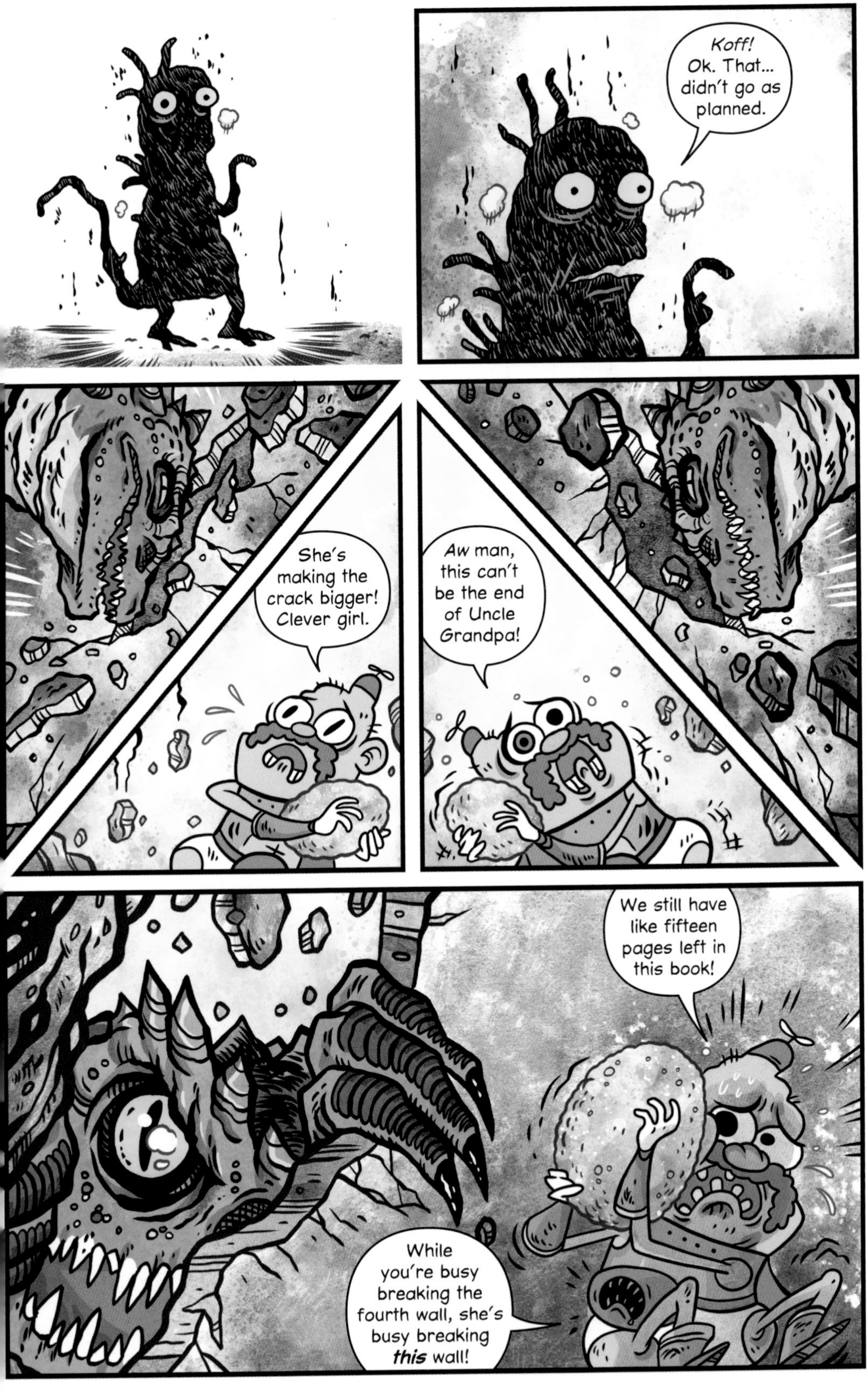
Koff! Ok. That... didn't go as planned.
She's making the crack bigger! Clever girl.
Aw man, this can't be the end of Uncle Grandpa!
We still have like fifteen pages left in this book!
While you're busy breaking the fourth wall, she's busy breaking *this* wall!

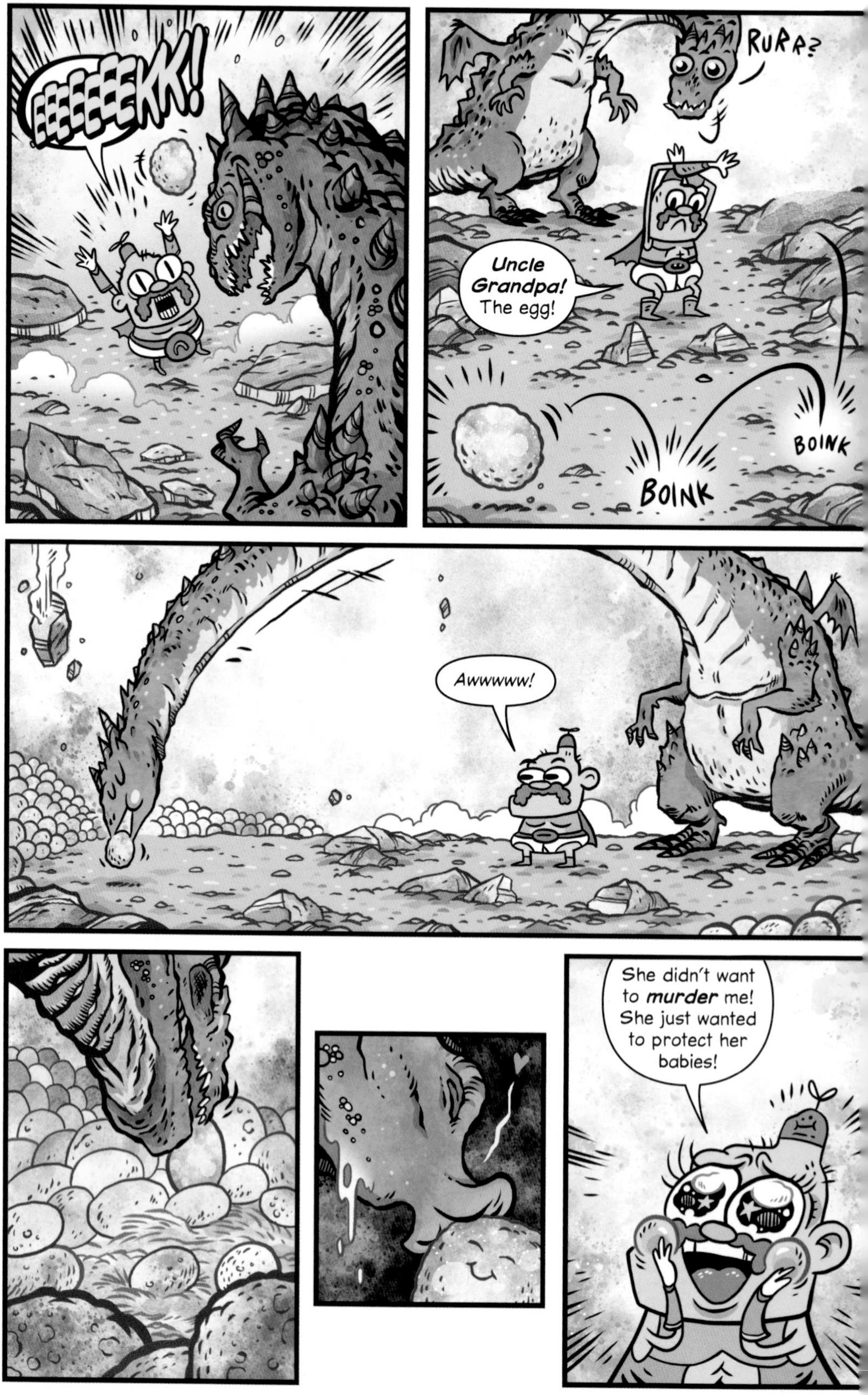
EEEEEEEEKK!
RURR?
Uncle Grandpa! The egg!
BOINK
BOINK
Awwwww!
She didn't want to murder me! She just wanted to protect her babies!

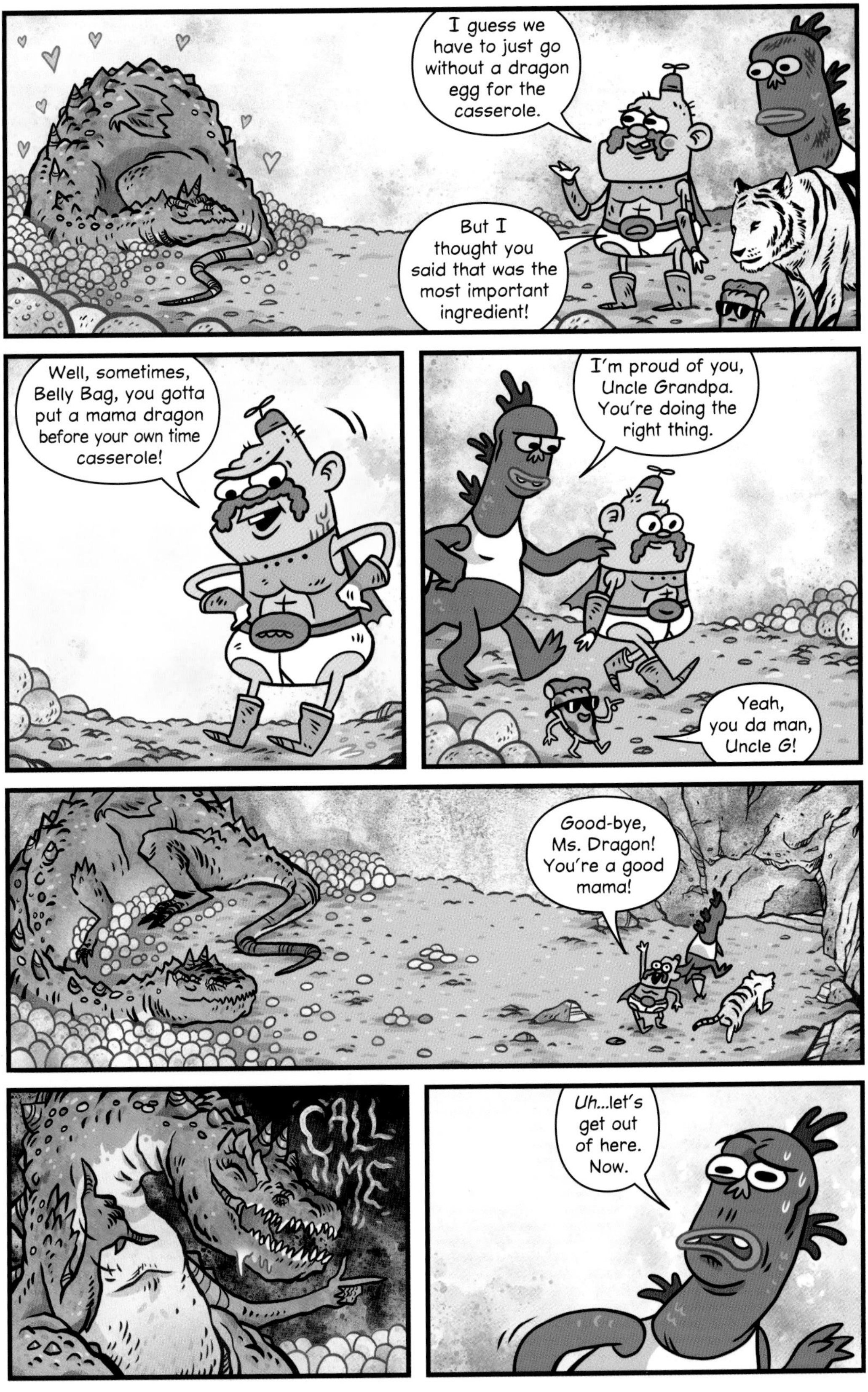
I guess we have to just go without a dragon egg for the casserole.
But I thought you said that was the most important ingredient!
Well, sometimes, Belly Bag, you gotta put a mama dragon before your own time casserole!
I'm proud of you, Uncle Grandpa. You're doing the right thing.
Yeah, you da man, Uncle G!
Good-bye, Ms. Dragon! You're a good mama!
CALL ME
Uh...let's get out of here. Now.

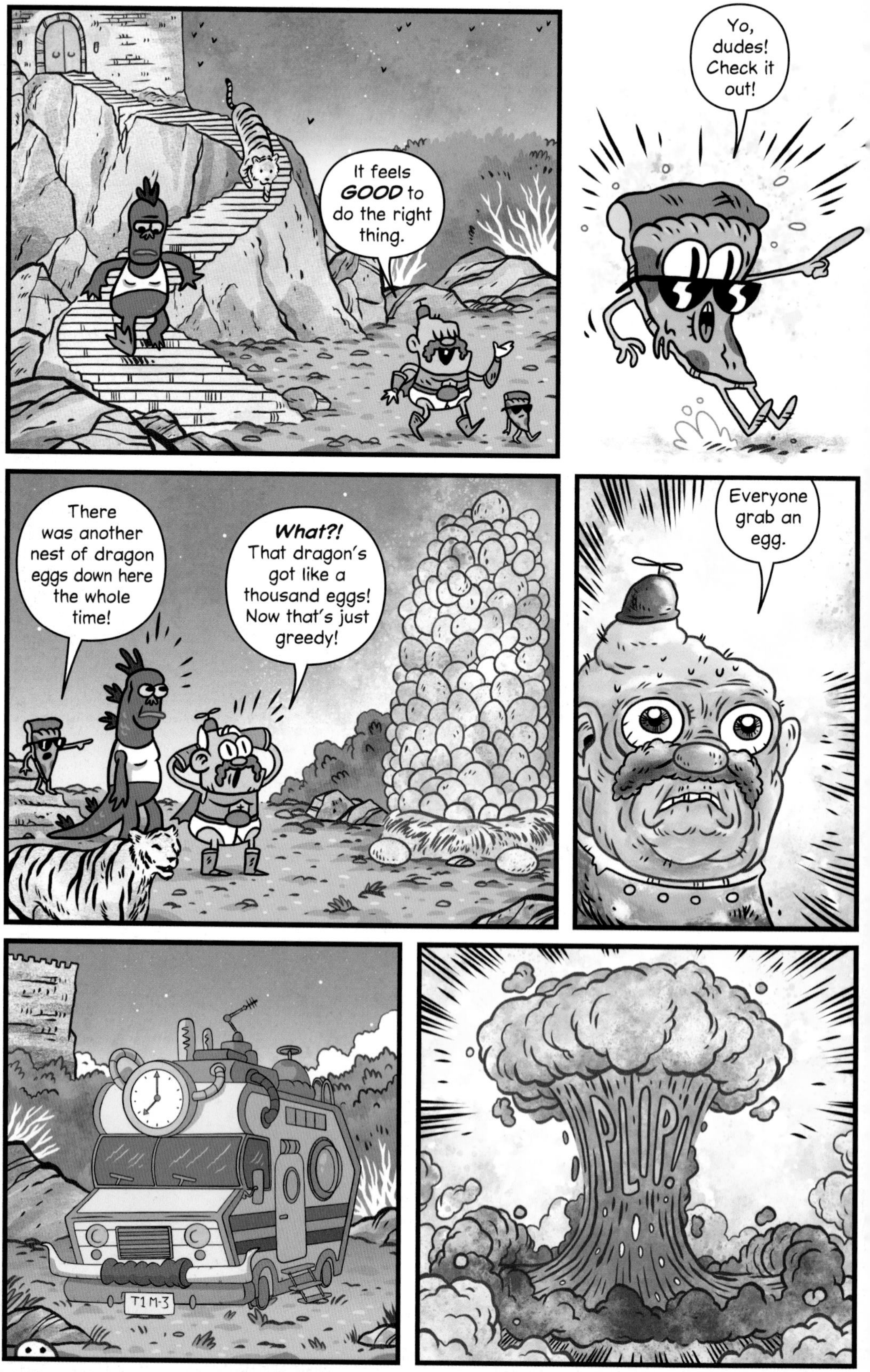
It feels GOOD to do the right thing.
Yo, dudes! Check it out!
There was another nest of dragon eggs down here the whole time!
What?! That dragon's got like a thousand eggs! Now that's just greedy!
Everyone grab an egg.
T1M-3
PLIP!

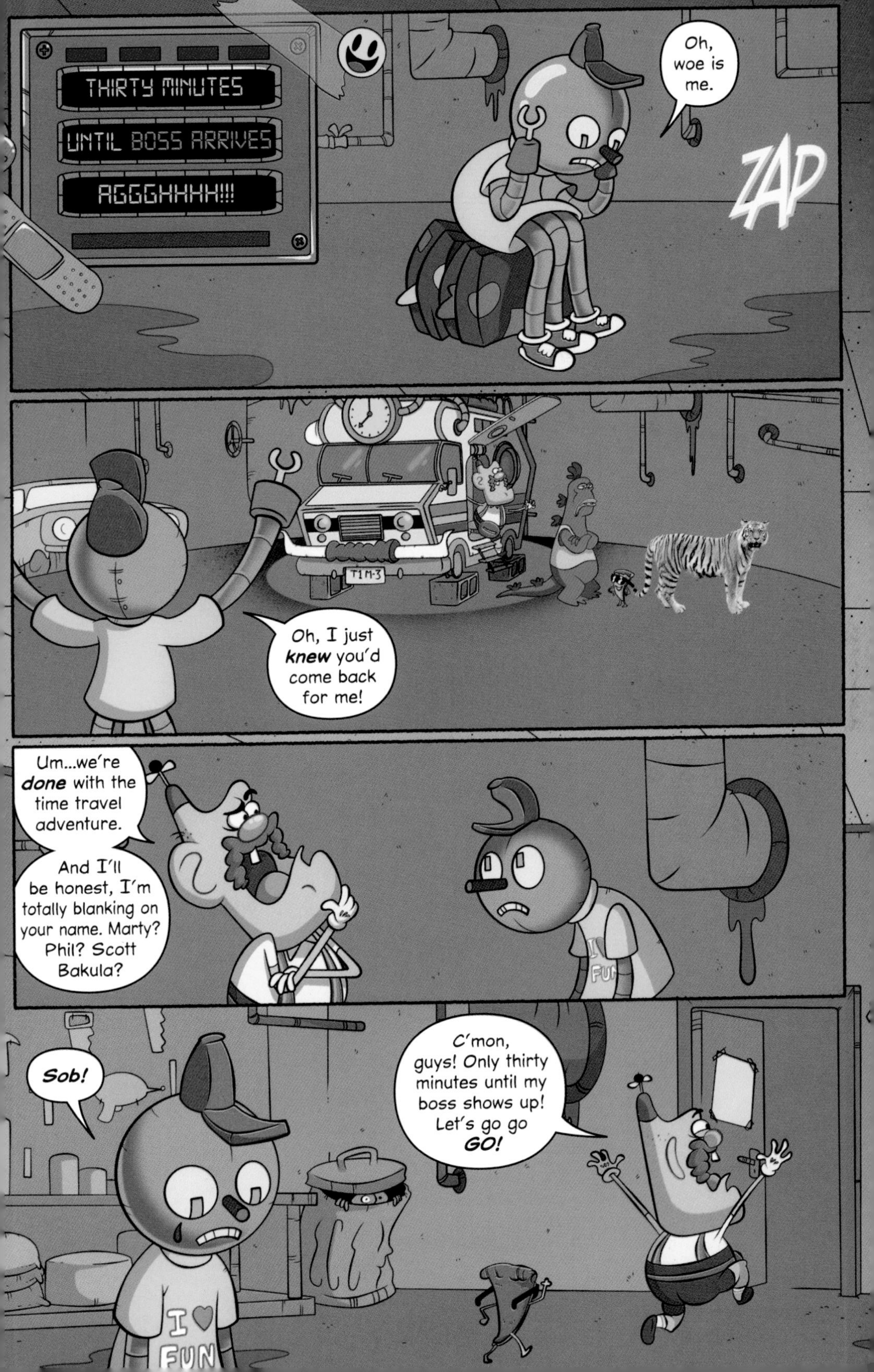
THIRTY MINUTES
UNTIL BOSS ARRIVES
AGGGHHHH!!!
Oh, woe is me.
ZAP
Oh, I just **knew** you'd come back for me!
T1M-3
Um...we're **done** with the time travel adventure.
And I'll be honest, I'm totally blanking on your name. Marty? Phil? Scott Bakula?
I ♥ FUN
Sob!
C'mon, guys! Only thirty minutes until my boss shows up! Let's go go **GO!**
I ♥ FUN

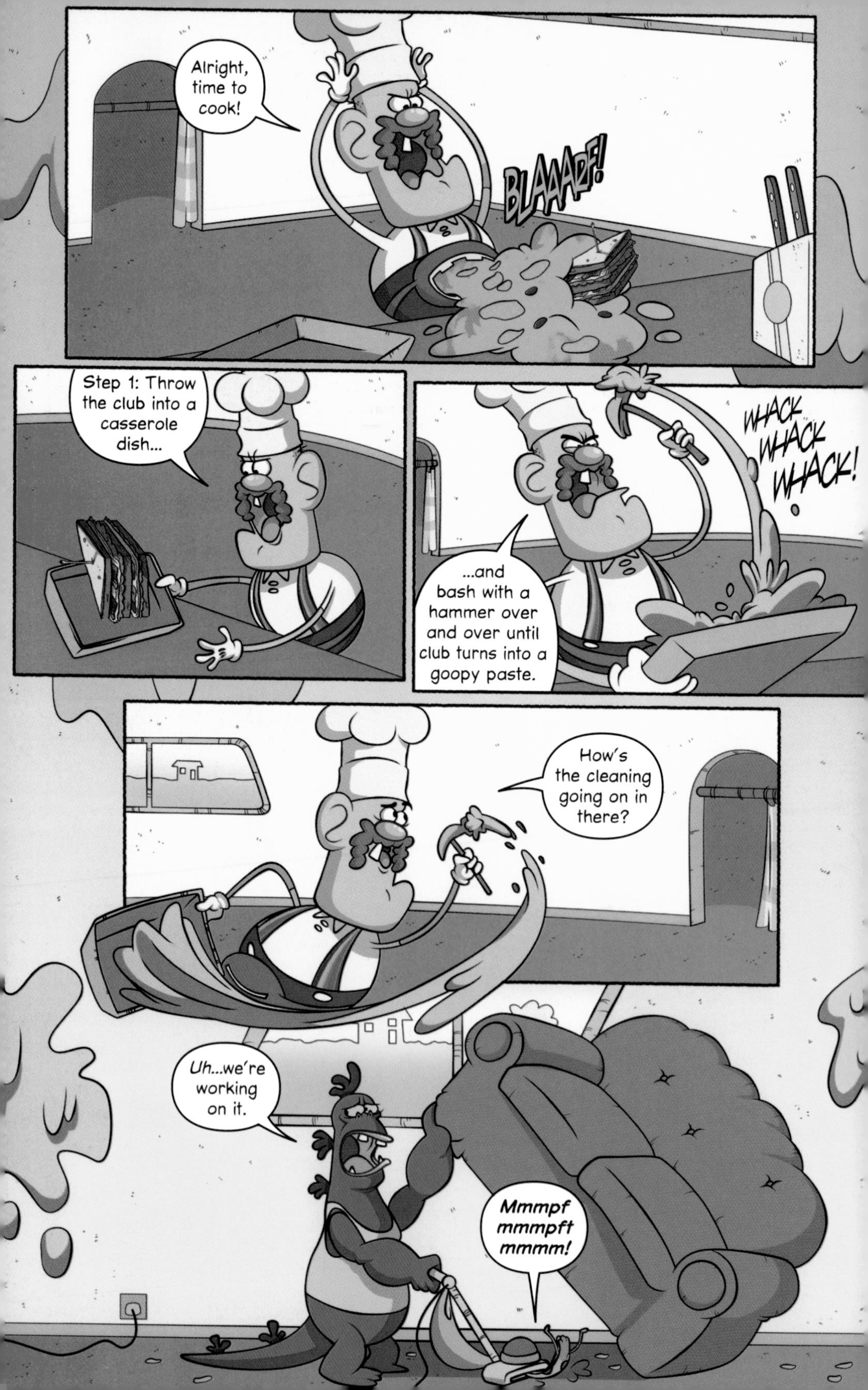

Alright, time to cook!
BLAAADF!
Step 1: Throw the club into a casserole dish...
WHACK WHACK WHACK!
...and bash with a hammer over and over until club turns into a goopy paste.
How's the cleaning going on in there?
Uh...we're working on it.
Mmmpf mmmpft mmmm!

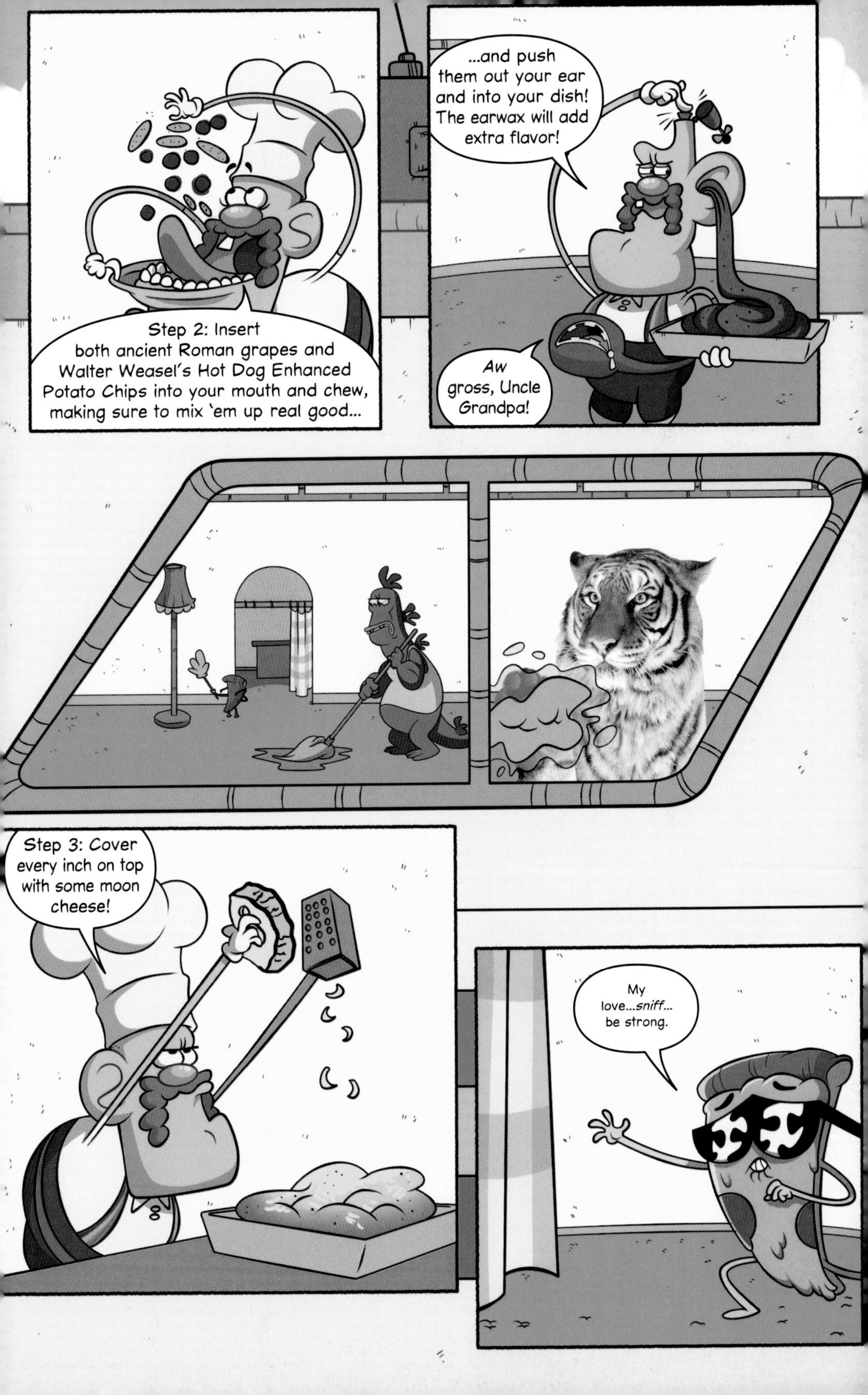
Step 2: Insert both ancient Roman grapes and Walter Weasel's Hot Dog Enhanced Potato Chips into your mouth and chew, making sure to mix 'em up real good...
...and push them out your ear and into your dish! The earwax will add extra flavor!
Aw gross, Uncle Grandpa!
Step 3: Cover every inch on top with some moon cheese!
My love...*sniff*... be strong.

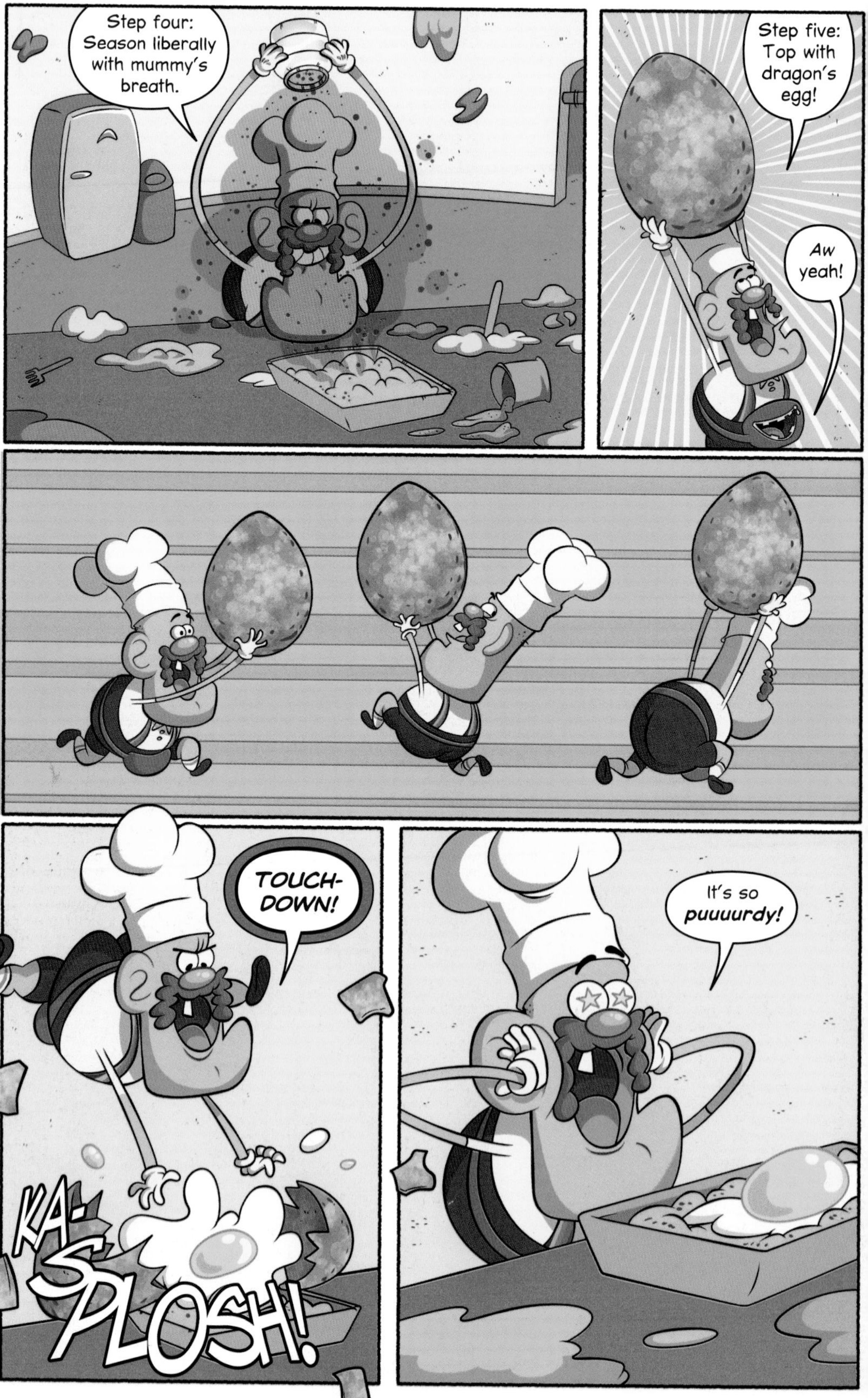
Step four: Season liberally with mummy's breath.
Step five: Top with dragon's egg!
Aw yeah!
TOUCH-DOWN!
KA-SPLOSH!
It's so puuuurdy!

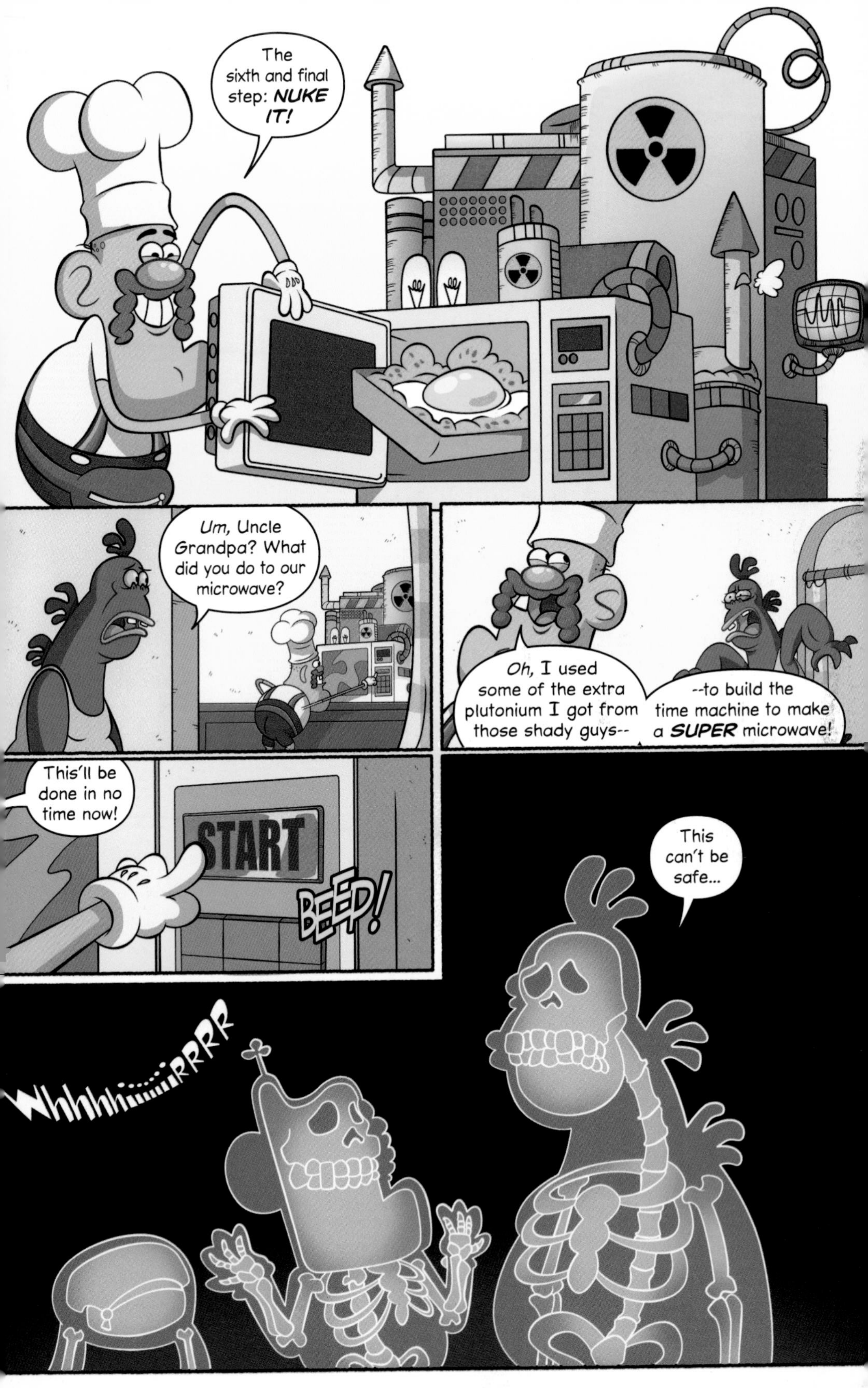

The sixth and final step: NUKE IT!
Um, Uncle Grandpa? What did you do to our microwave?
Oh, I used some of the extra plutonium I got from those shady guys--
--to build the time machine to make a SUPER microwave!
This'll be done in no time now!
START
BEEP!
This can't be safe...
Whhhhiiiiiiiiiiiirrrr

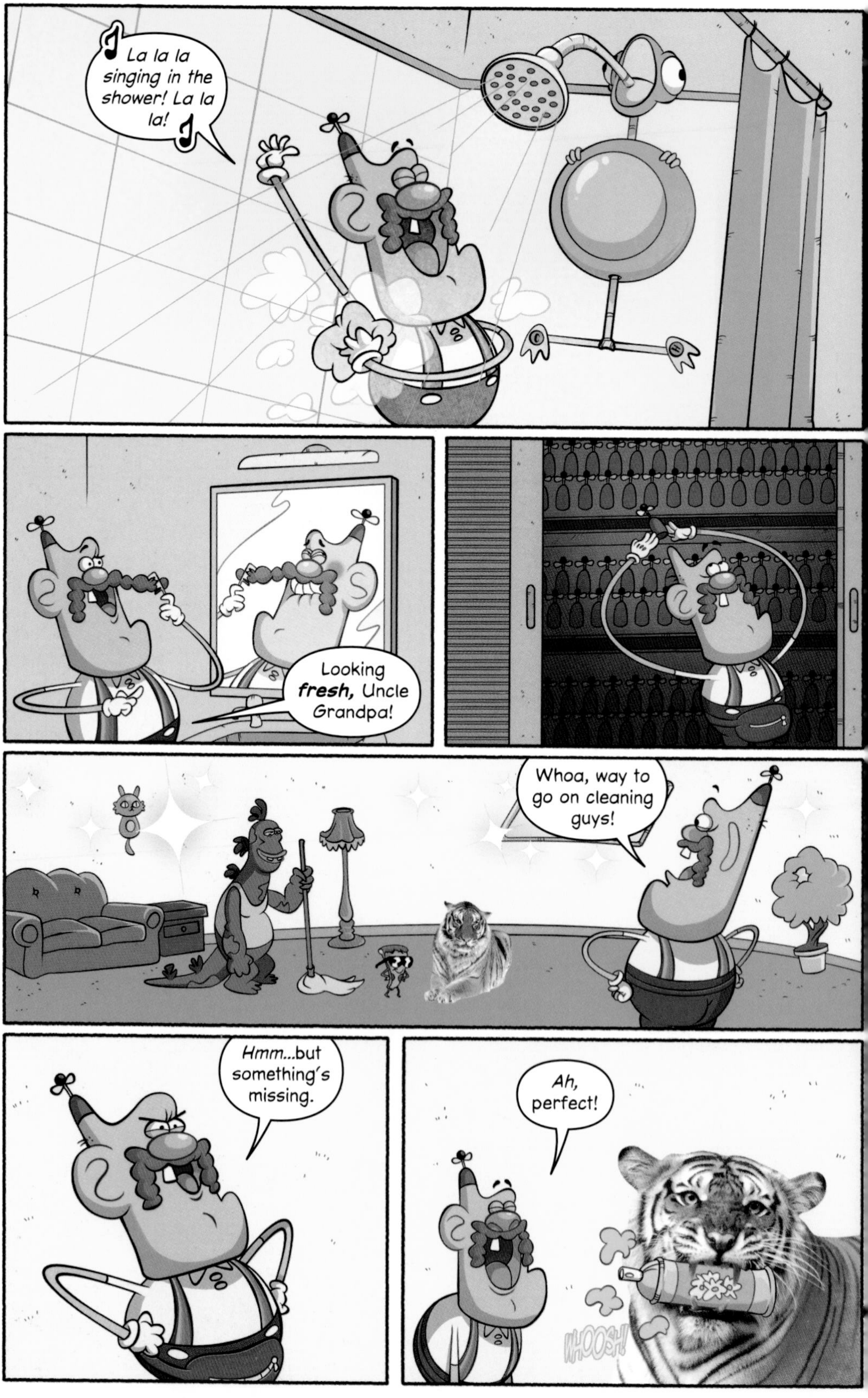

La la la singing in the shower! La la la!
Looking *fresh,* Uncle Grandpa!
Whoa, way to go on cleaning guys!
Hmm...but something's missing.
Ah, perfect!
WHOOSH!

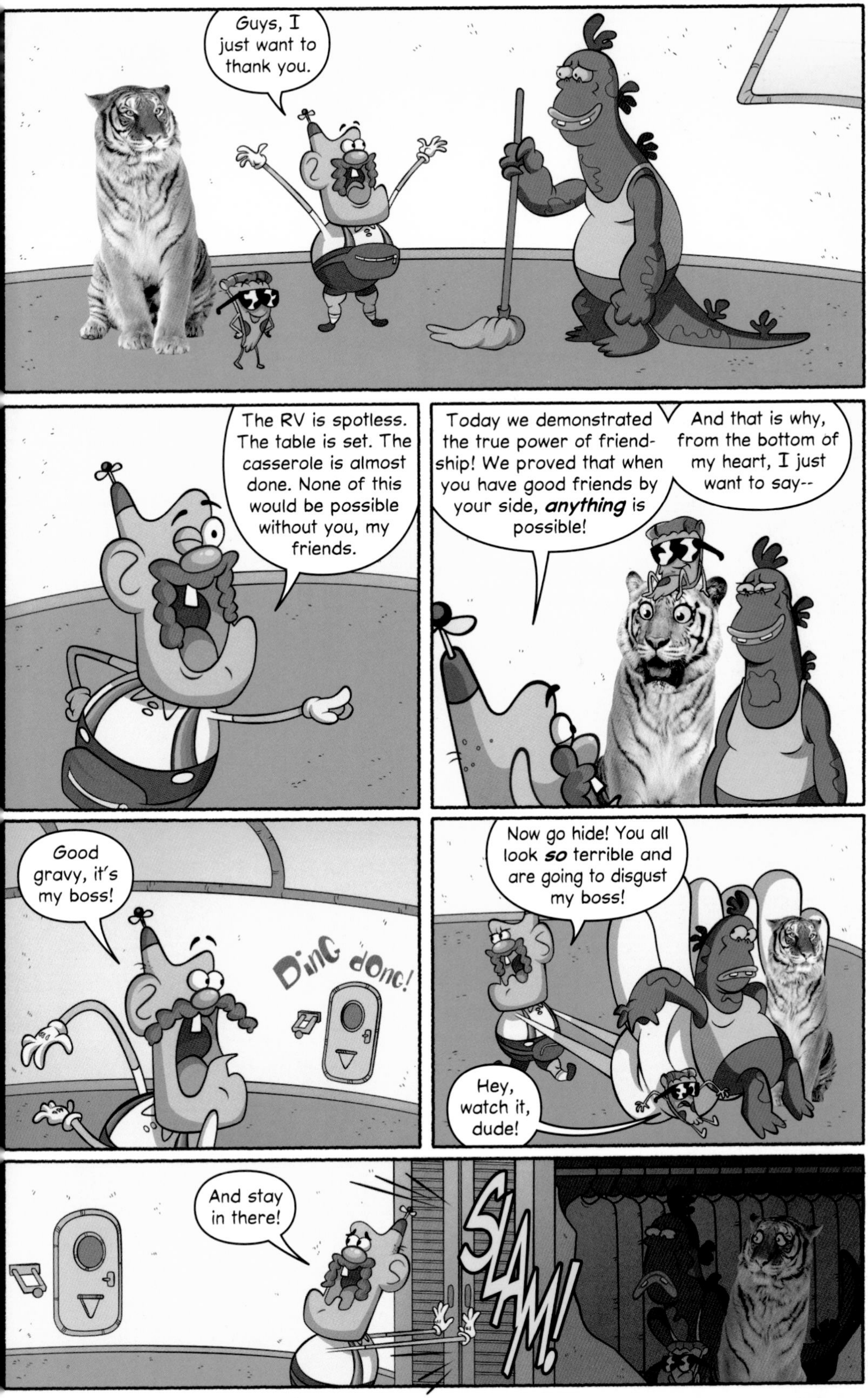
Guys, I just want to thank you.
The RV is spotless. The table is set. The casserole is almost done. None of this would be possible without you, my friends.
Today we demonstrated the true power of friendship! We proved that when you have good friends by your side, ***anything*** is possible!
And that is why, from the bottom of my heart, I just want to say--
Good gravy, it's my boss!
DinG dOnG!
Now go hide! You all look ***so*** terrible and are going to disgust my boss!
Hey, watch it, dude!
And stay in there!
SLAM!

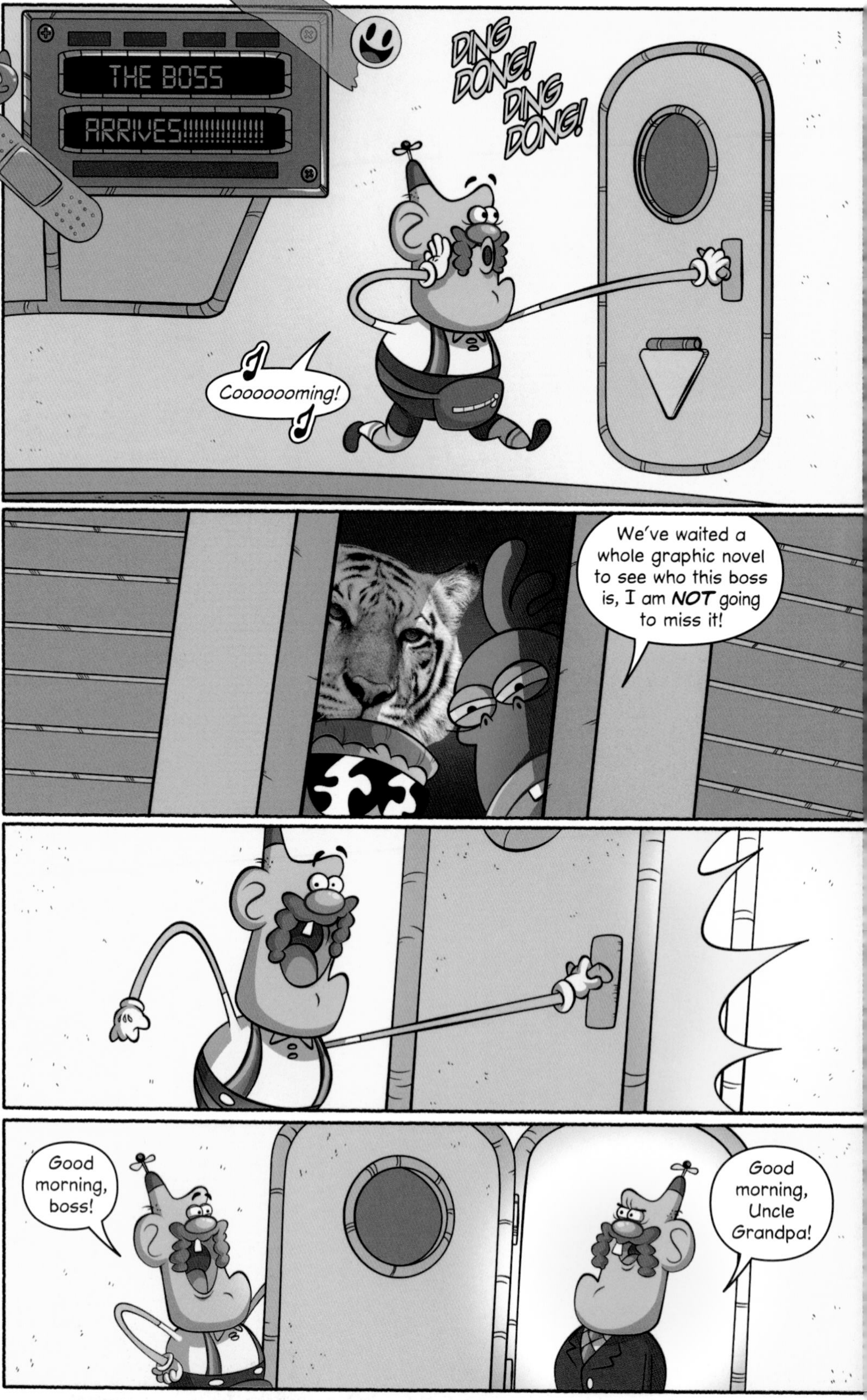
THE BOSS
ARRIVES!!!!!!!!!!!!!!!!
DING DONG! DING DONG!
Cooooooming!
We've waited a whole graphic novel to see who this boss is, I am ***NOT*** going to miss it!
Good morning, boss!
Good morning, Uncle Grandpa!

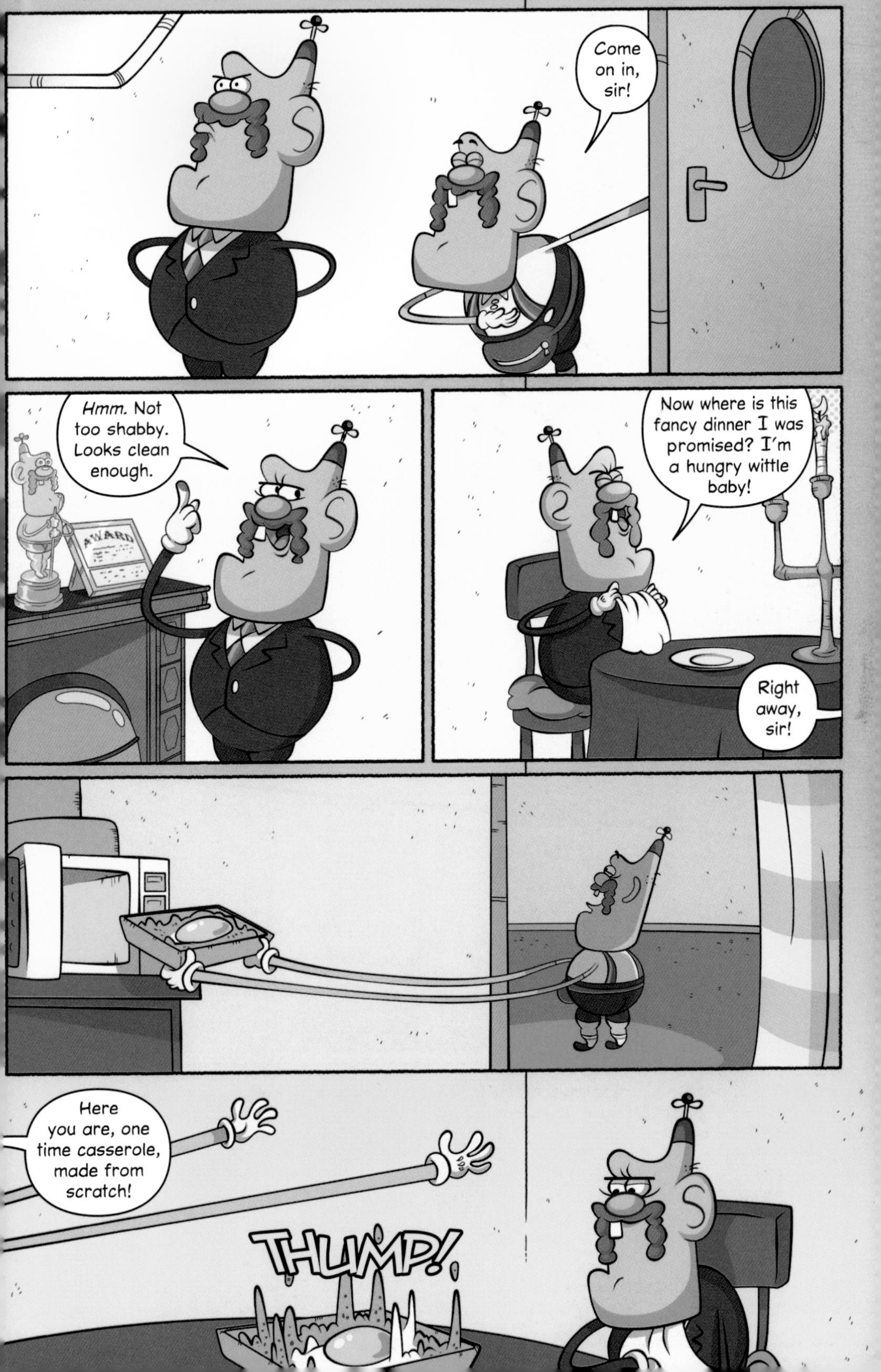
Come on in, sir!
Hmm. Not too shabby. Looks clean enough.
AWARD
Now where is this fancy dinner I was promised? I'm a hungry wittle baby!
Right away, sir!
Here you are, one time casserole, made from scratch!
THUMP!

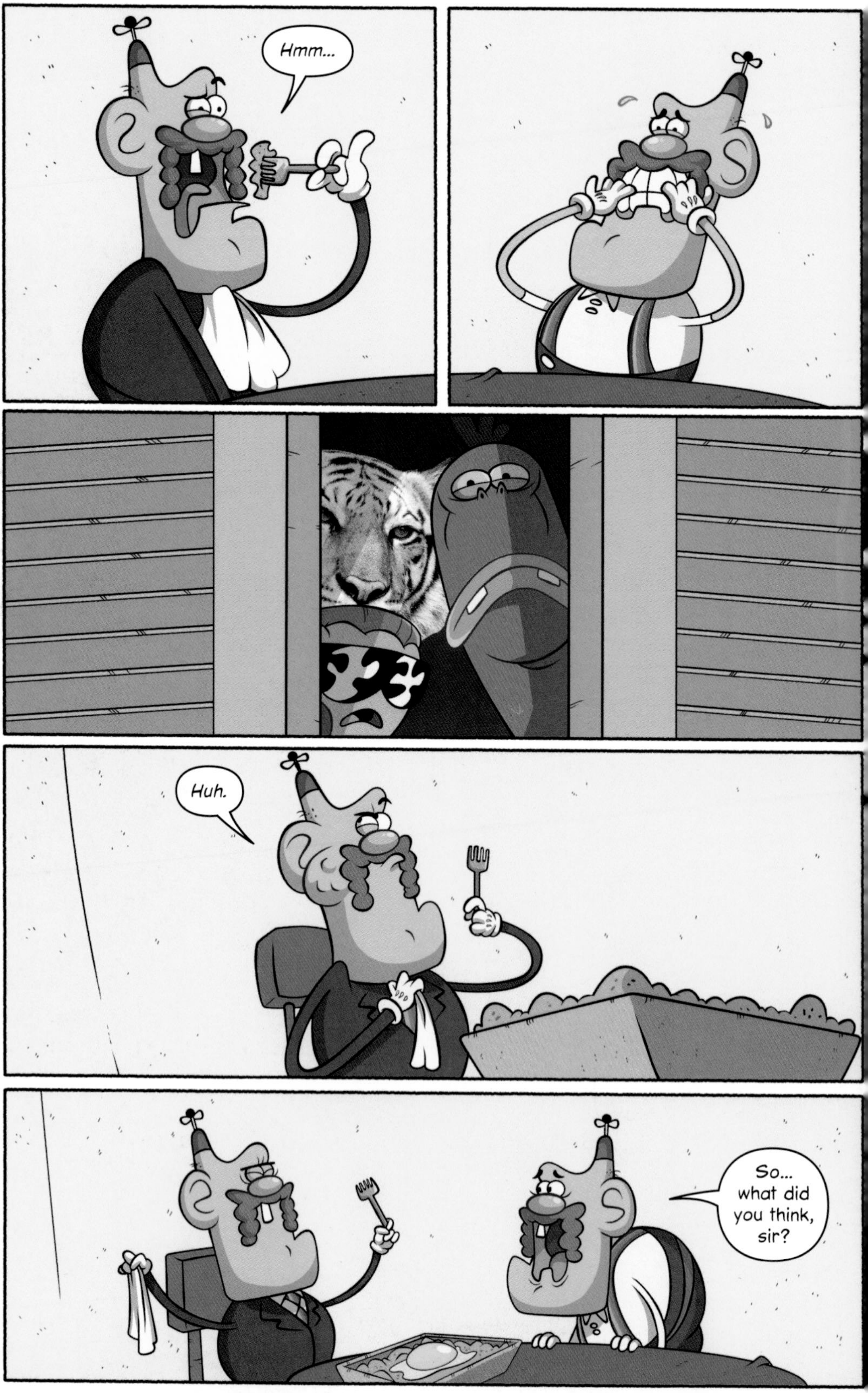
Hmm...
Huh.
So... what did you think, sir?

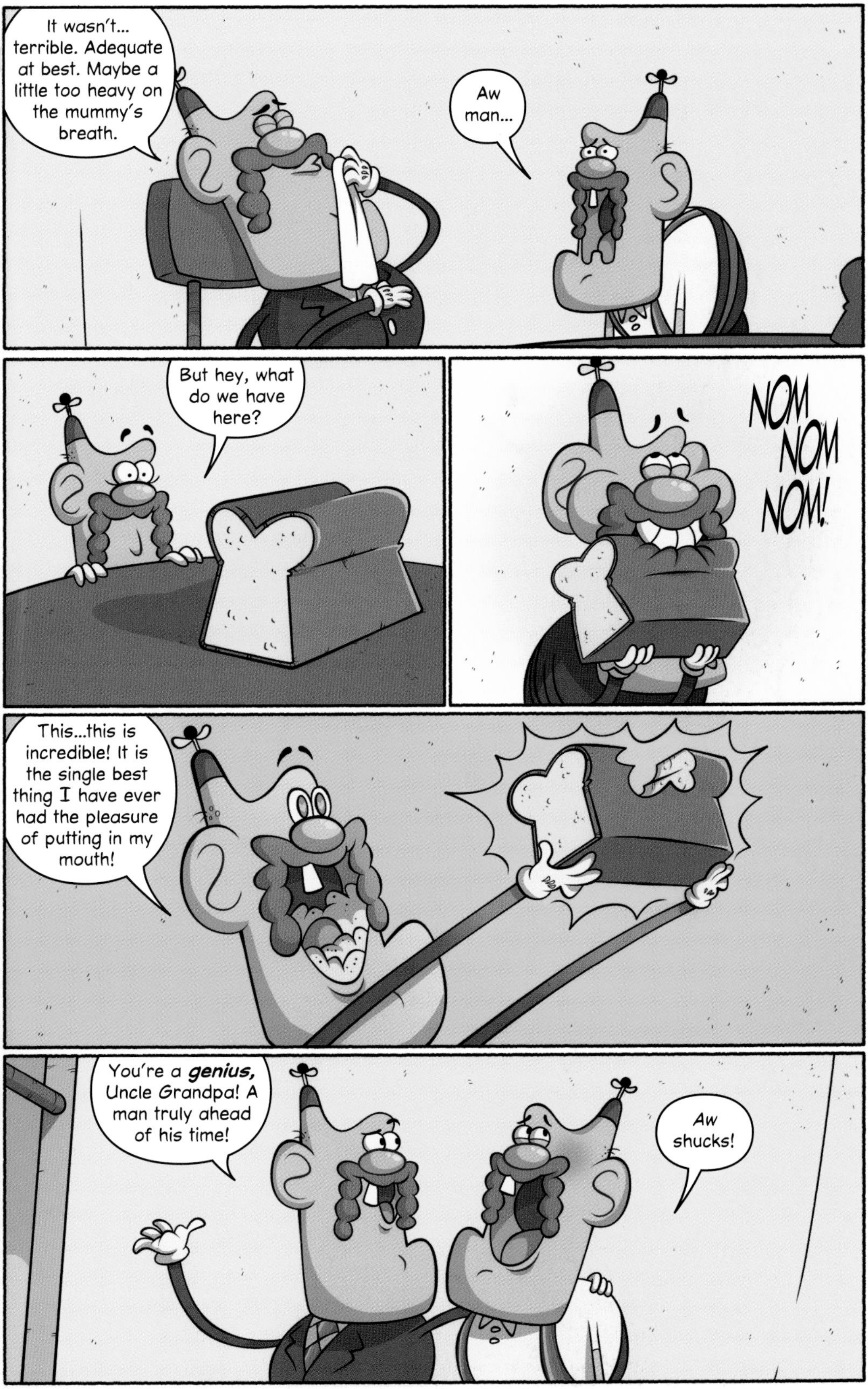
It wasn't... terrible. Adequate at best. Maybe a little too heavy on the mummy's breath.
Aw man...
But hey, what do we have here?
NOM NOM NOM!
This...this is incredible! It is the single best thing I have ever had the pleasure of putting in my mouth!
You're a ***genius,*** Uncle Grandpa! A man truly ahead of his time!
Aw shucks!

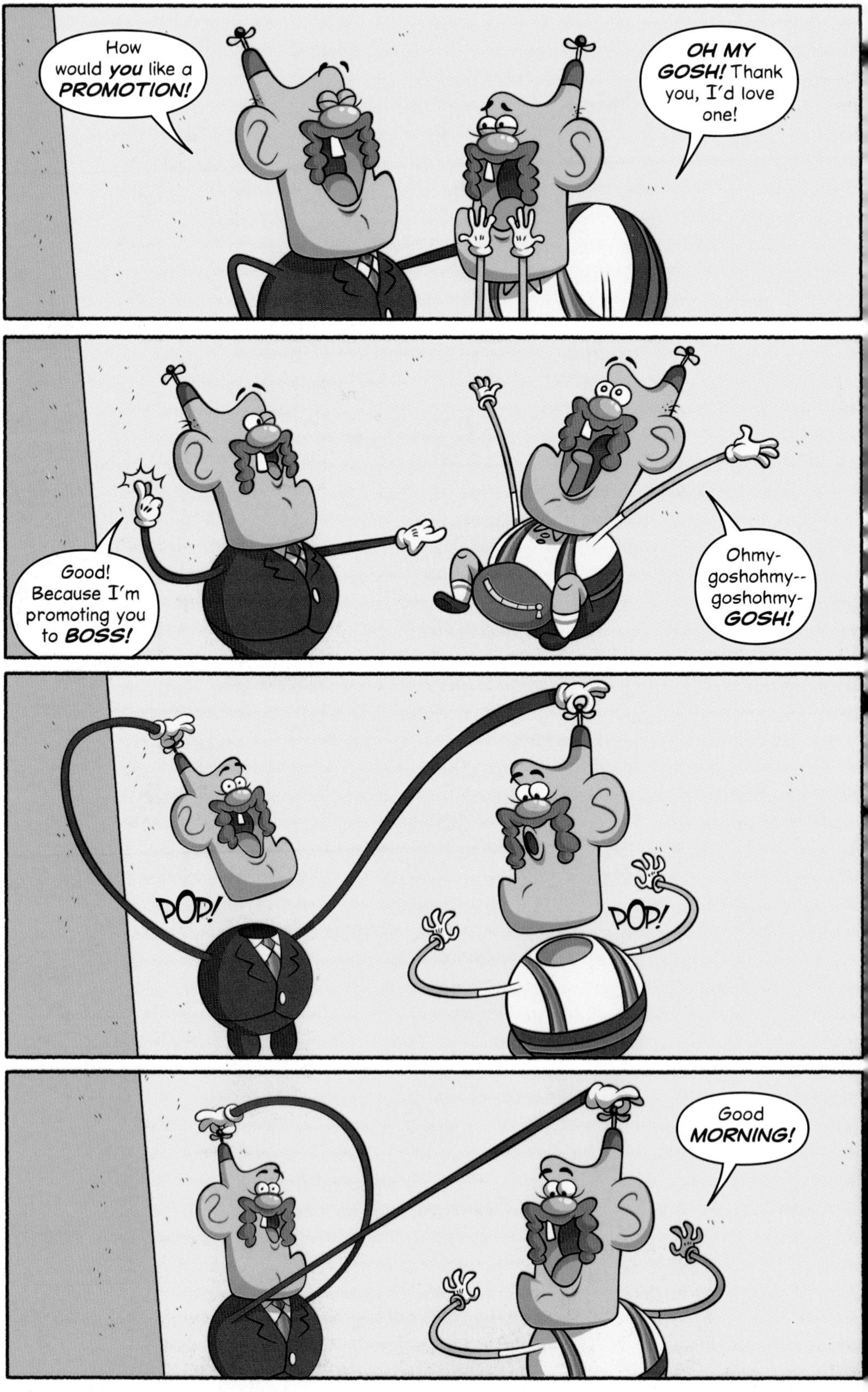
How would you like a PROMOTION!
OH MY GOSH! Thank you, I'd love one!
Good! Because I'm promoting you to BOSS!
Ohmy-goshohmy--goshohmy-GOSH!
POP!
POP!
Good MORNING!

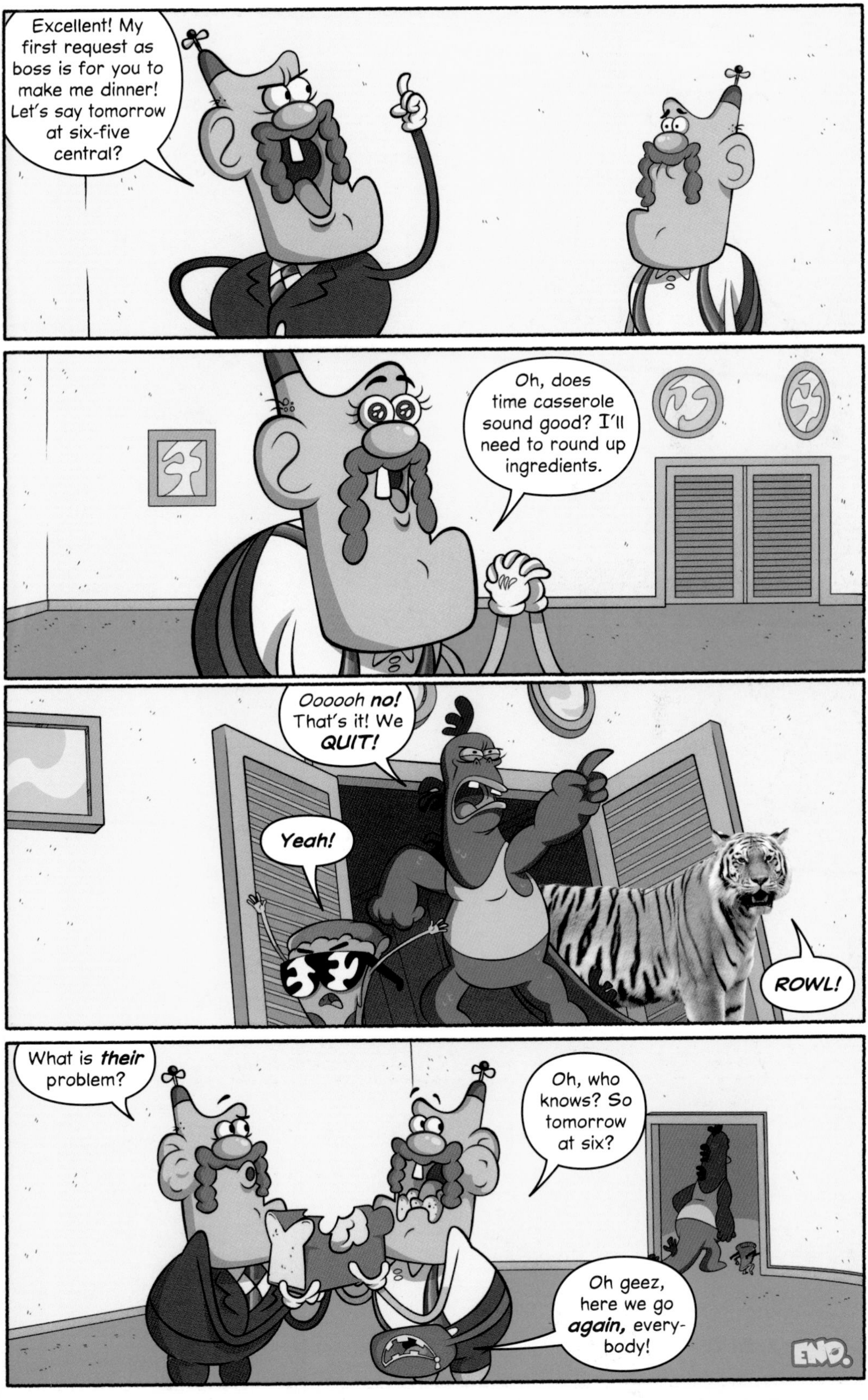
Excellent! My first request as boss is for you to make me dinner! Let's say tomorrow at six-five central?
Oh, does time casserole sound good? I'll need to round up ingredients.
Oooooh no! That's it! We QUIT!
Yeah!
ROWL!
What is their problem?
Oh, who knows? So tomorrow at six?
Oh geez, here we go again, every-body!
END.